'A visually stunning book...
packed with unexpected delig[...]
The Sunday Age

'I often lose myself in the world of Scarygirl.
I adore the amazing artwork filled with
numerous hidden details. There's a great
theme of friendship and love – the two
most important things in the world.'
Matias Roskos, www.visualblog.de

'Nathan Jurevicius has a cult online following
for his character, Scarygirl, and her world —
through an online comic, game, artwork and
designer toys. The reader is taken on a
Wizard of Oz-style adventure/quest with
her and a crew of scary/cute companions.
There is no denying Jurevicius' talent...'
Angela Meyer, *Bookseller* & *Publisher*

'A true riot of visual splendour...
intoxicating, endlessly visually stunning.'
www.kids-bookreview.com

'A universe filled with eccentric creatures,
deep secrets and common objects that
routinely come to life. It's a spectacle that,
like a luscious confection, makes you
want more and more and more.'
Gina Garan, www.thisisblythe.com

NATHAN JUREVICIUS

THE ADVENTURES OF

ScaryGirl

ALLEN&UNWIN
SYDNEY · MELBOURNE · AUCKLAND · LONDON

First published in 2012

Allen & Unwin
83 Alexander Street
Crows Nest NSW 2065
Australia
Phone: (612) 8425 0100
Fax: (612) 9906 2218
Email: info@allenandunwin.com
Web: www.allenandunwin.com

A Cataloguing-in-Publication
entry is available from the
National Library of Australia
www.trove.nla.gov.au

ISBN 9 781 74237 293 8

Cover and text design by
Nathan Jurevicius and Bruno Herfst
This book was printed in August
2012 at Prosperous Printing
(Shenzhen) Co. Ltd., Hong Mian
Road, Heng Gang Town, Long
Gang district, Shenzhen, P.R. China.

10 9 8 7 6 5 4 3 2 1

For my family

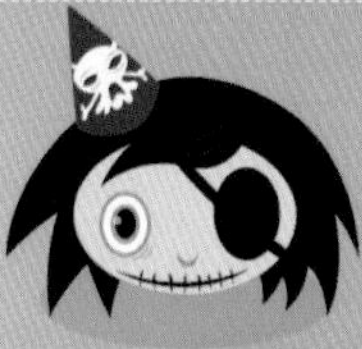

SCARYGIRL

Abandoned on a deserted peninsula, Scarygirl, with determination and resourcefulness, is on a mission to find the man behind her haunting dreams.

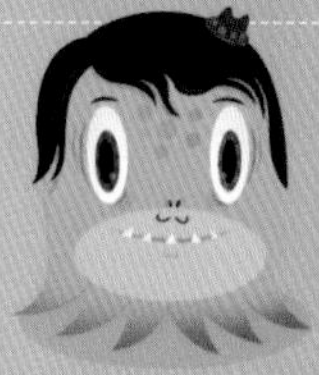

BLISTER

The last of his species, Blister, a super-intelligent giant octopus, is Scarygirl's guardian. Unfortunately he has no solid facts about the mysterious Dr Maybee.

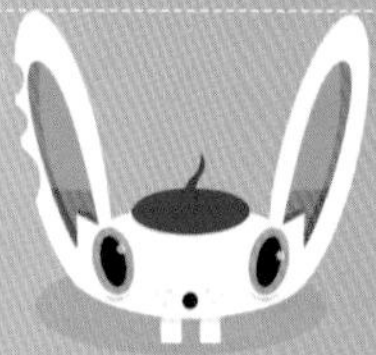

BUNNIGURU

Quick-witted and funny, Bunniguru offers confusing advice on everything from carrot soup recipes to ingrown hairs. It's best, though, to take all he says with a grain of salt.

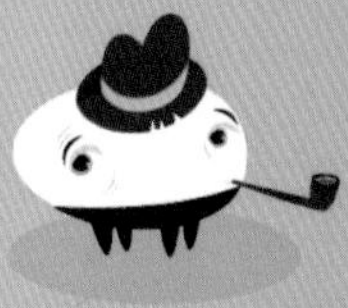

EGG

Acting as Bunniguru's silent conscience,
Egg is a reliable companion through thick and thin.

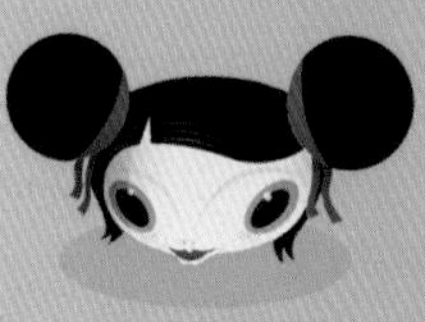

TREEDWELLER

Impish and mischievous, Treedweller lures travellers to her master, the Tree of Knowledge. What happens after is anyone's guess, as no one has ever returned to tell of the adventure.

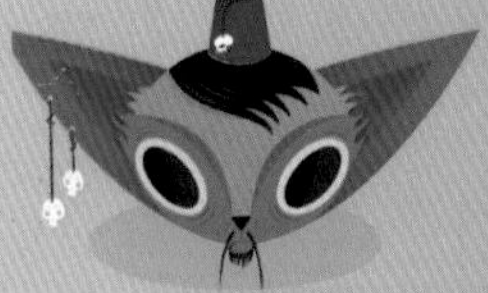

CHIHOOHOO

A major figure in the highly prized squid-ink trade, Chihoohoo is ruthless with anyone trying to disrupt his monopoly ... especially little girls dressed like pirates!

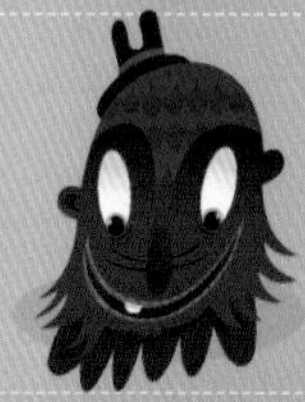

SEWER GIANT

Sometimes referred to as Steve, the Sewer Giant is a helpful and harmless soul who wanders diligently through the city's waste, collecting lost dreams.

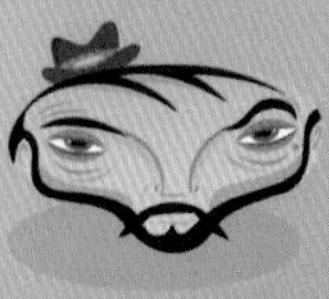

DR MAYBEE

This man holds the answers to all of Scarygirl's questions. He lives beyond the great city in a water-logged mansion deep in the ocean, where he conducts secret experiments.

PART ONE

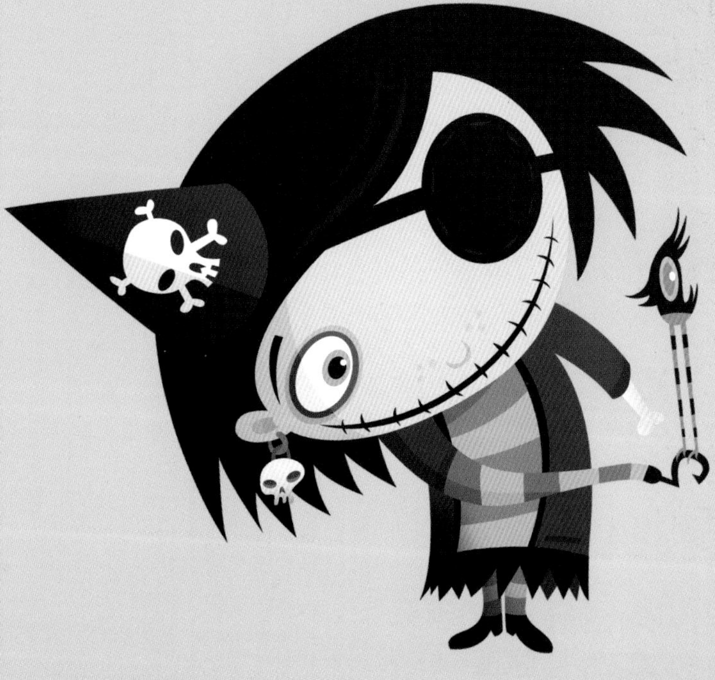

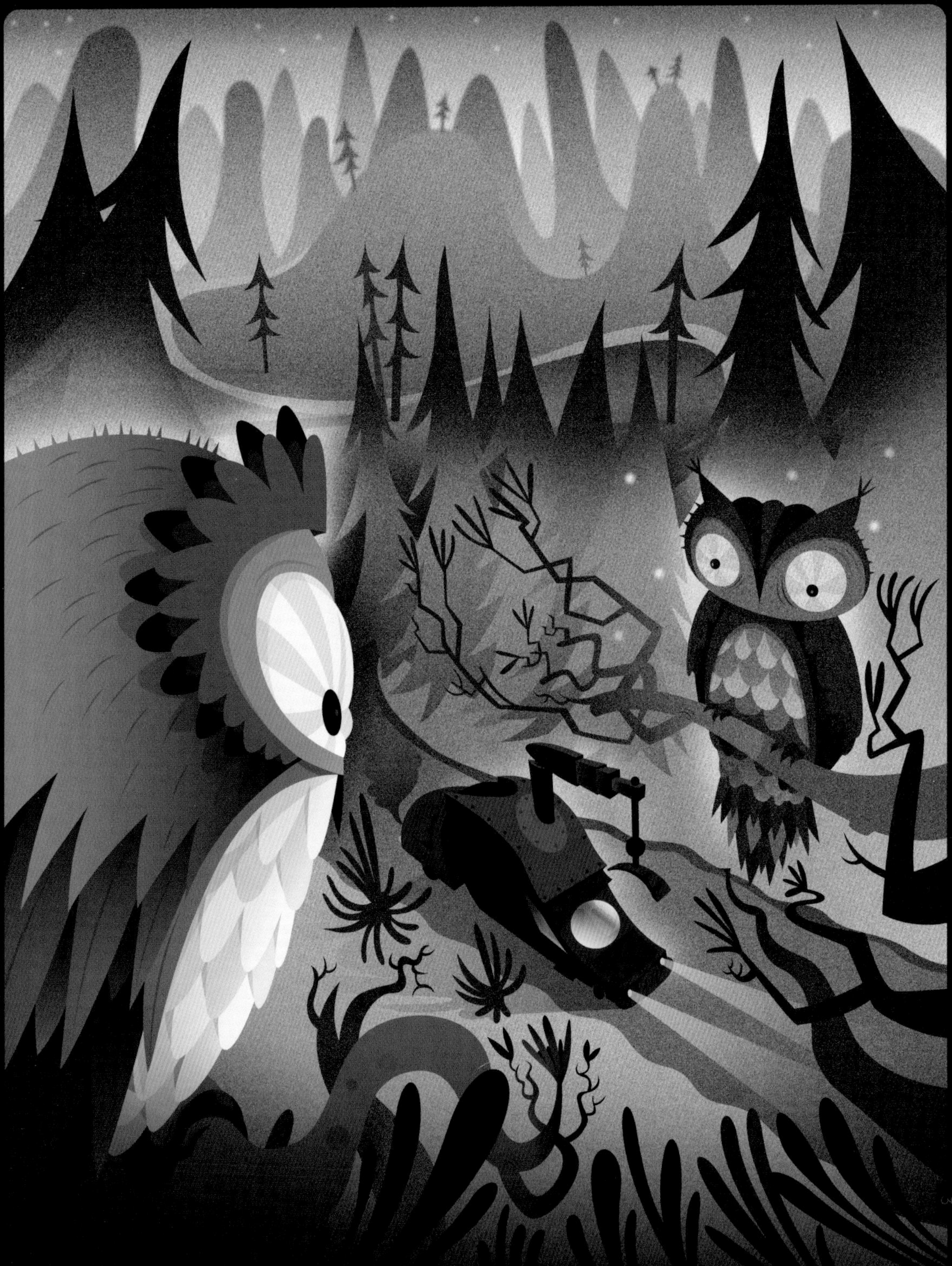

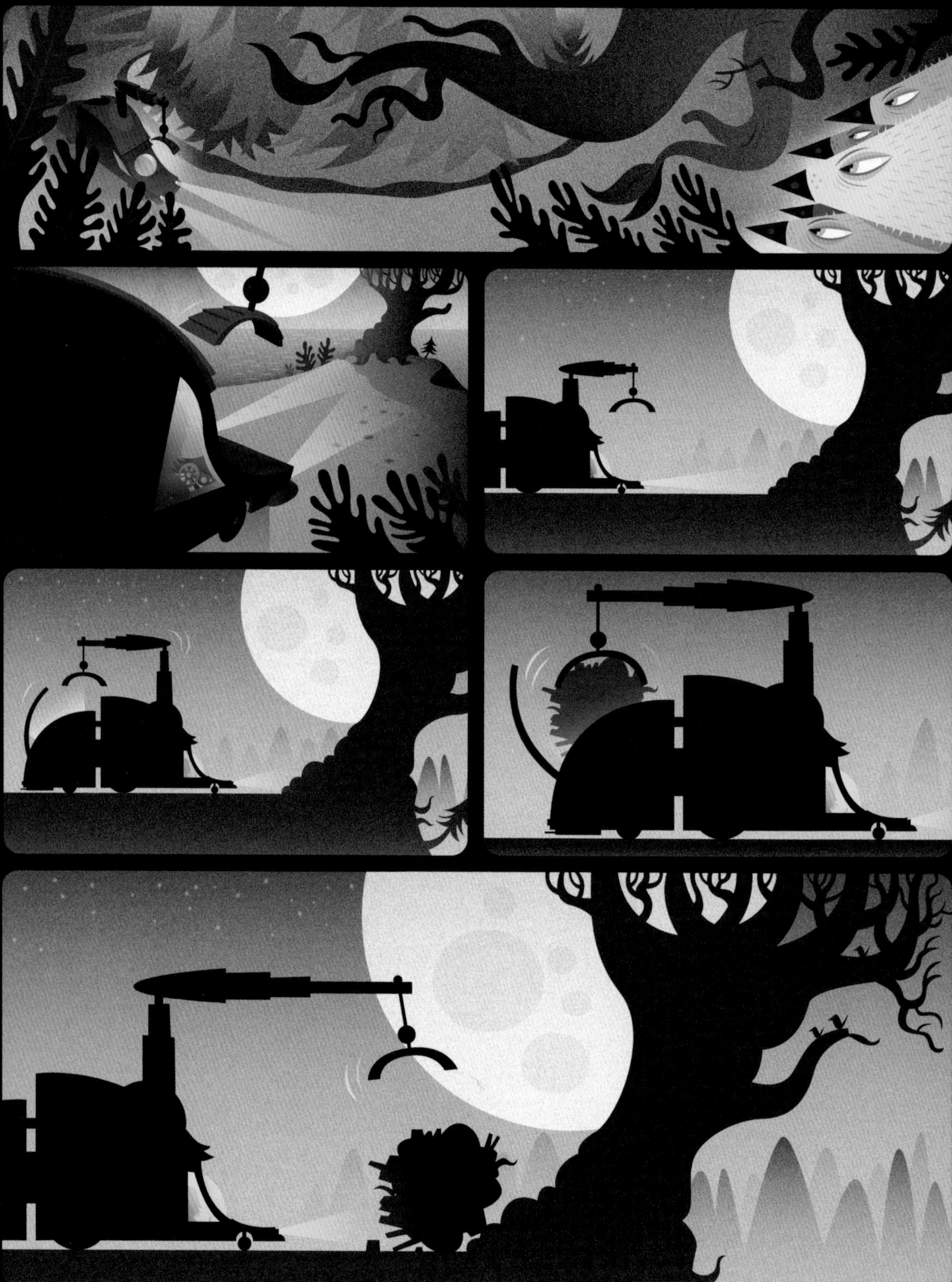

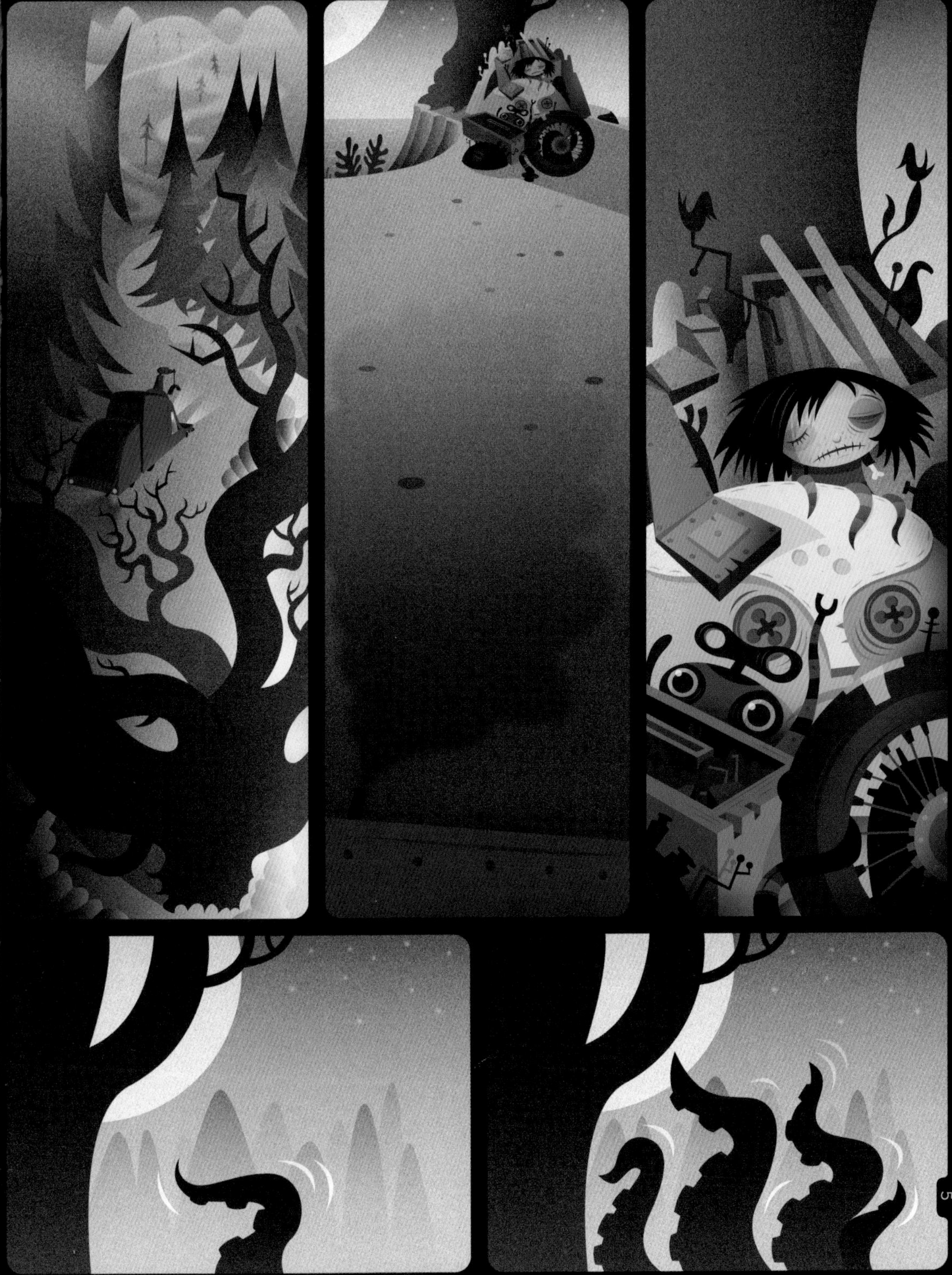

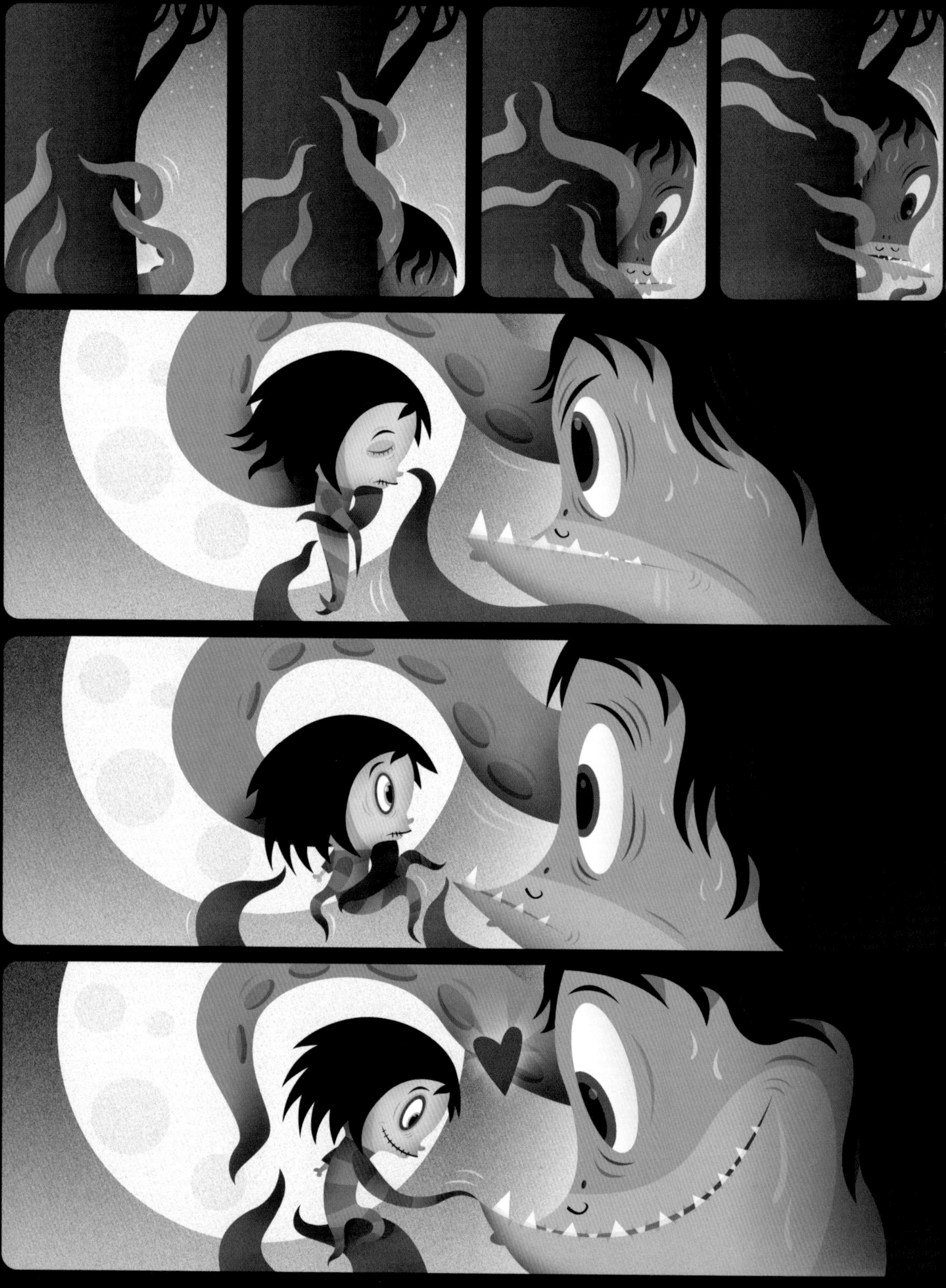

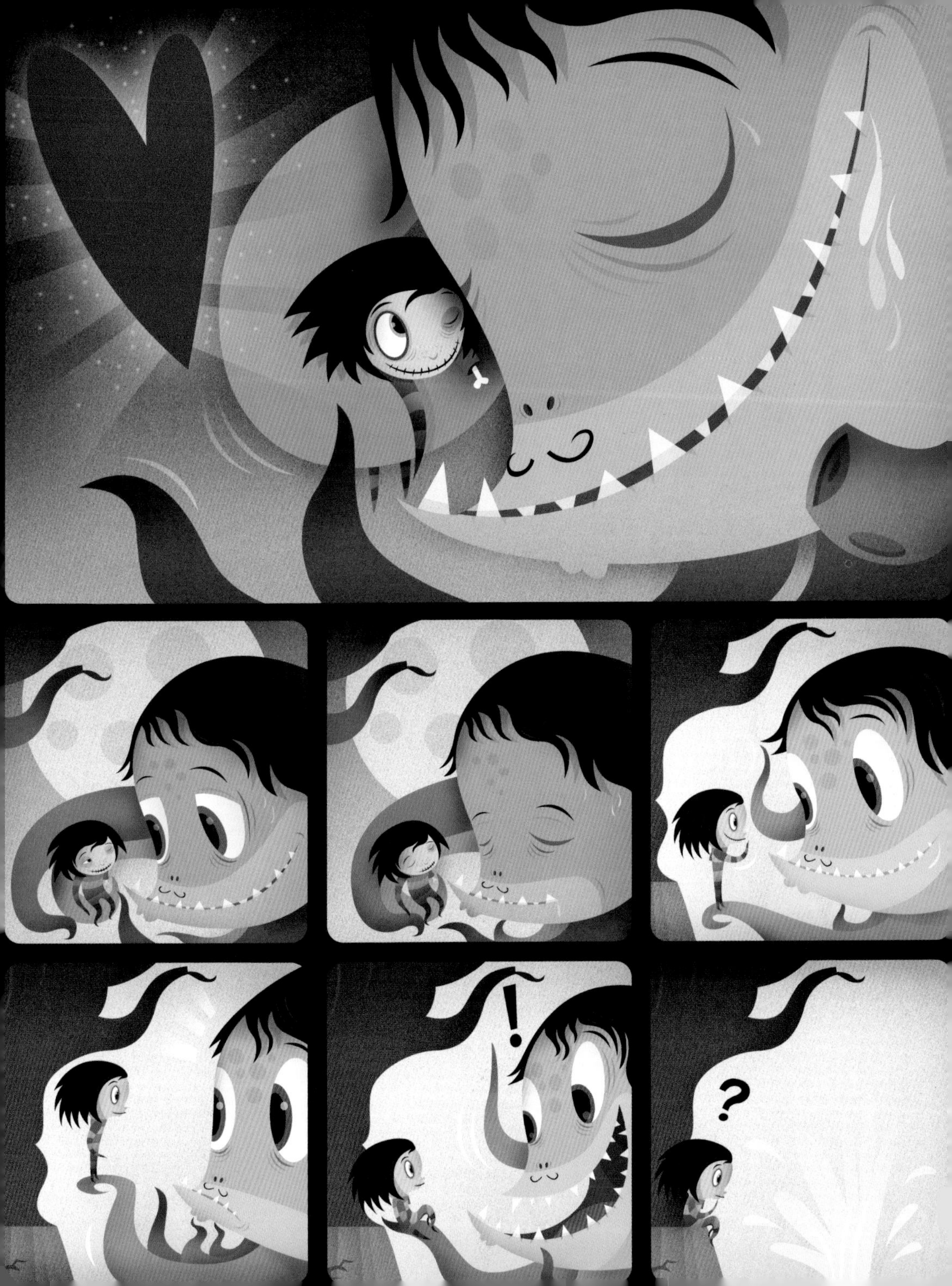
!
?

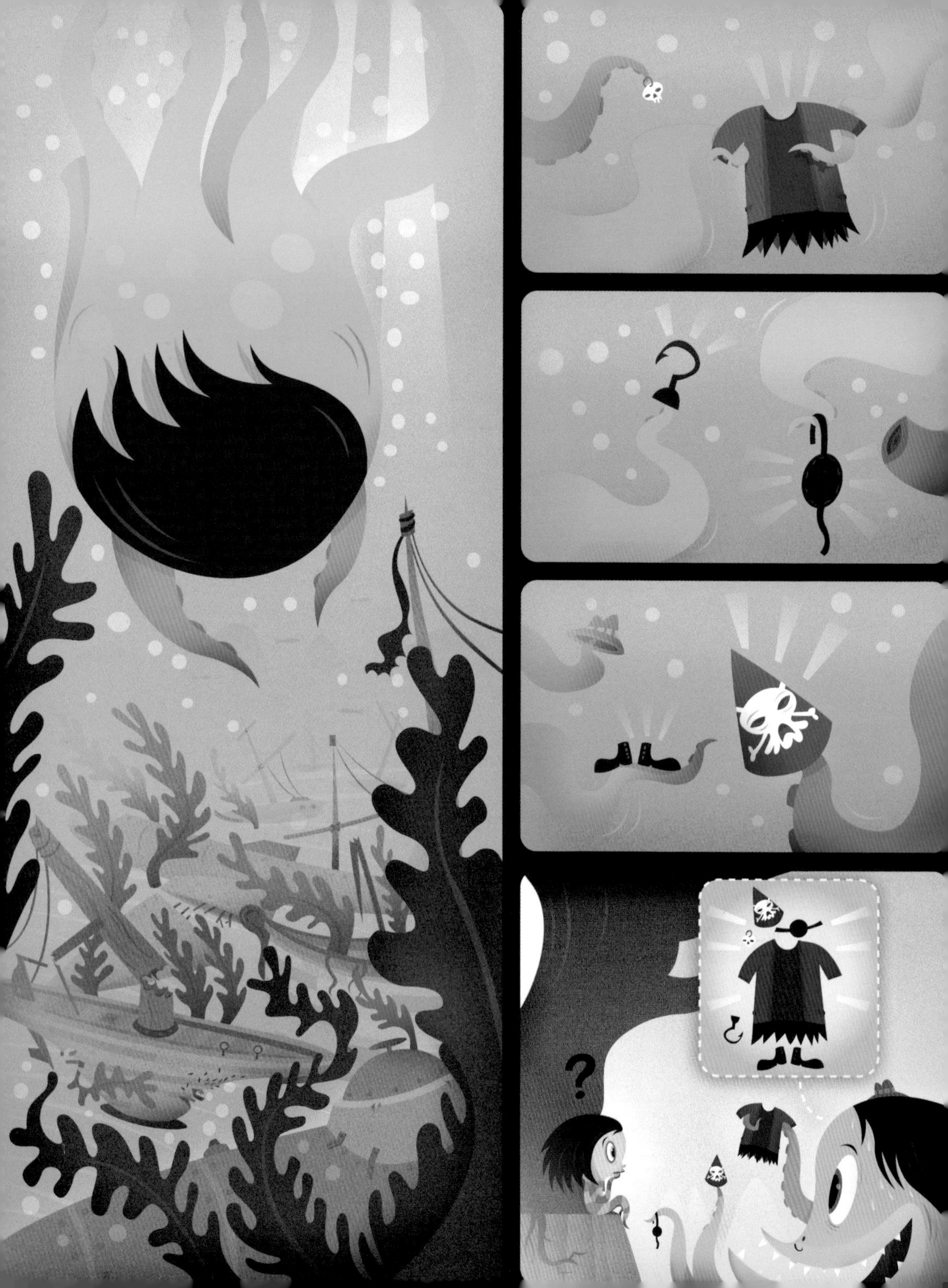

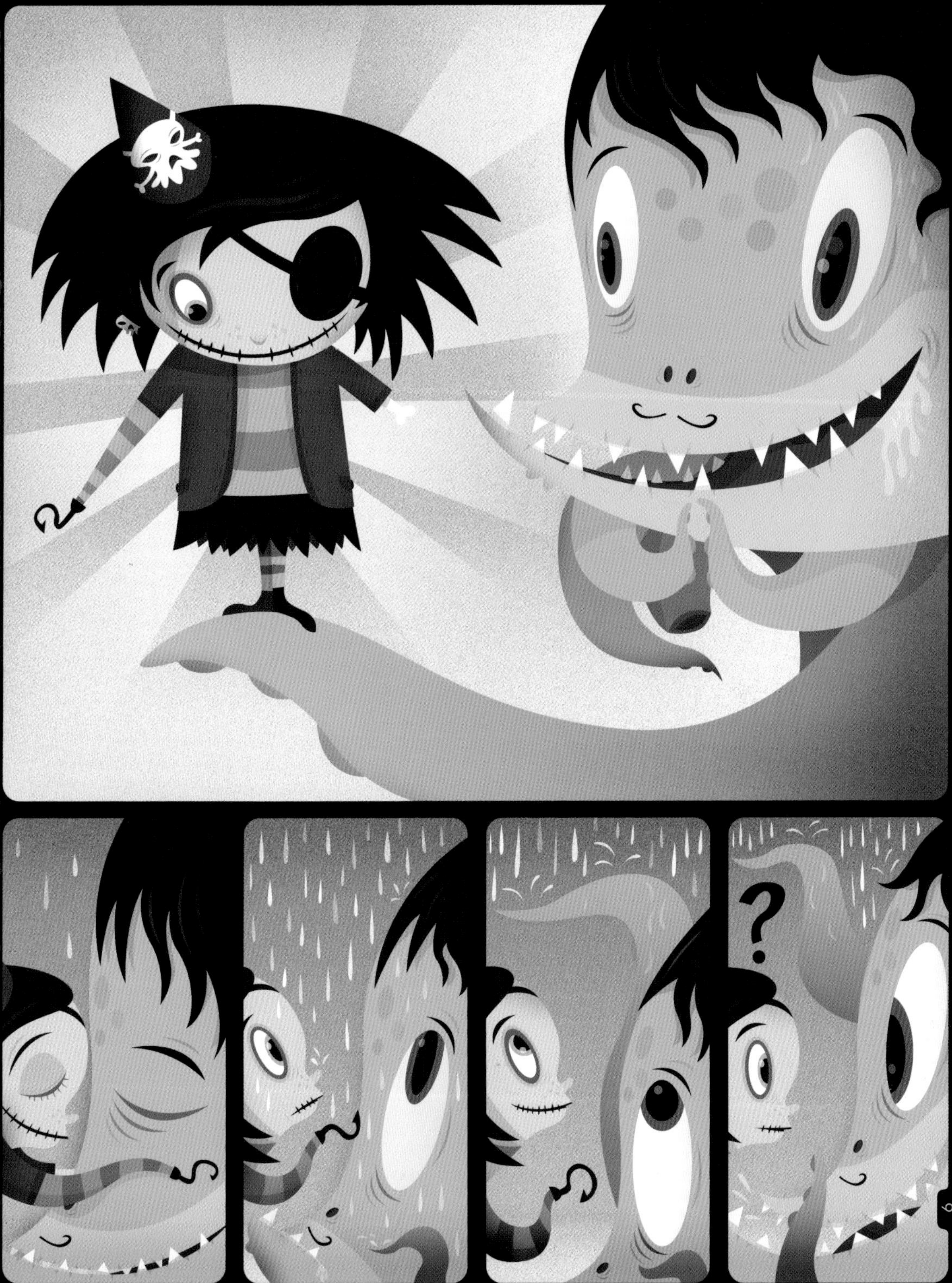
?

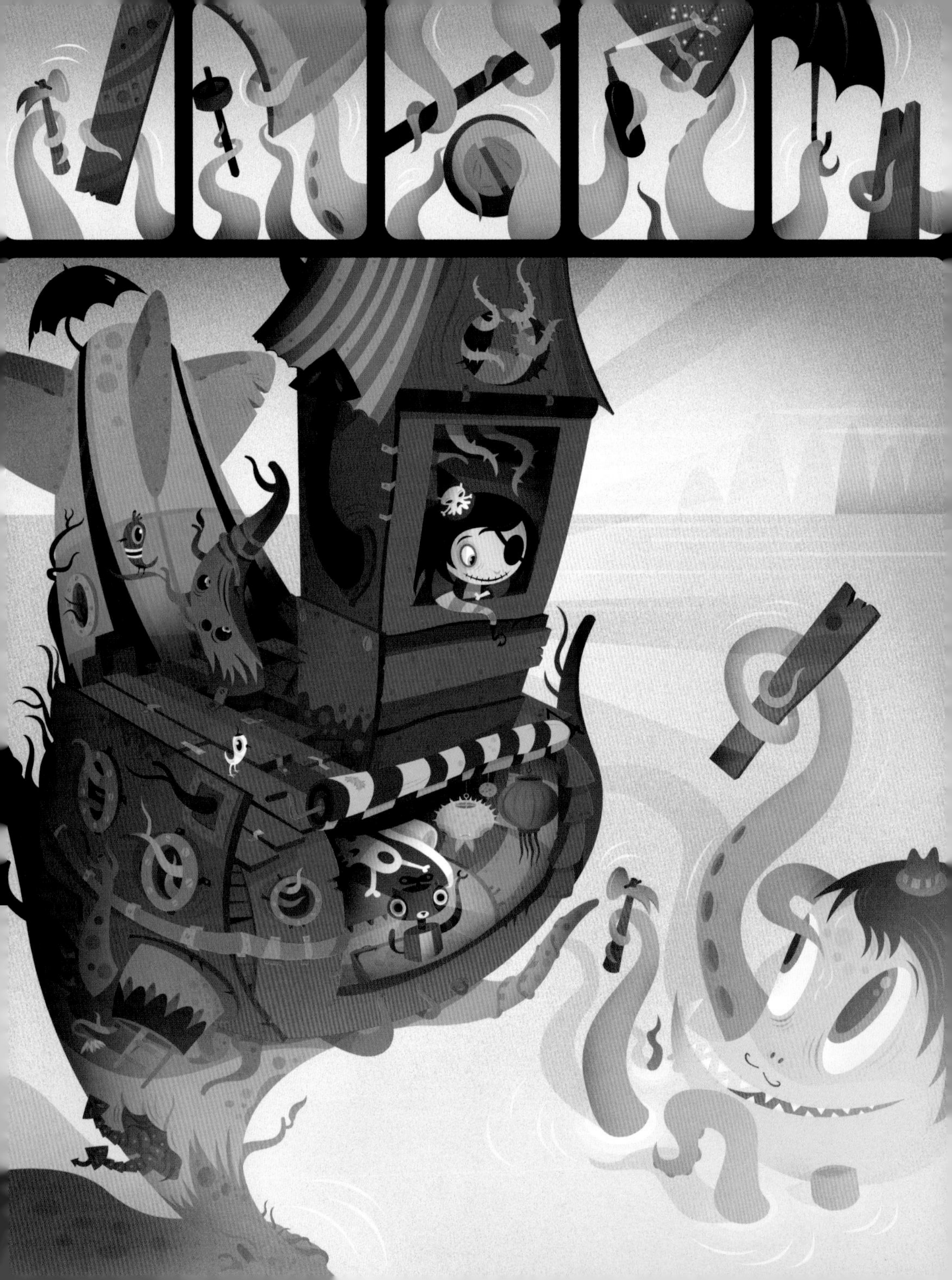

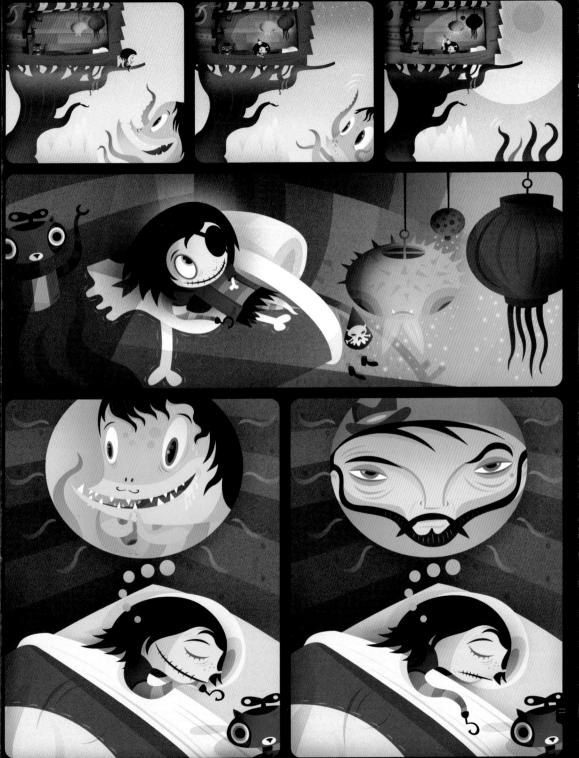

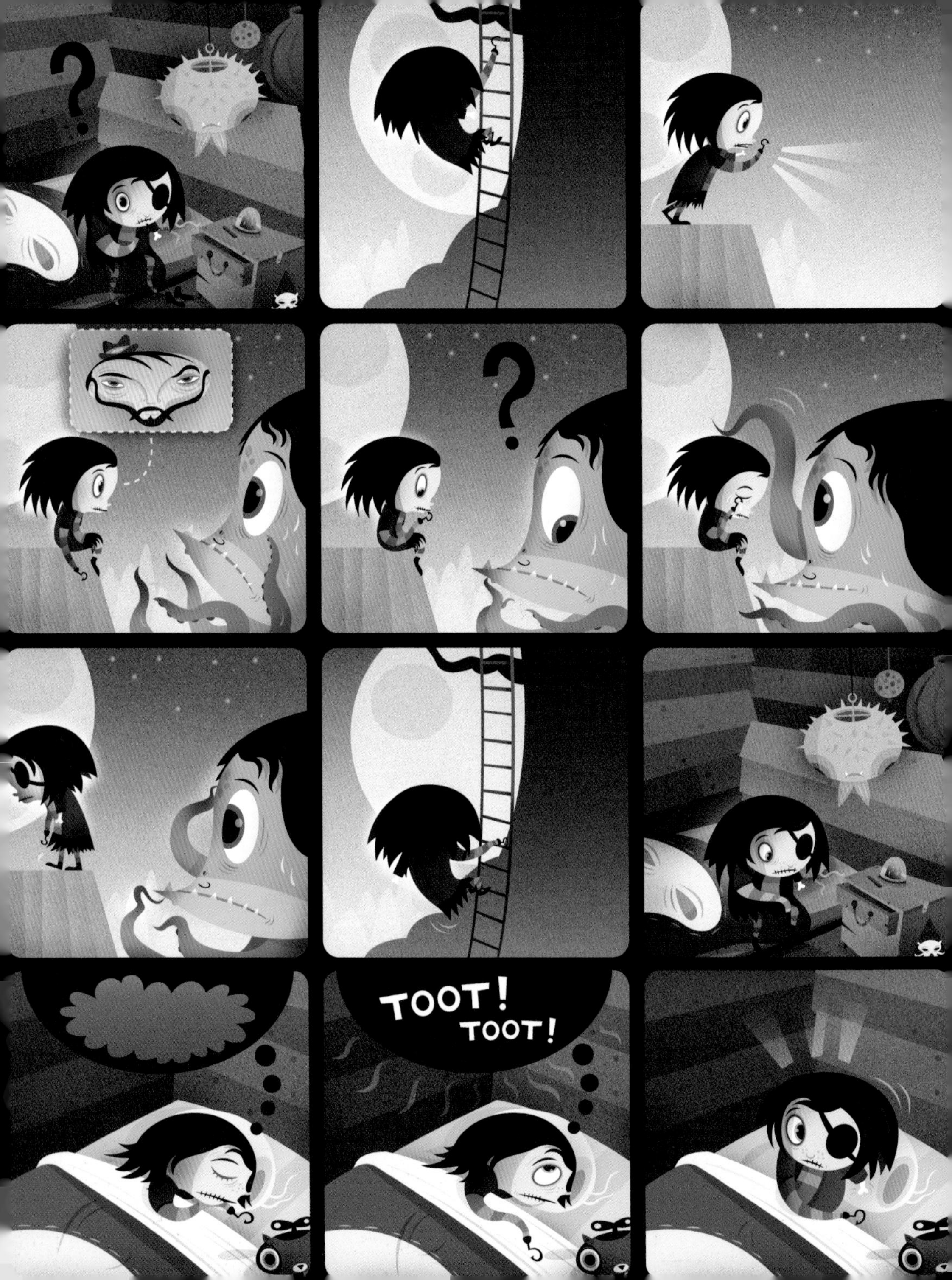
TOOT!
TOOT!

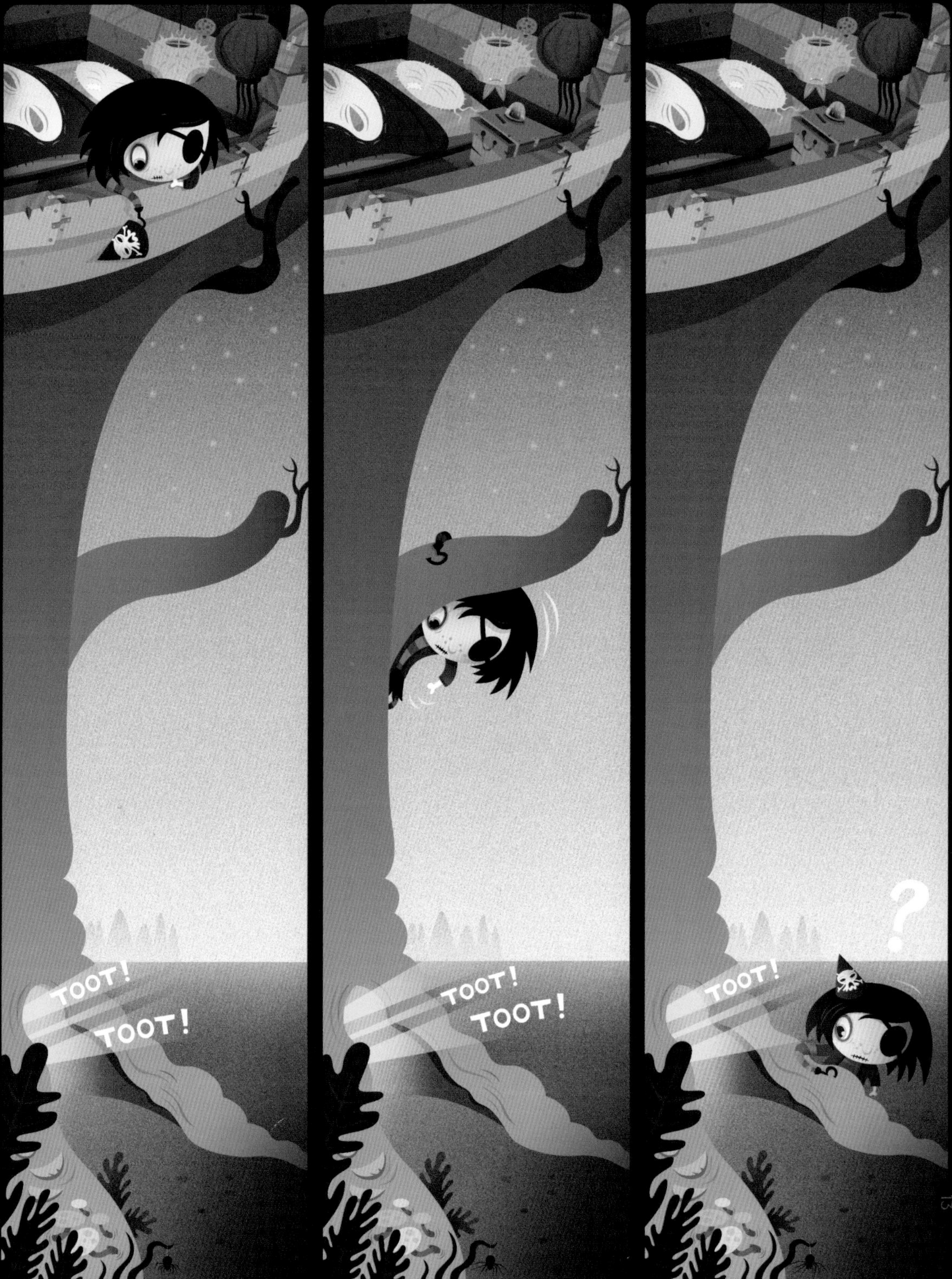
TOOT!
TOOT!
TOOT!
TOOT!
TOOT!
?

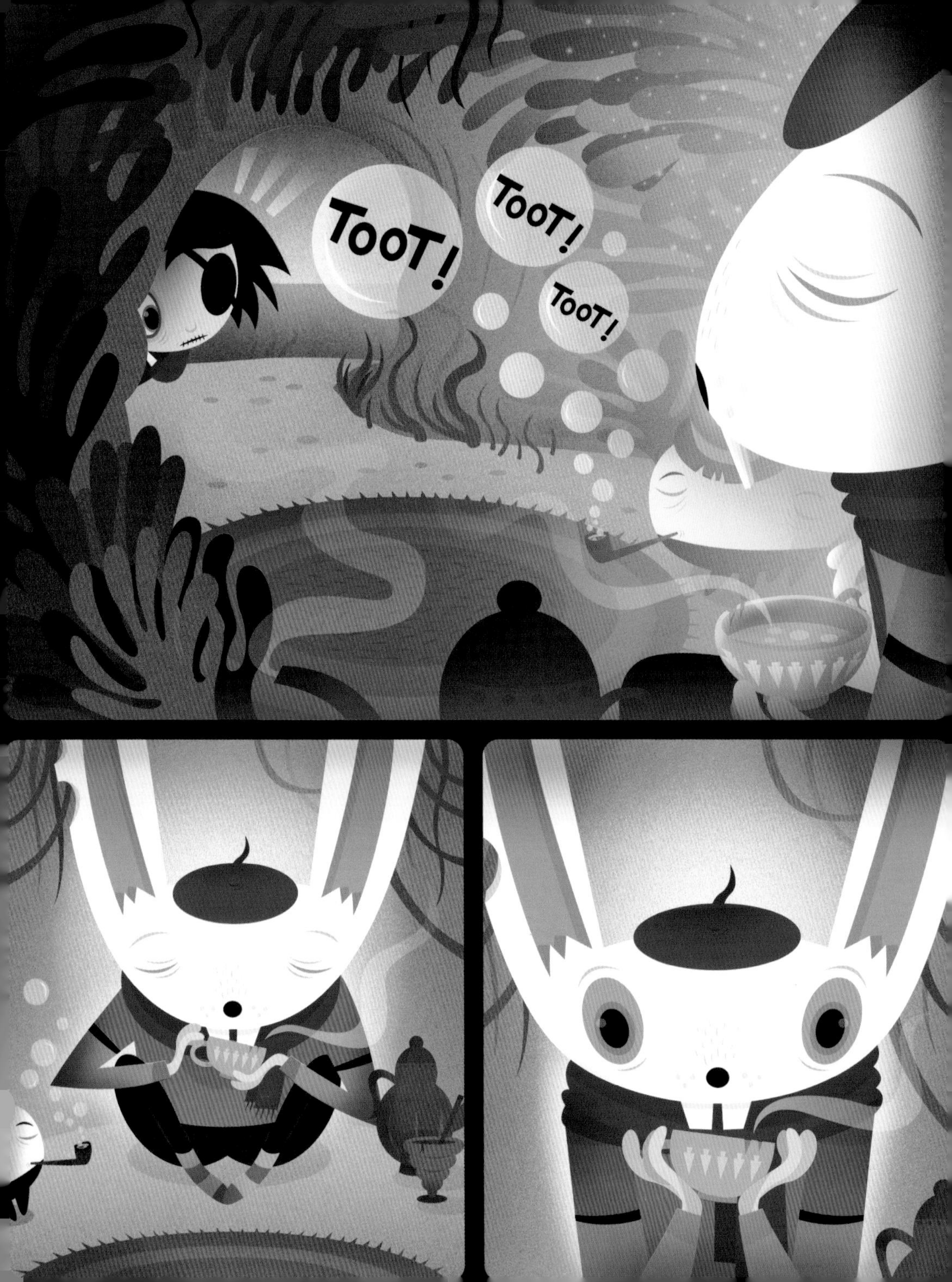
TOOT!
TOOT!
TOOT!

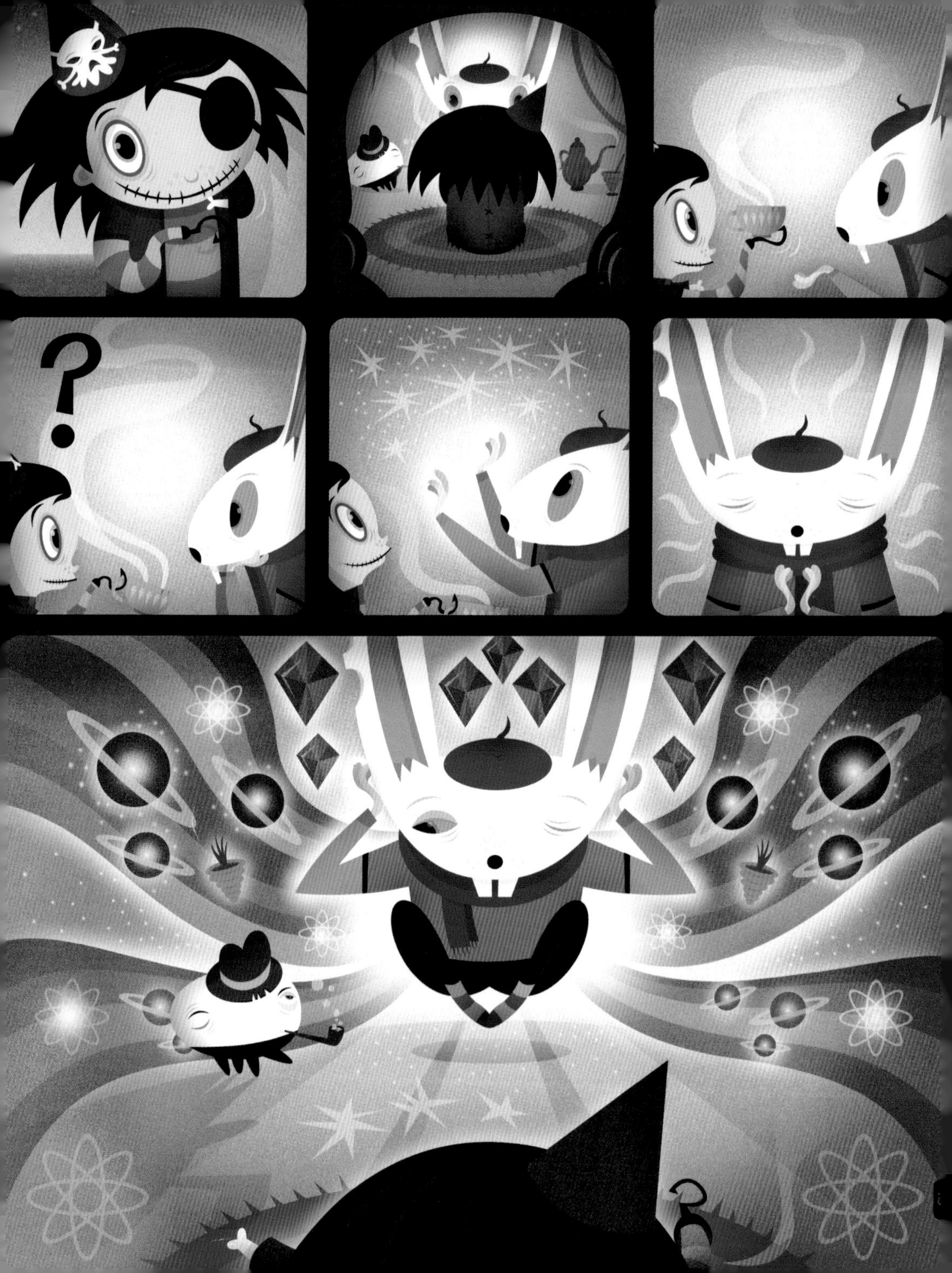

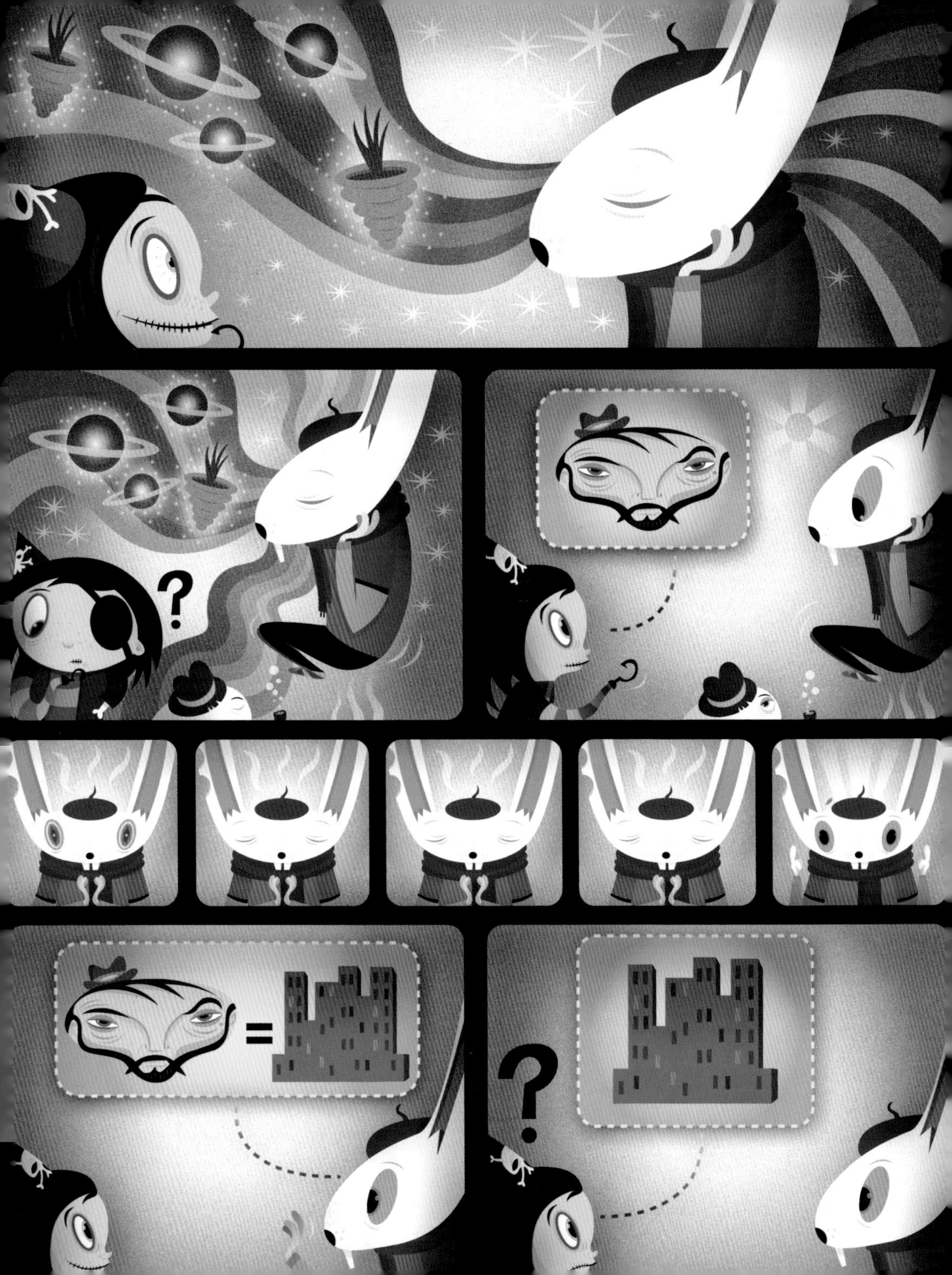

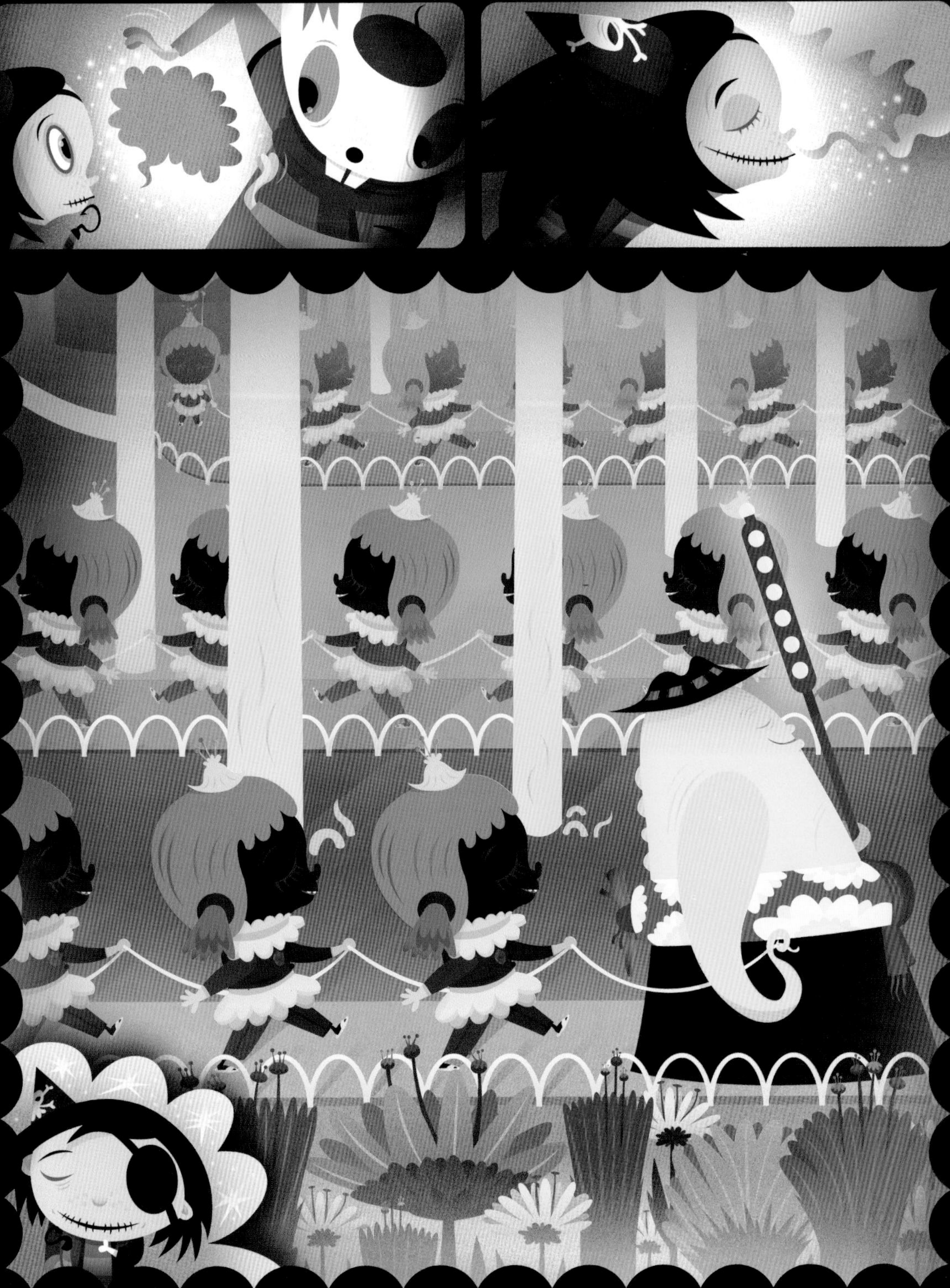

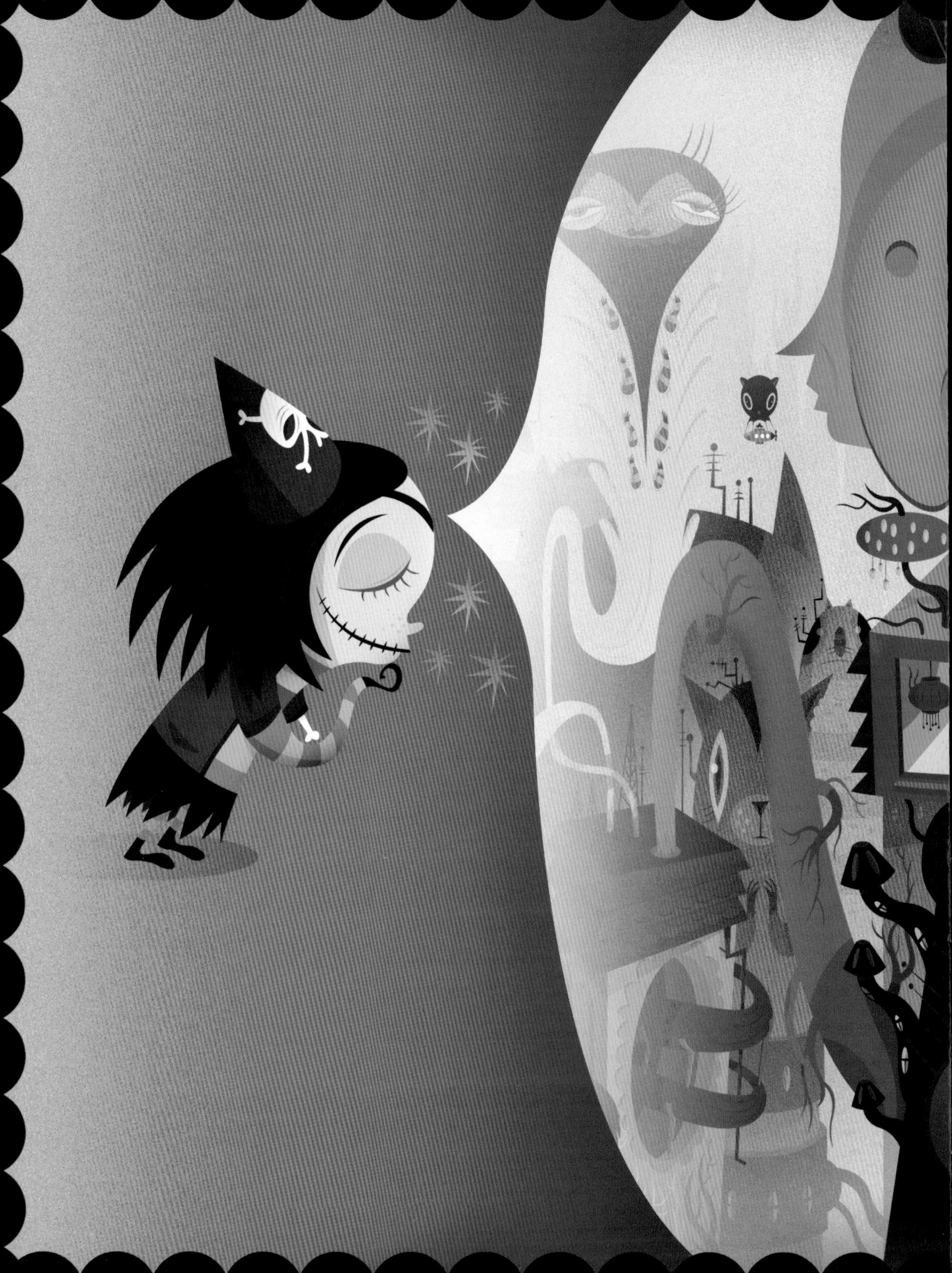

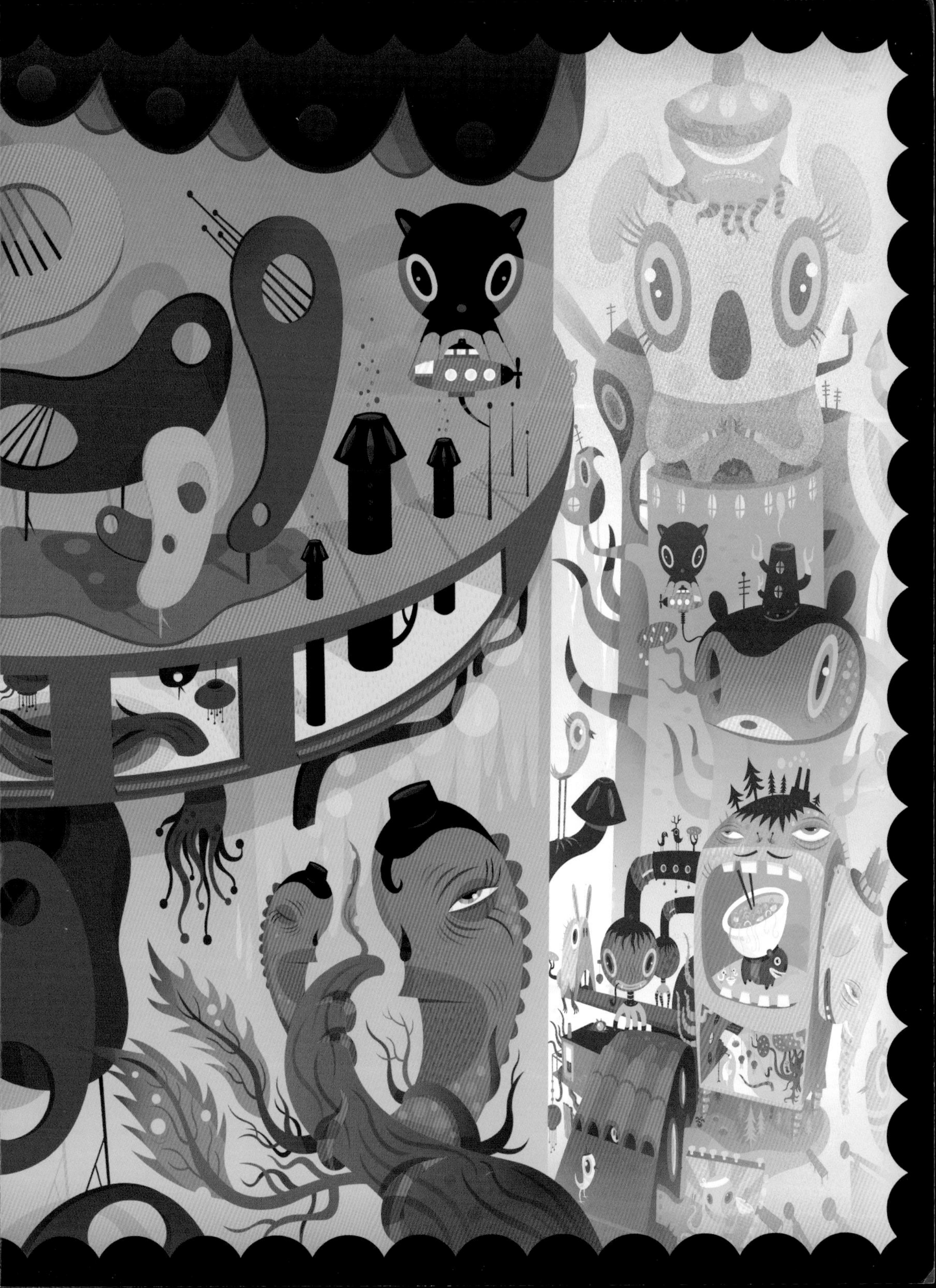

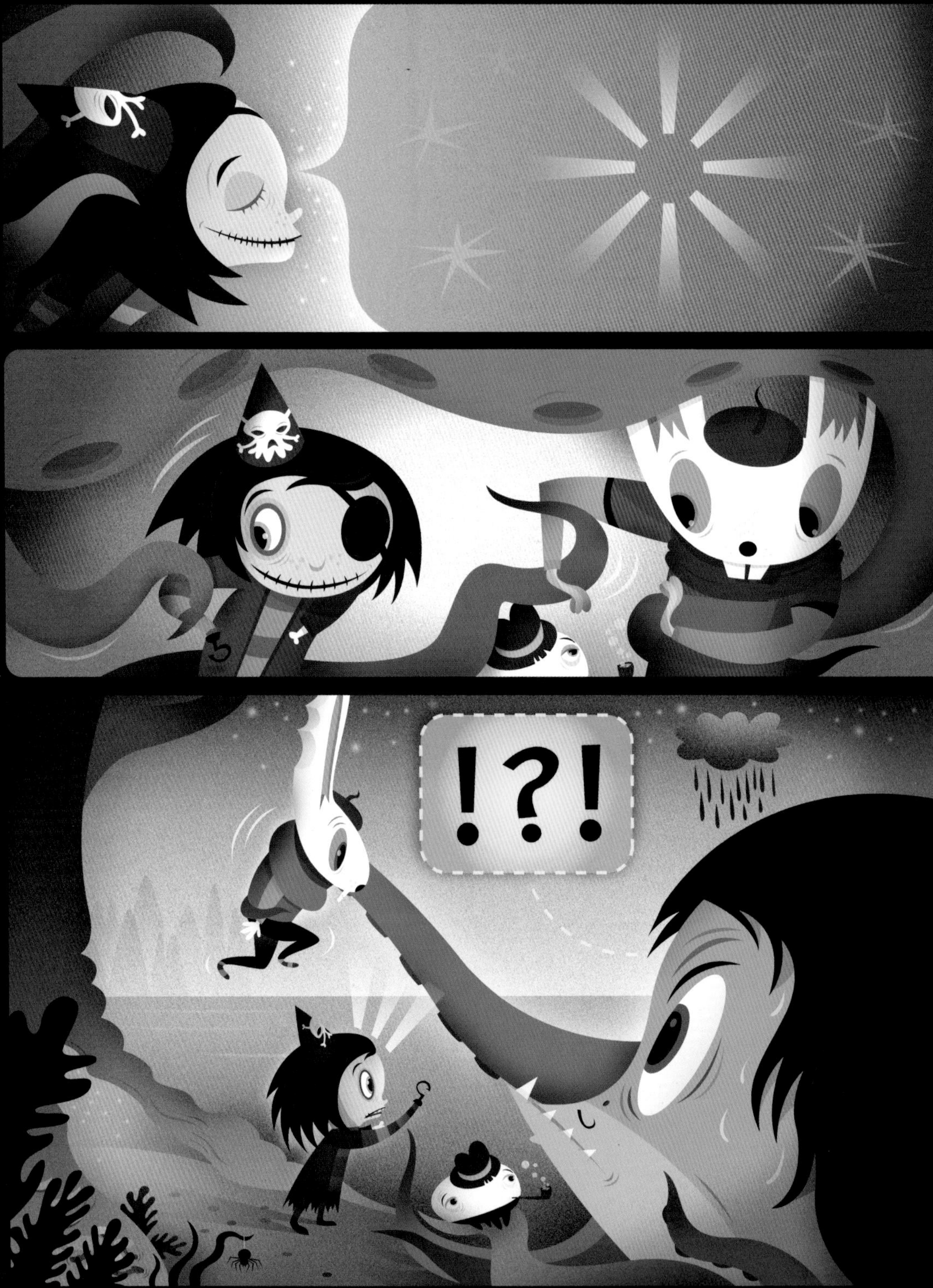
!?!

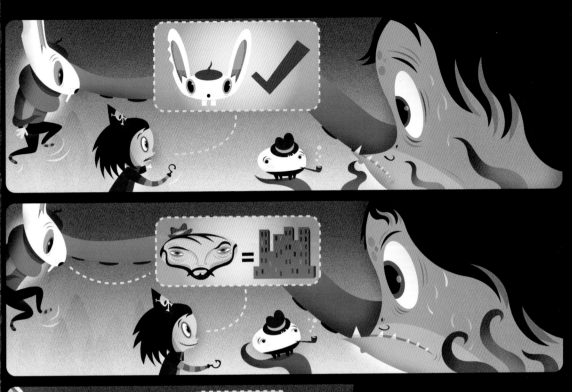

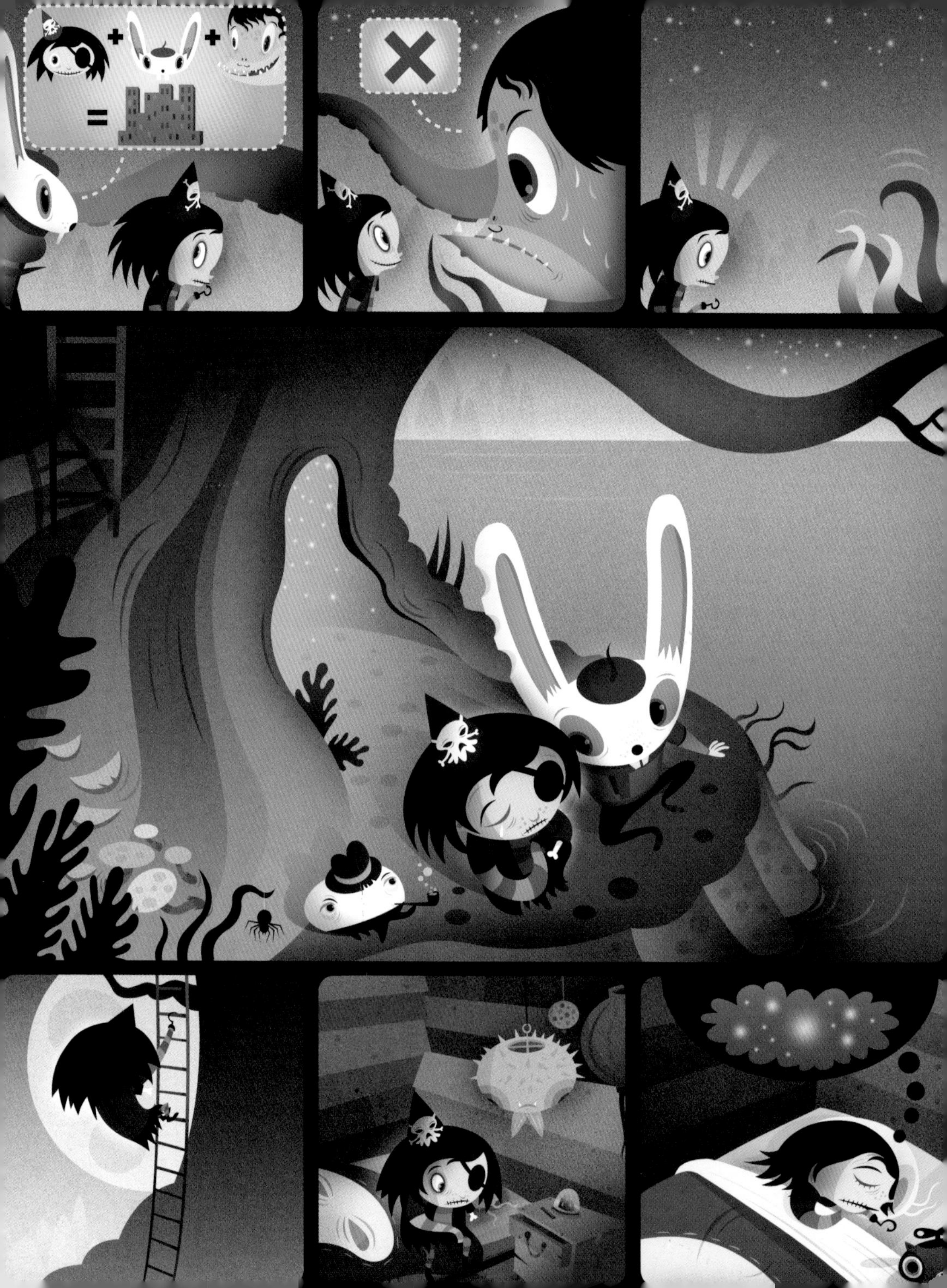

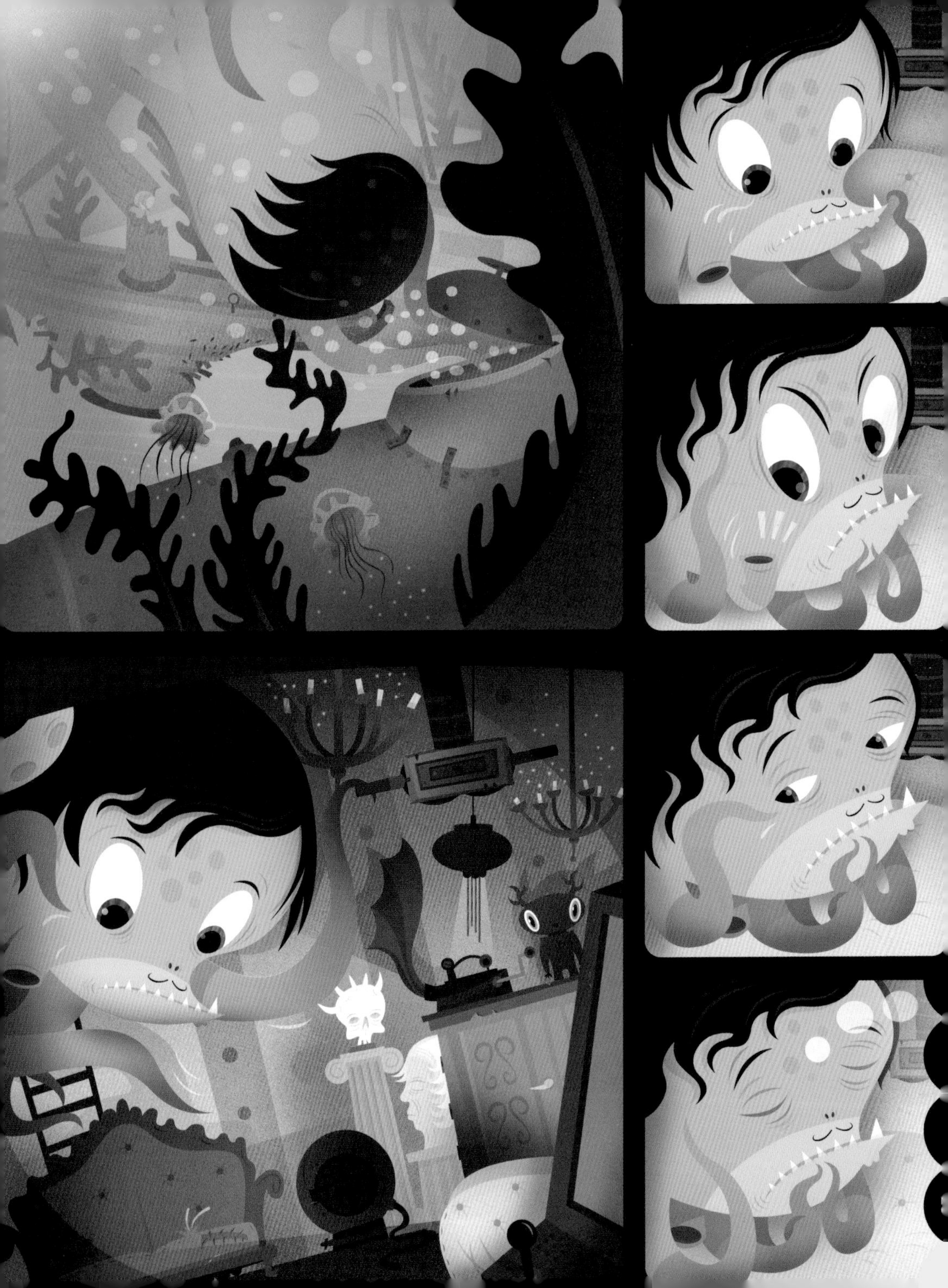

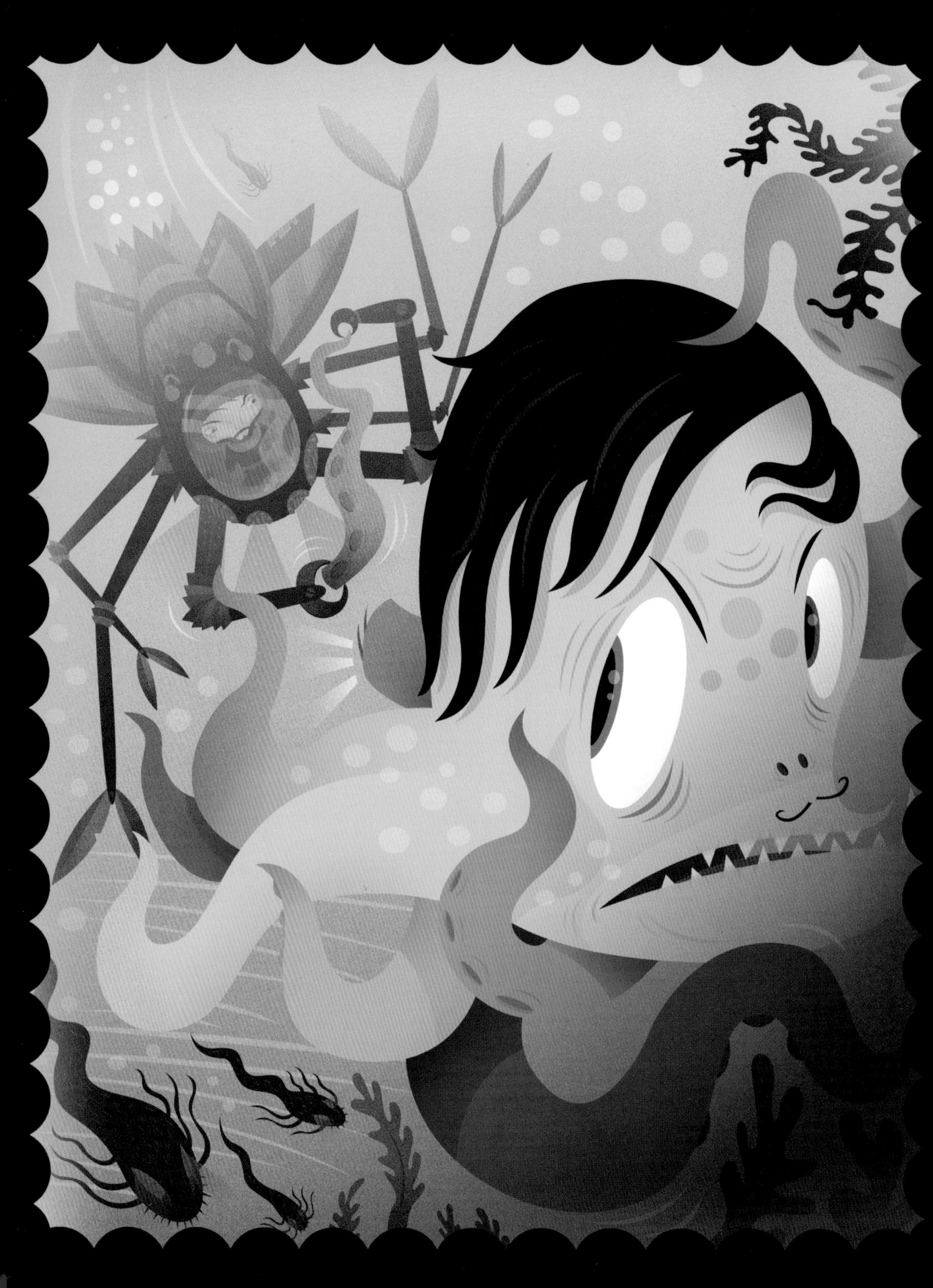

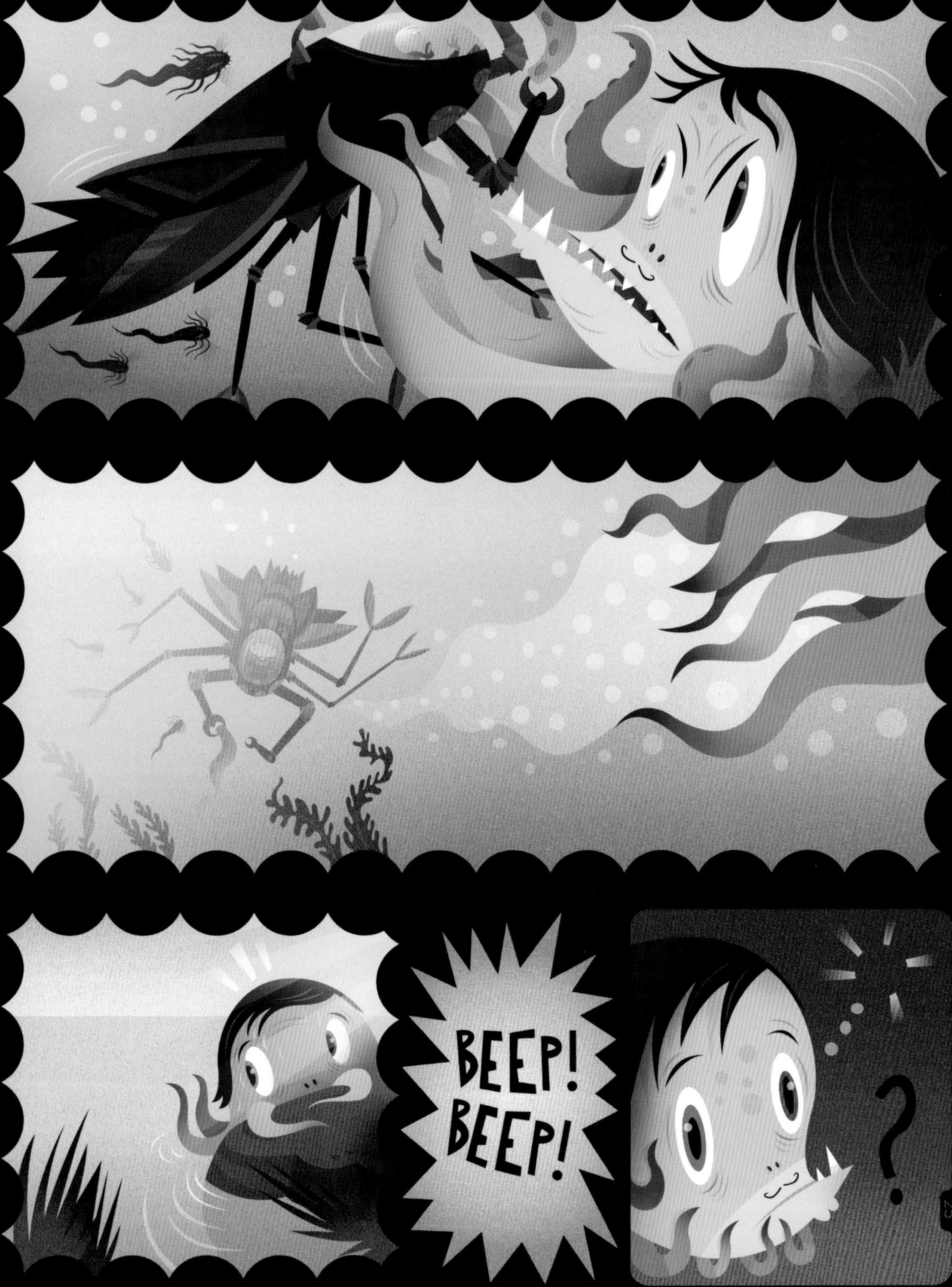
BEEP! BEEP!

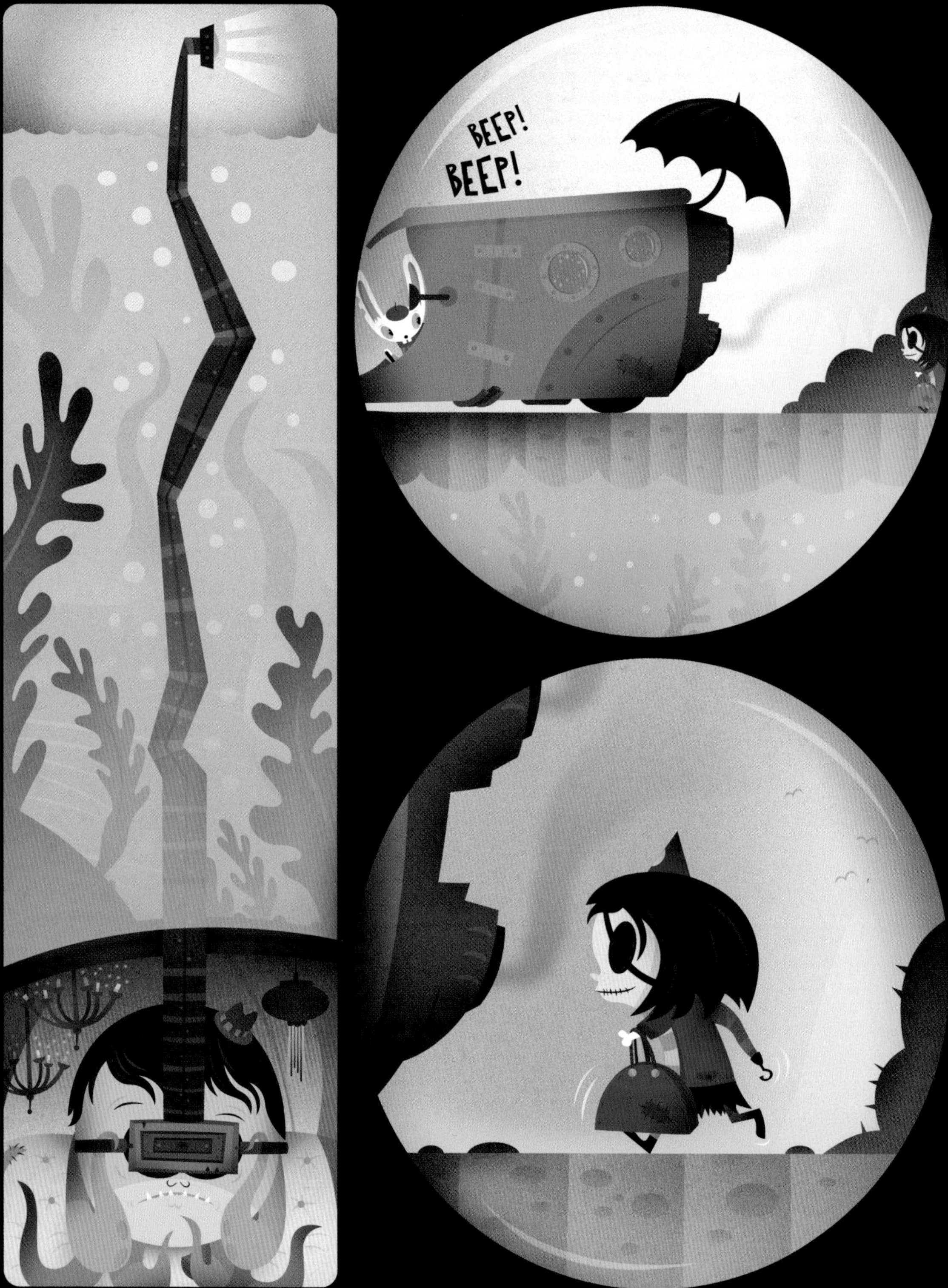
BEEP!
BEEP!

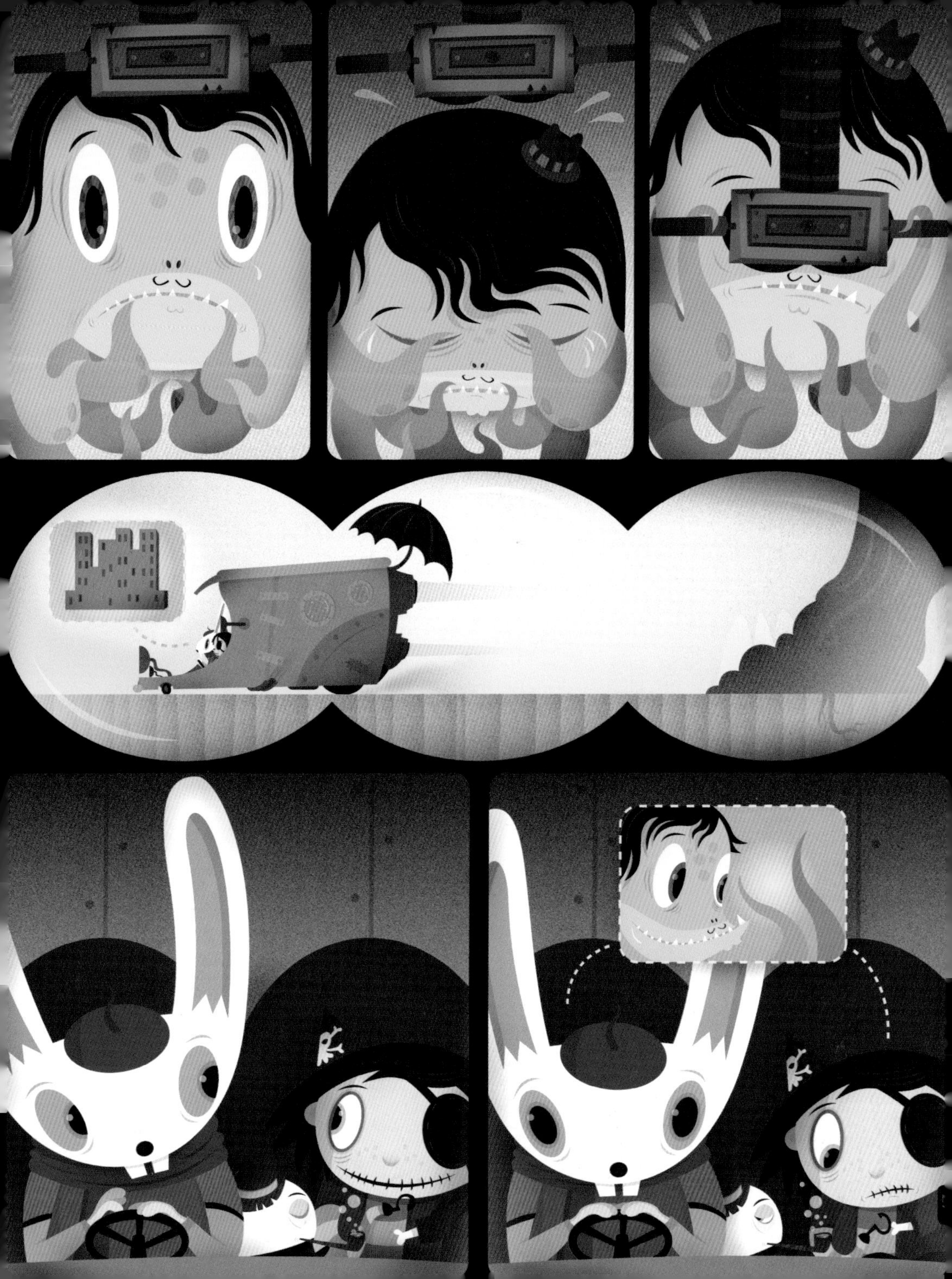

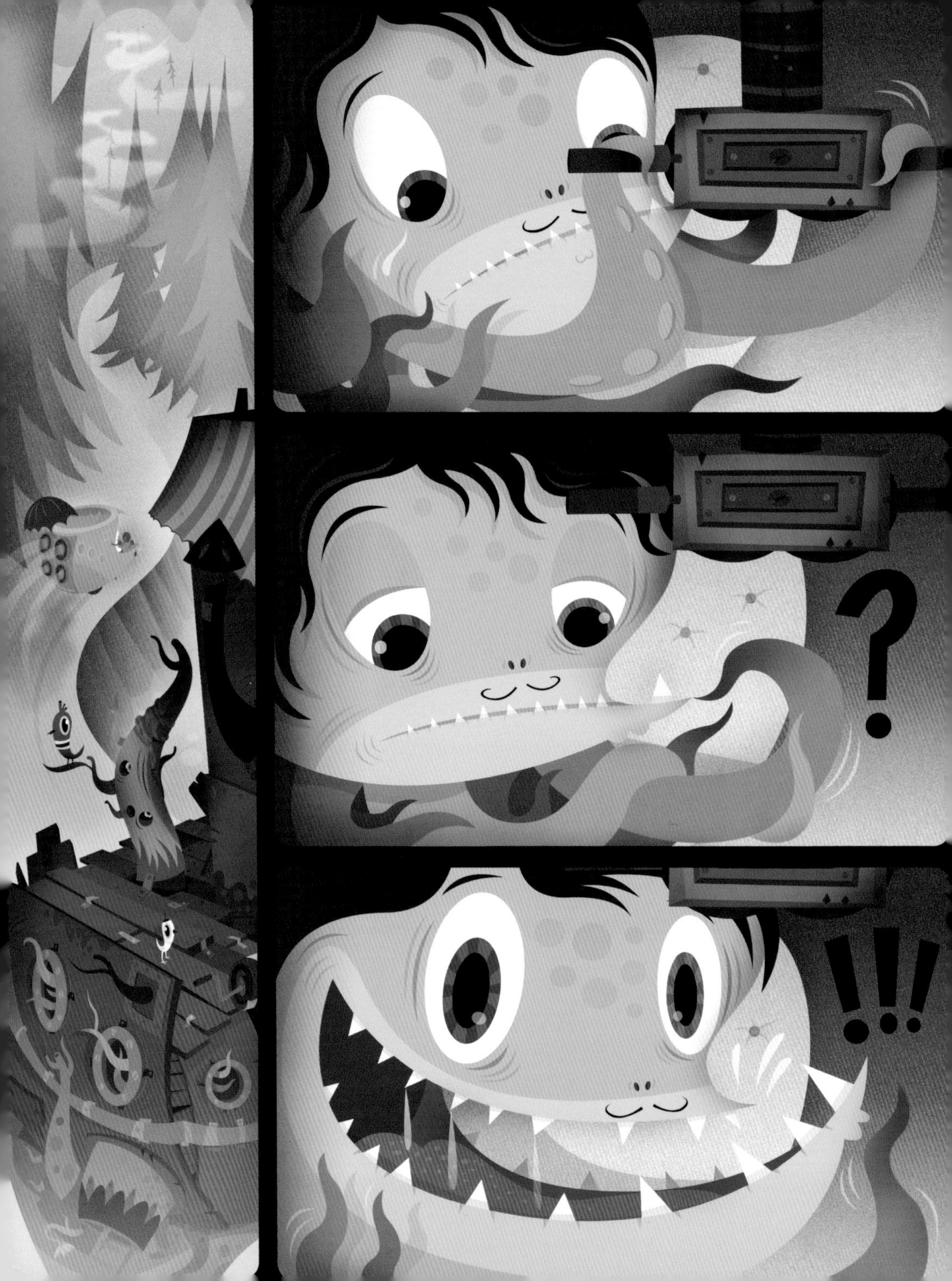
?
!!!

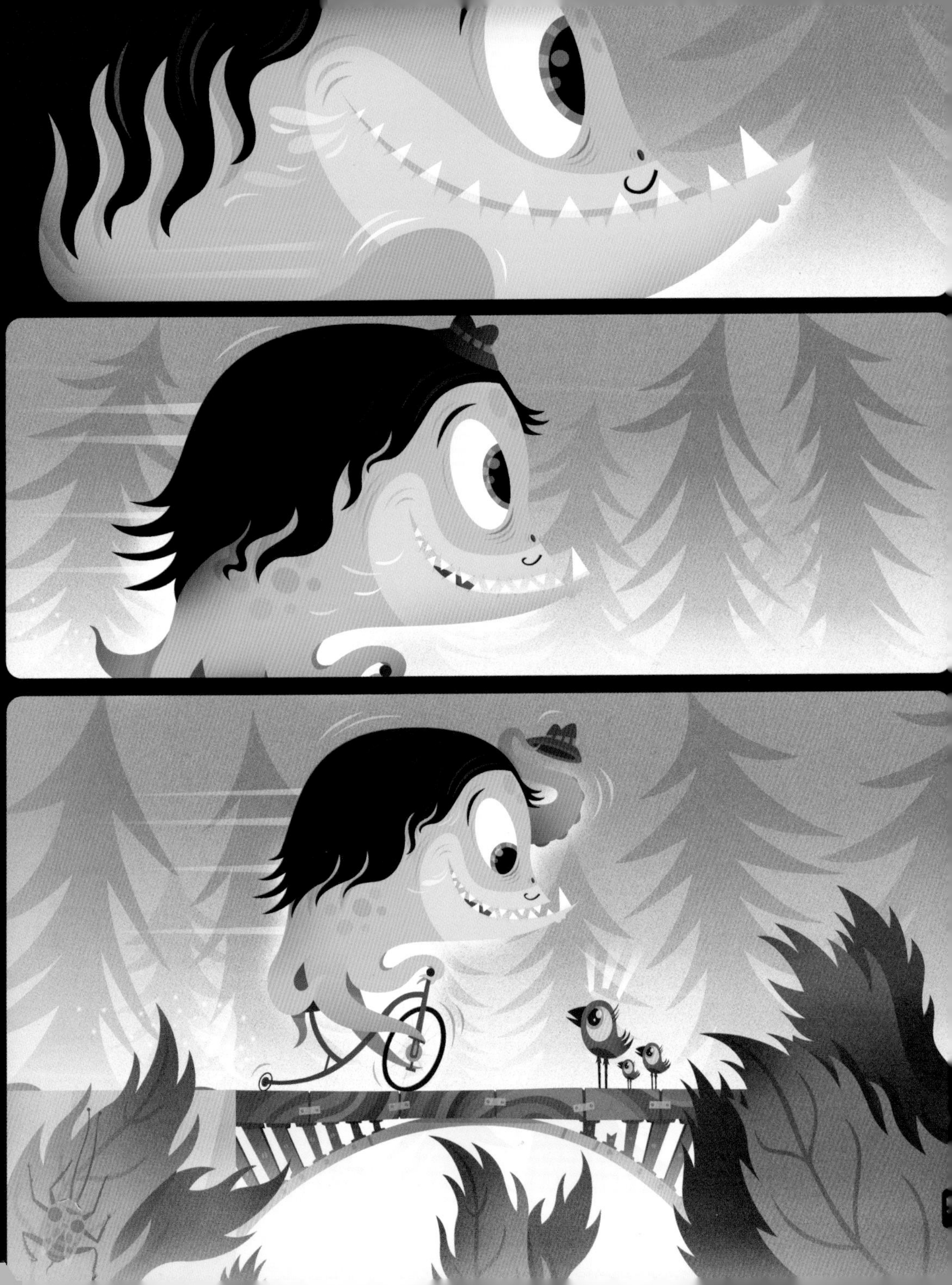

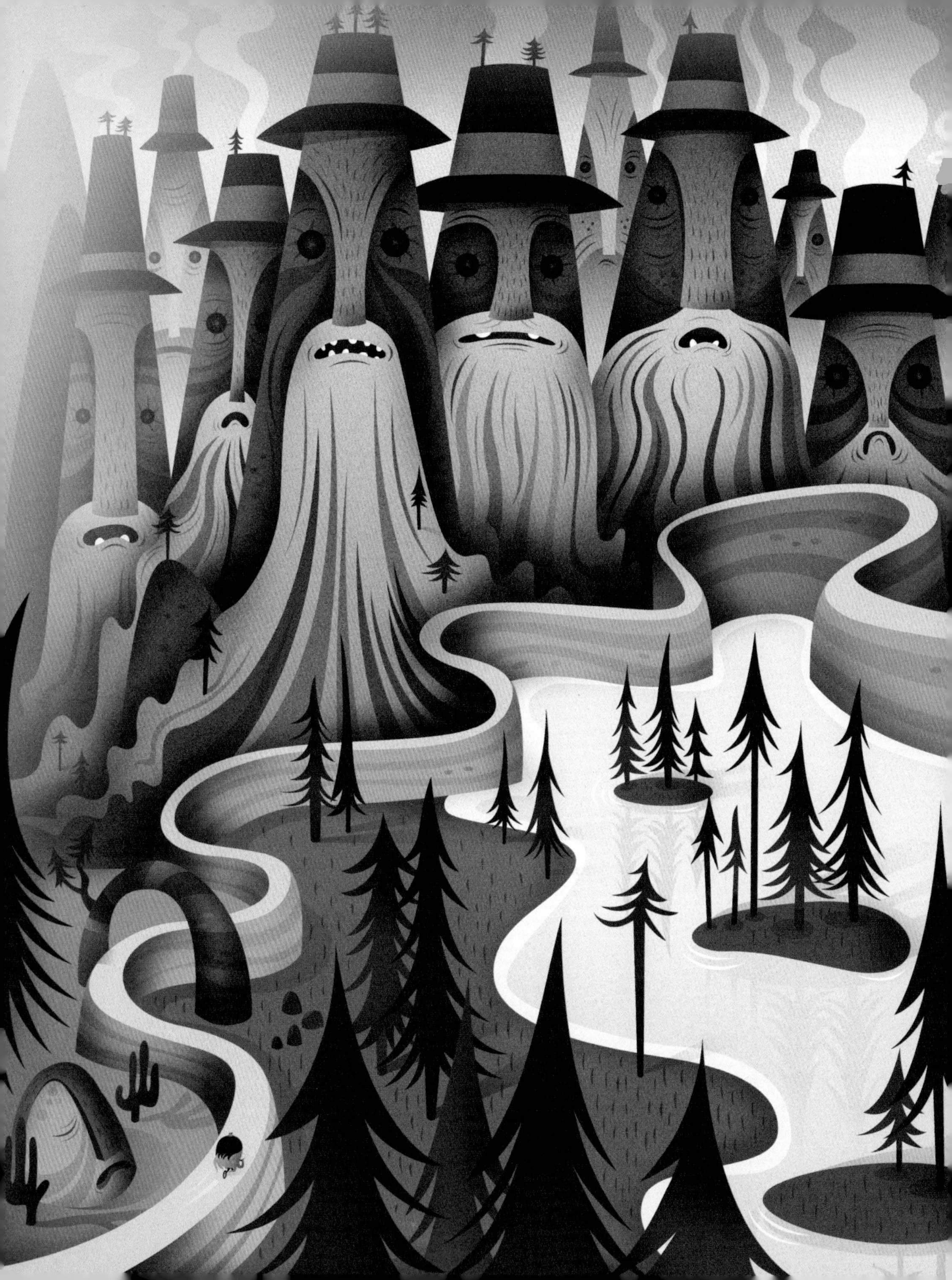

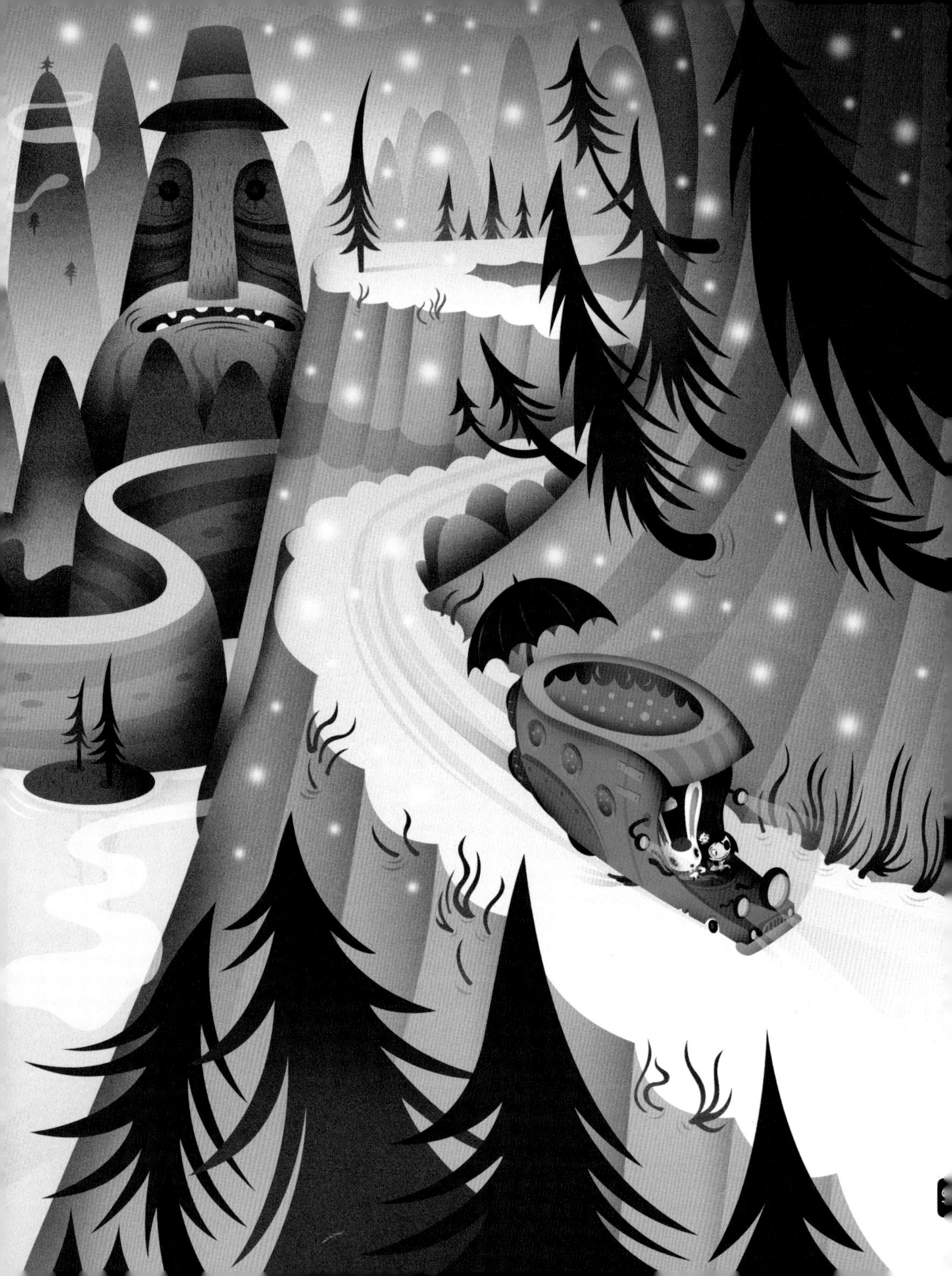

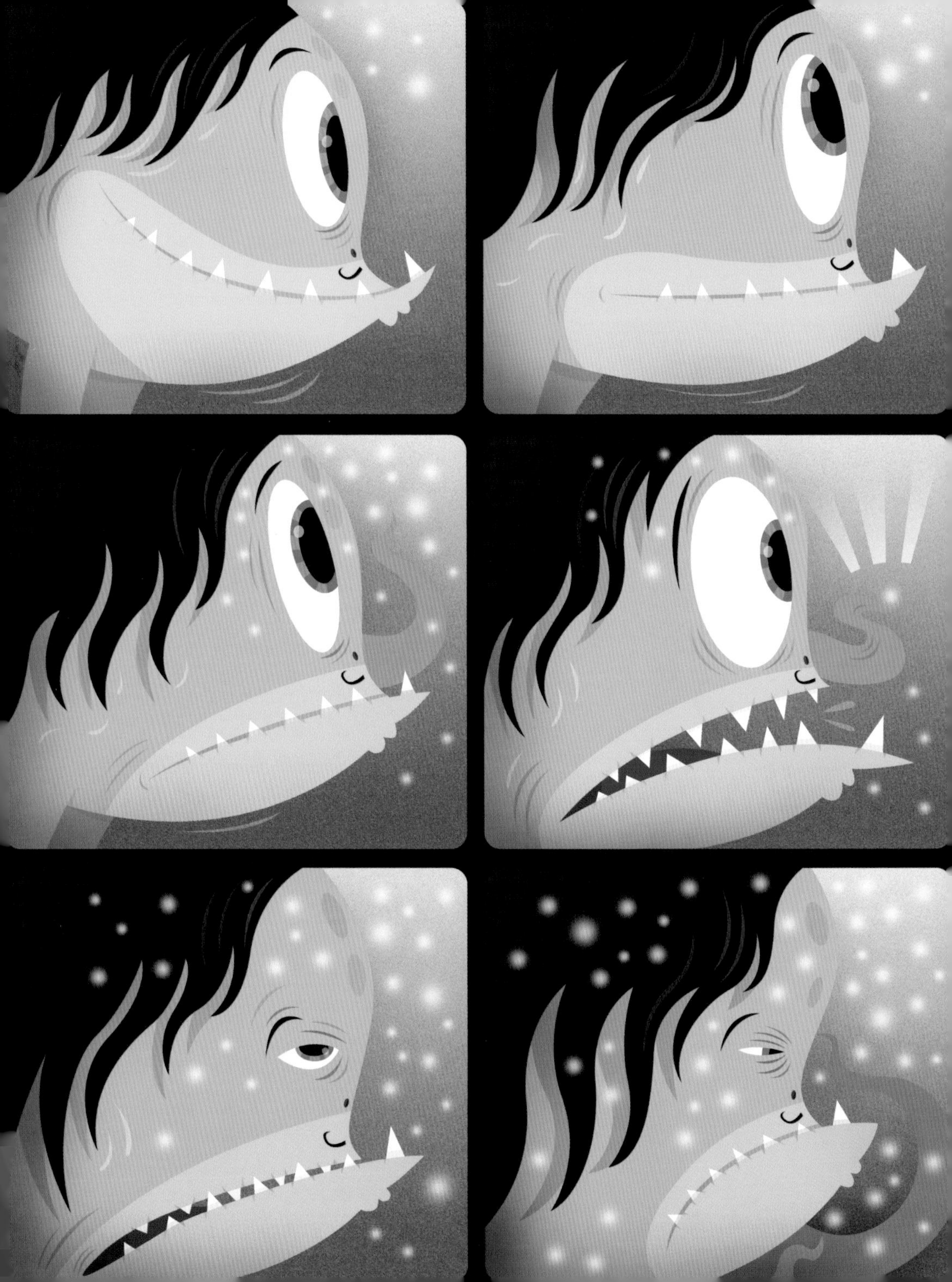

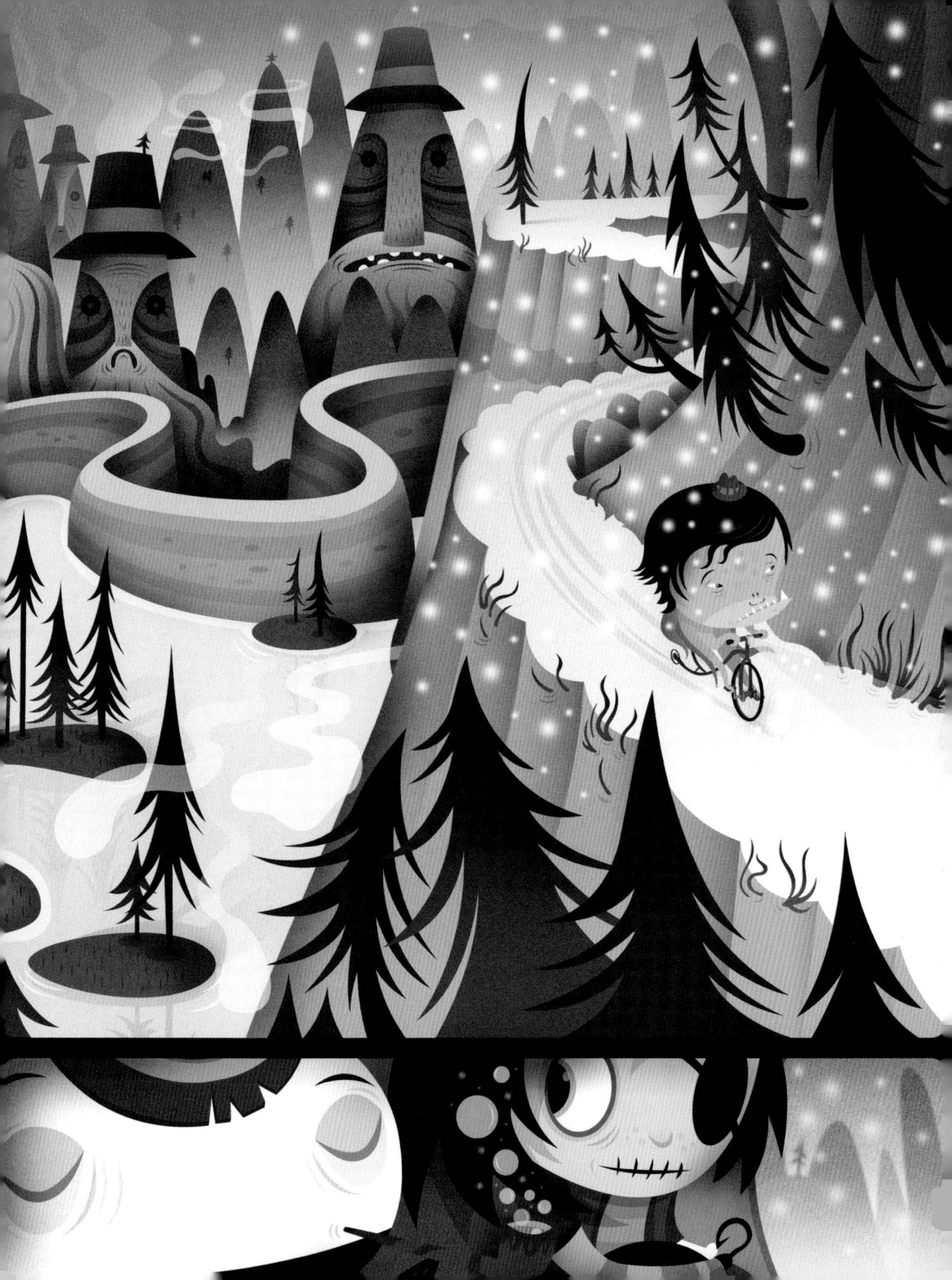

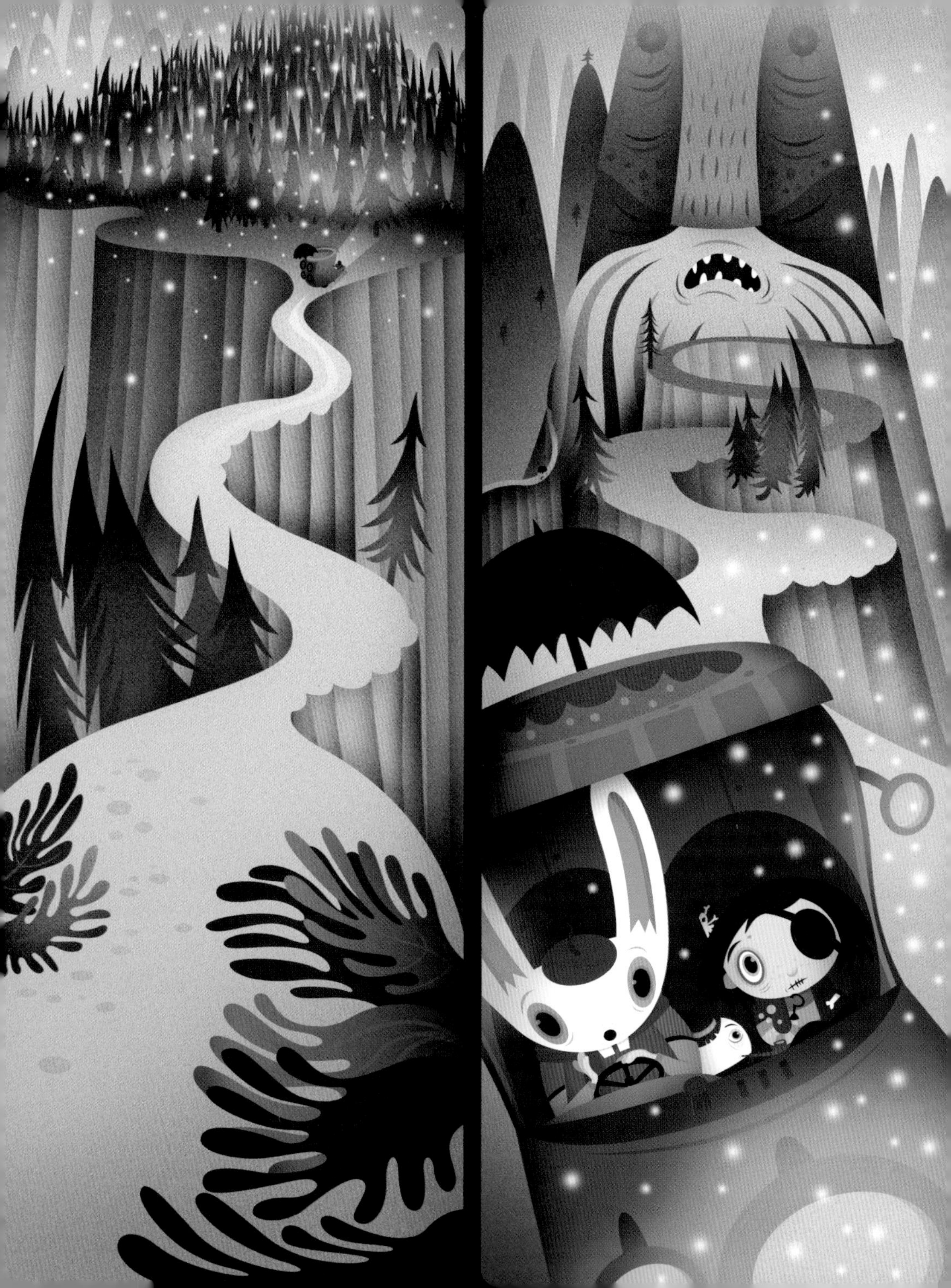

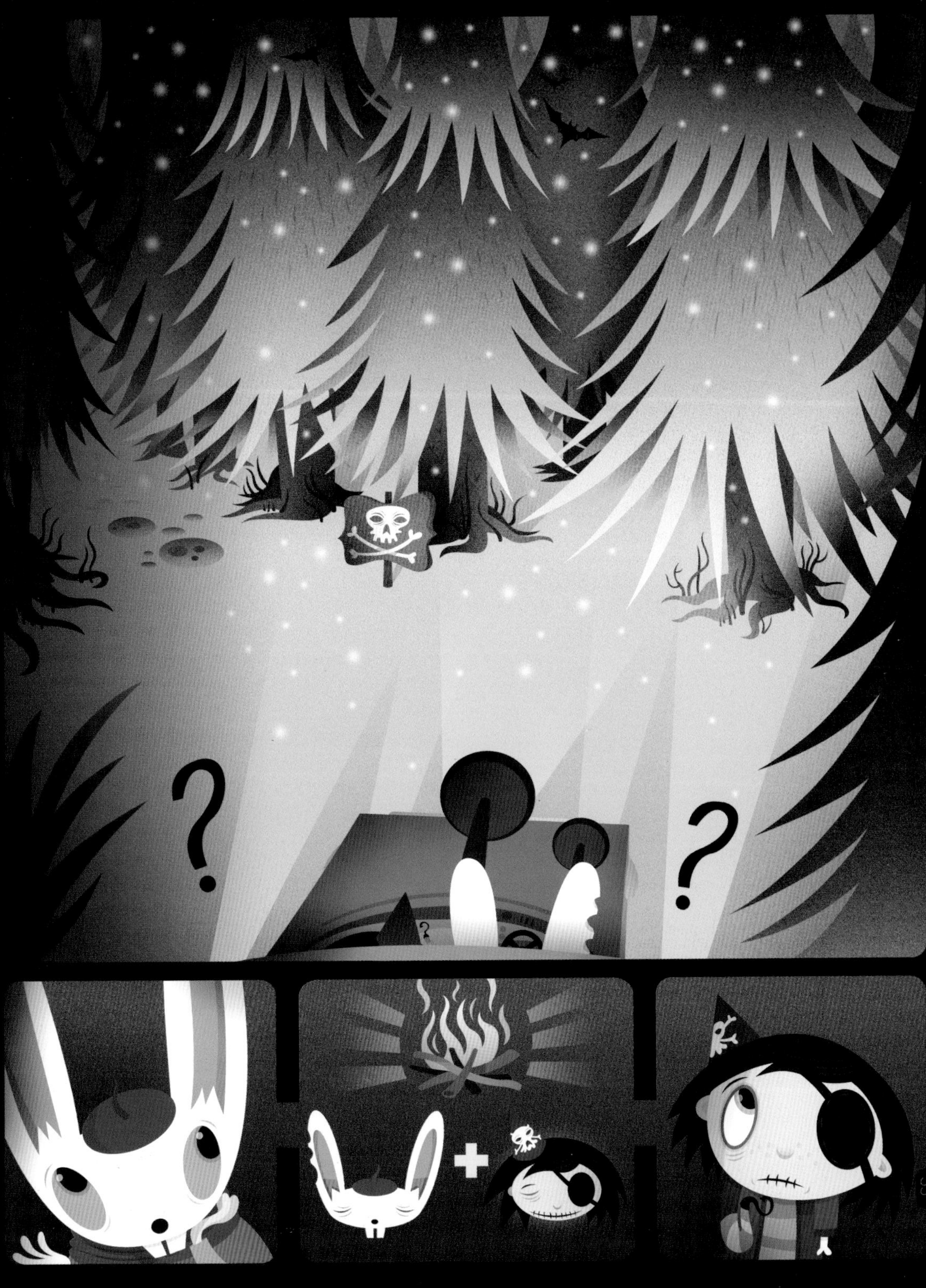

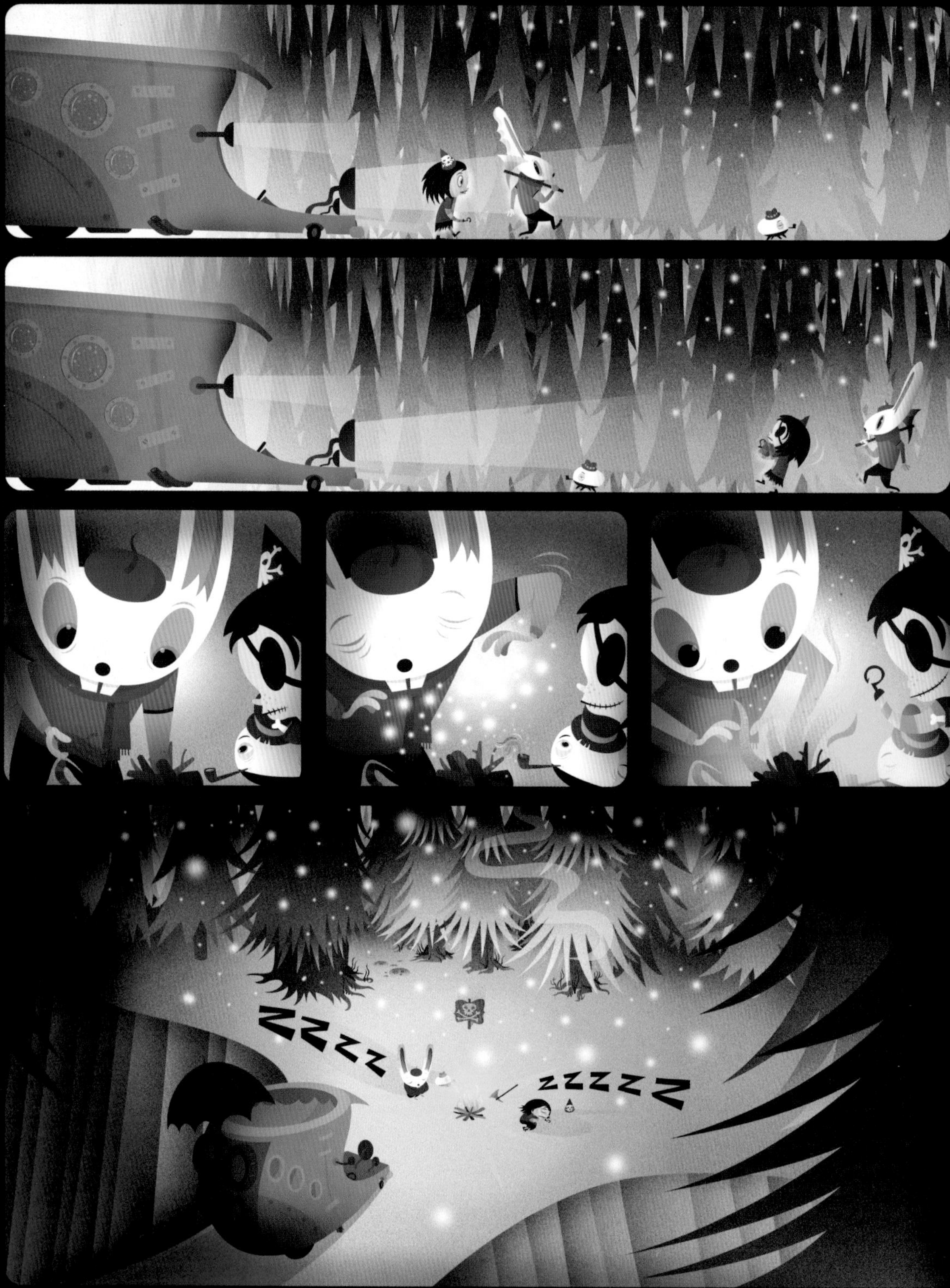
ZZZZZ
ZZZZZ

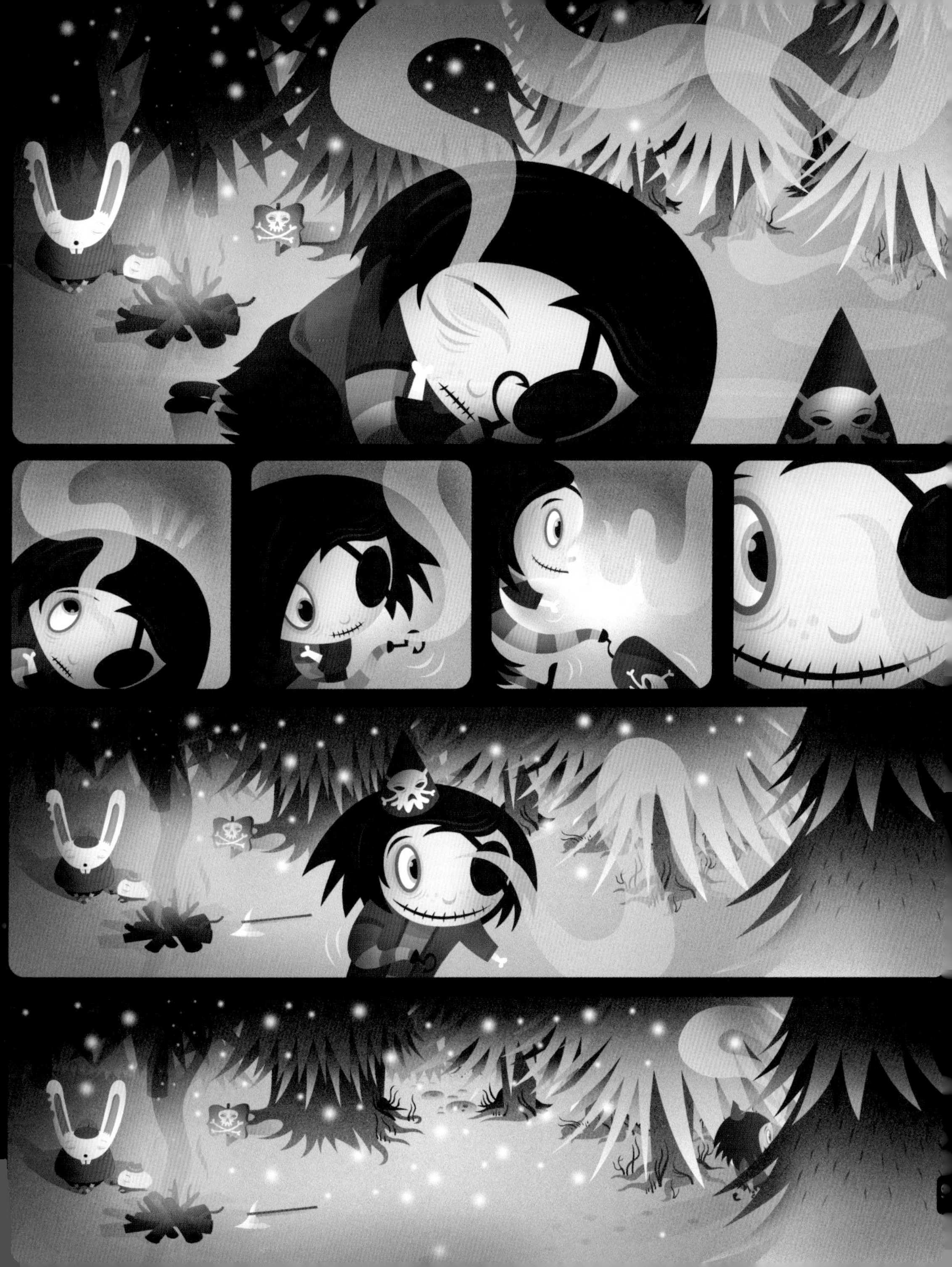

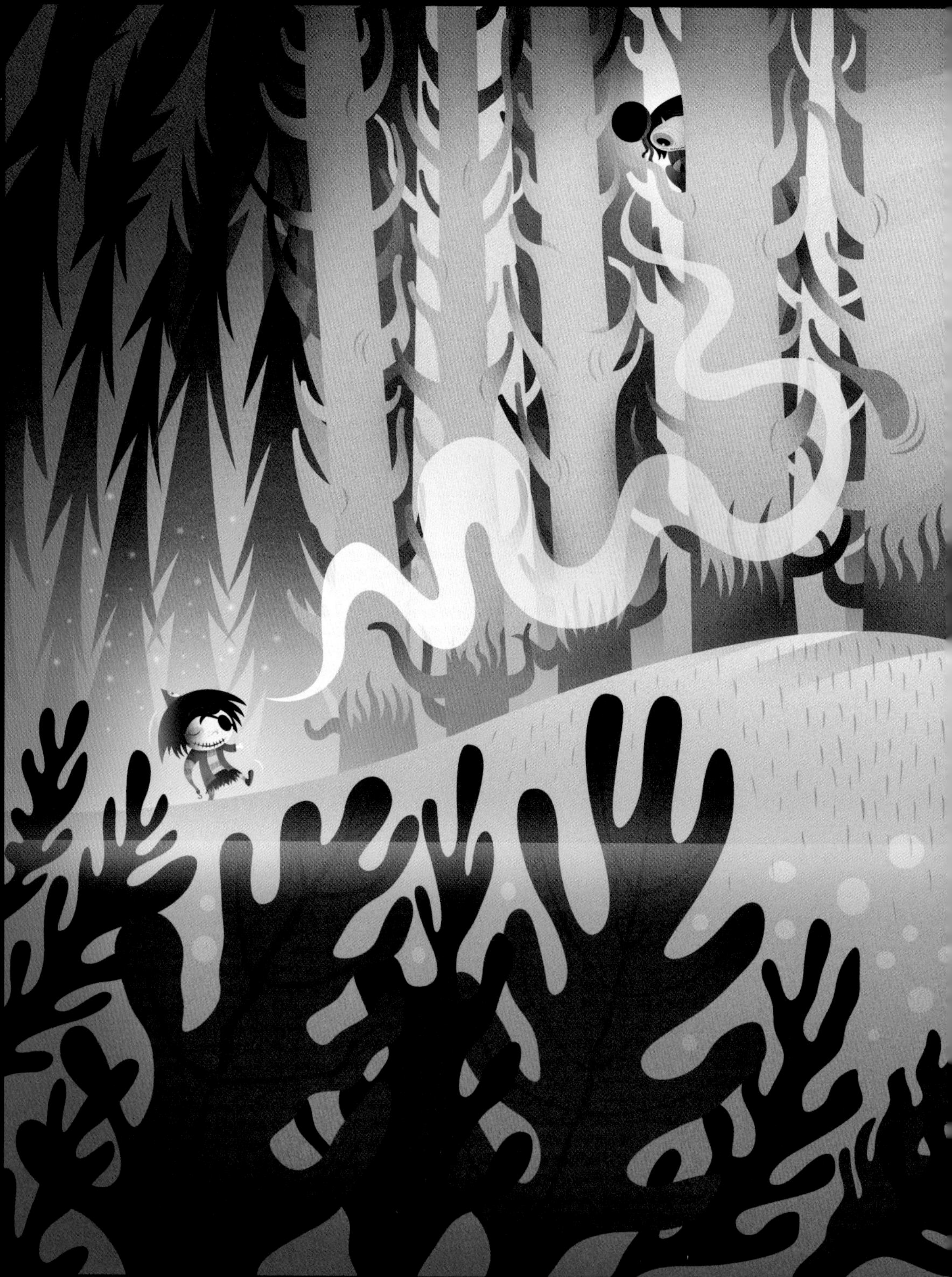

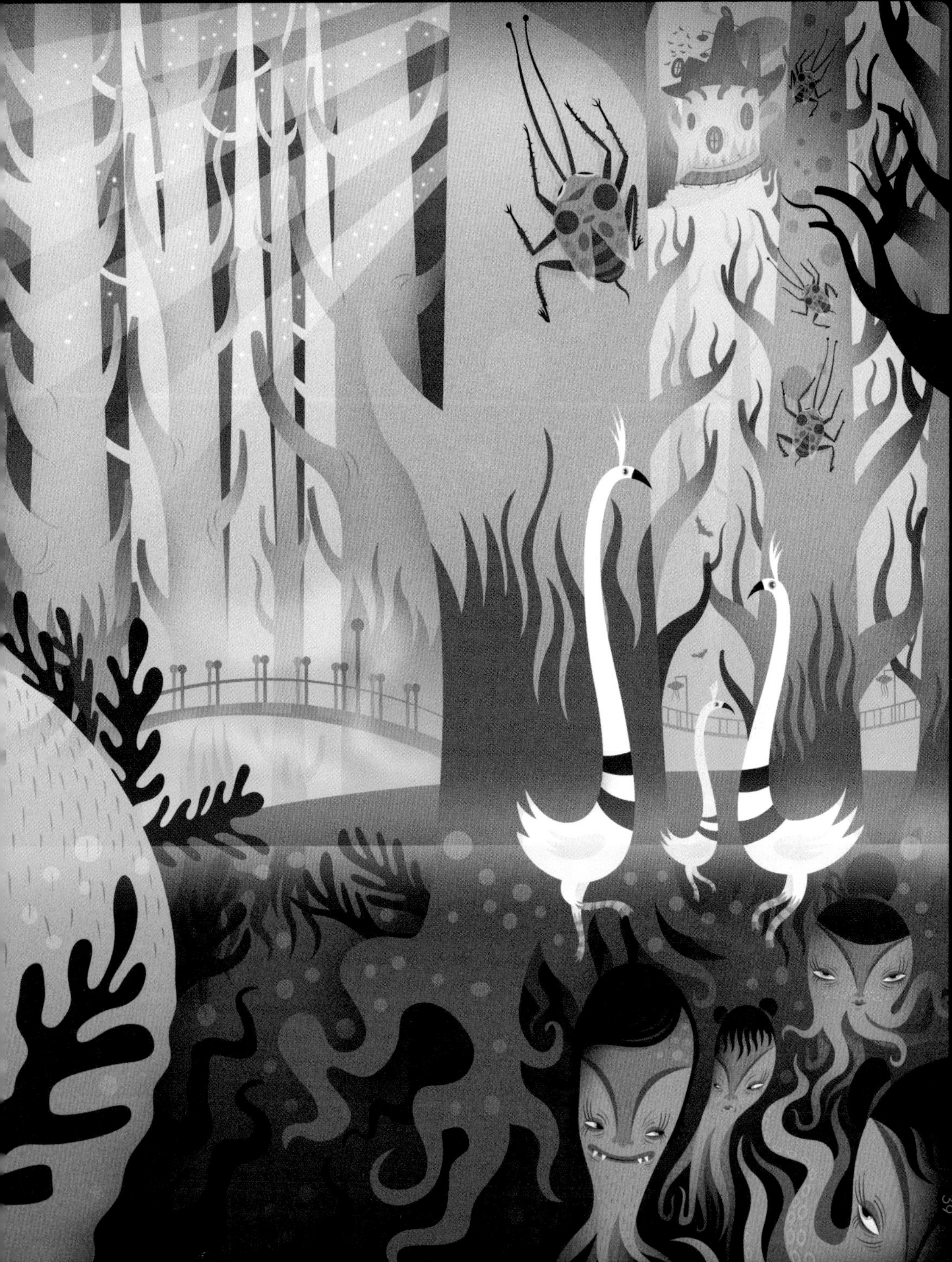

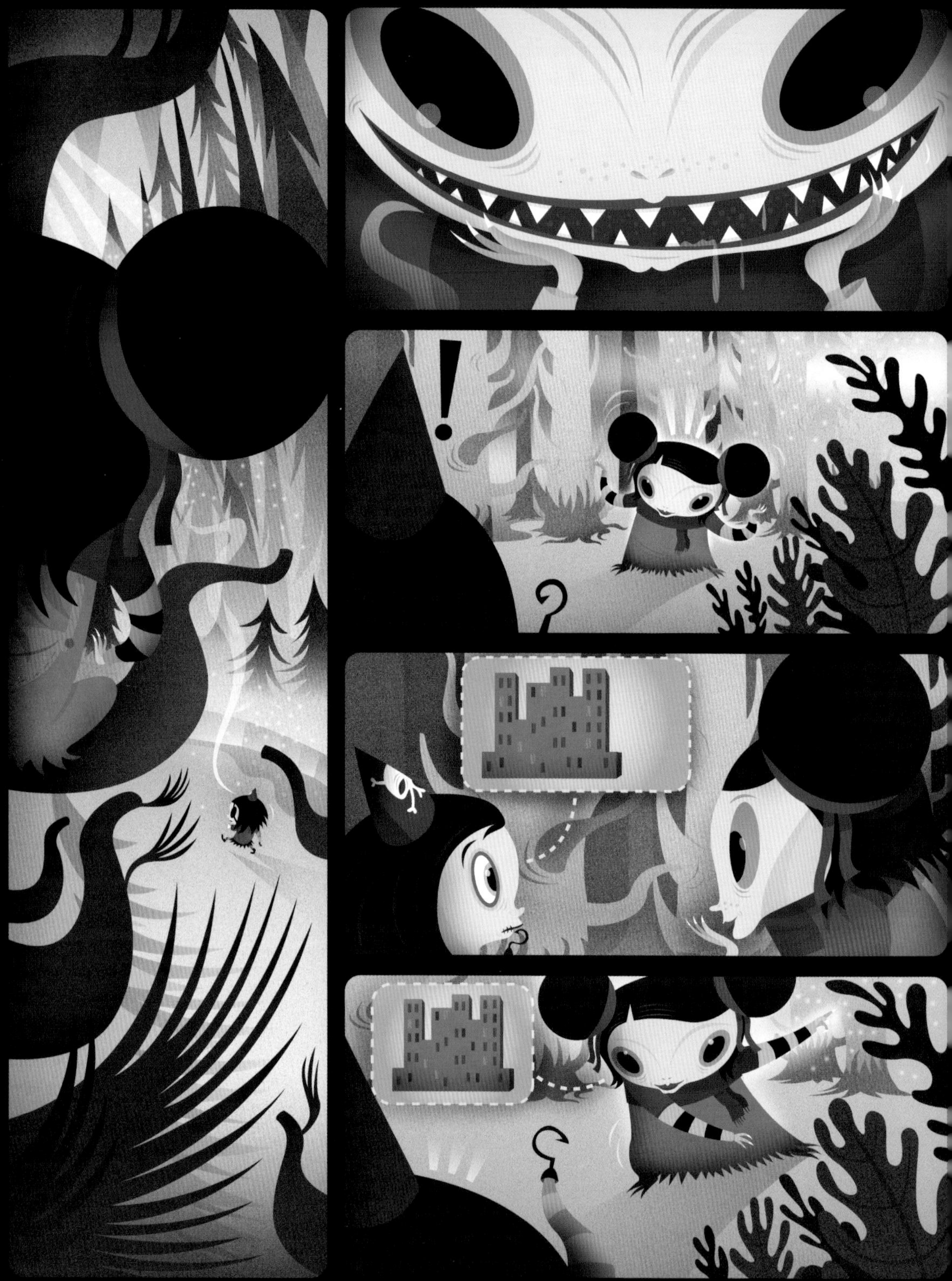
!

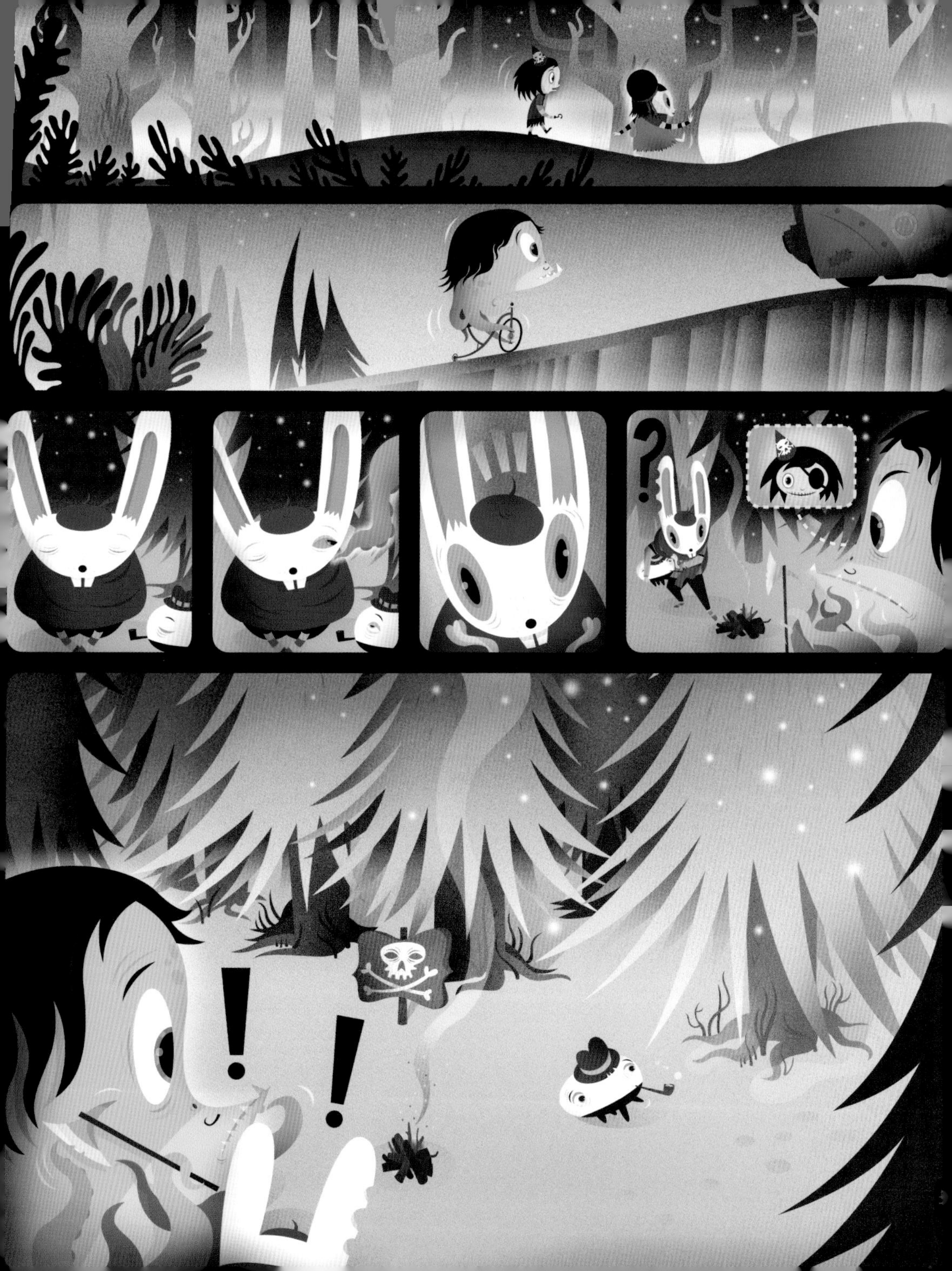

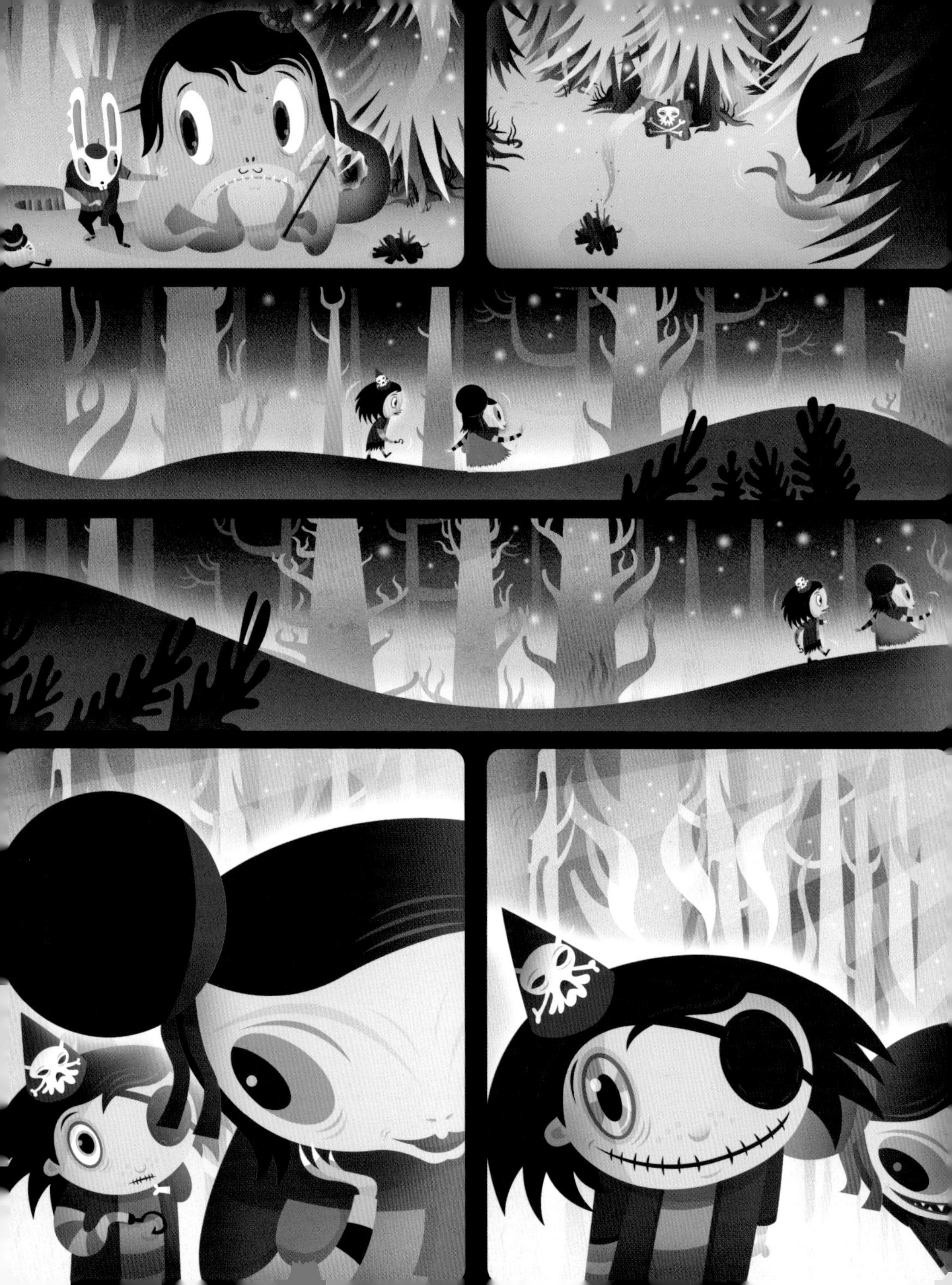

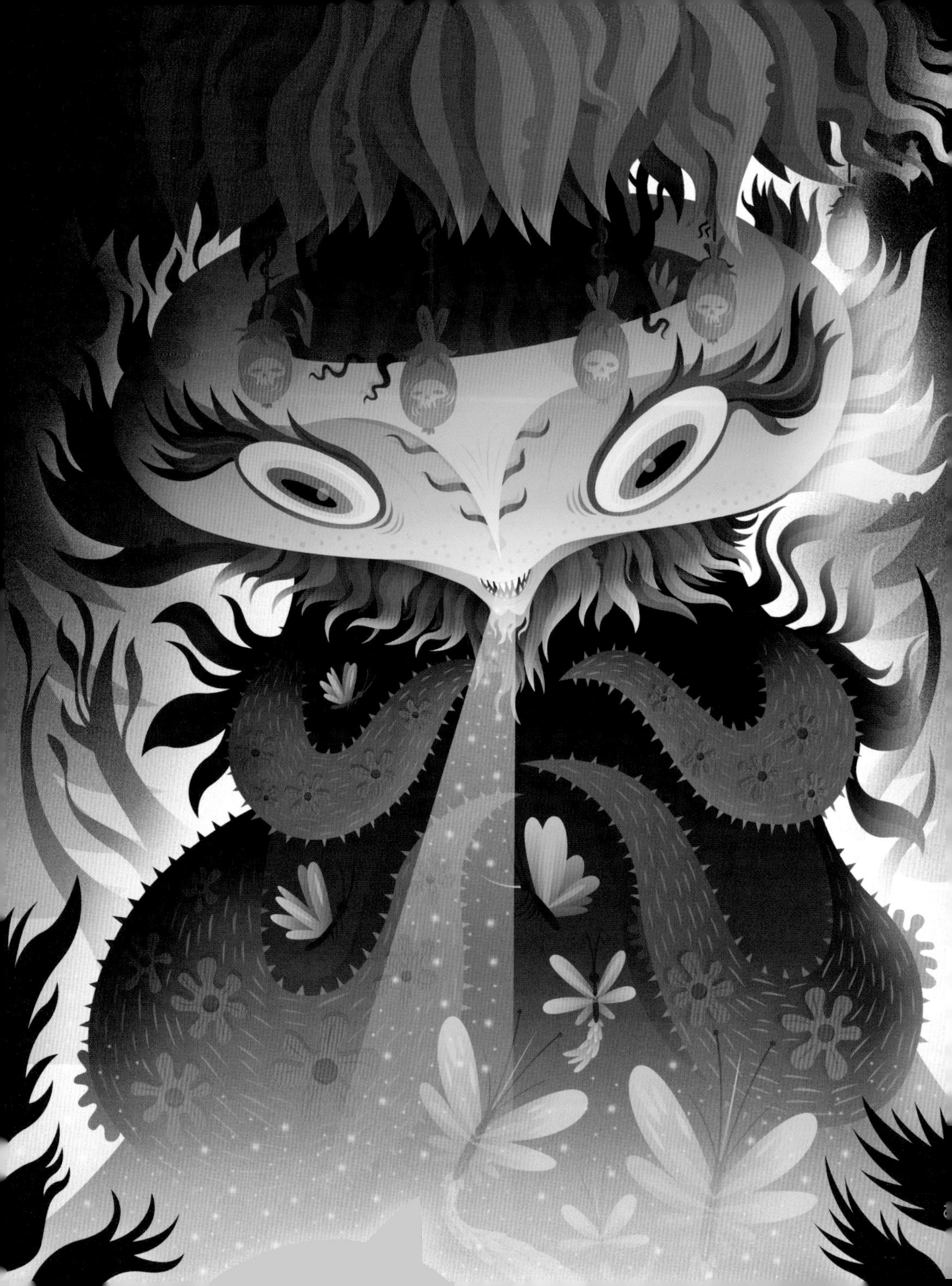

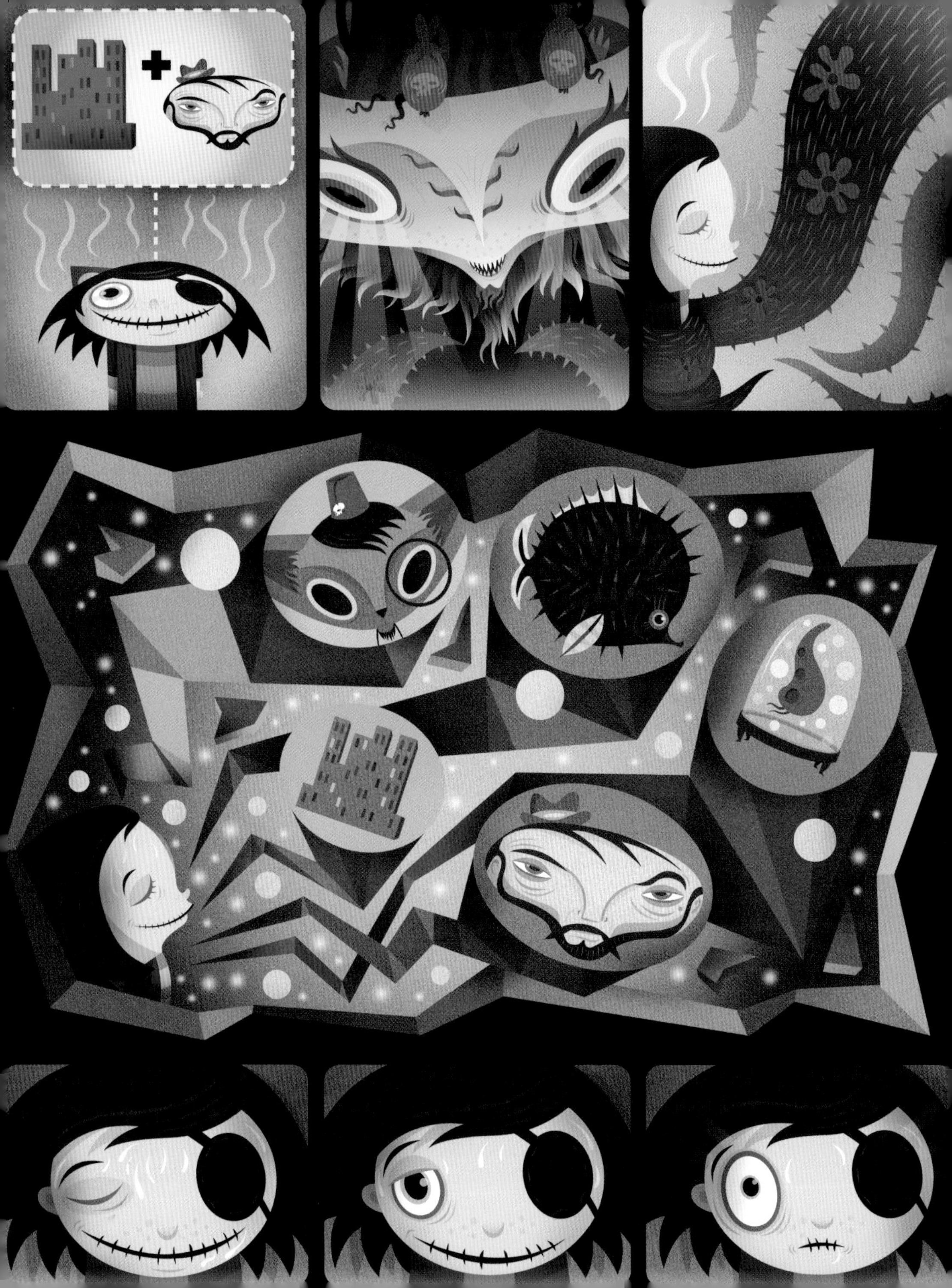

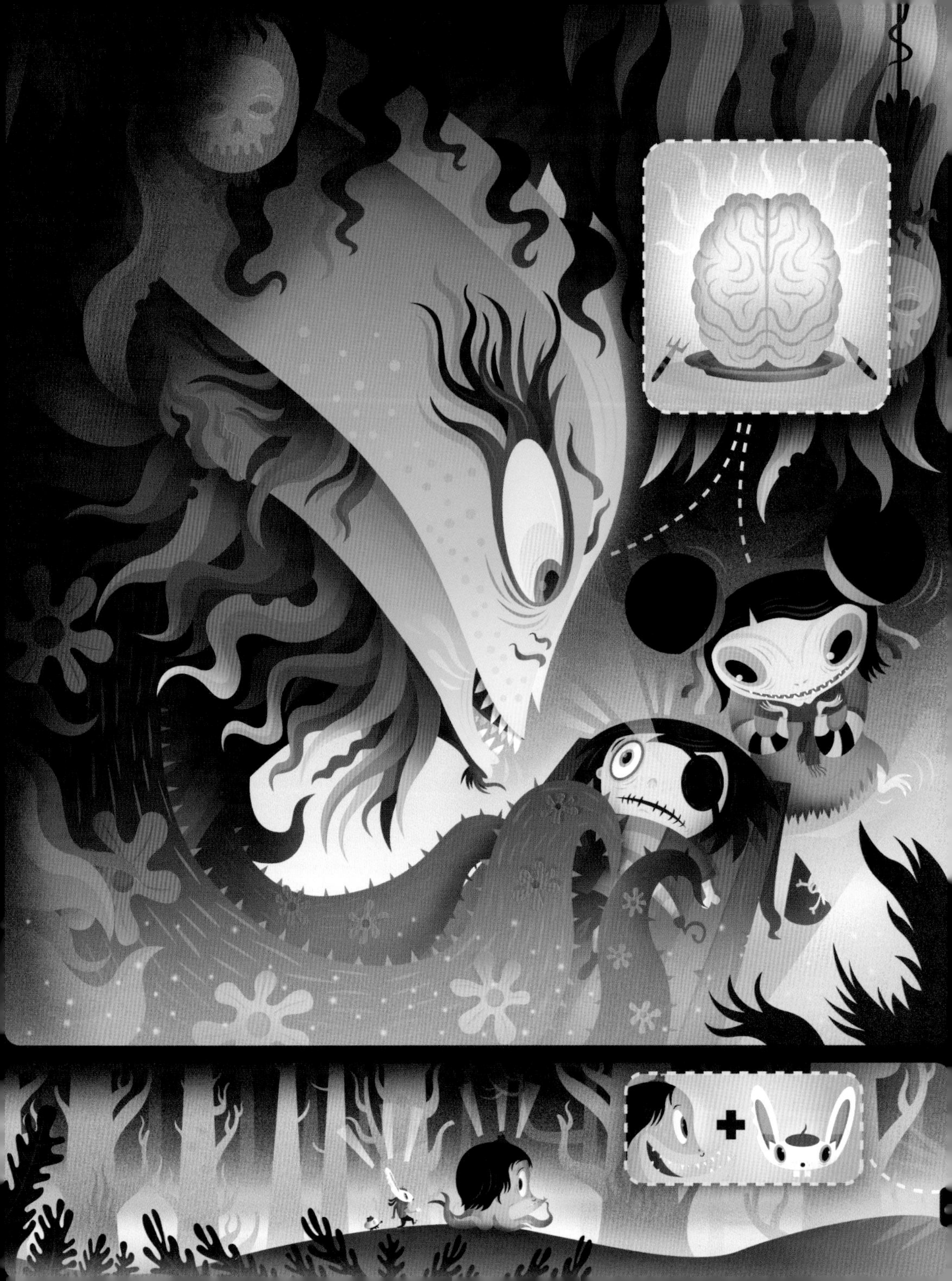

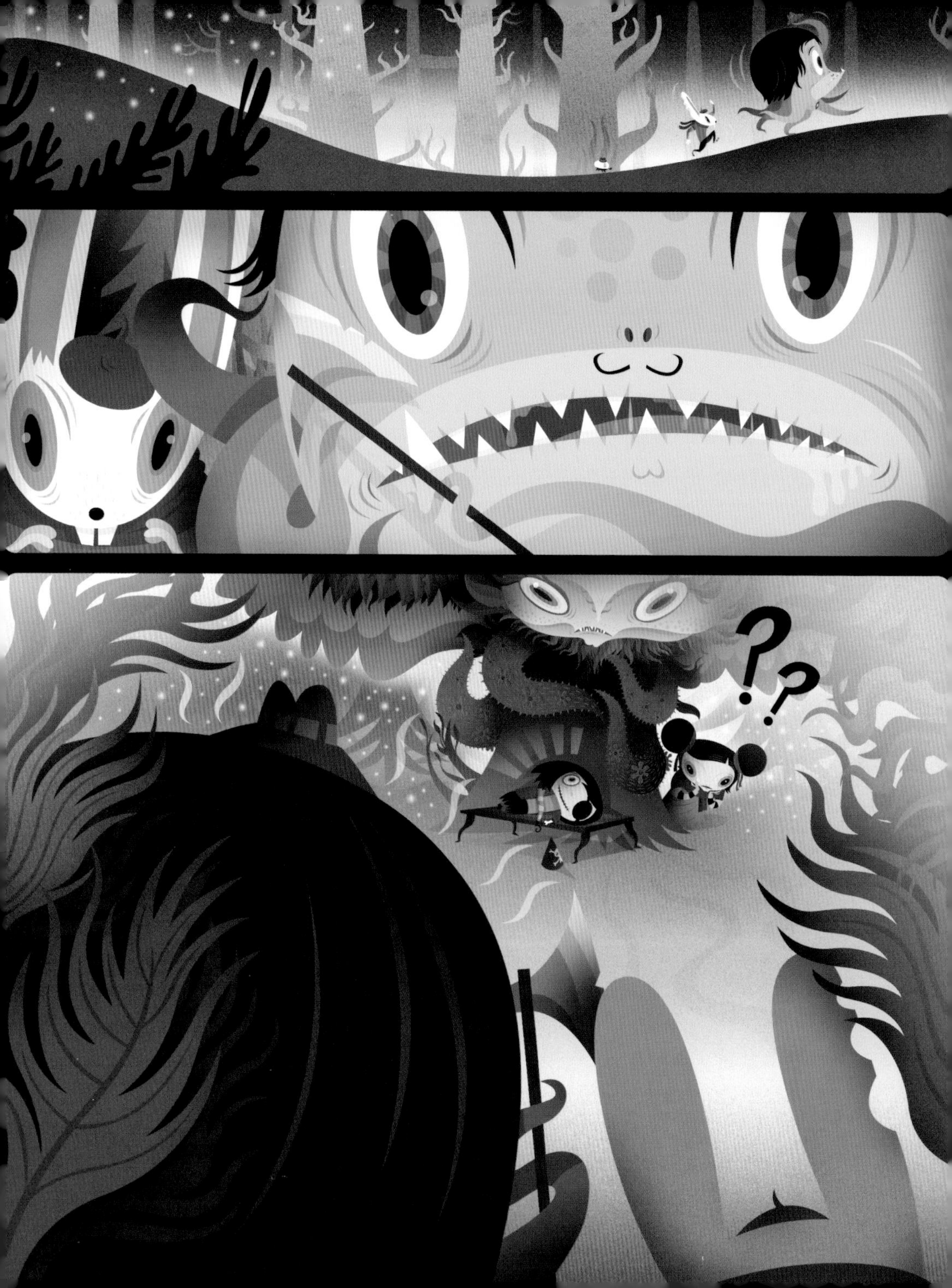

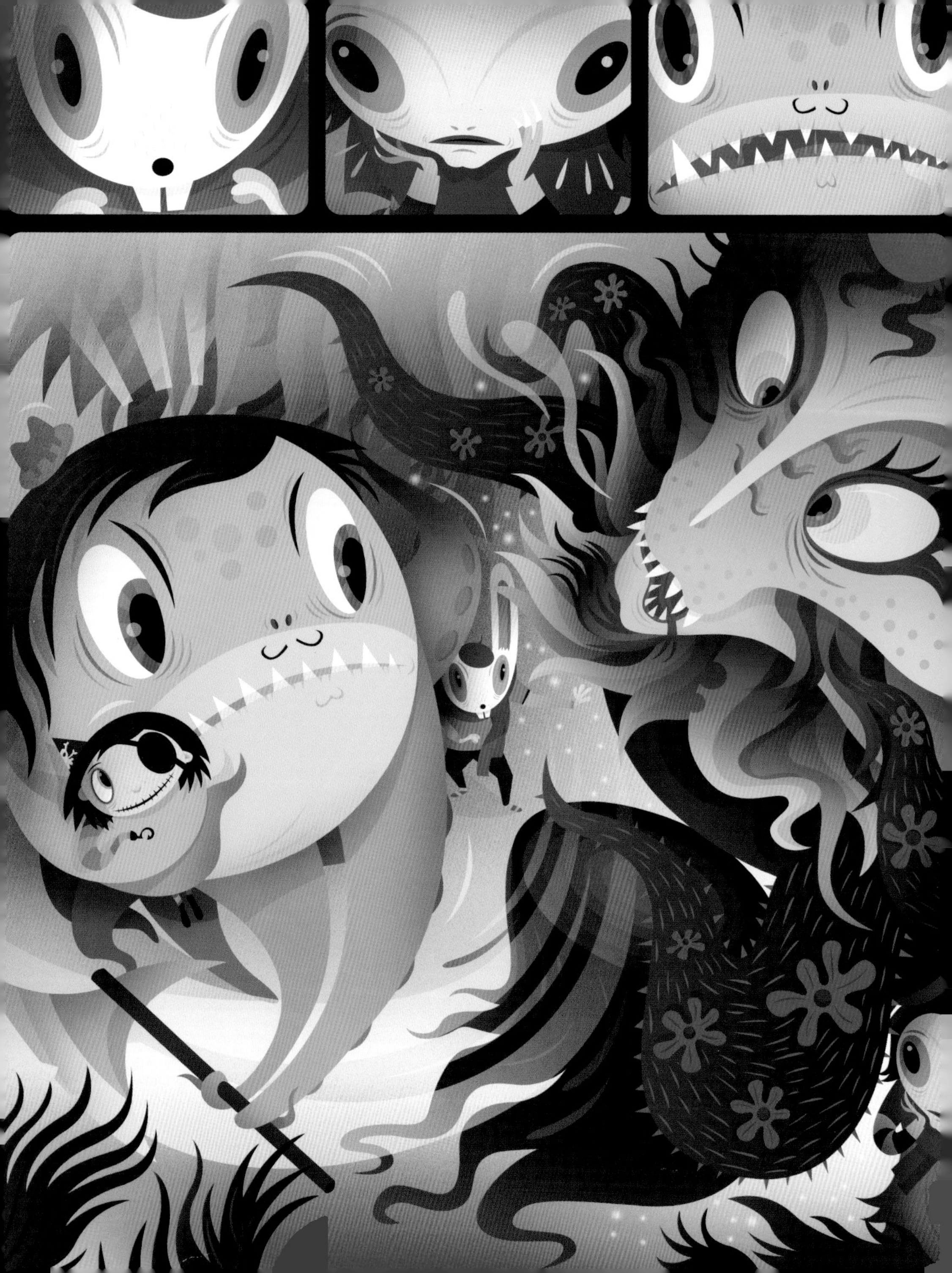

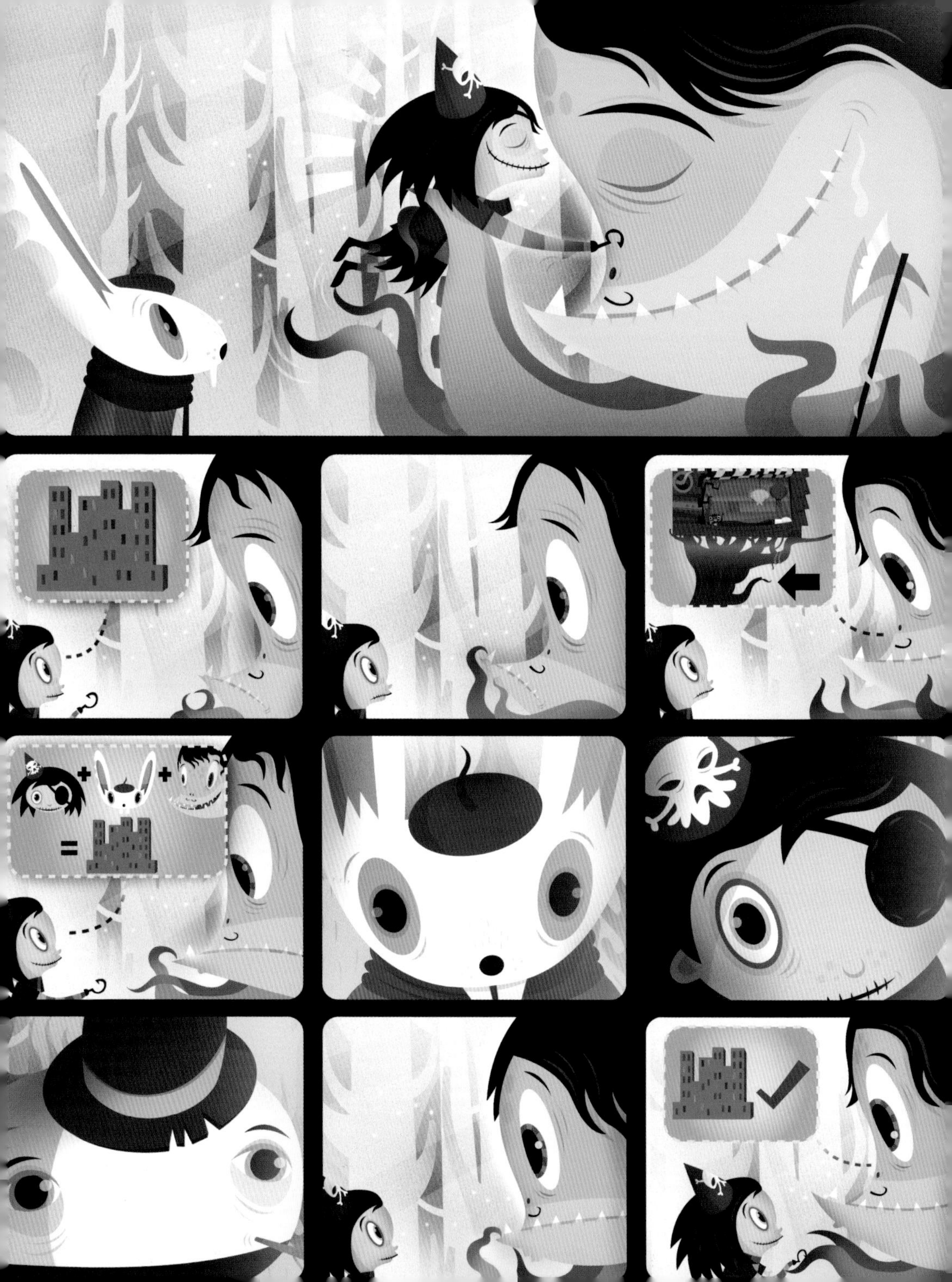

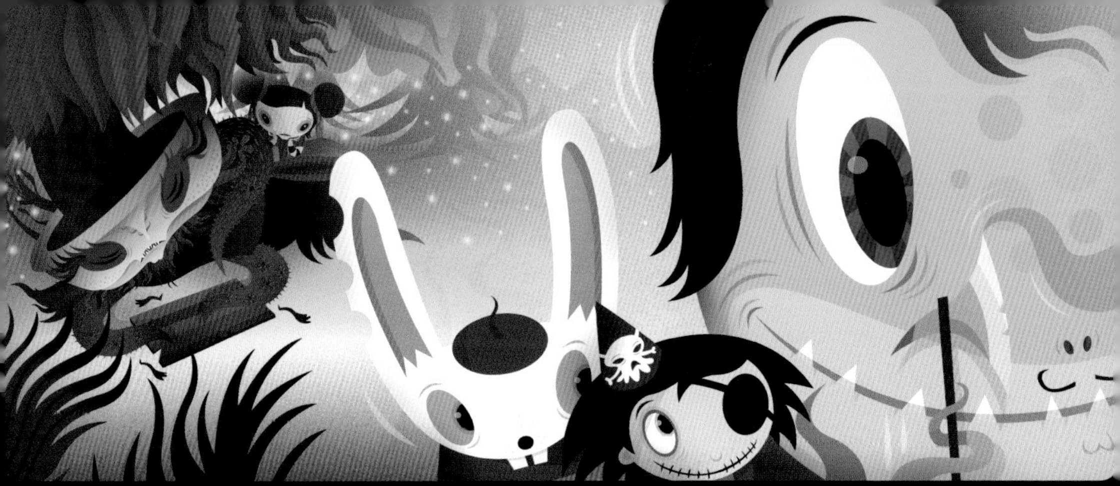

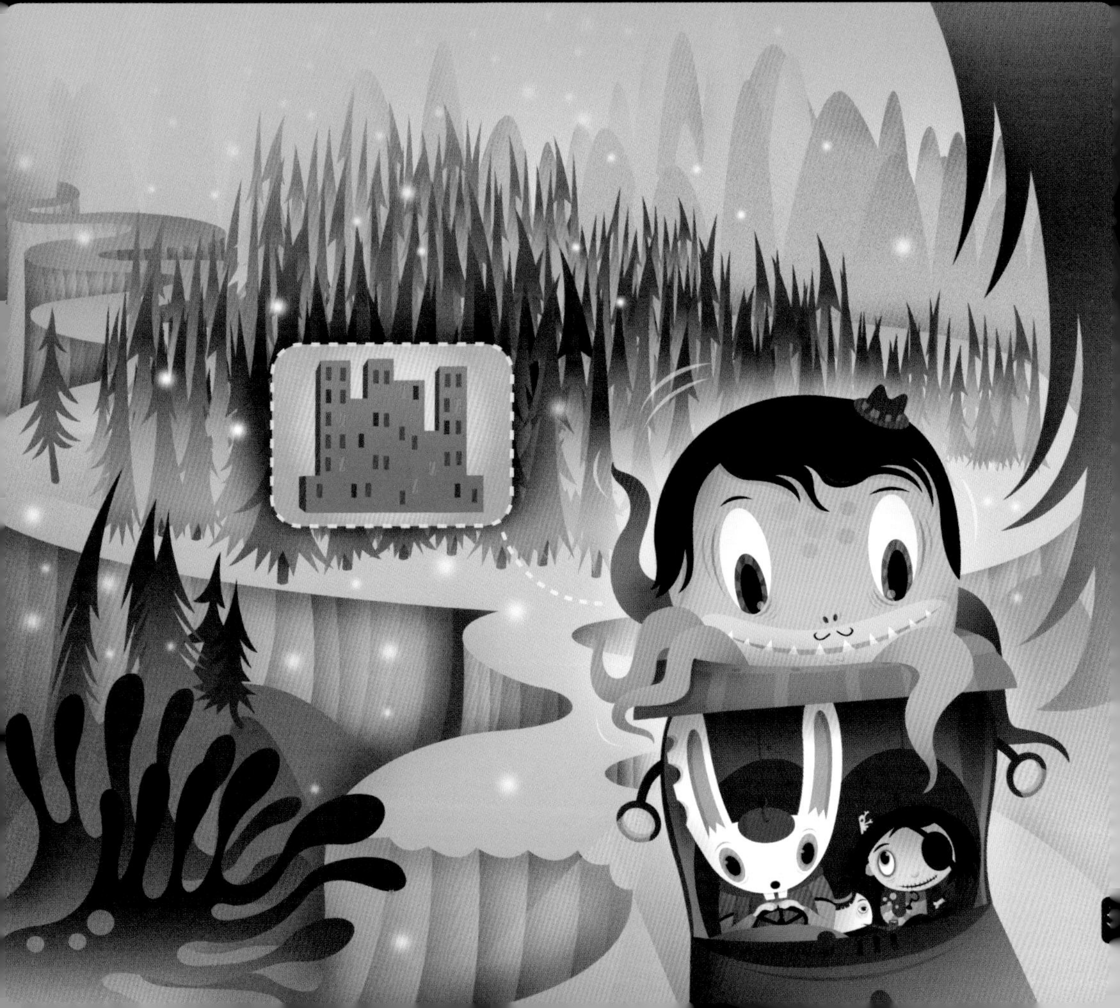

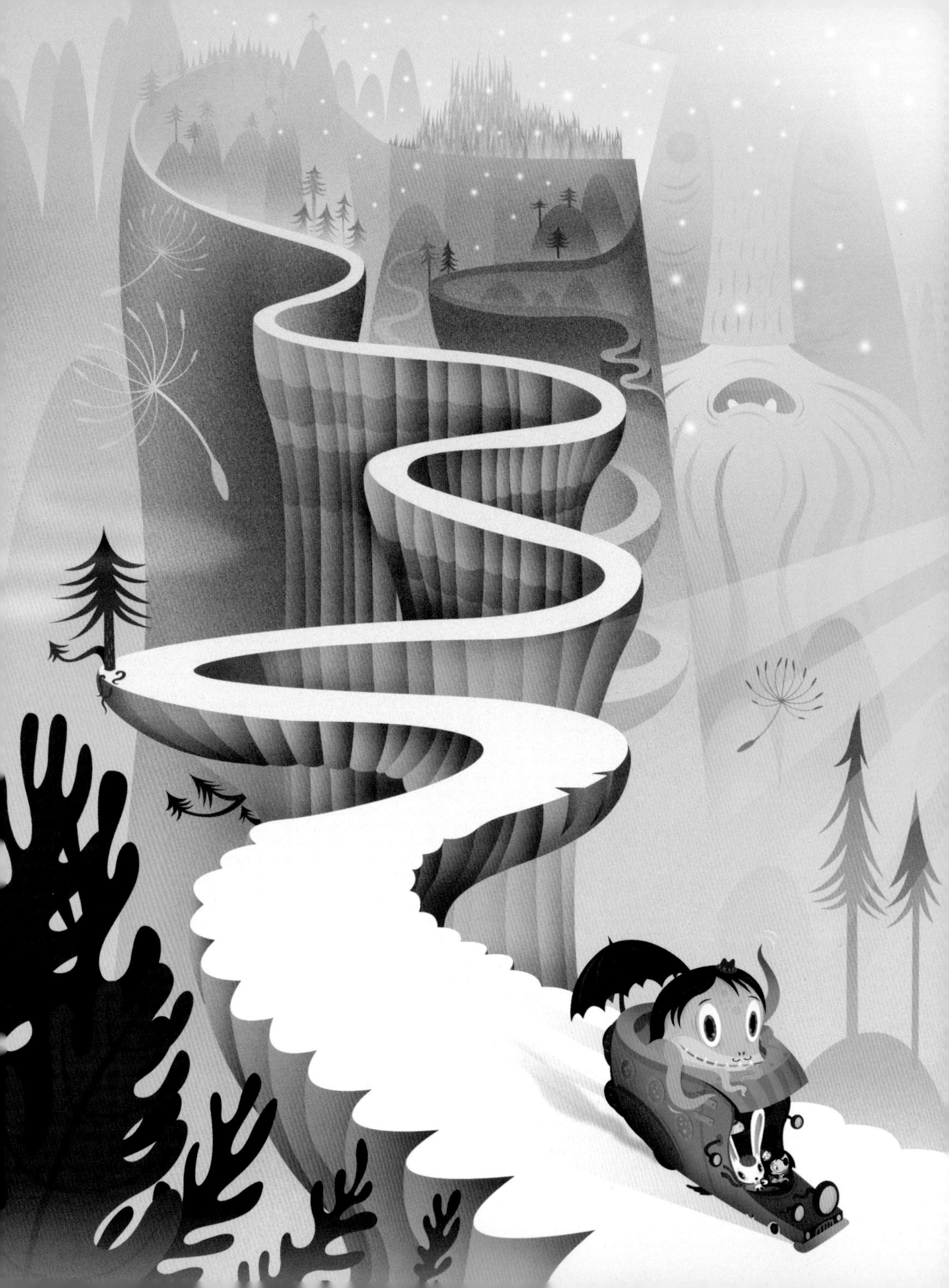

PART TWO

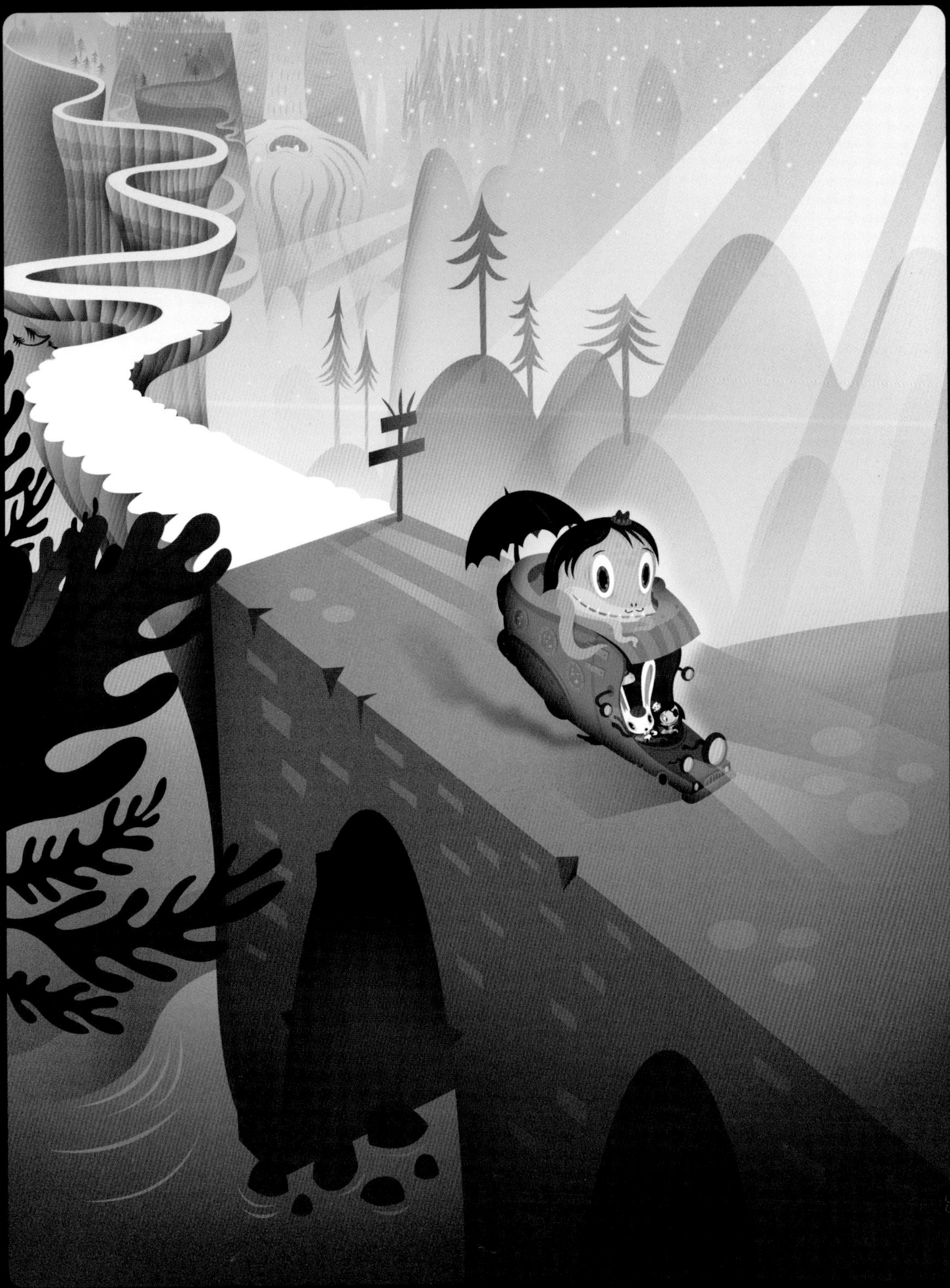

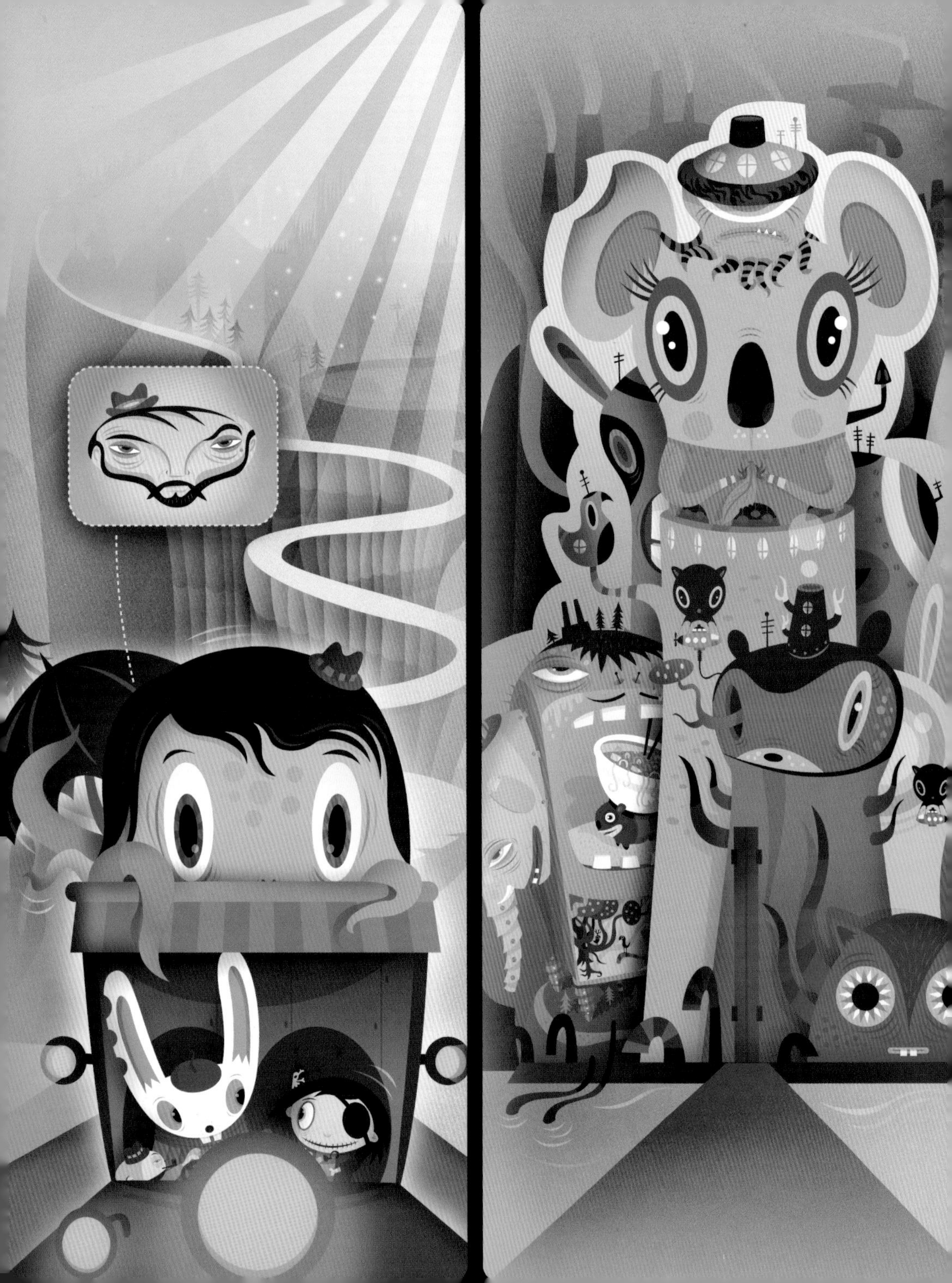

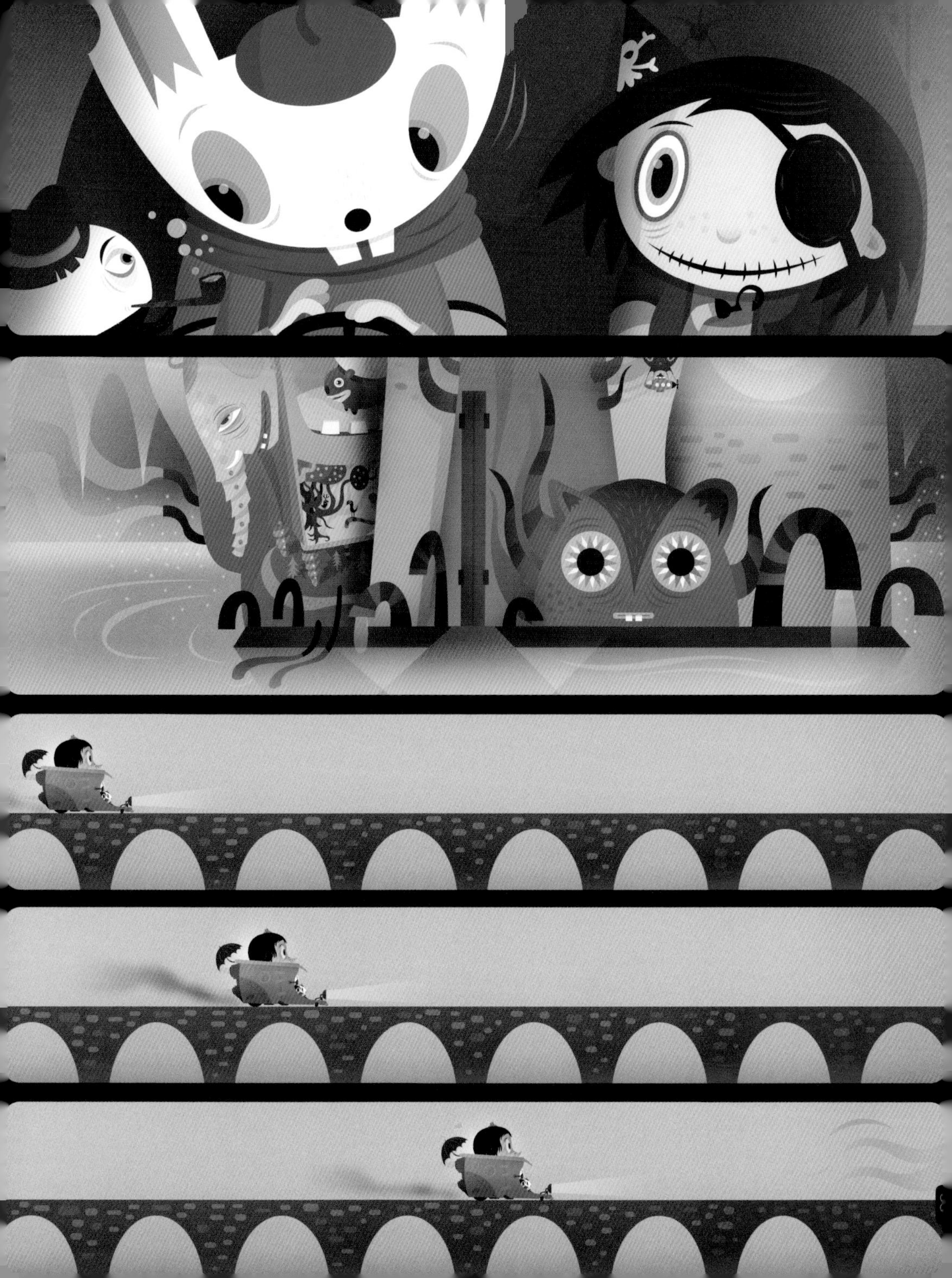

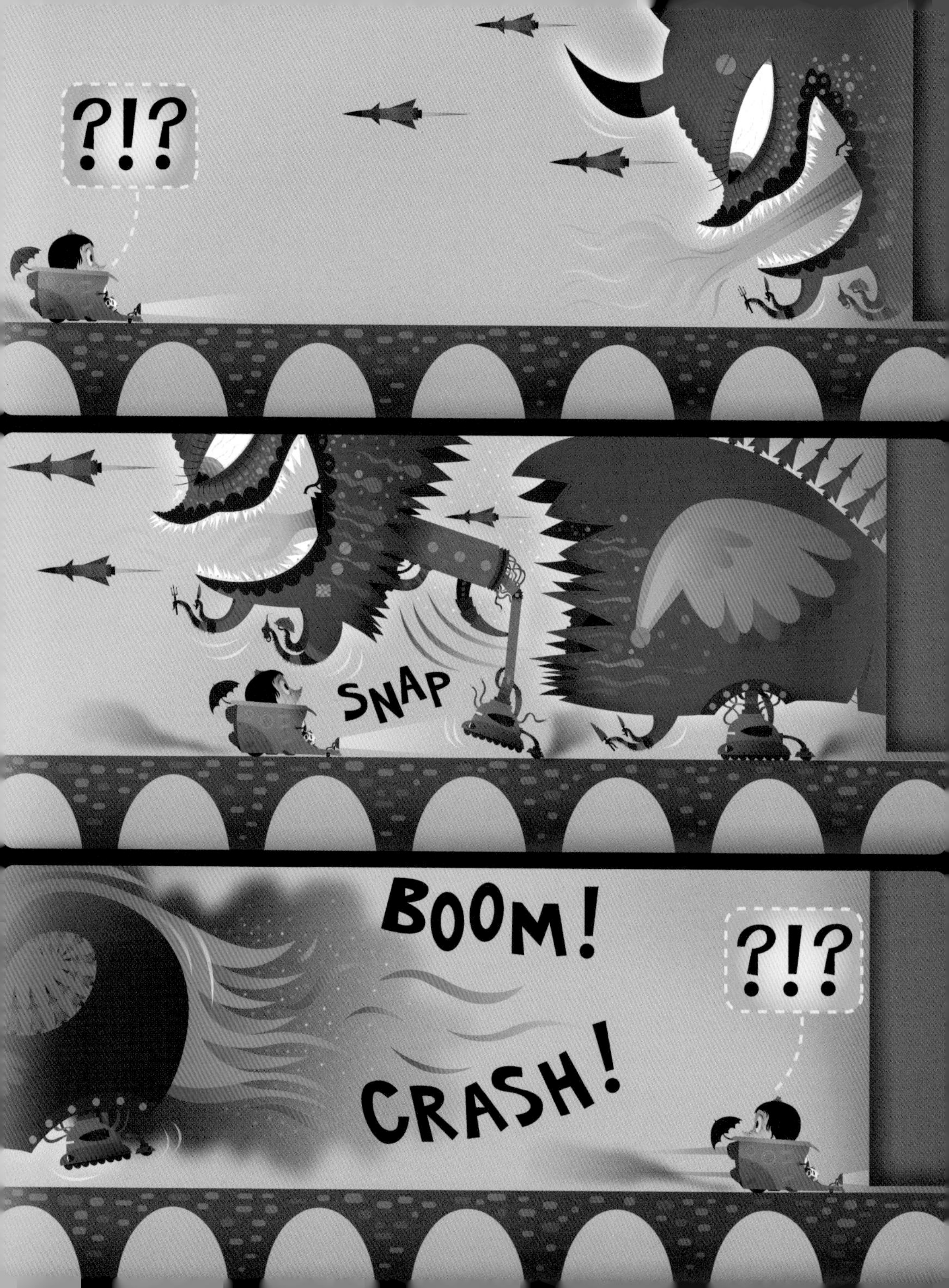
?!?
SNAP
BOOM!
CRASH!
?!?

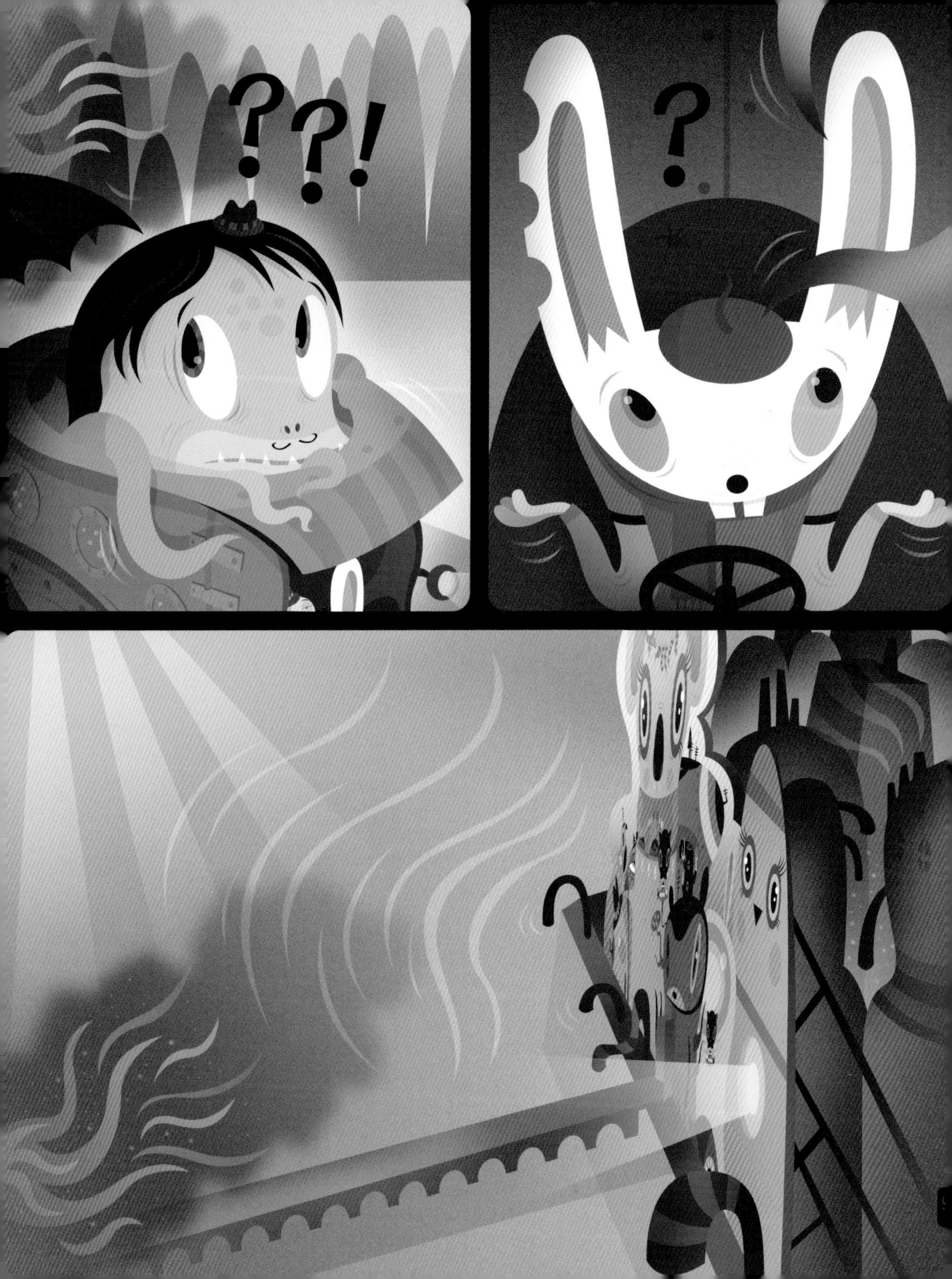
??!
?

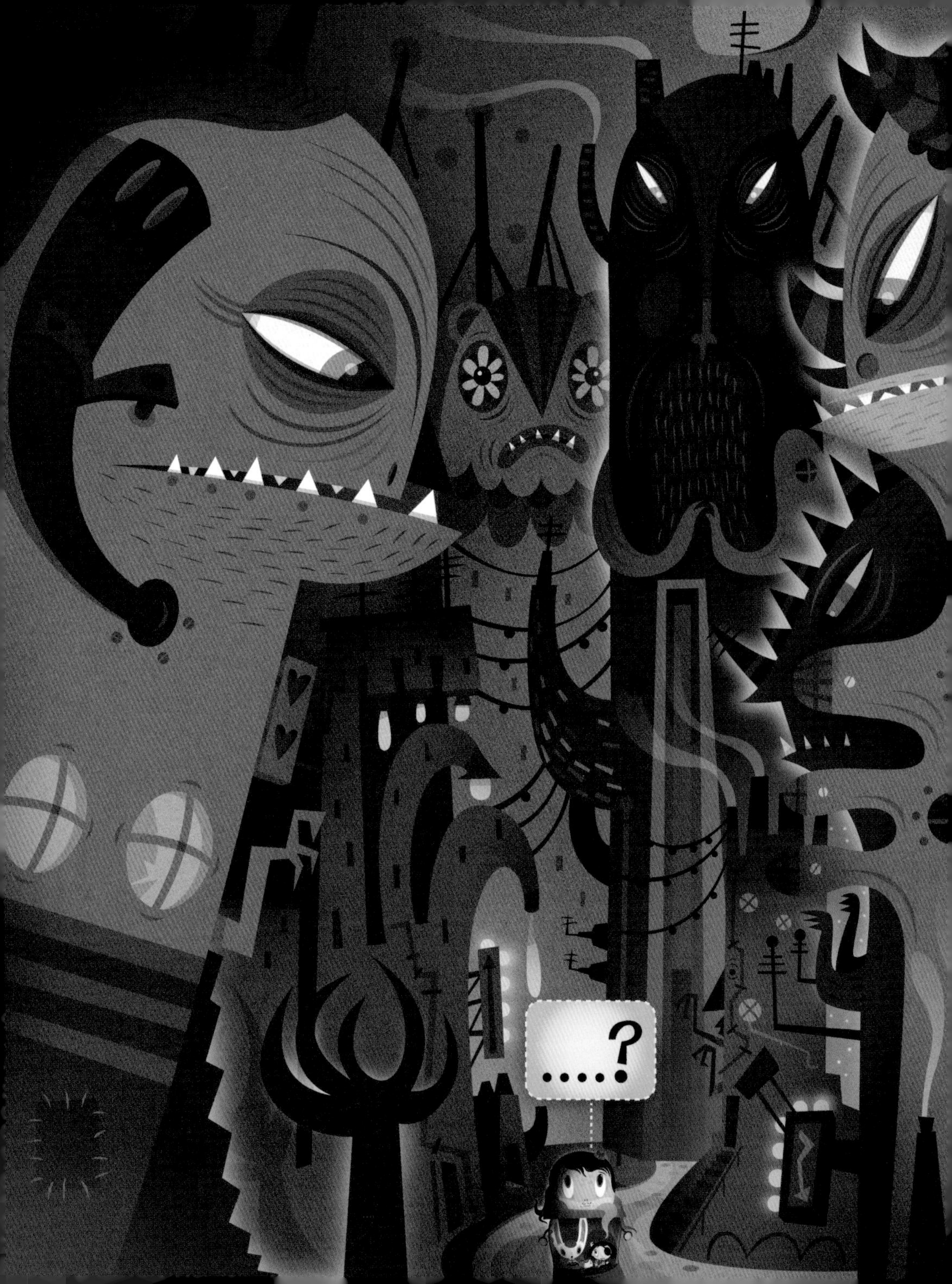
....?

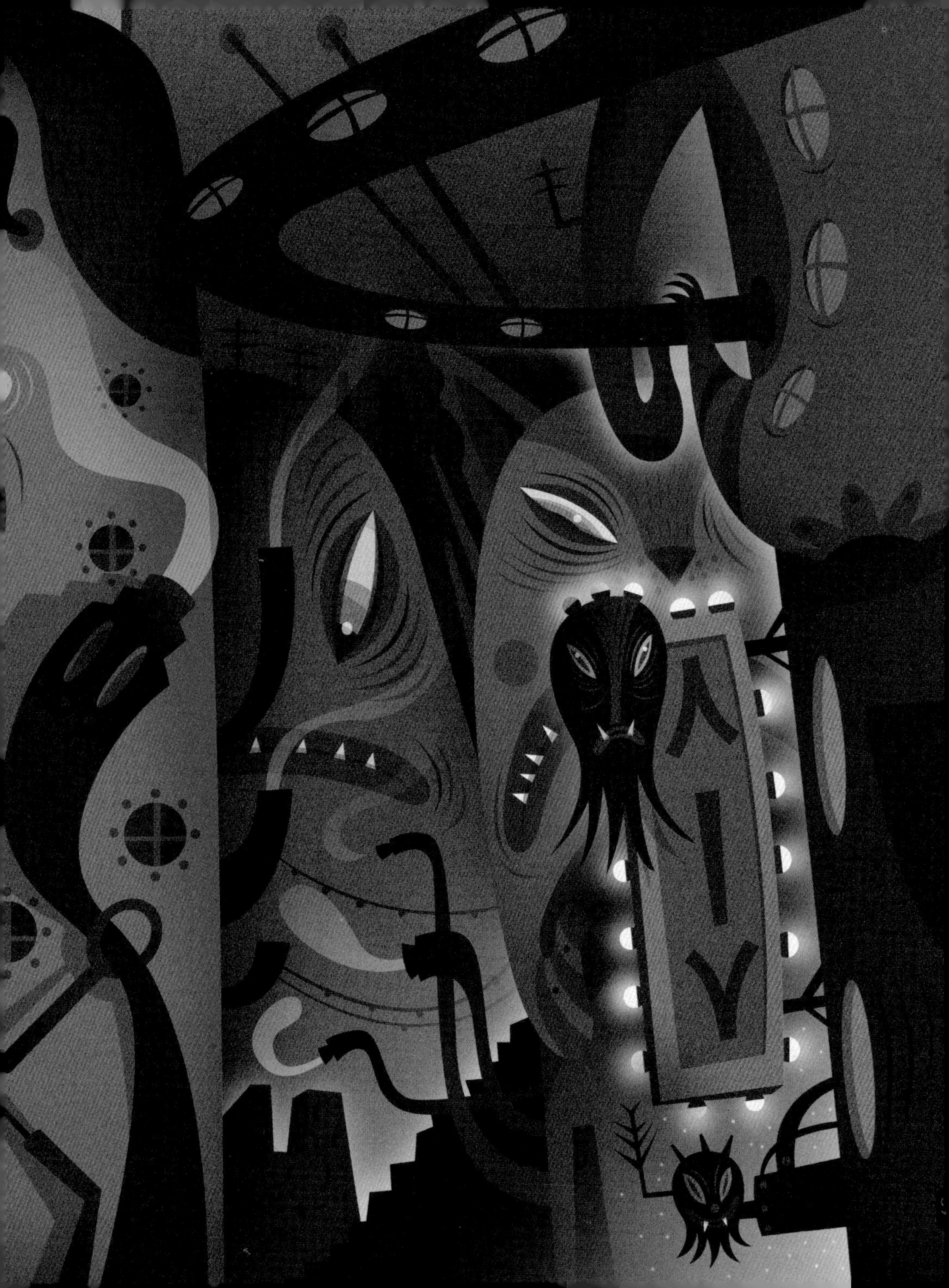

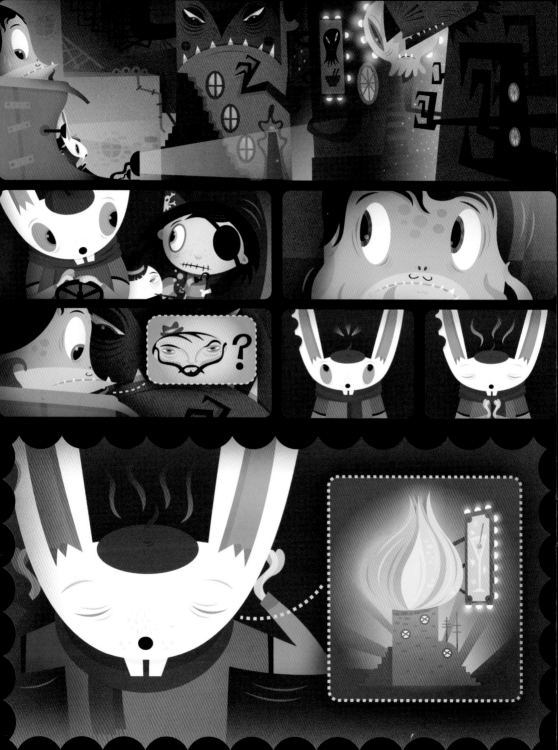

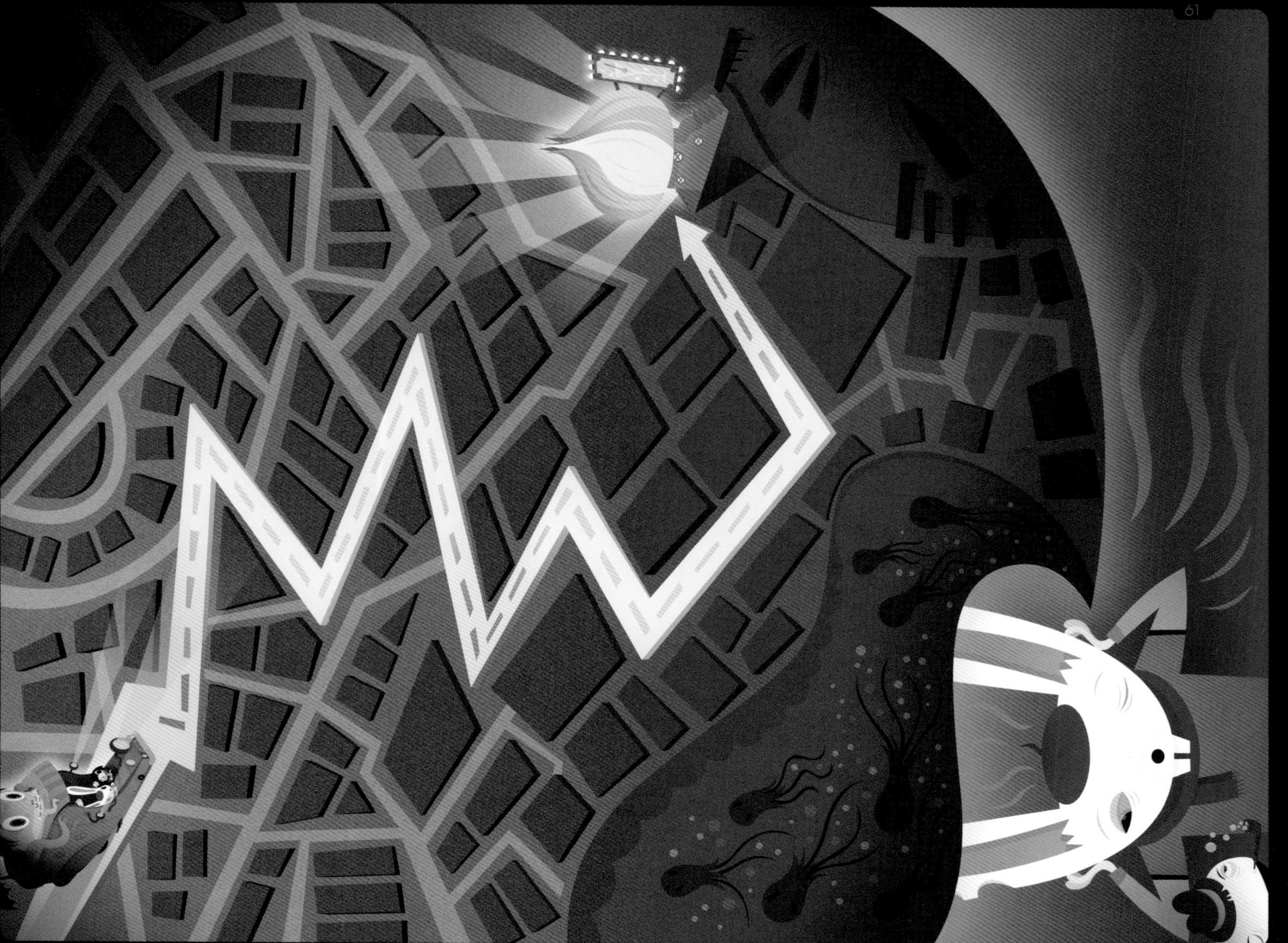

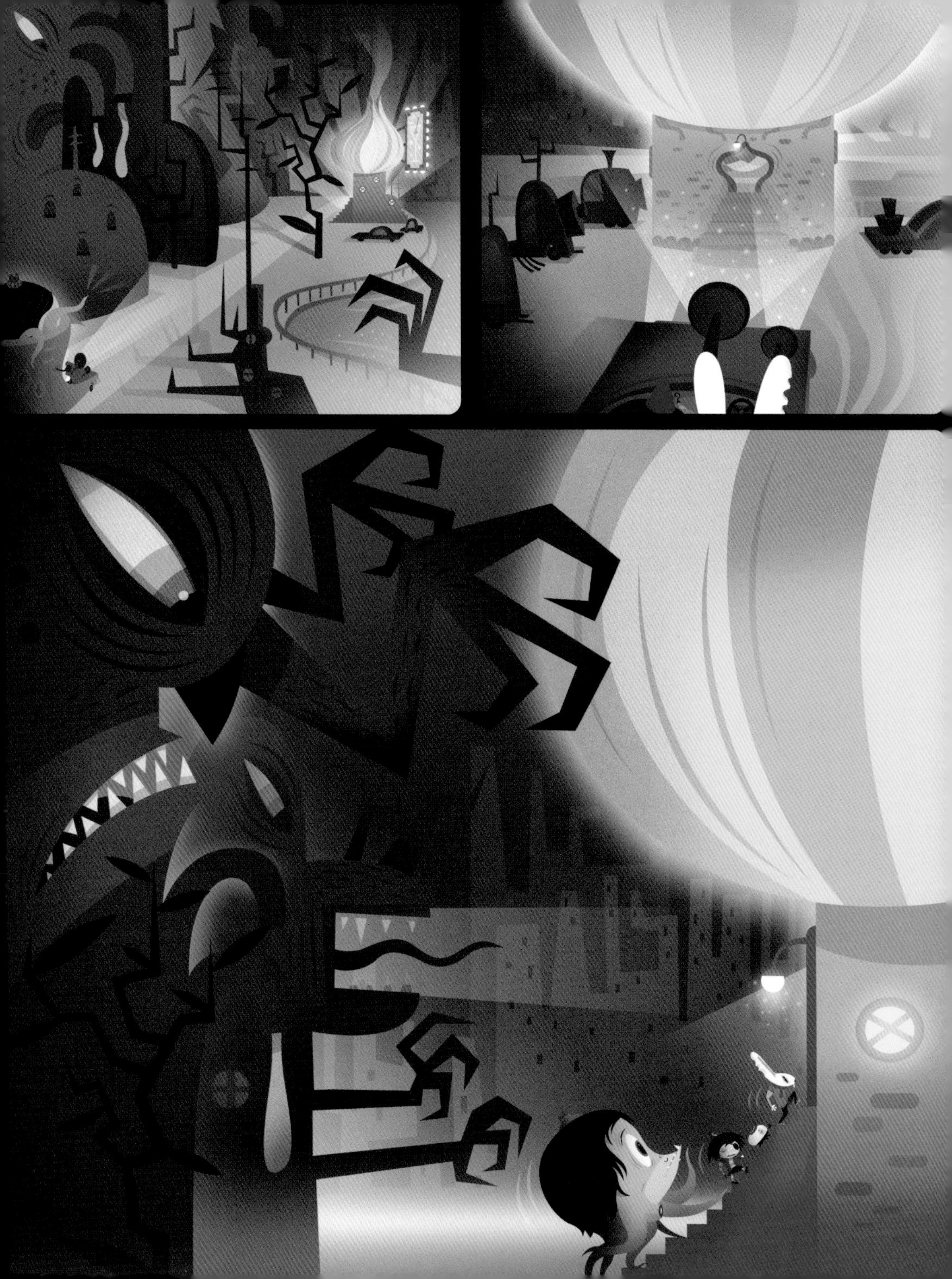

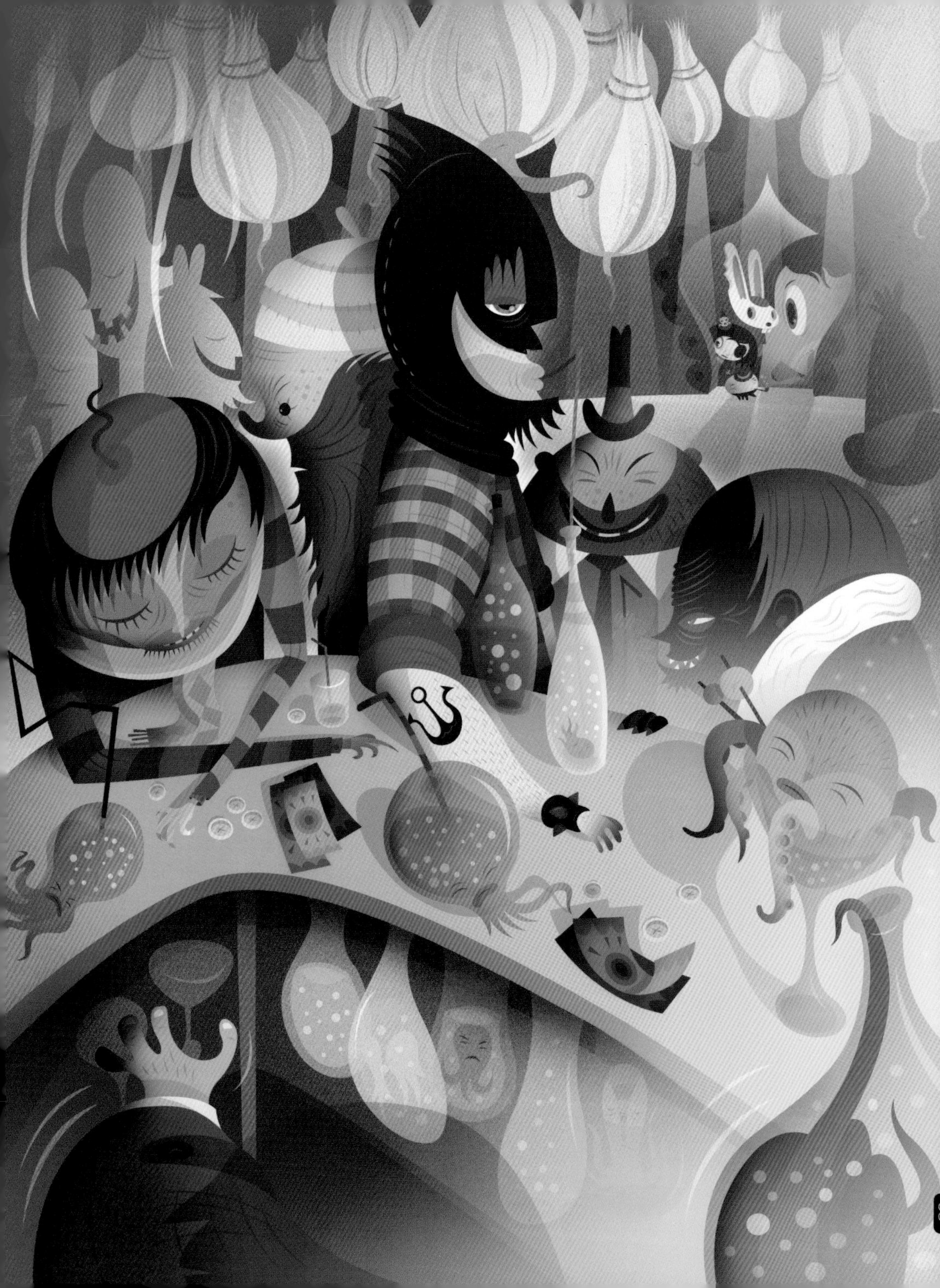

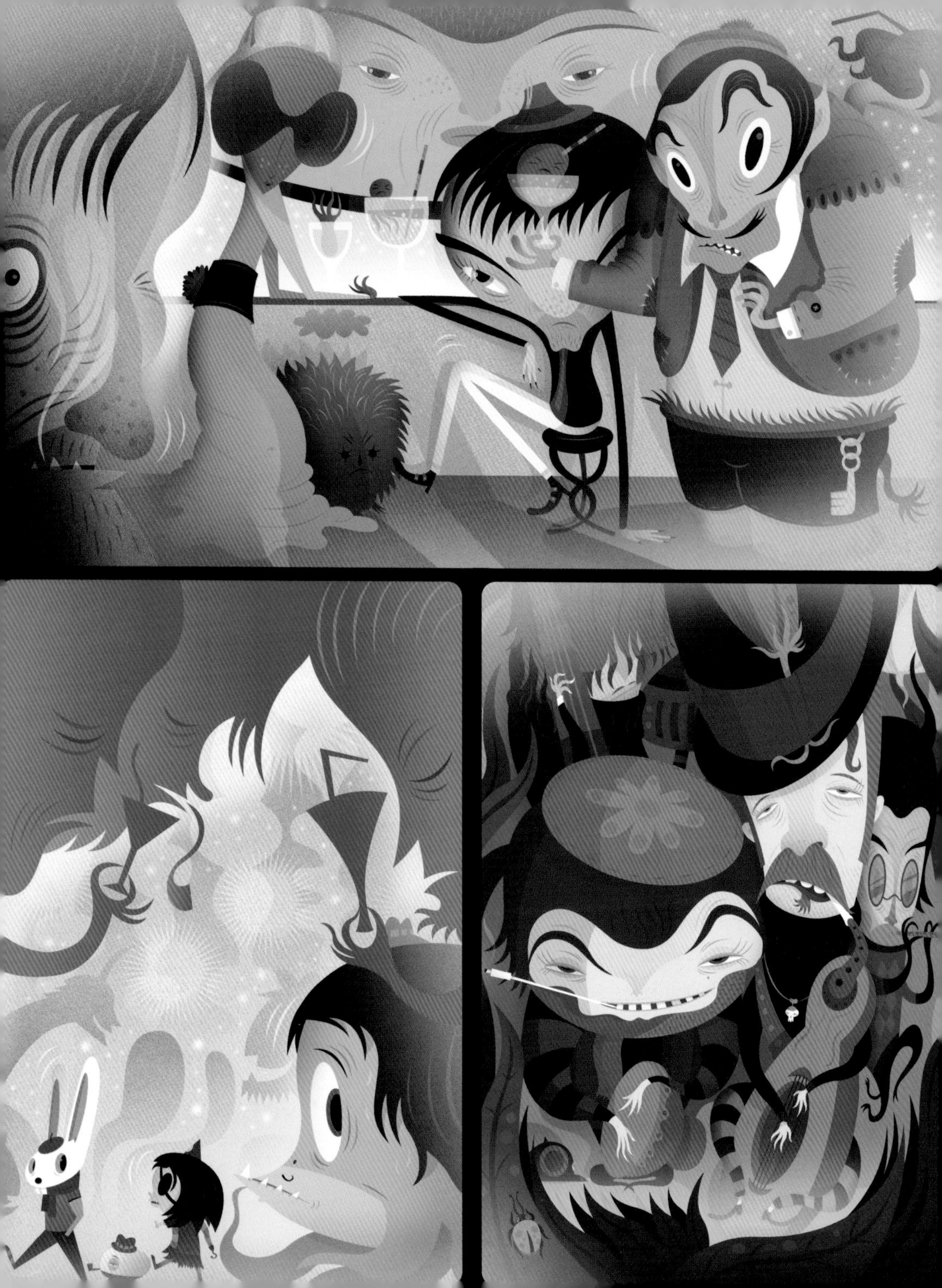

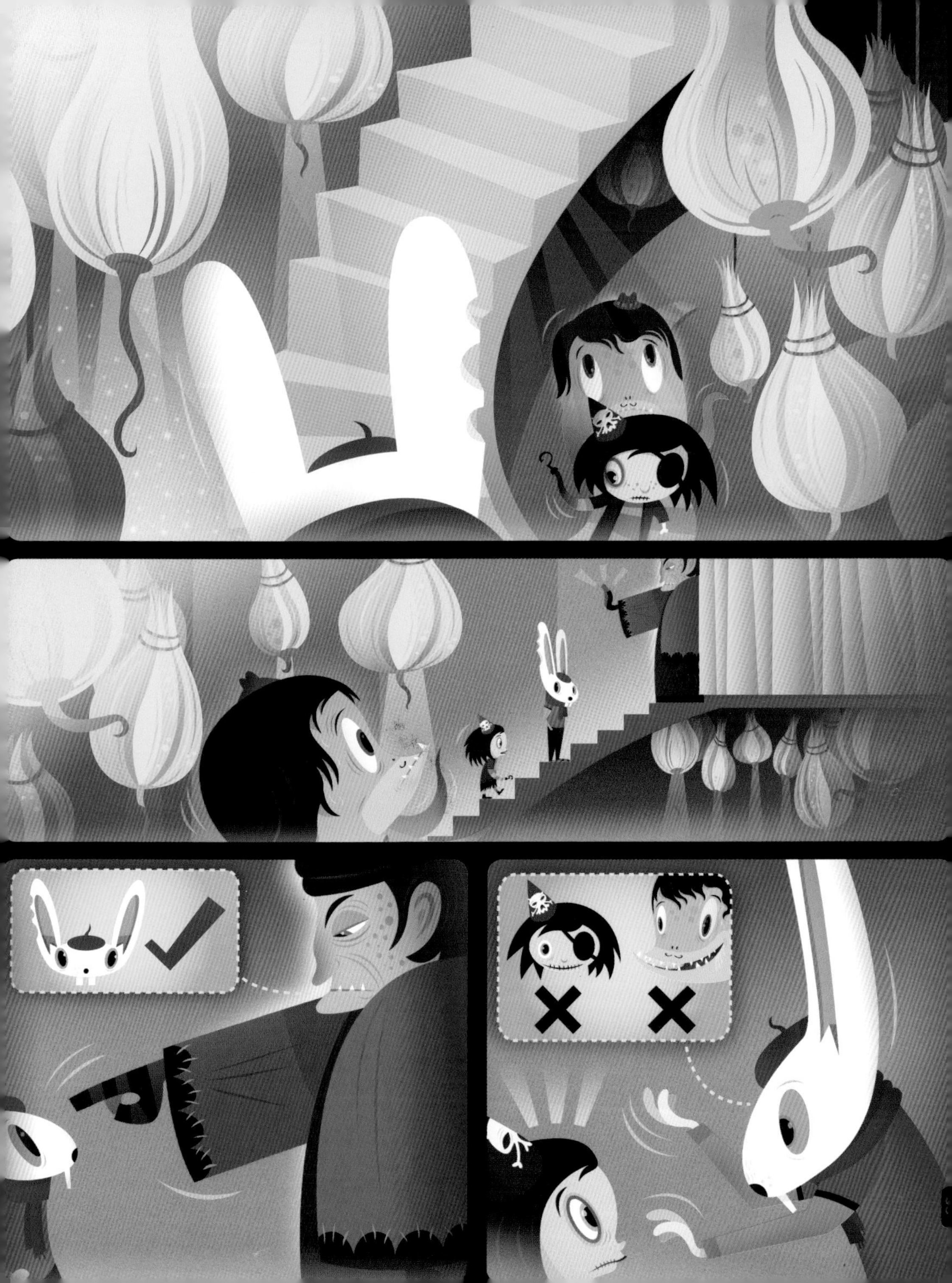

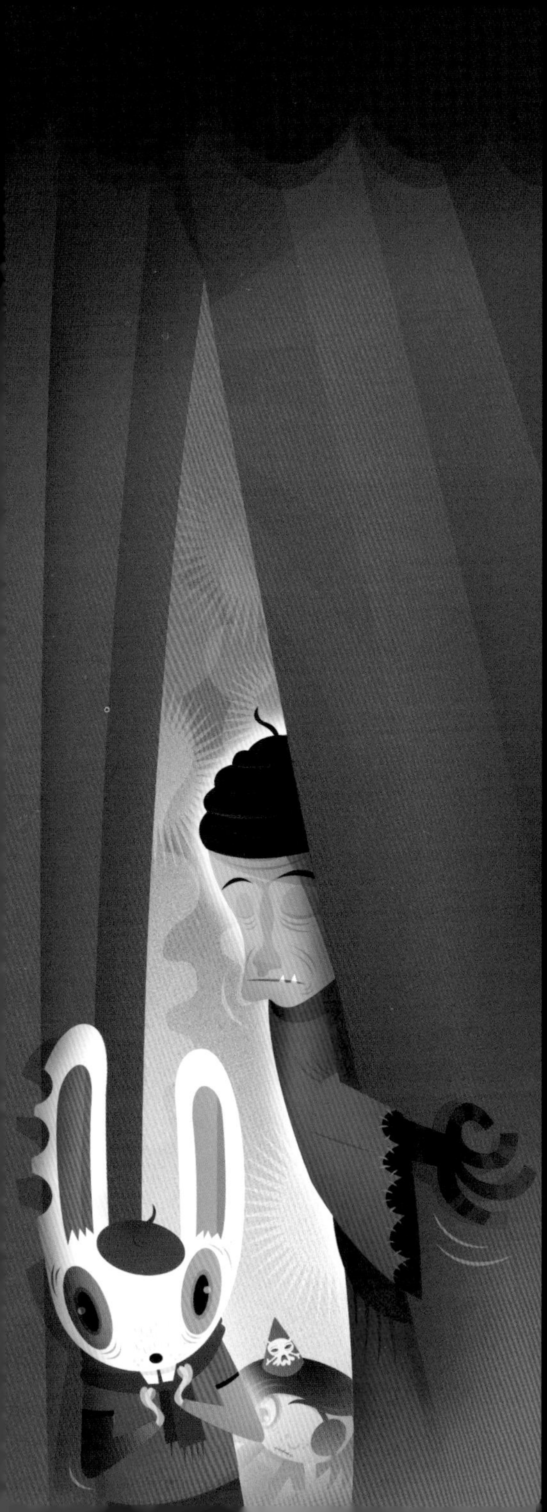

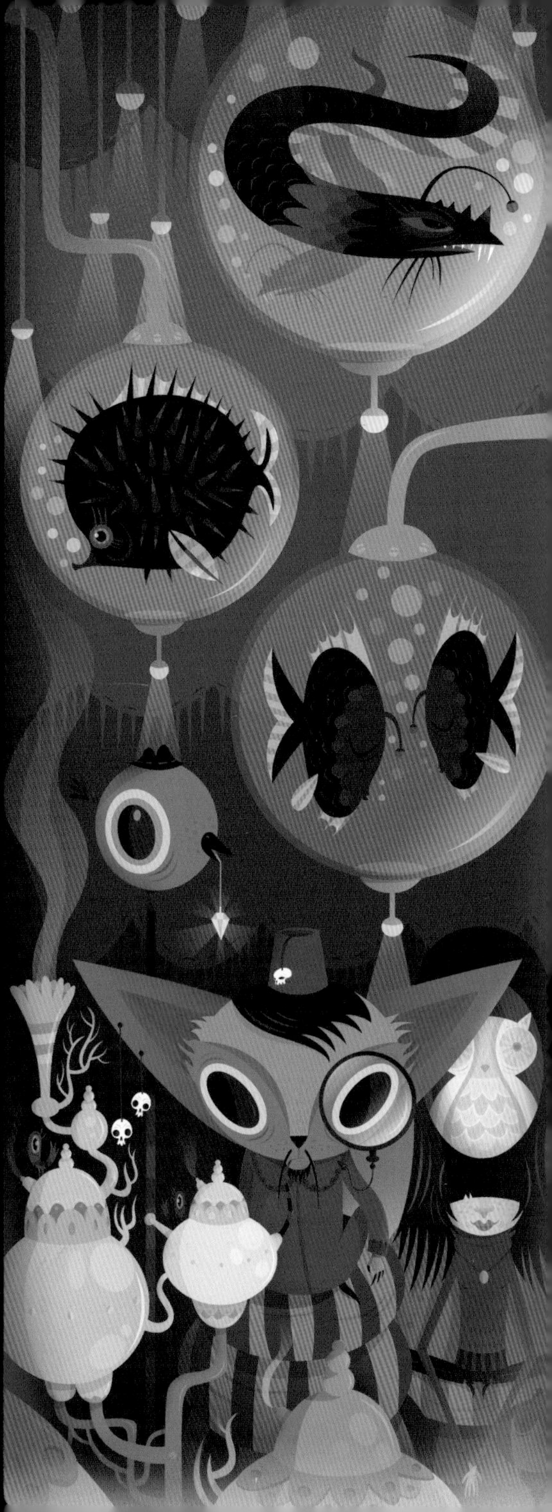

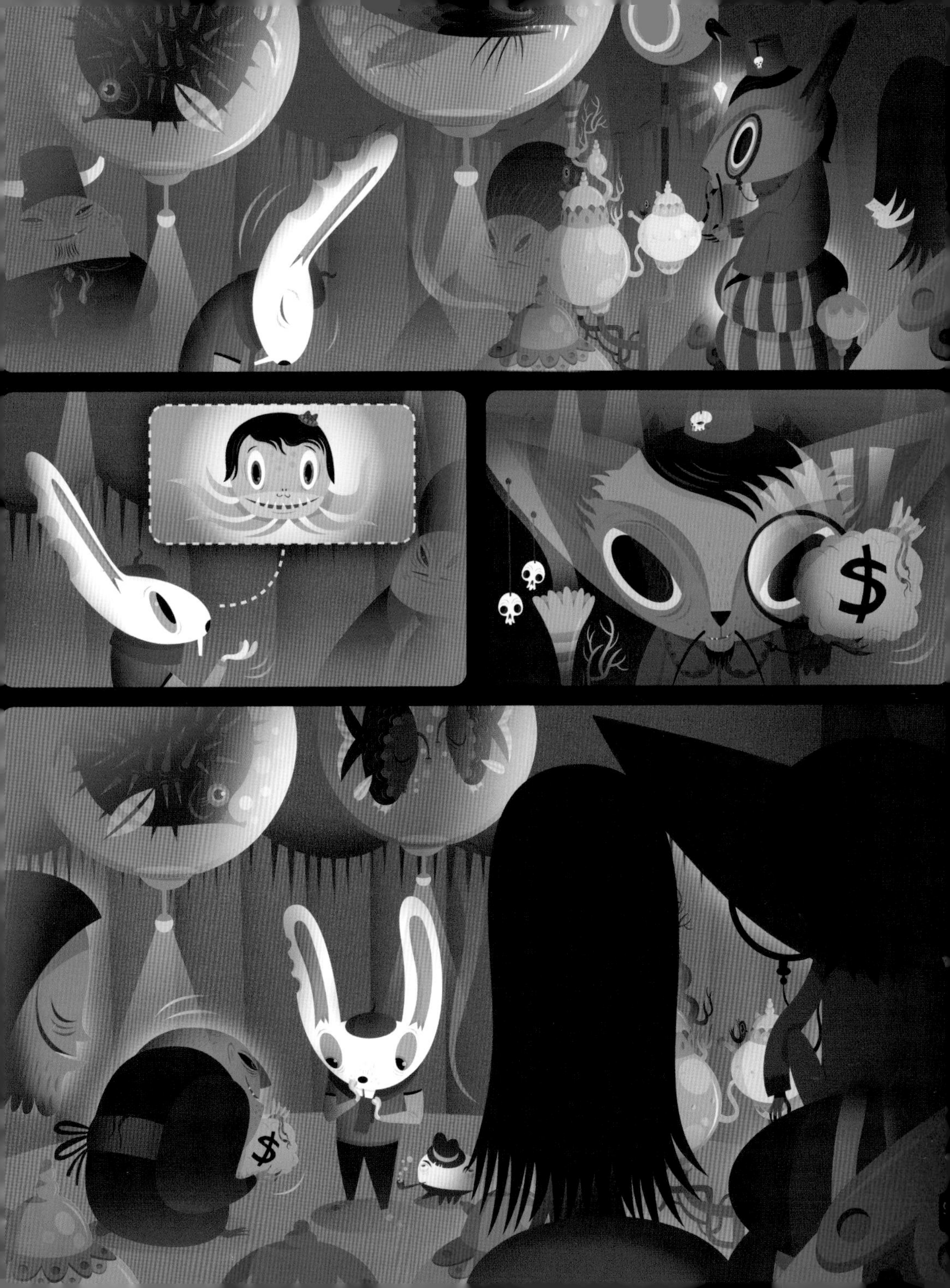

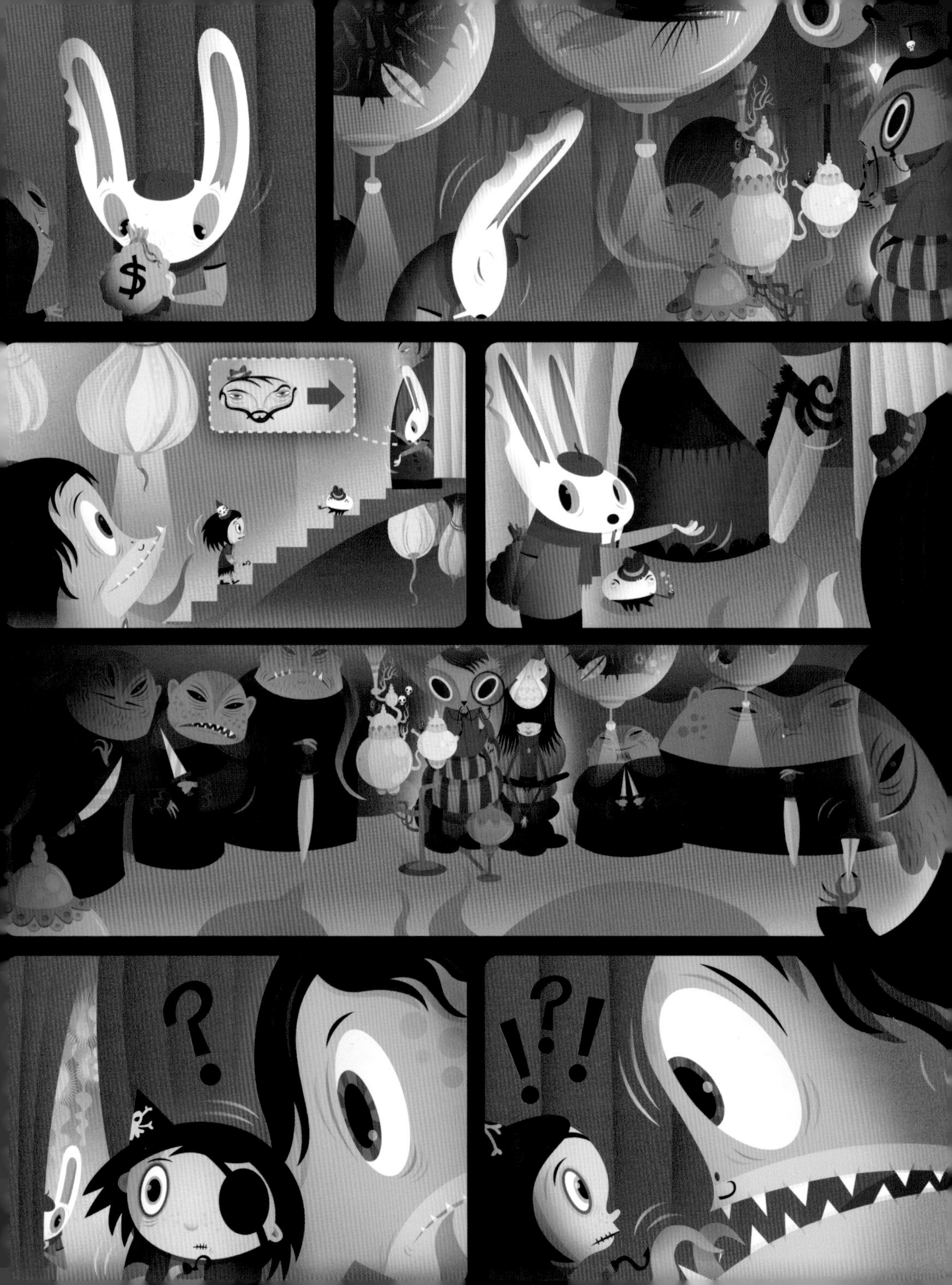
$
?
!?!

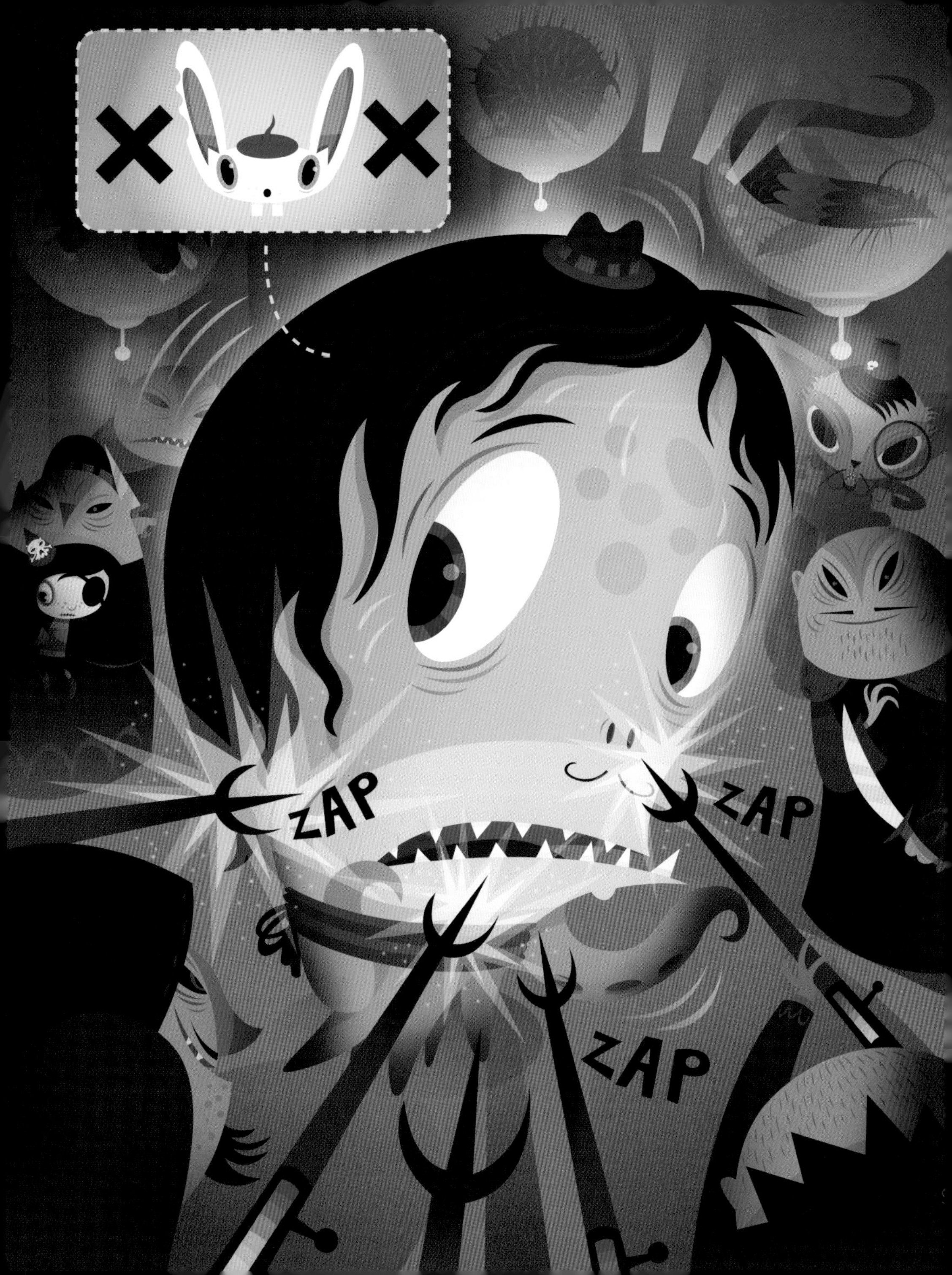
ZAP
ZAP
ZAP

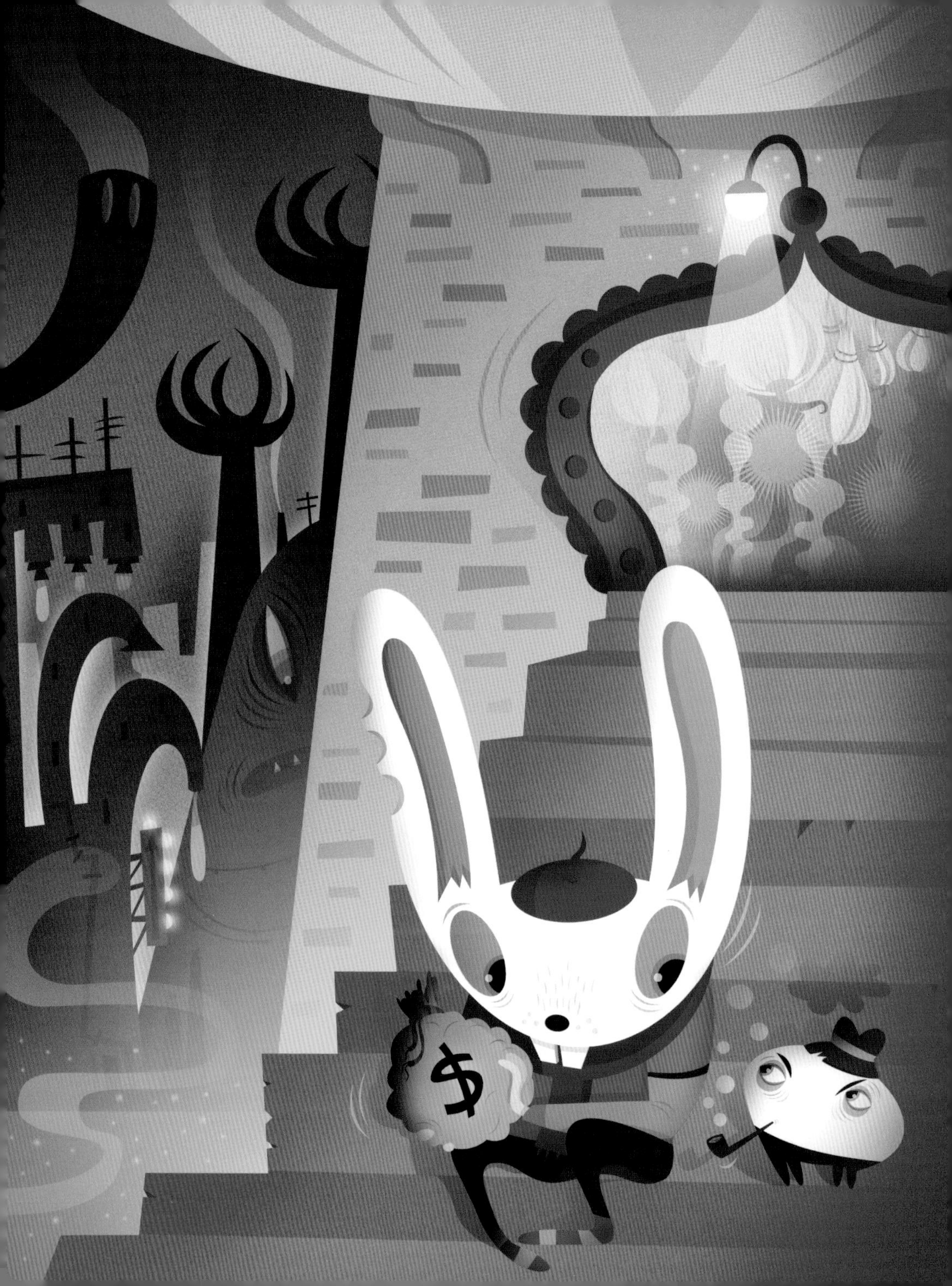

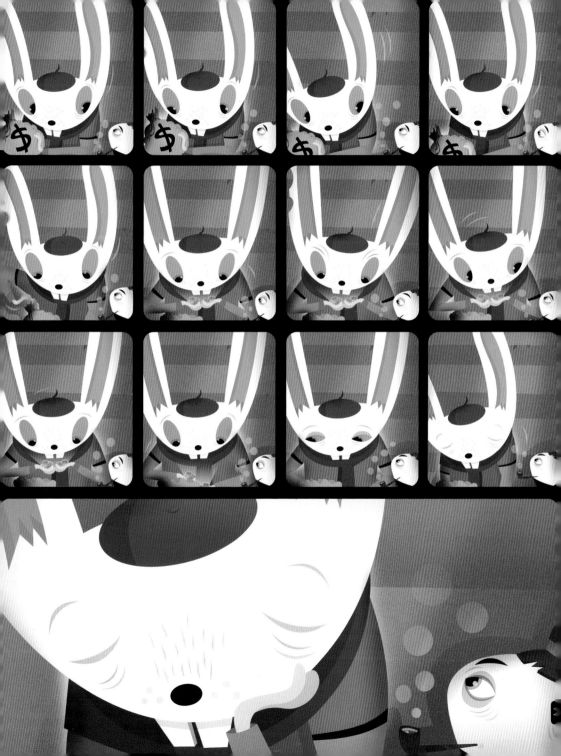

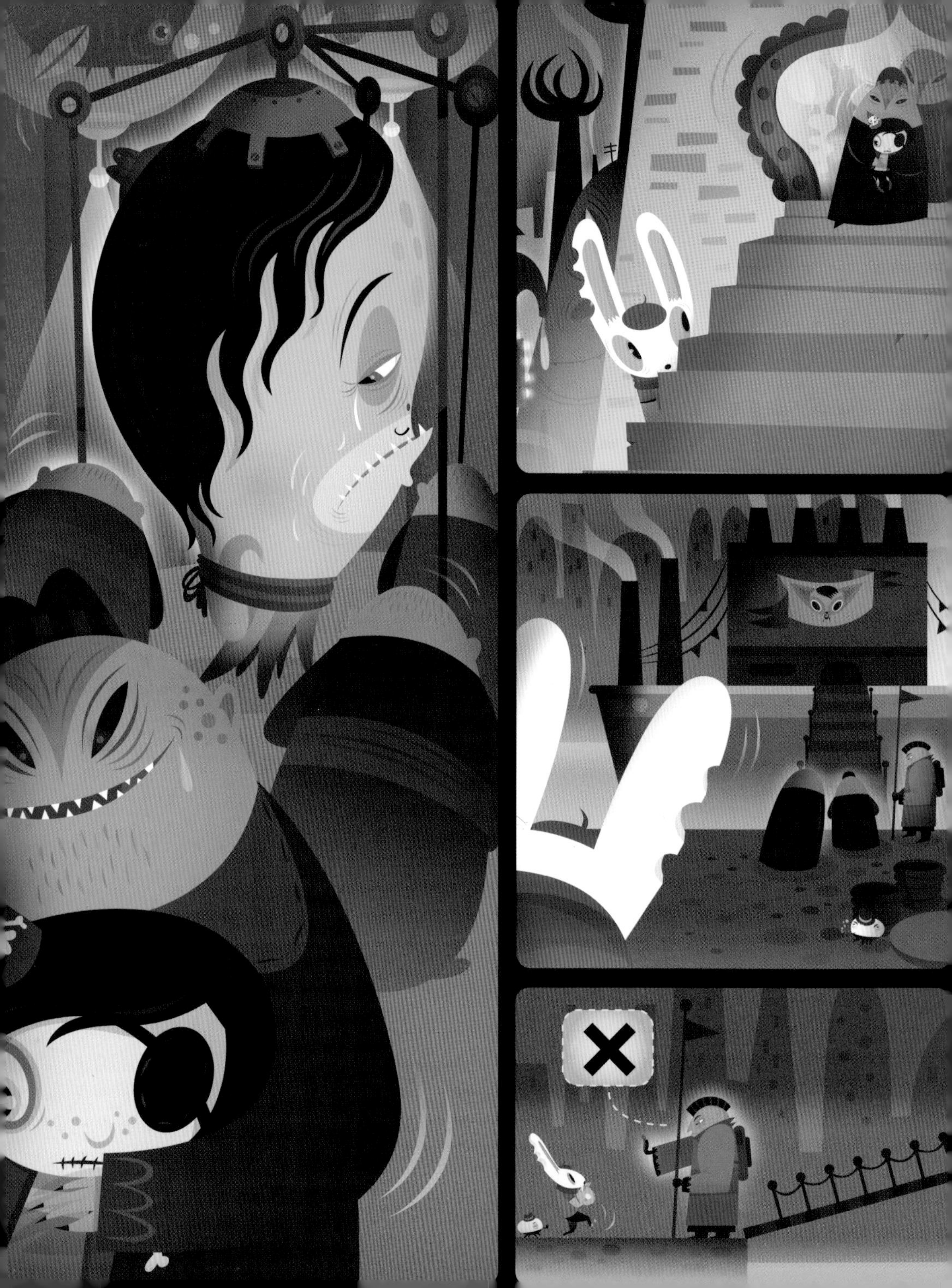

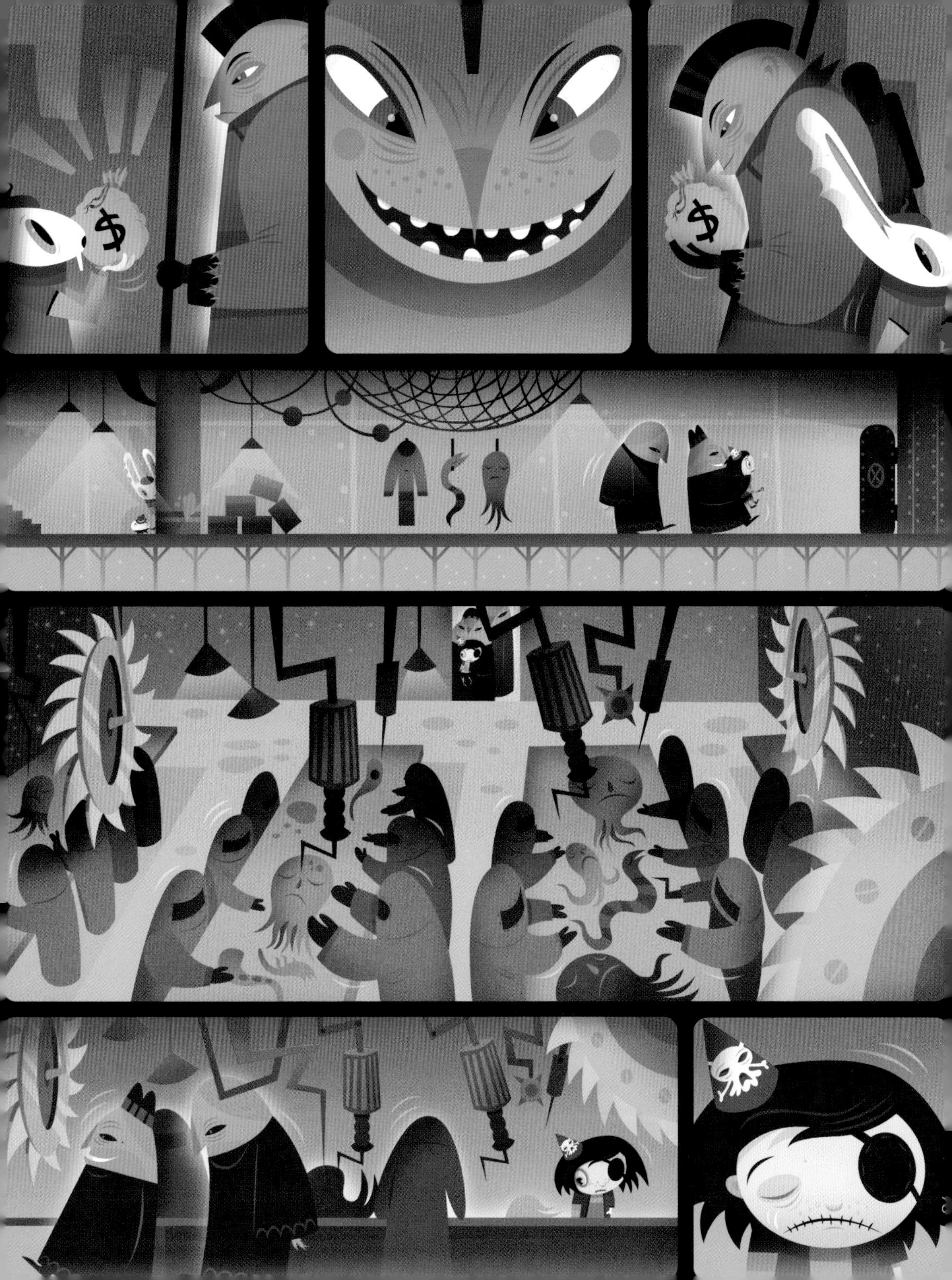

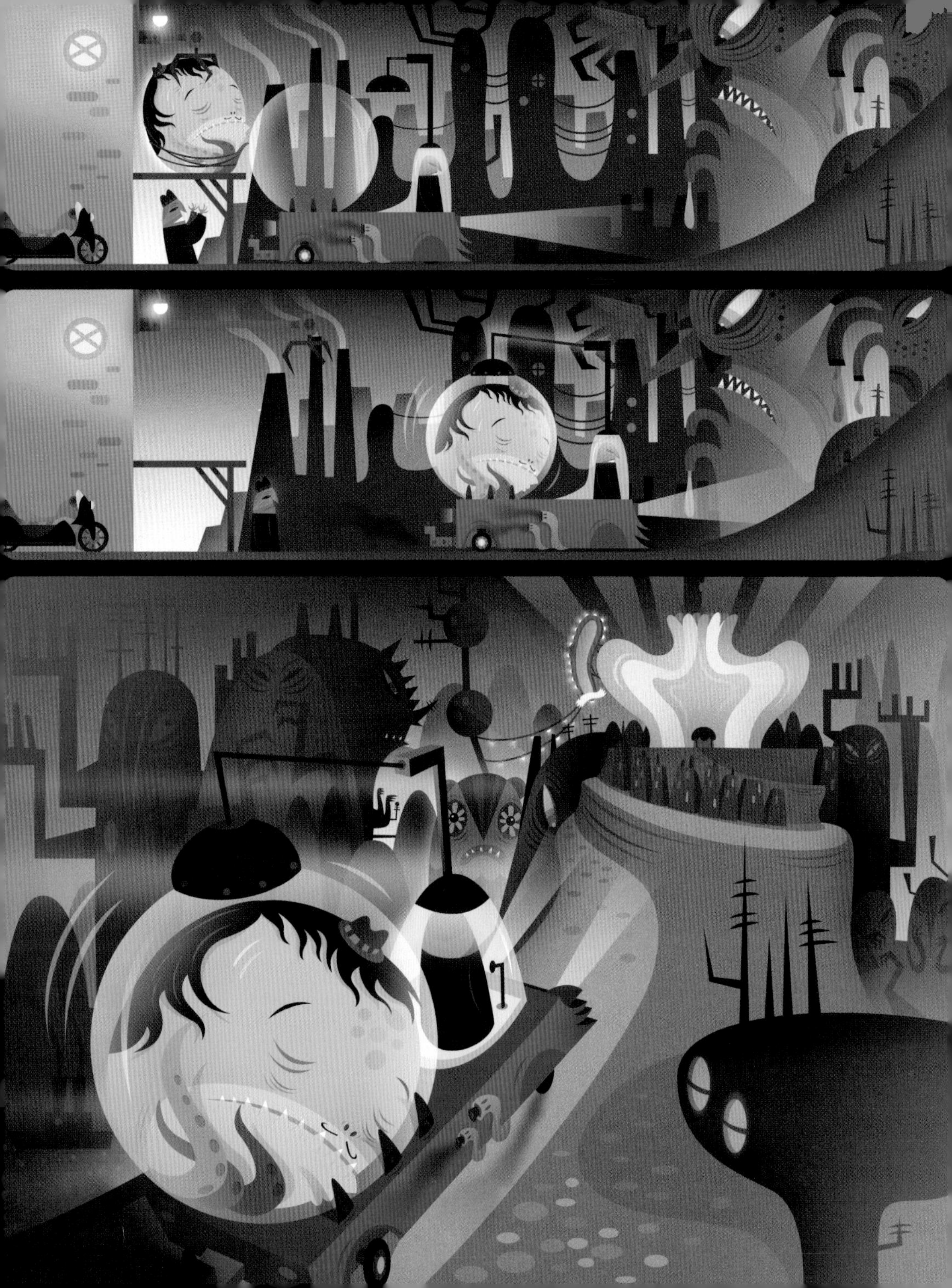

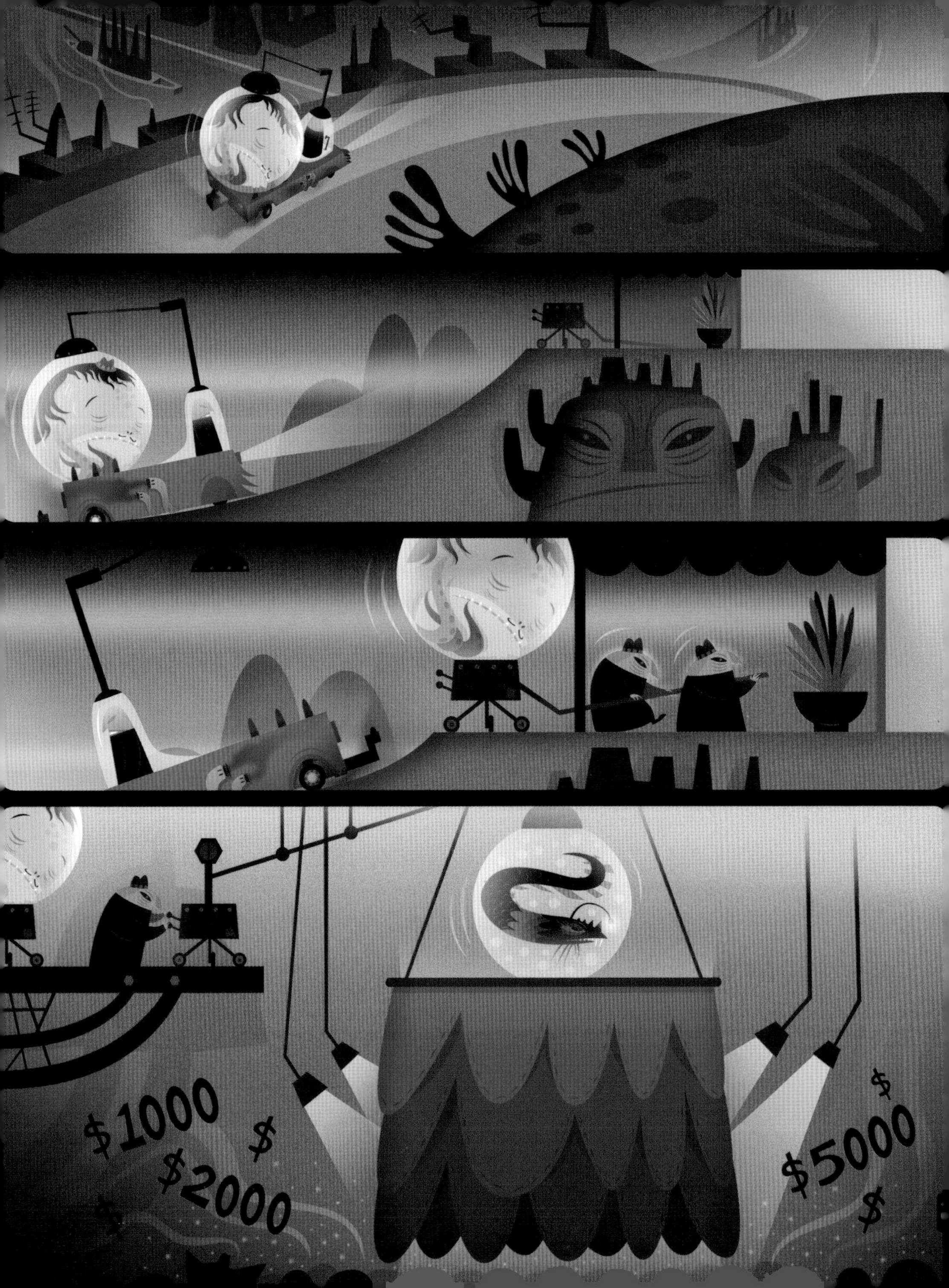

$1000
$
$2000
$
$5000
$

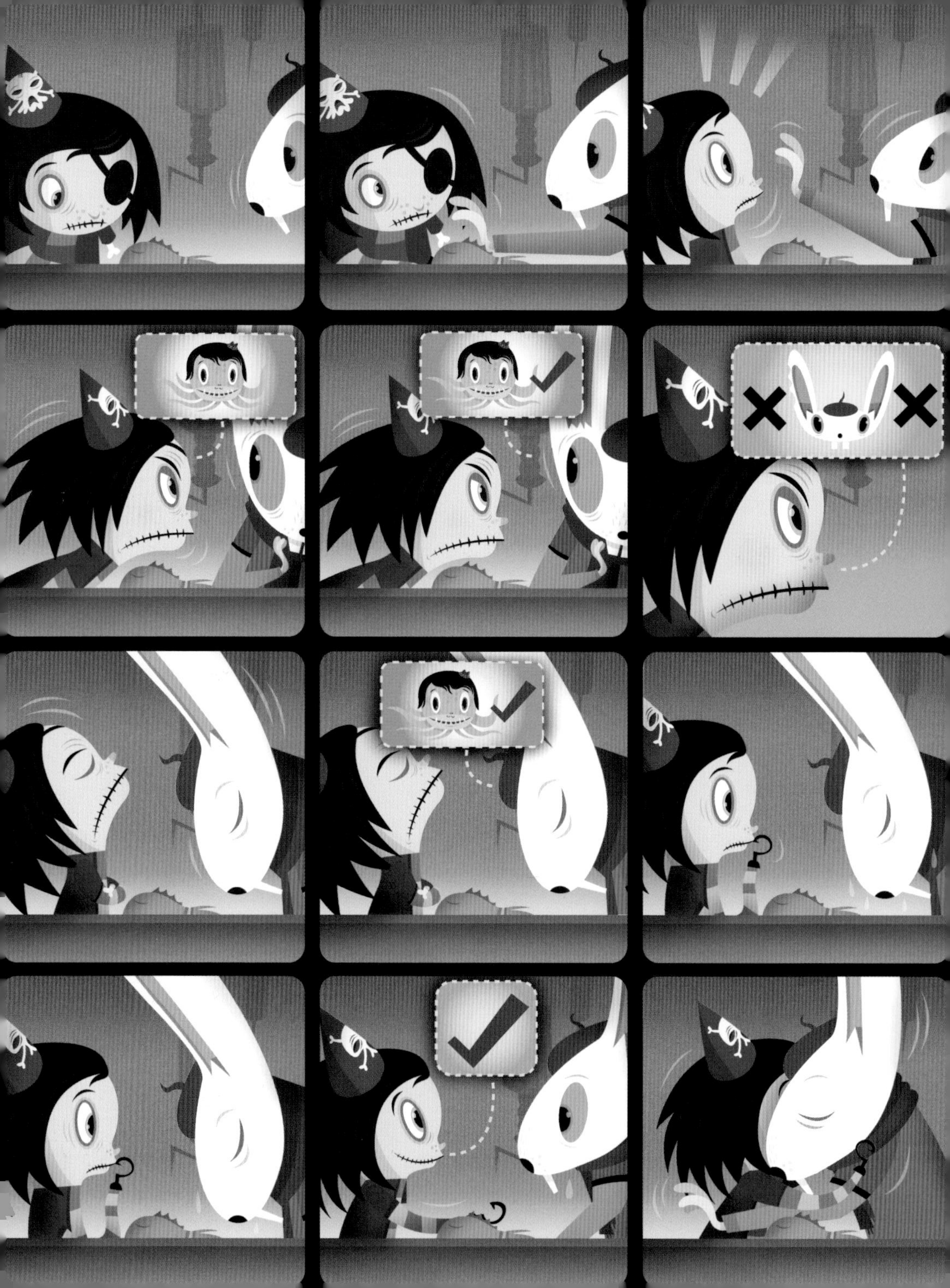

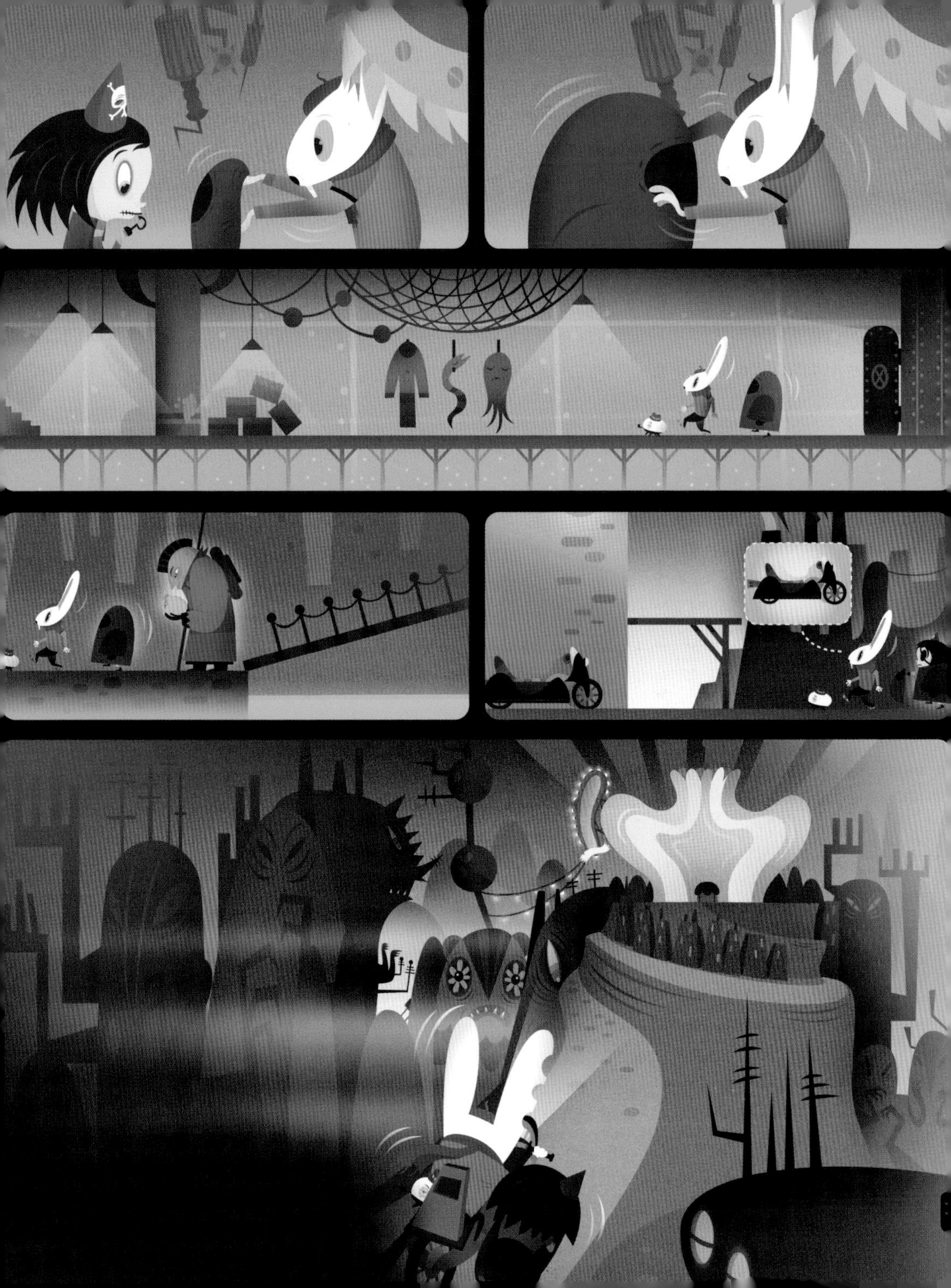

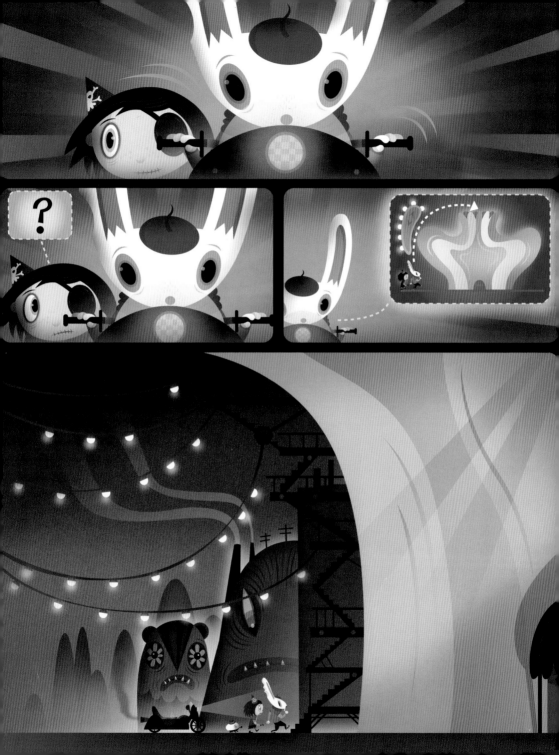

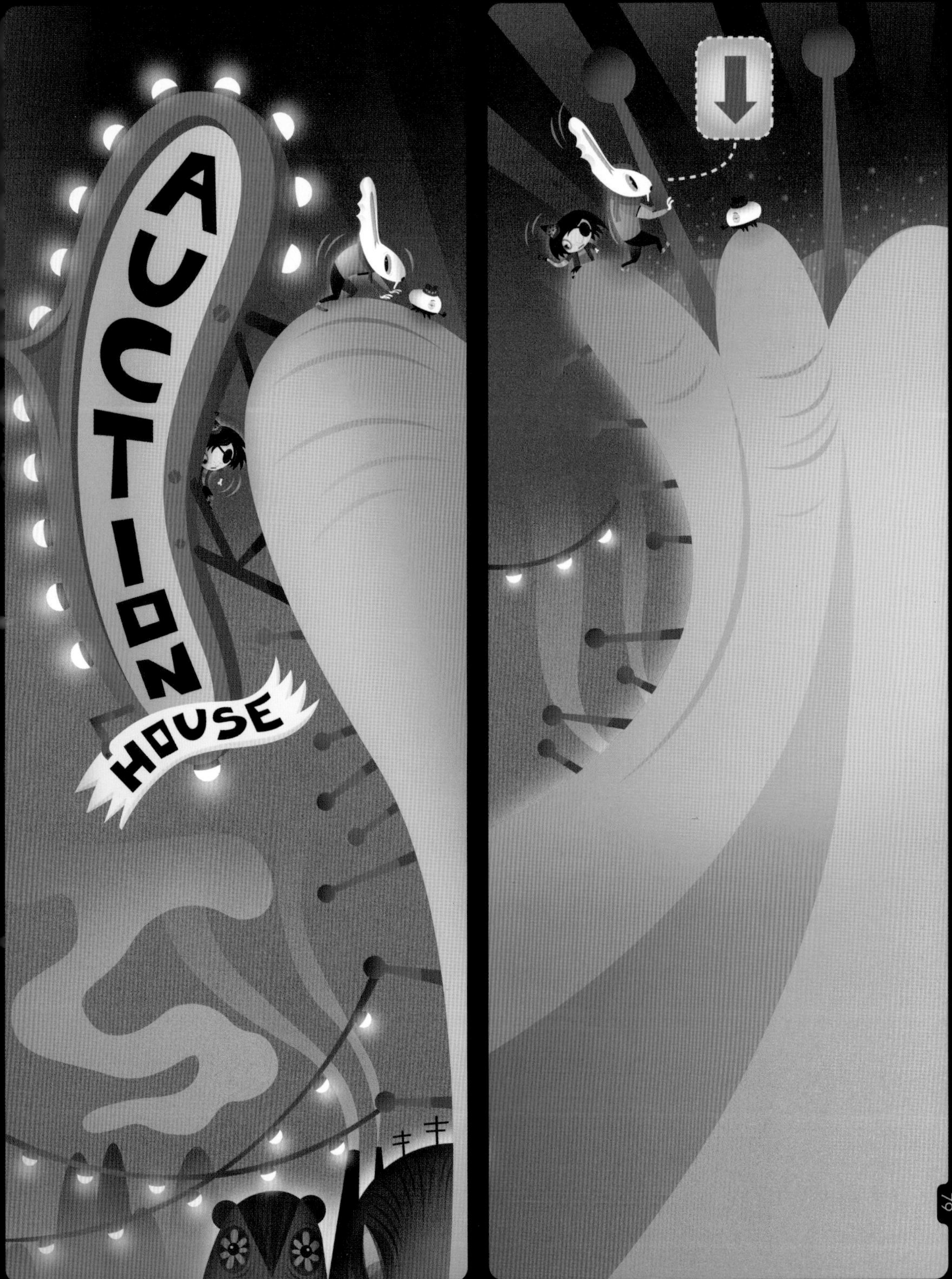
AUCTION
HOUSE

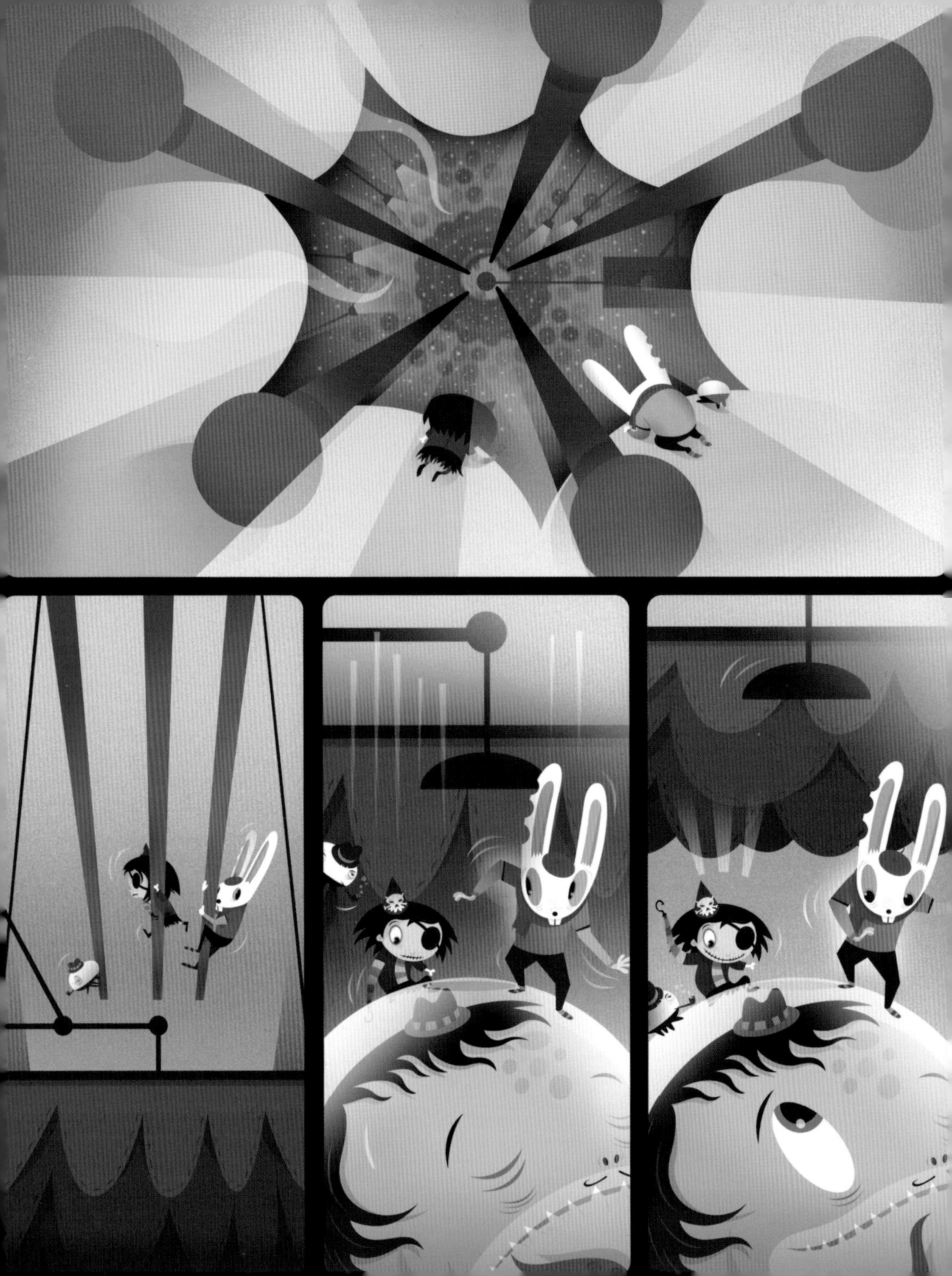

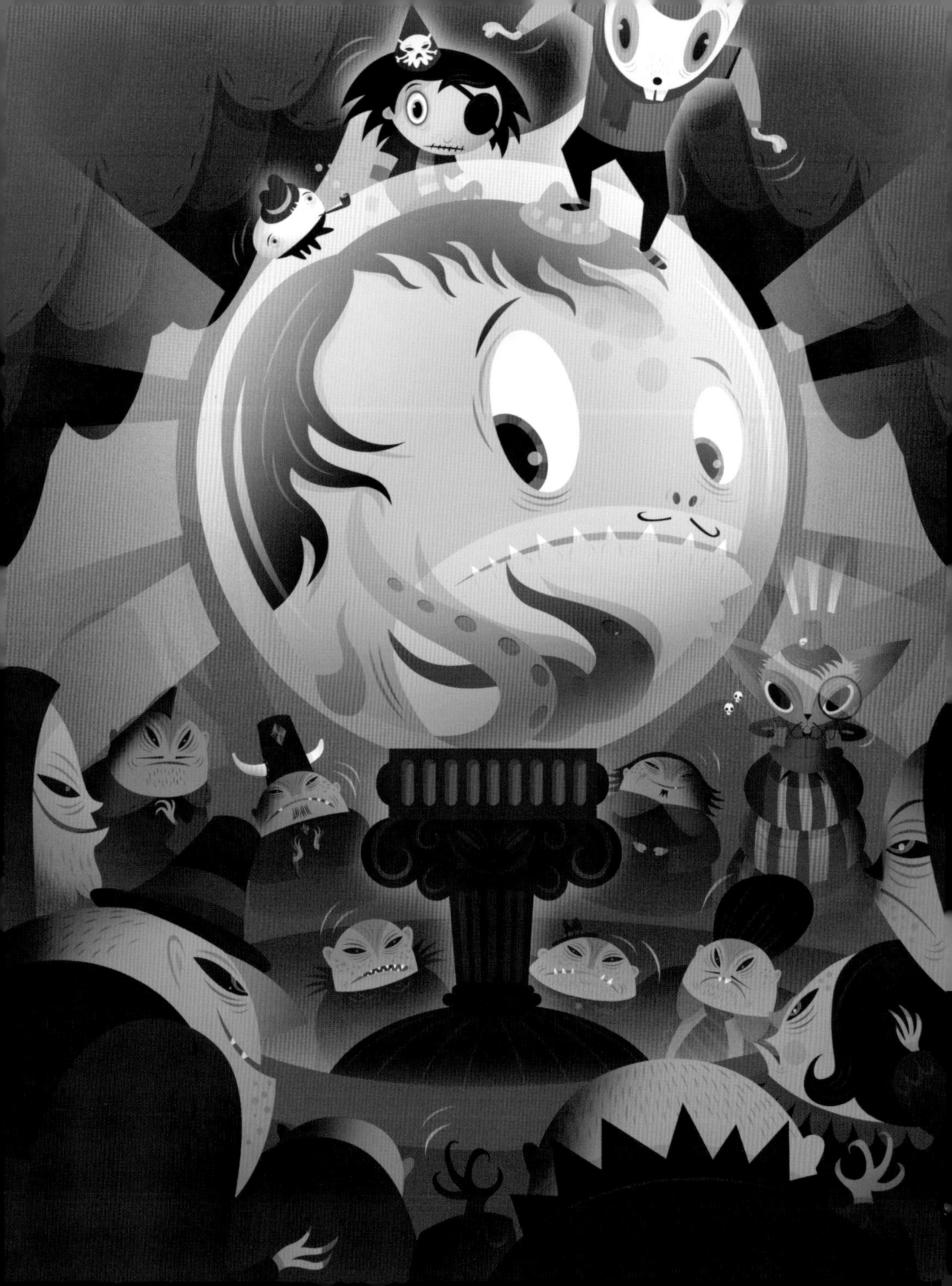

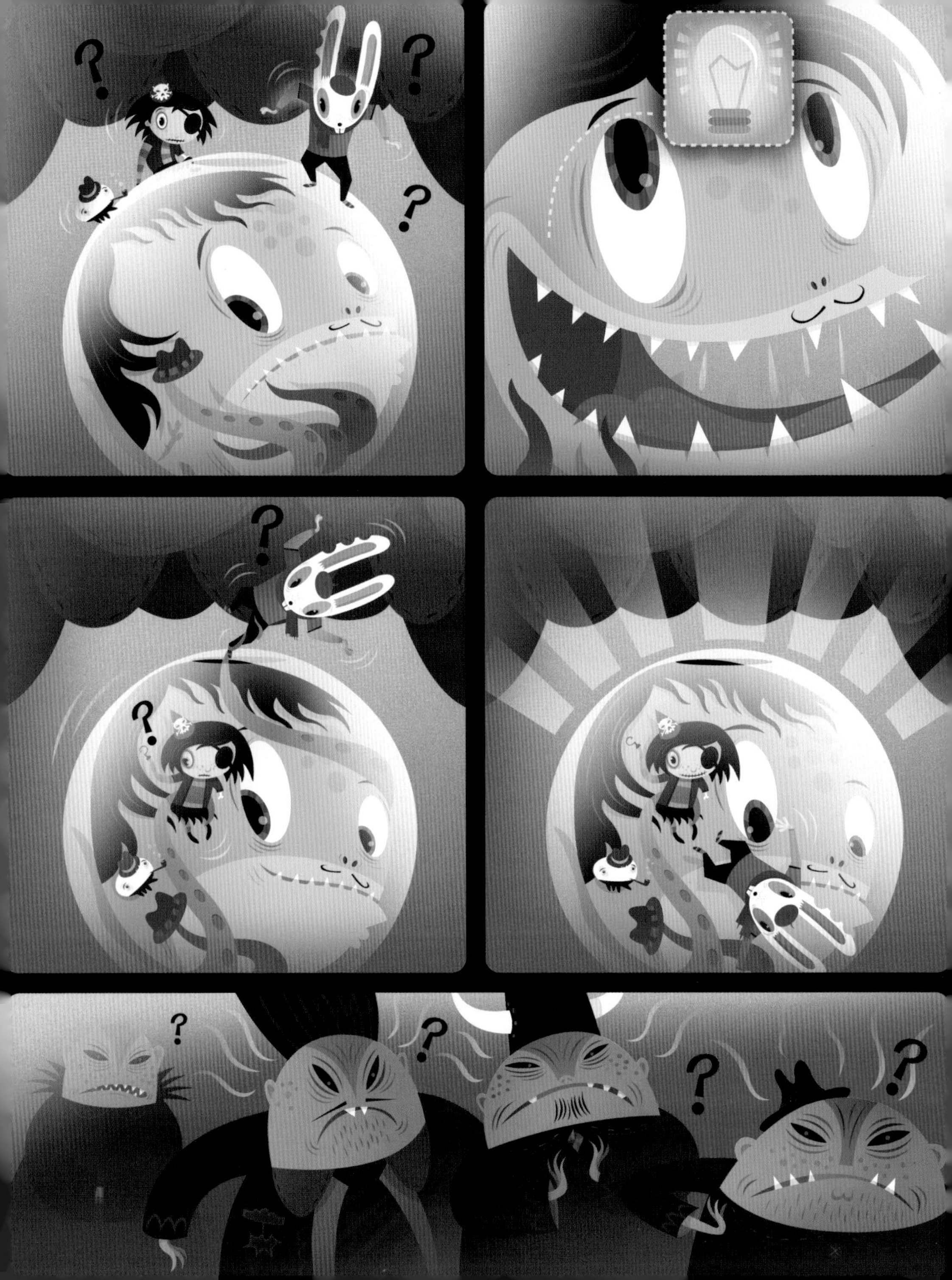

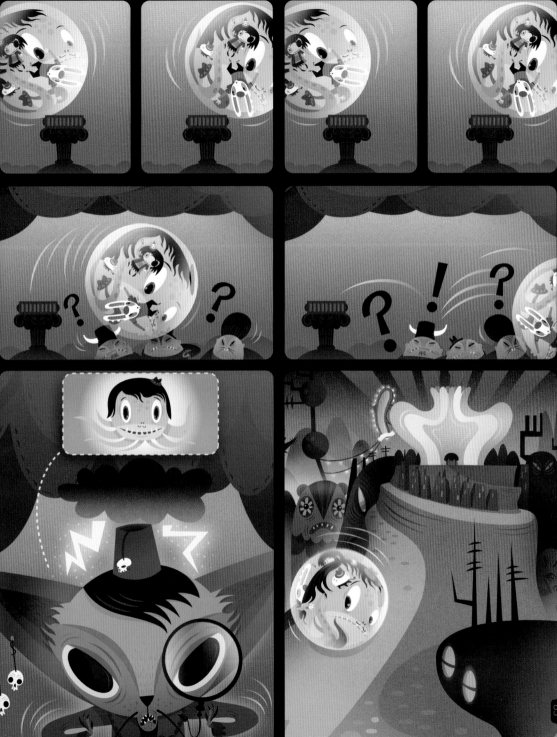

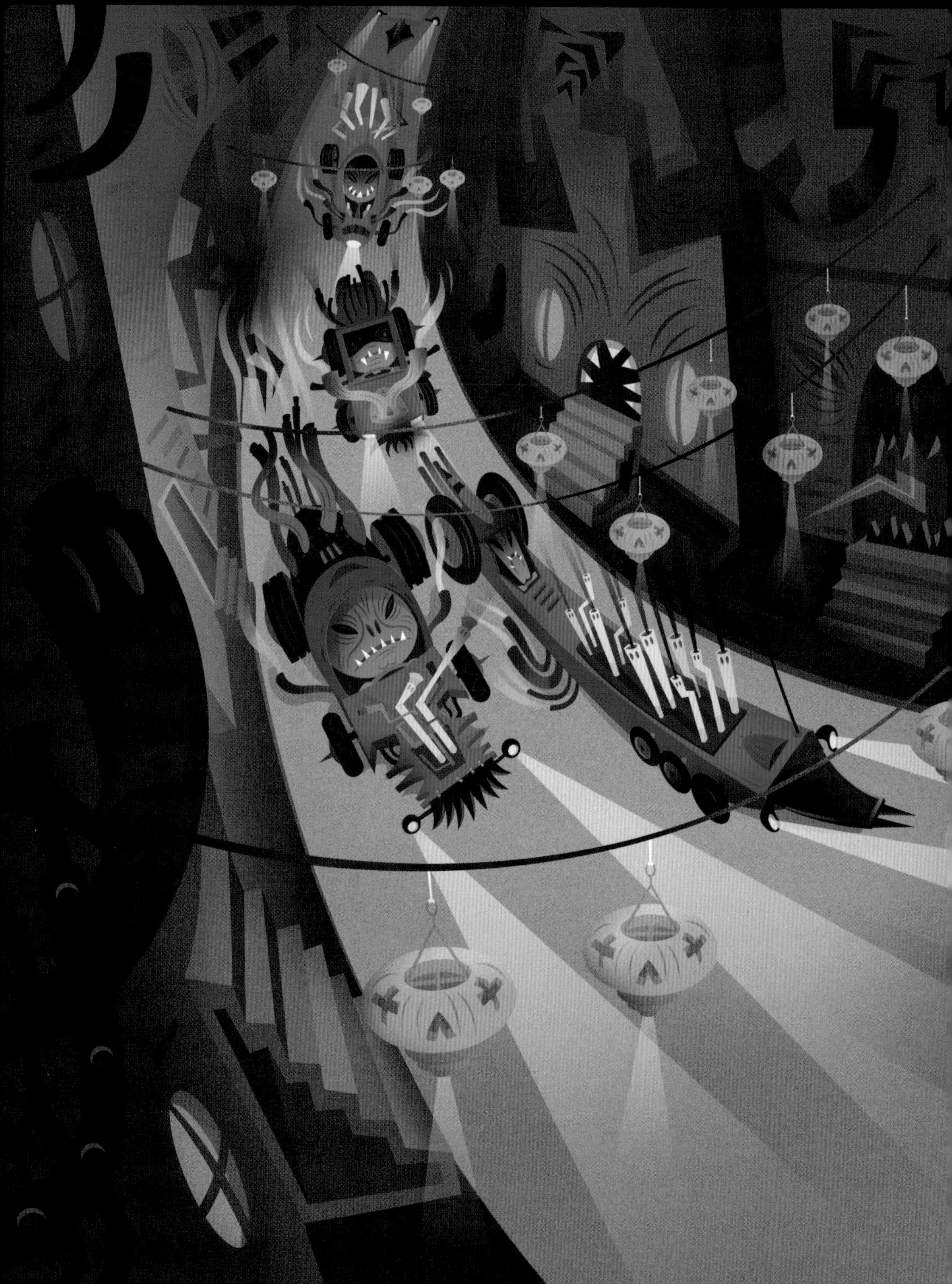

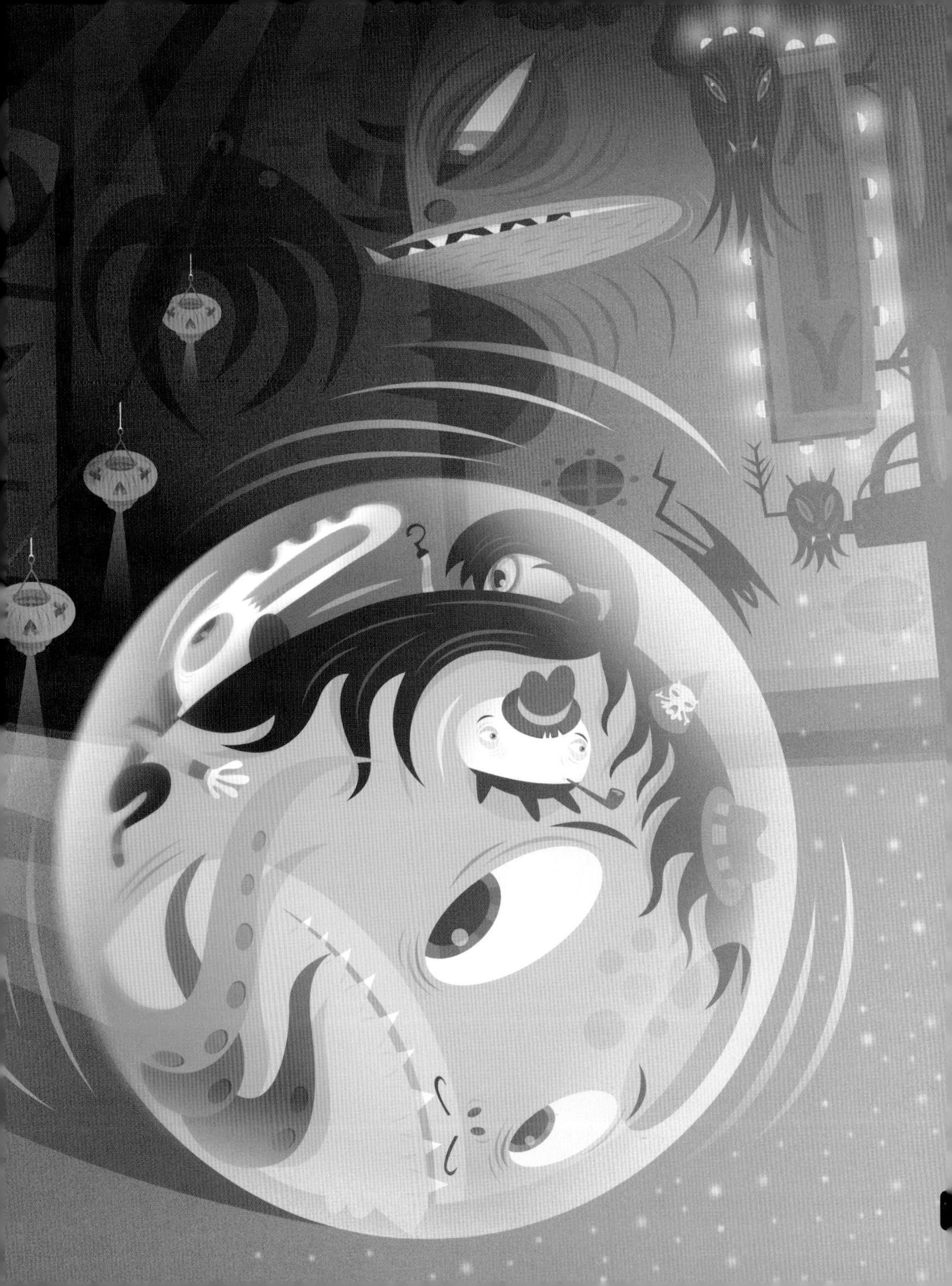

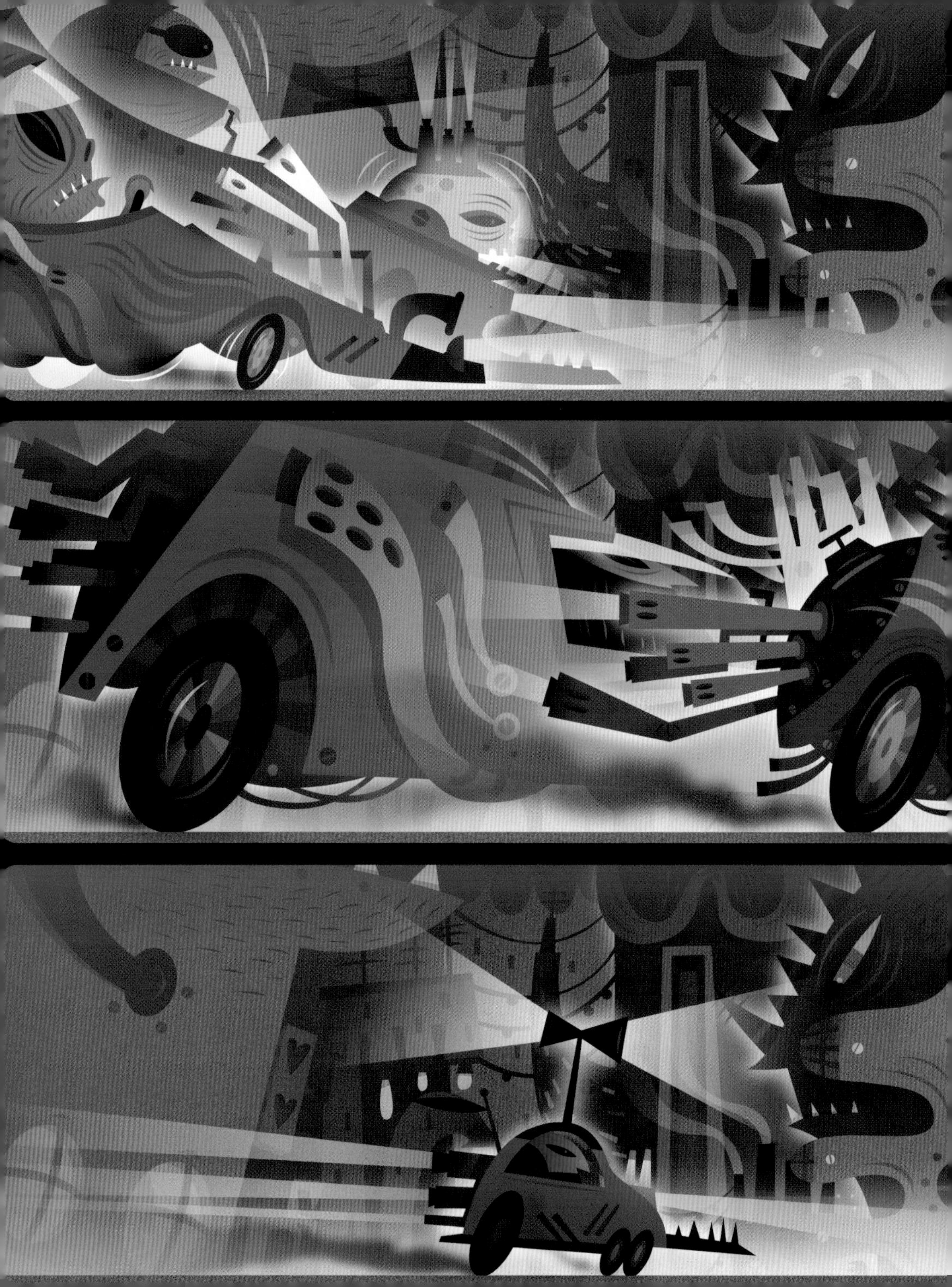

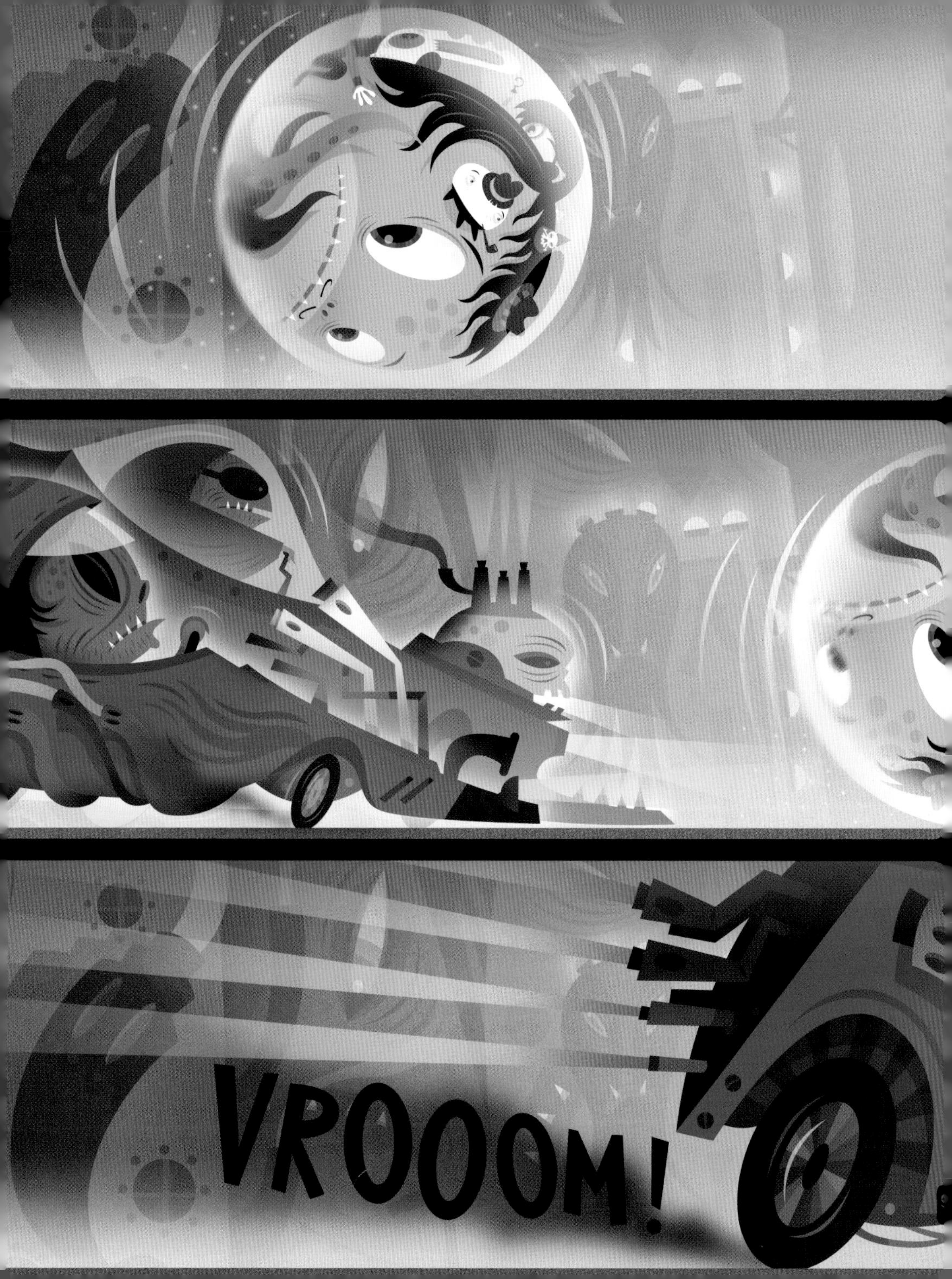
VROOOM!

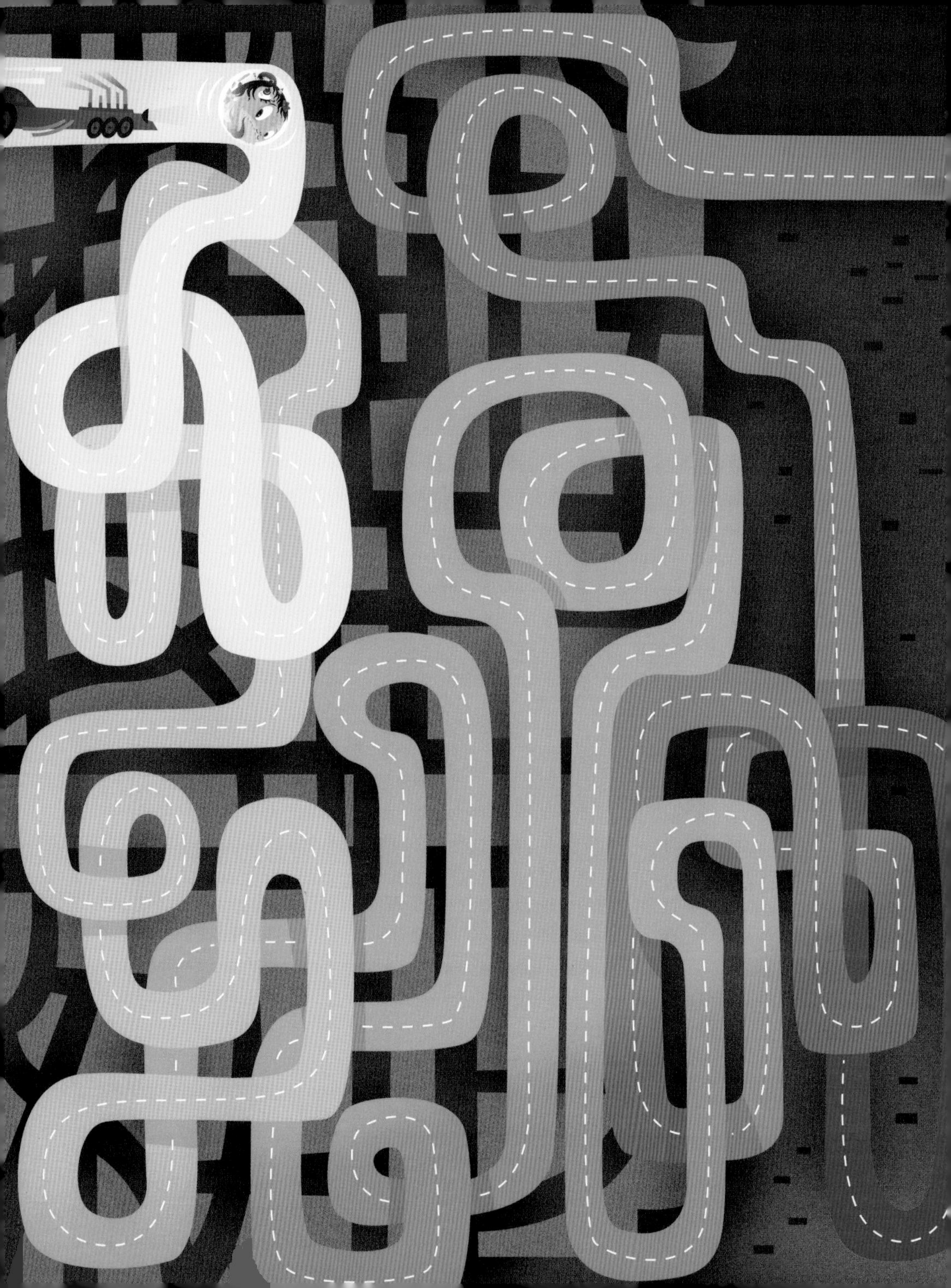

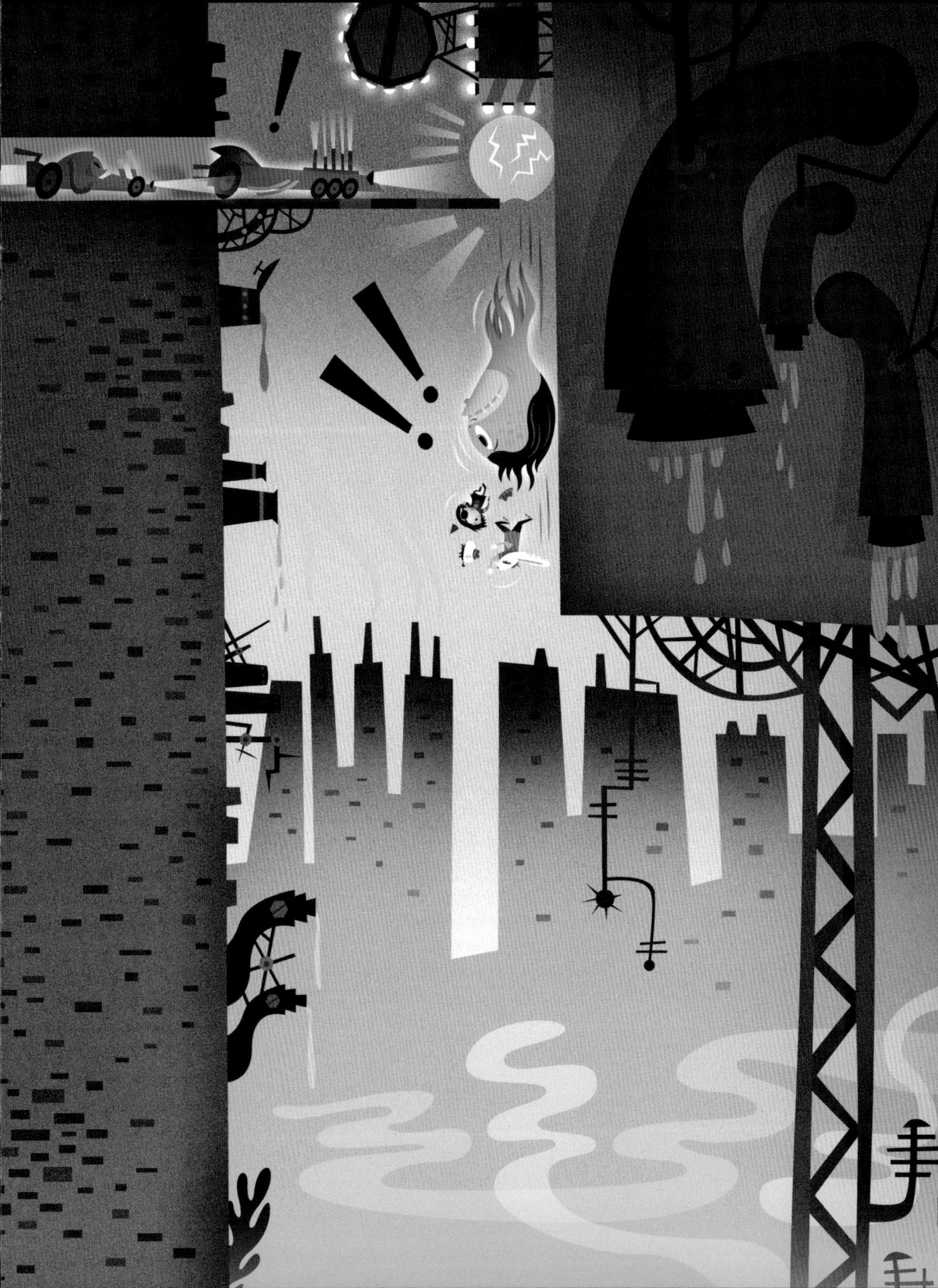

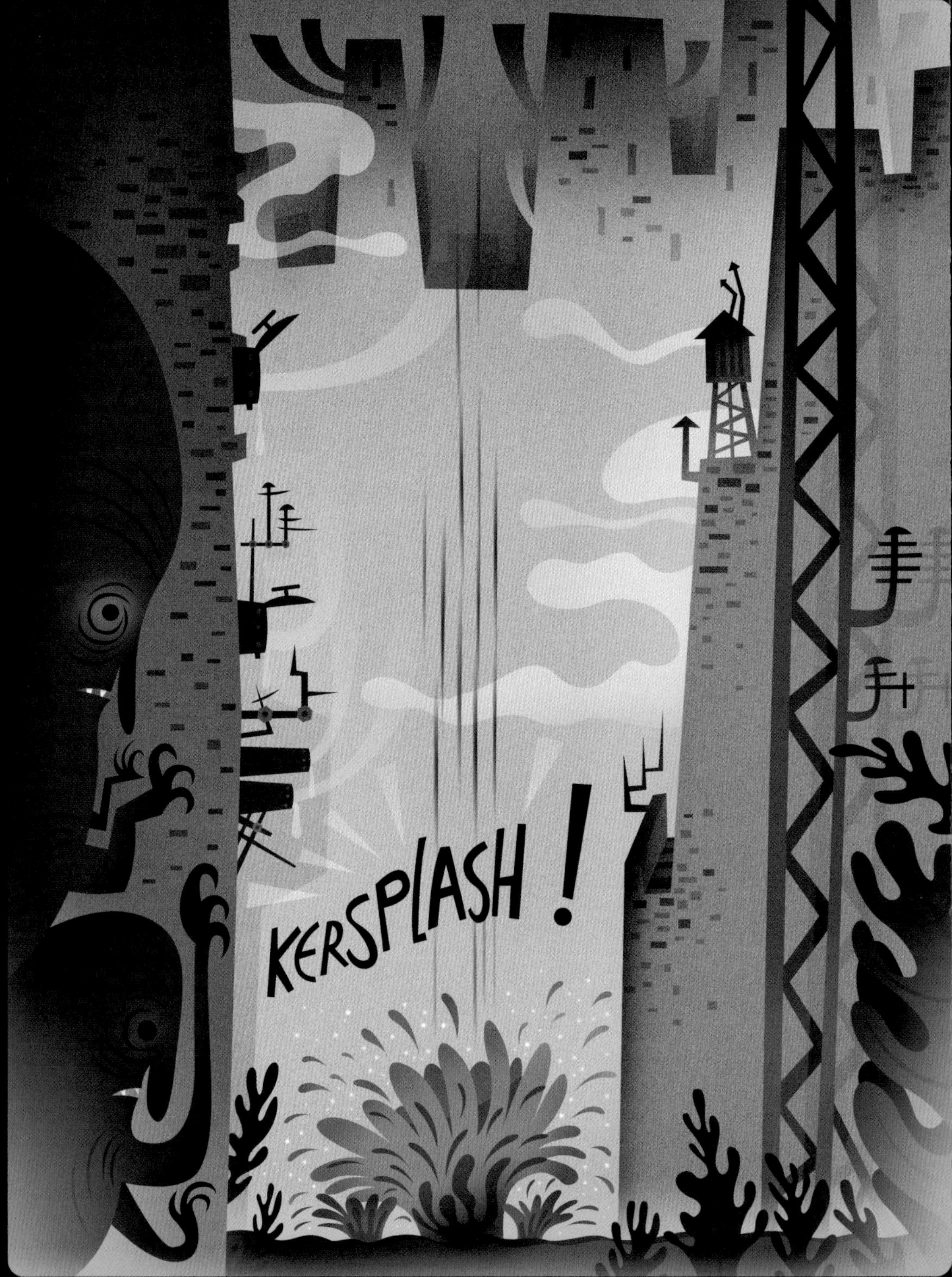
KERSPLASH!

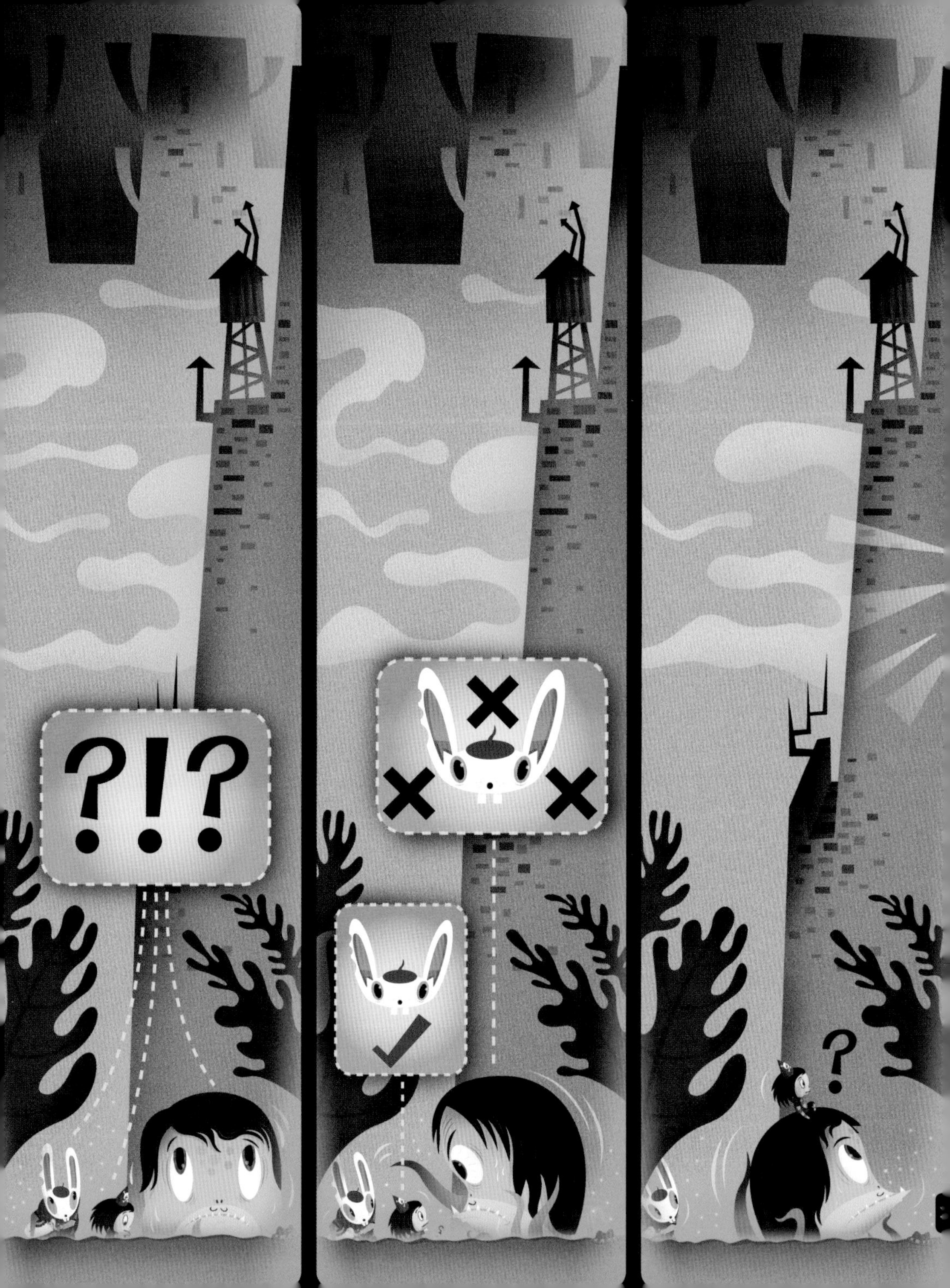
?!?
?

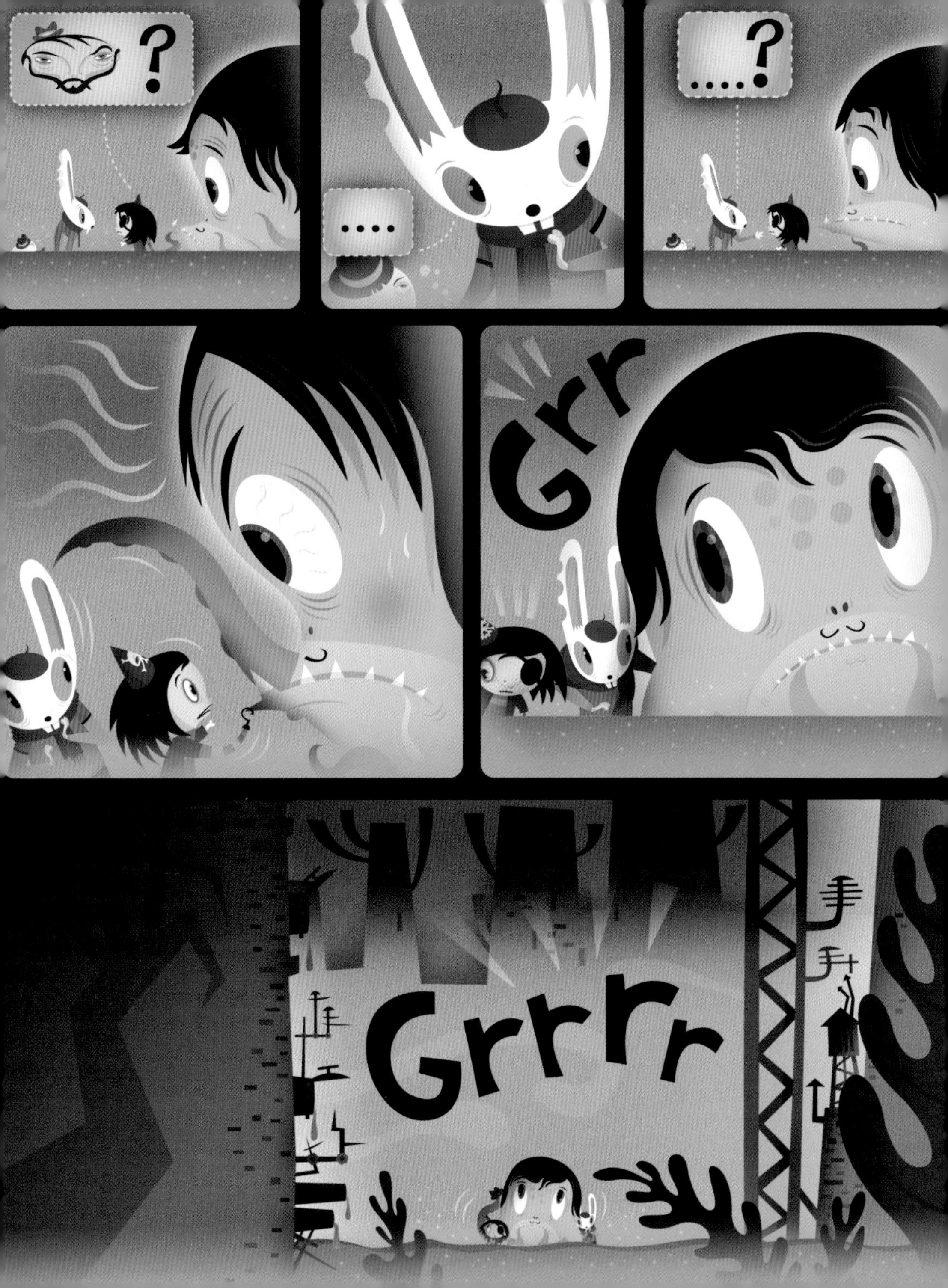
?
....
....?
Grr
Grrrr

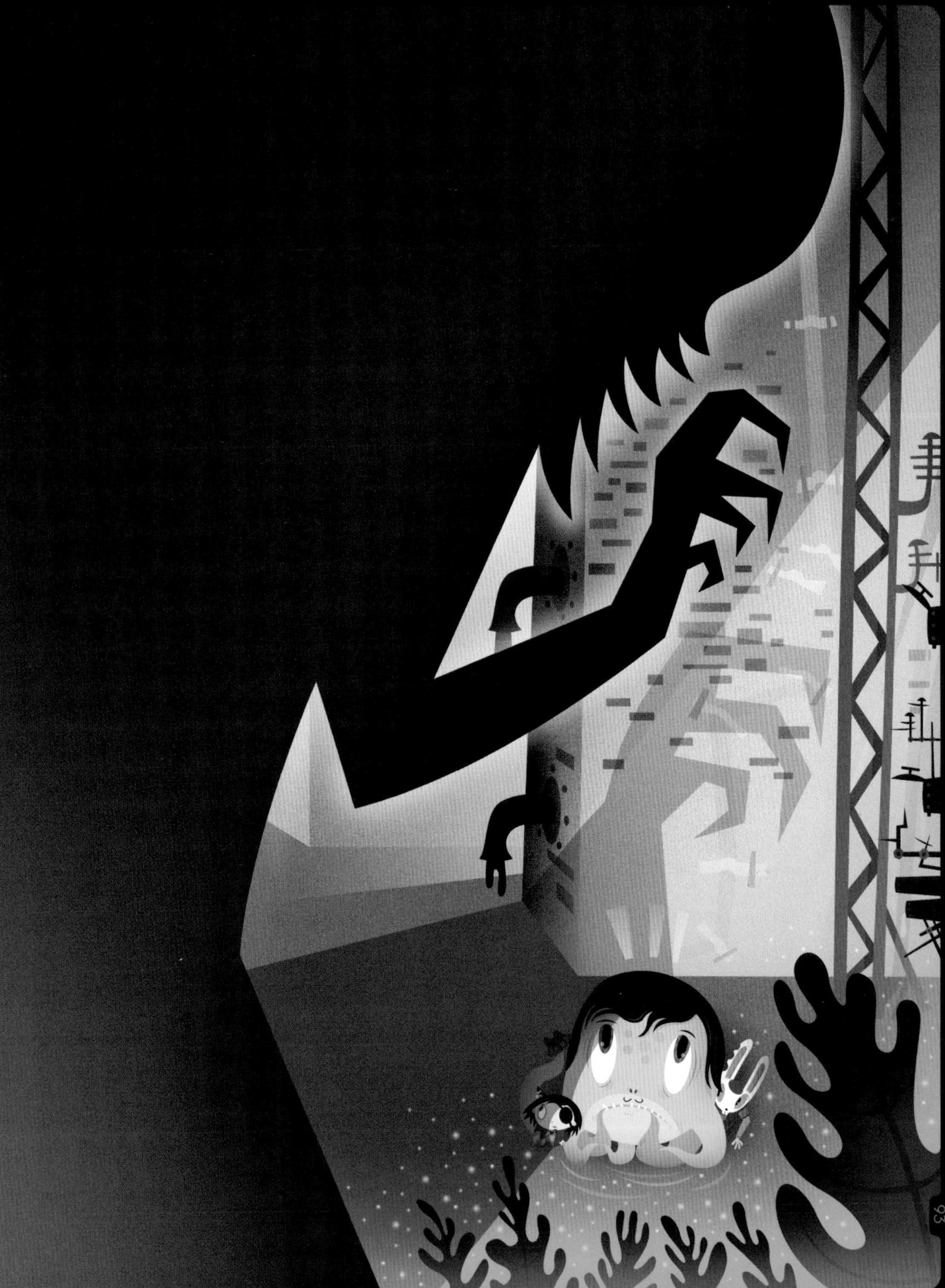

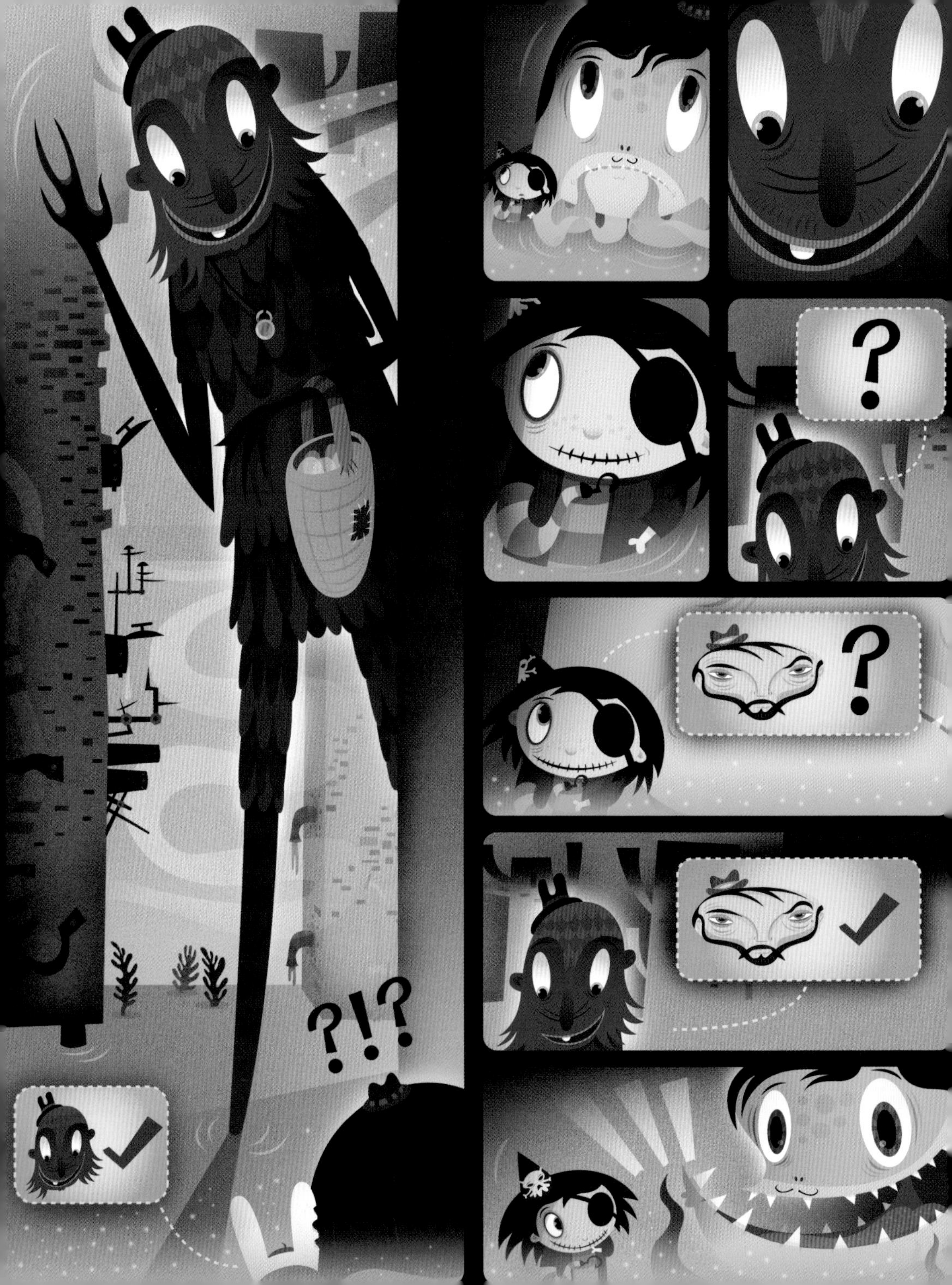
?
?
?!?

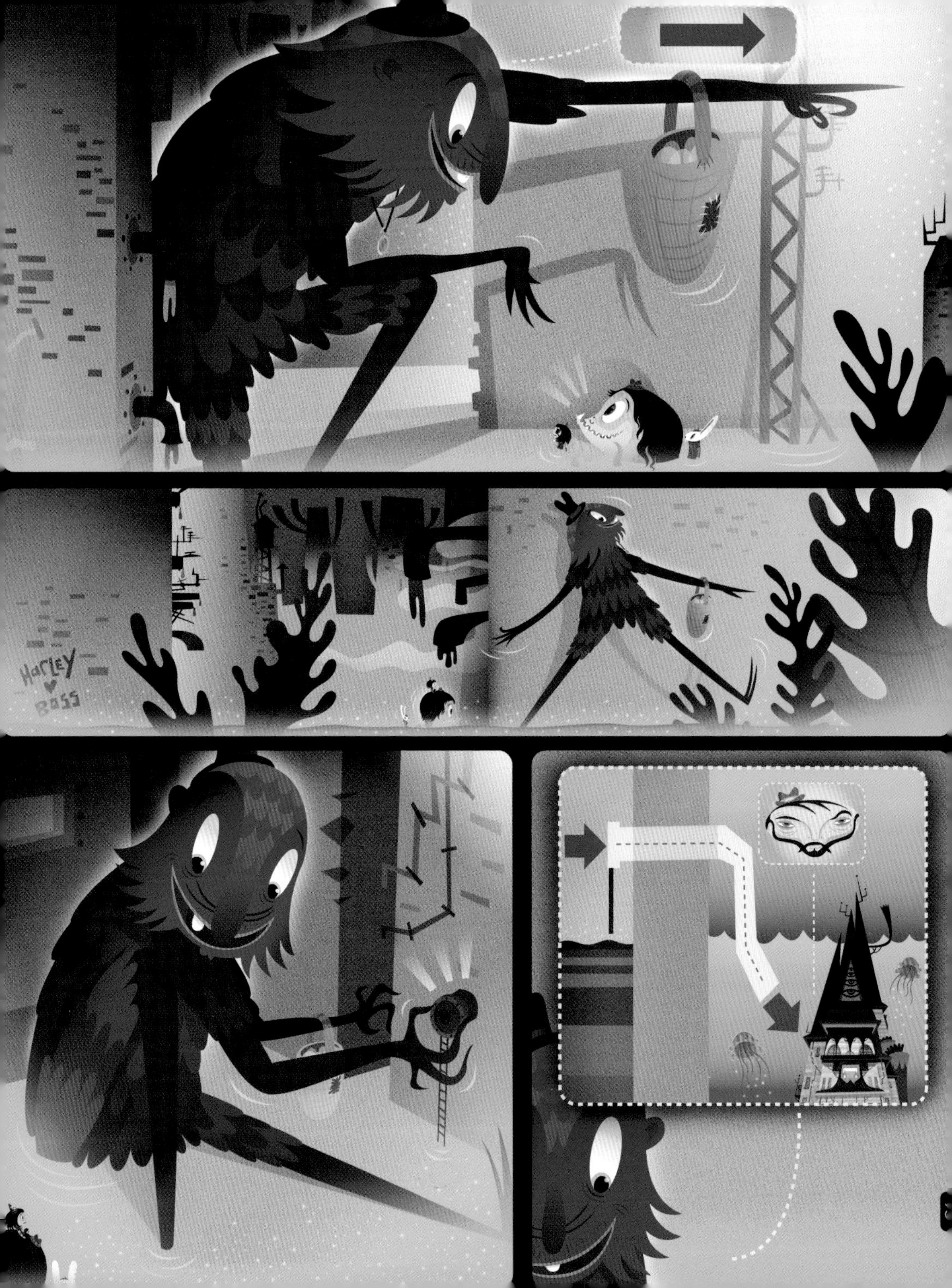
HarLey ♥ Boss

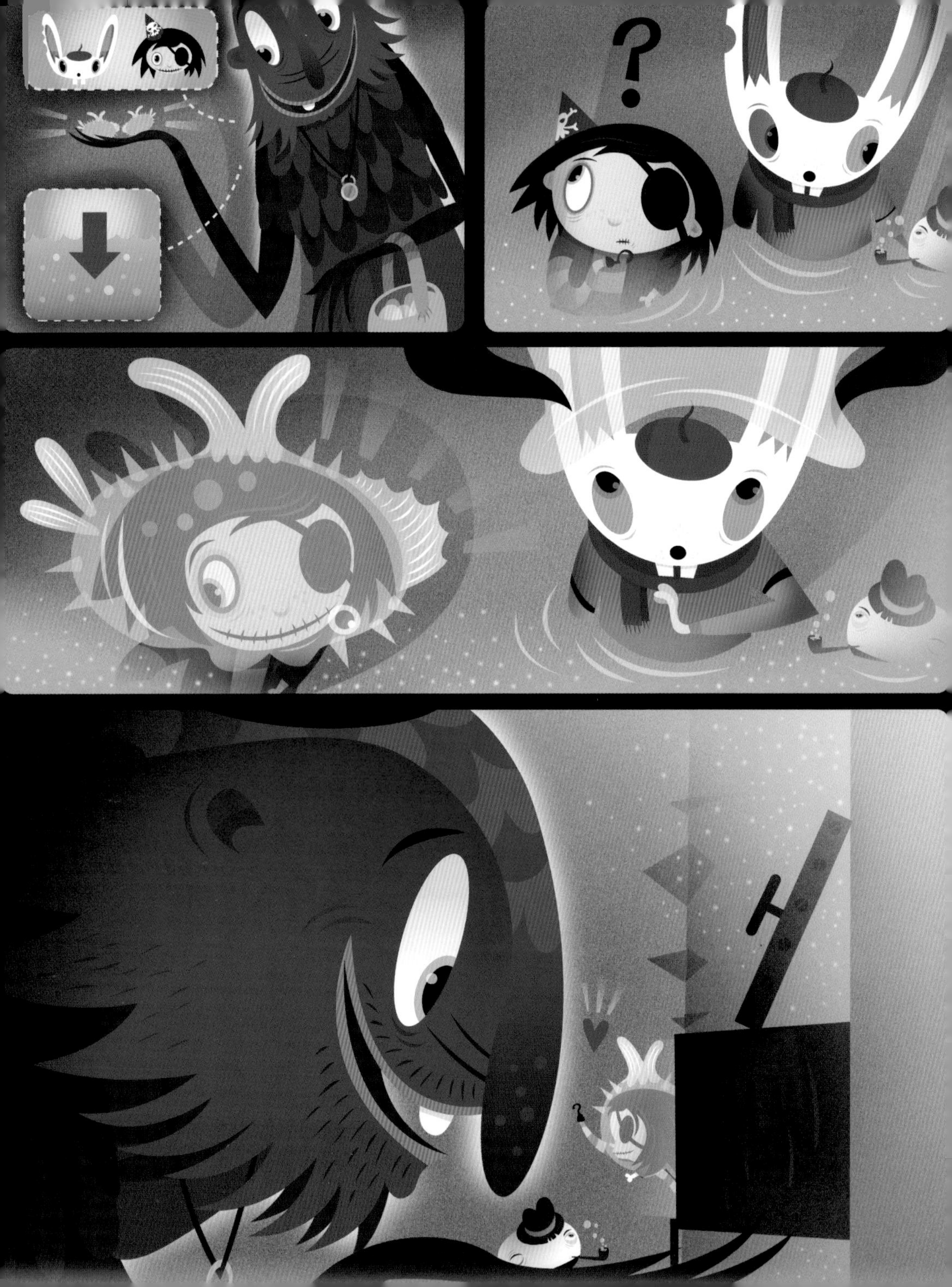

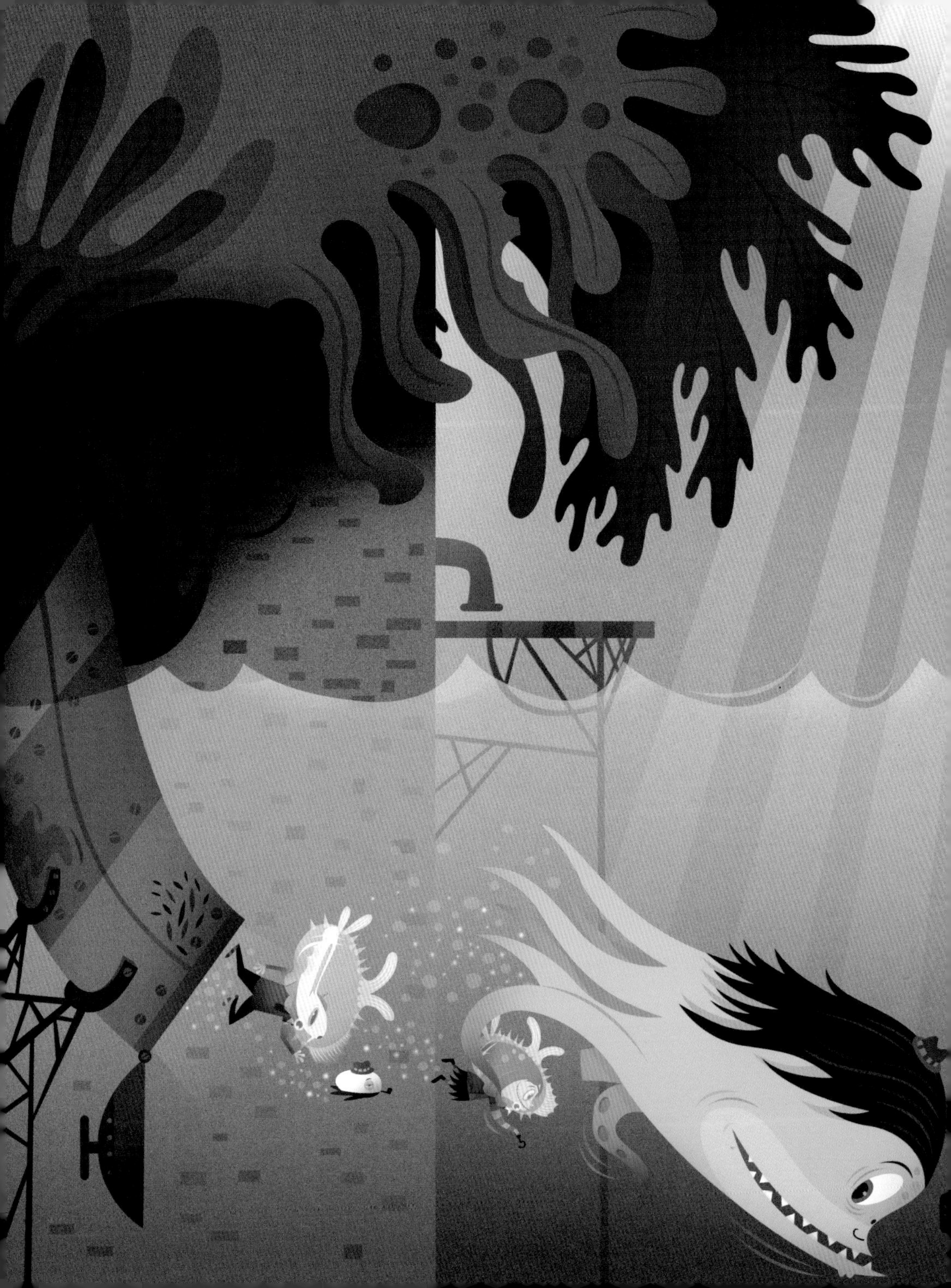

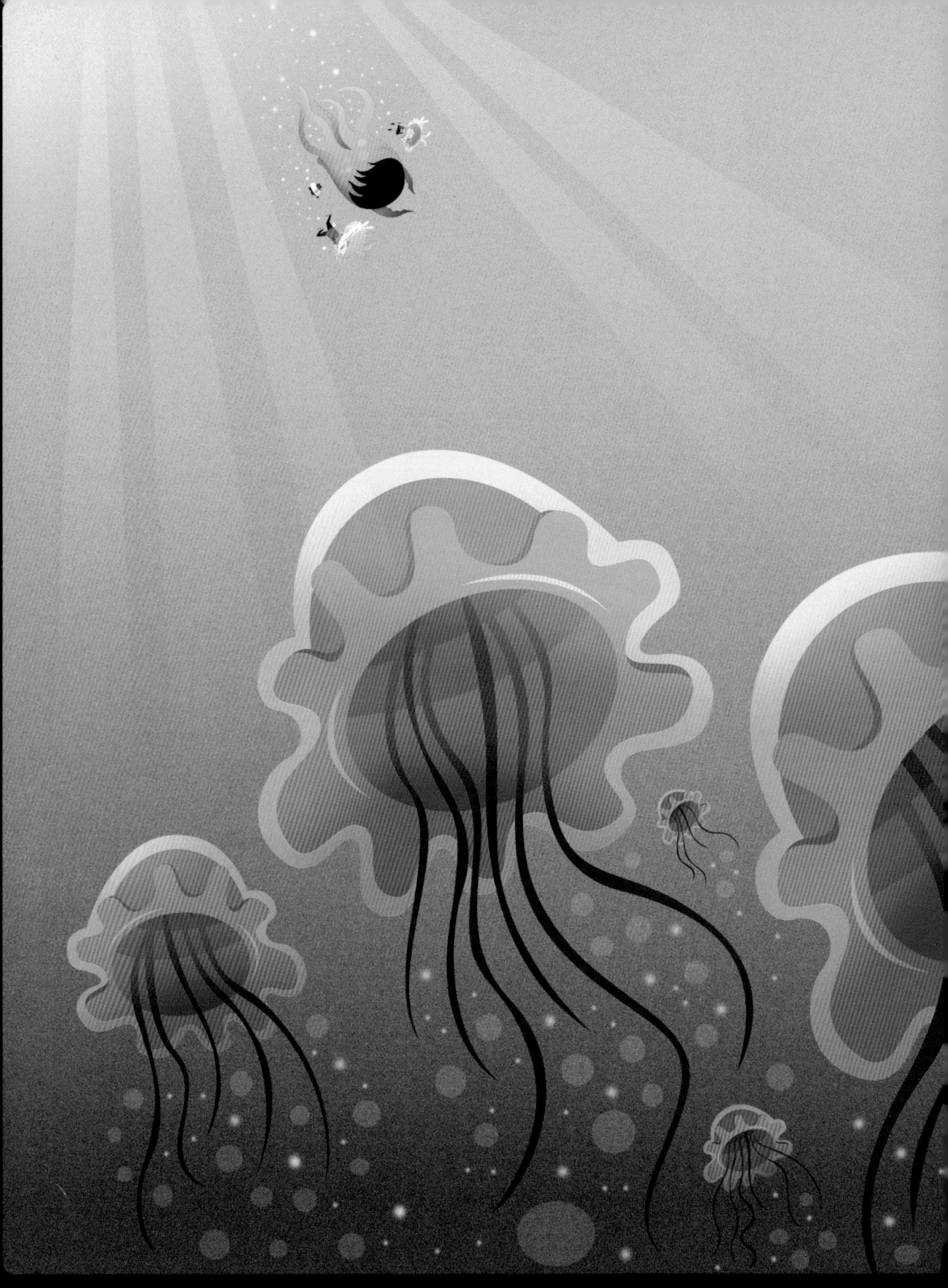

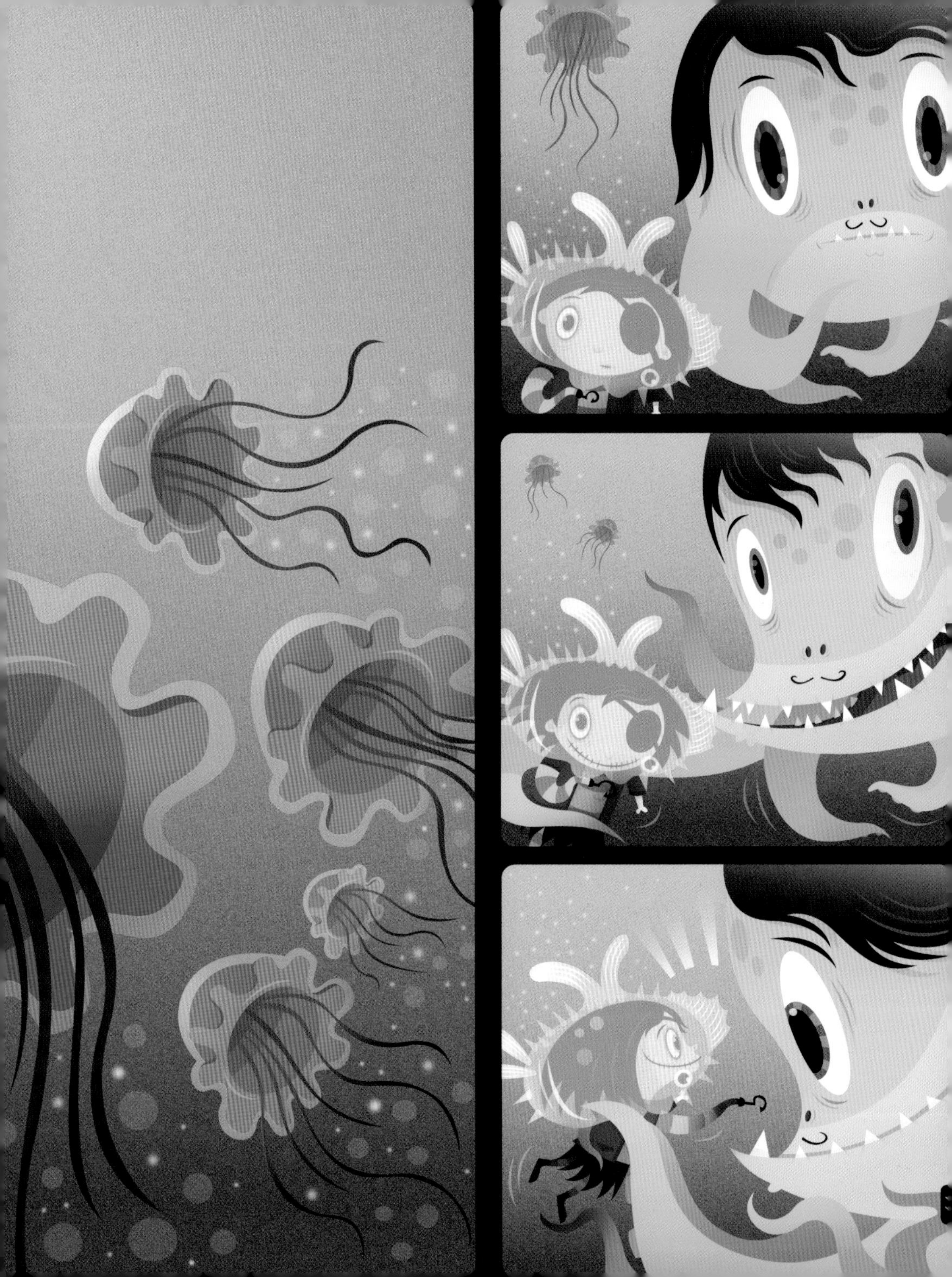

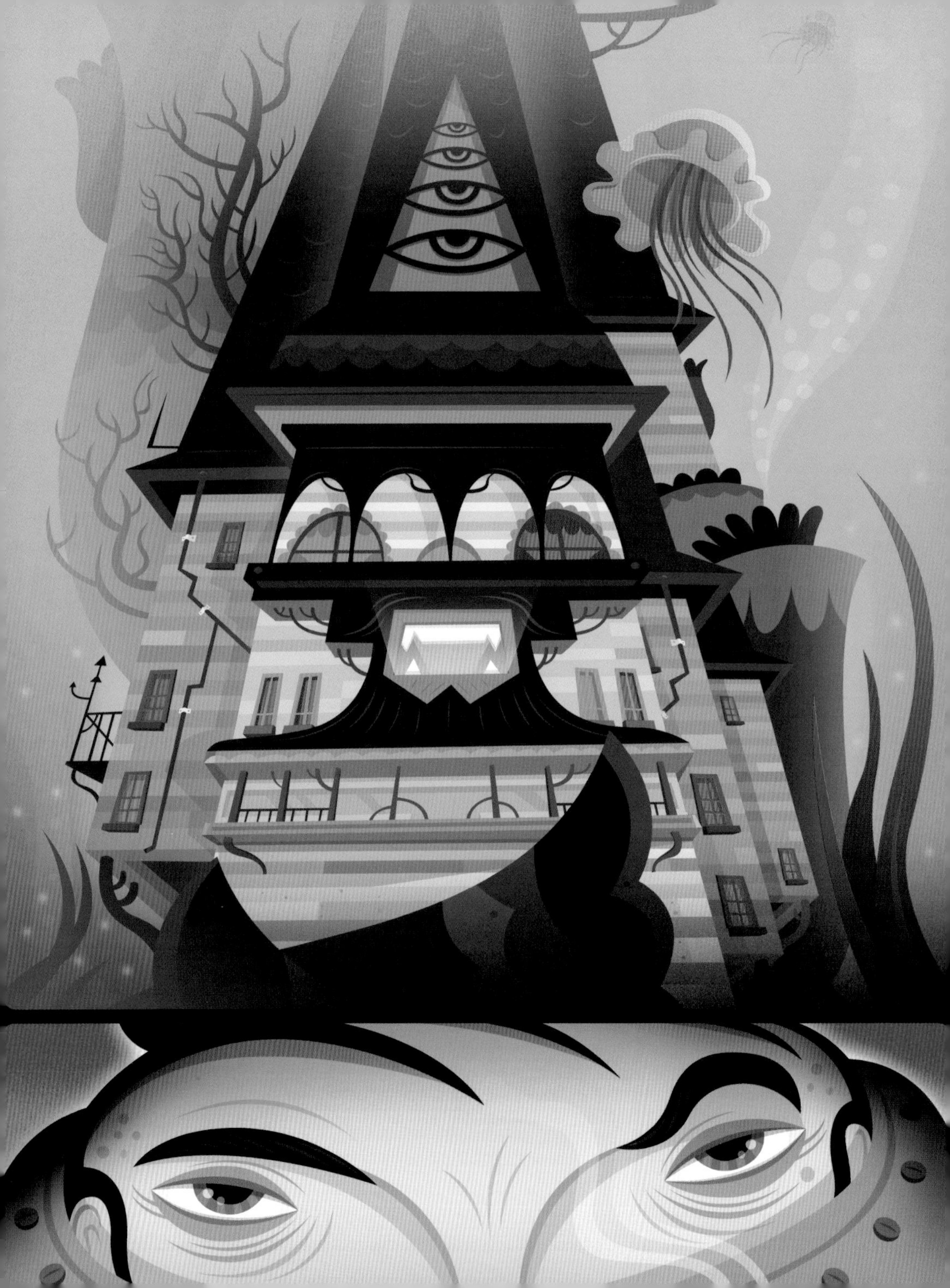

PART THREE

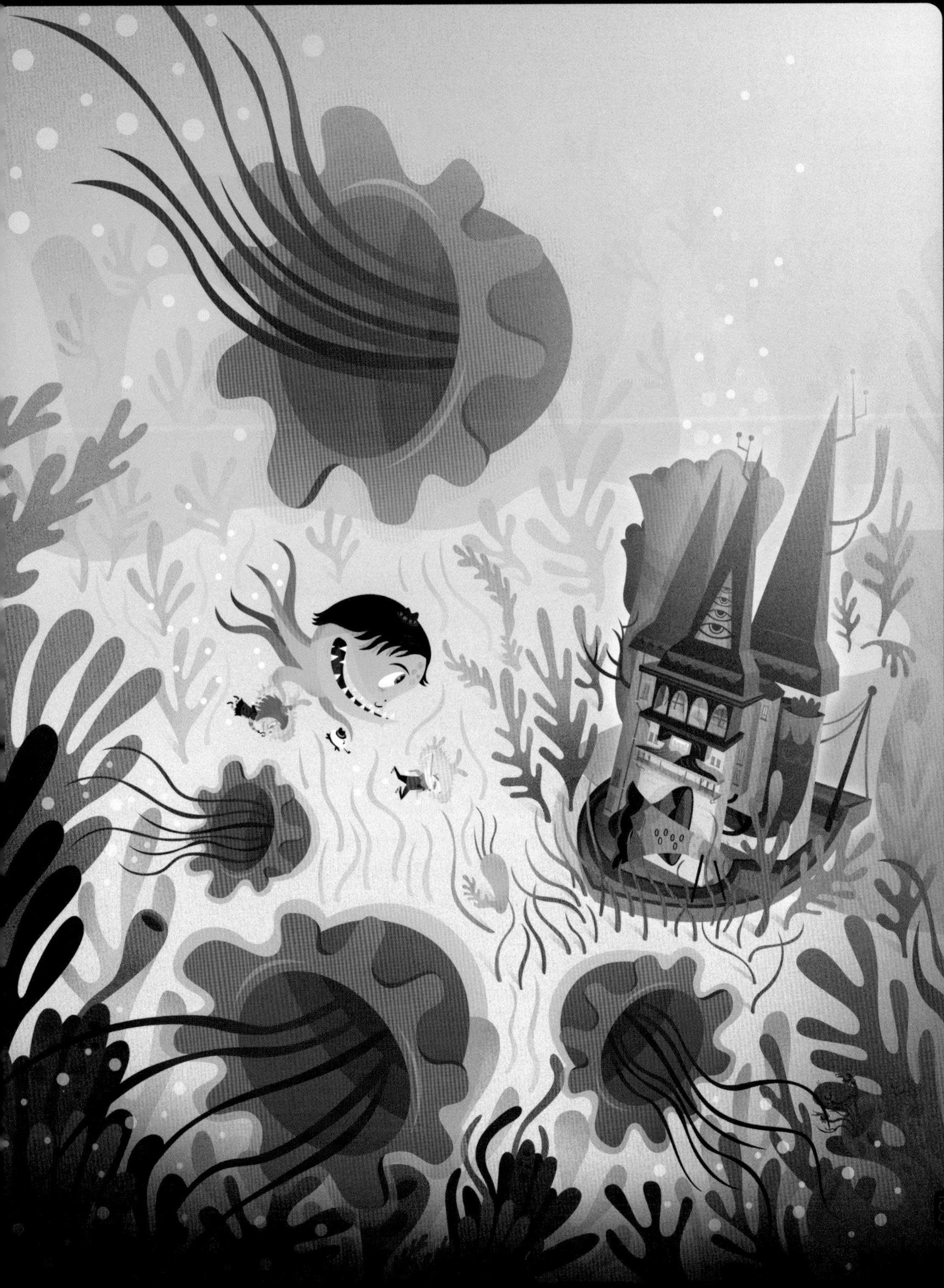

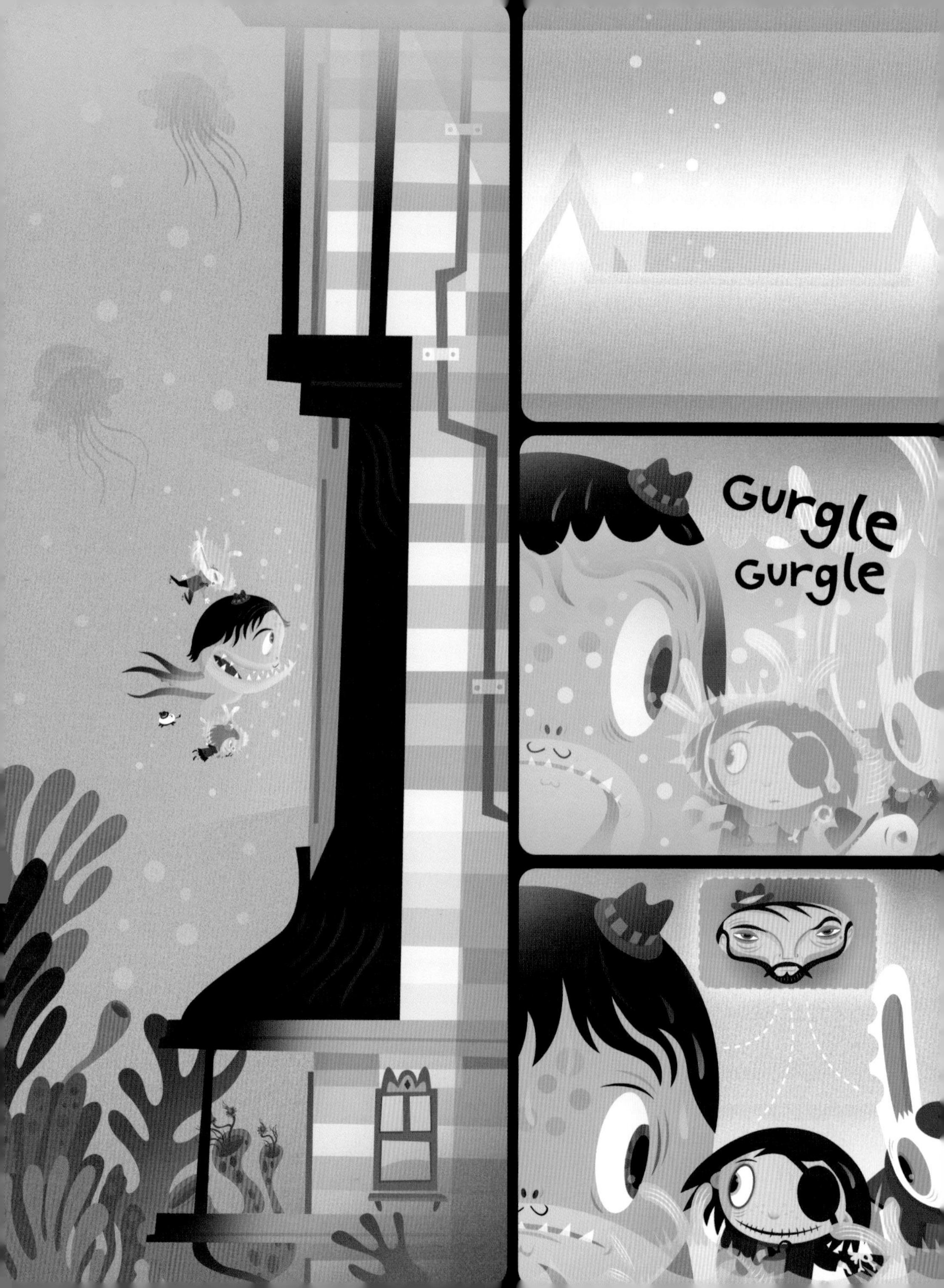
Gurgle
Gurgle

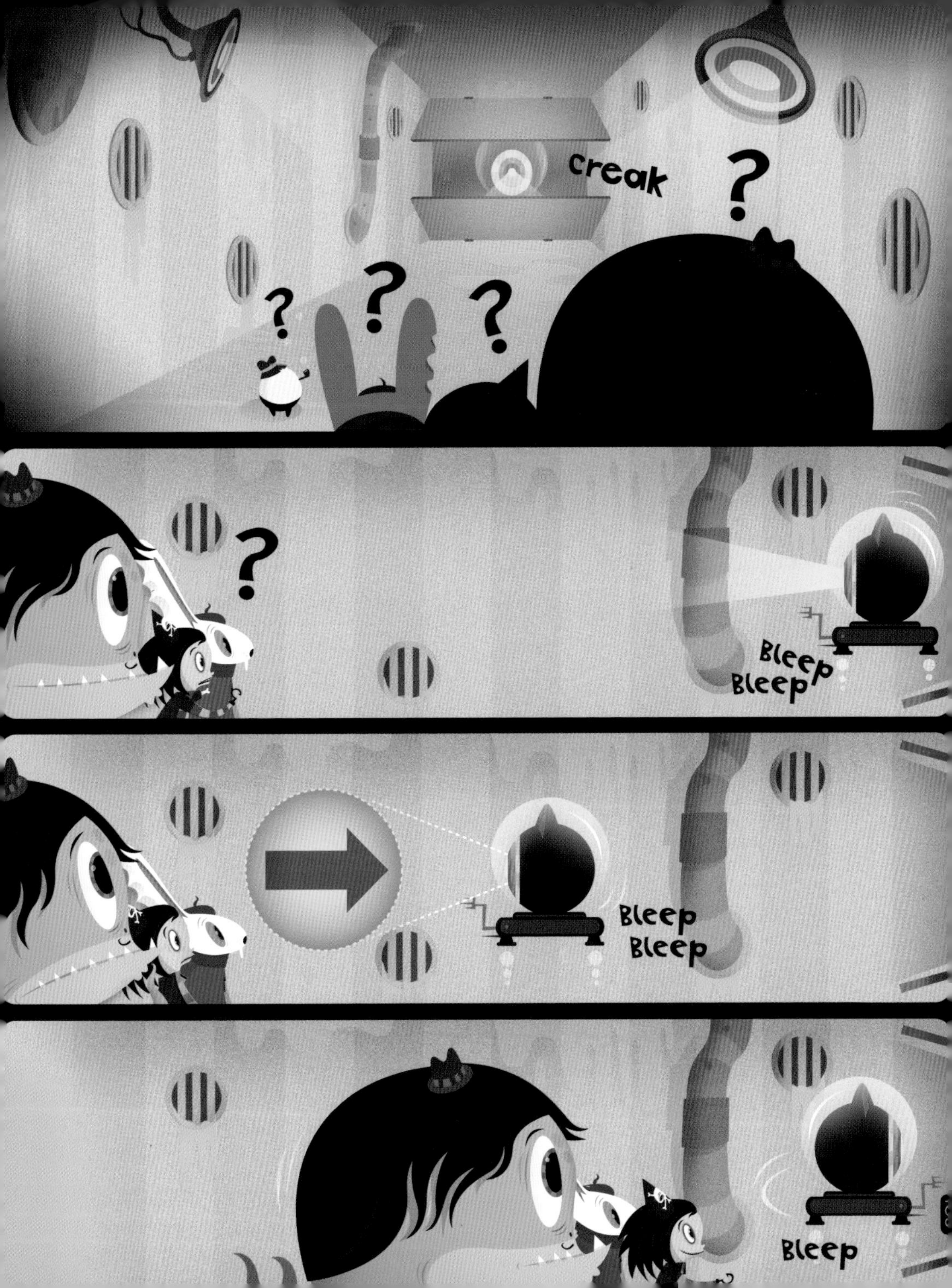
creak
?
?
?
?
?
Bleep
Bleep
Bleep
Bleep
Bleep

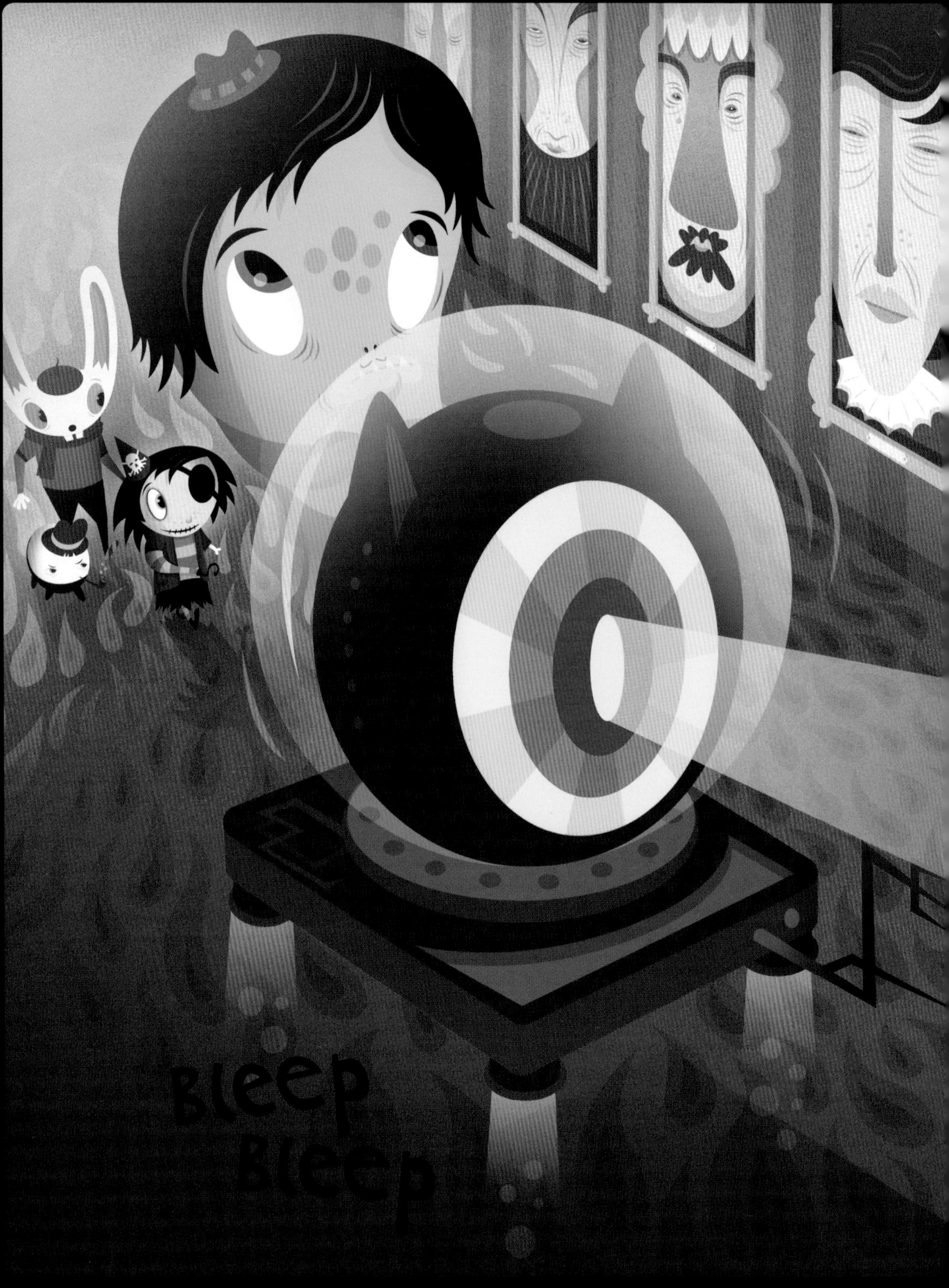
Bleep
Bleep

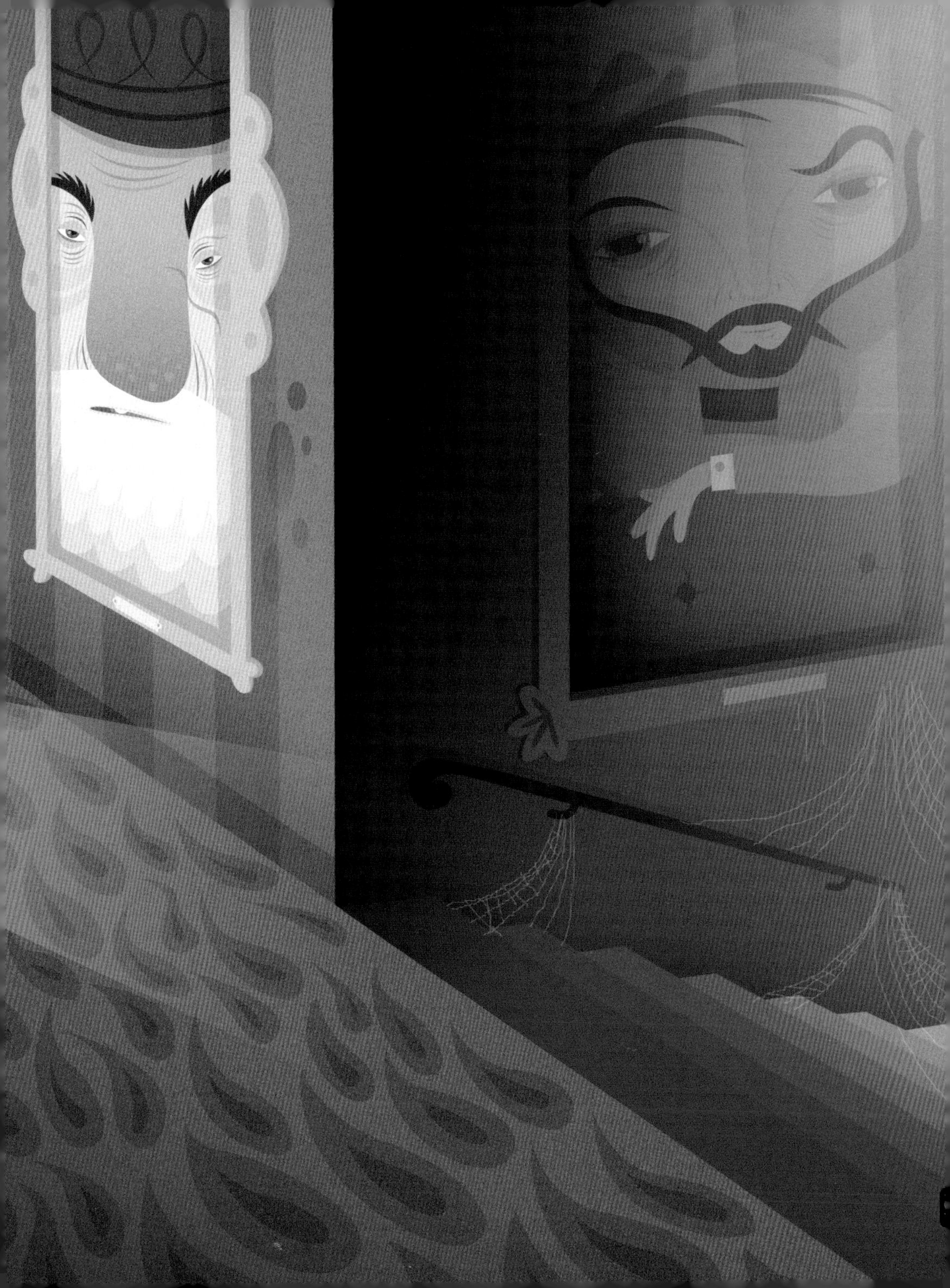

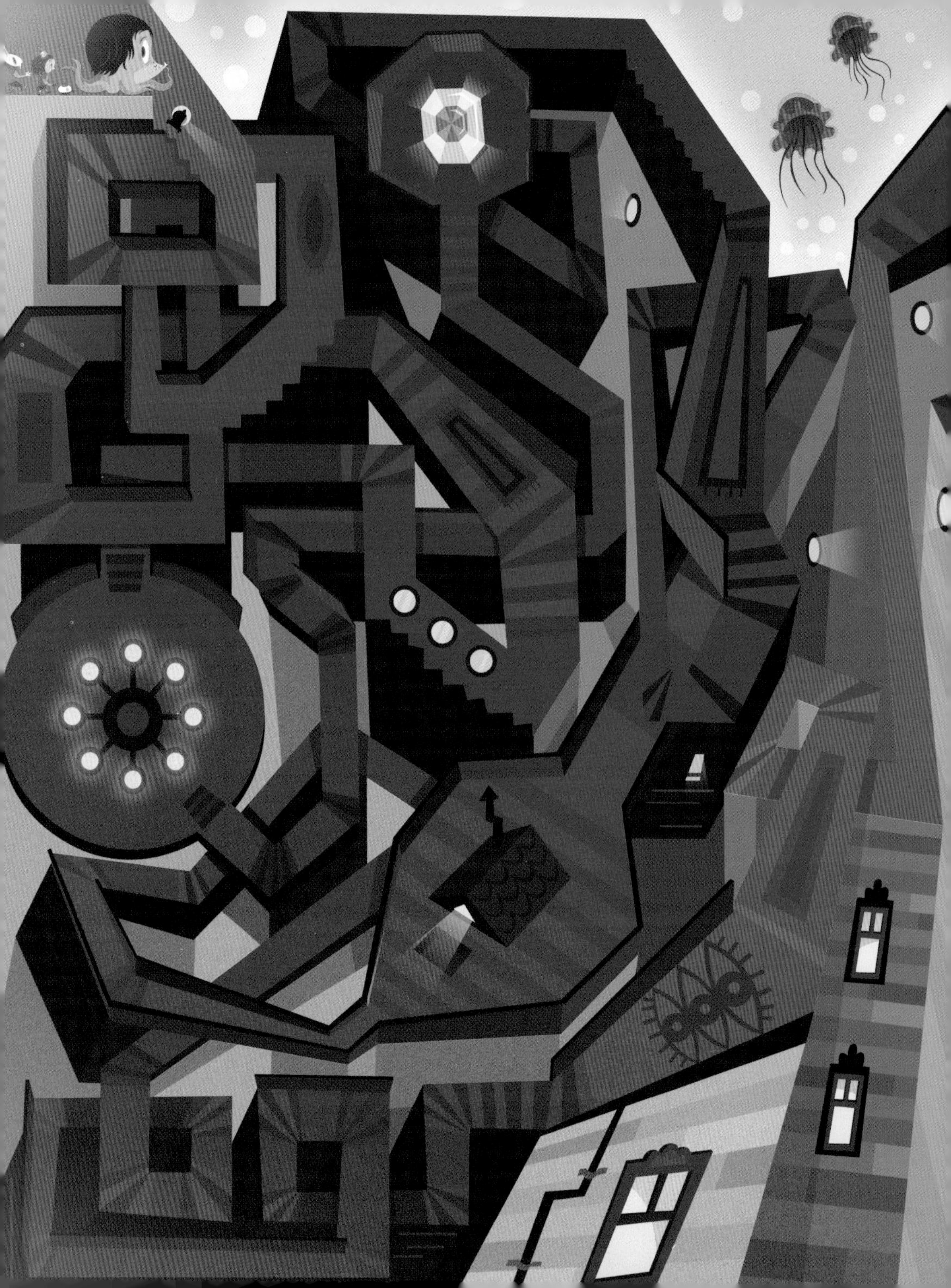

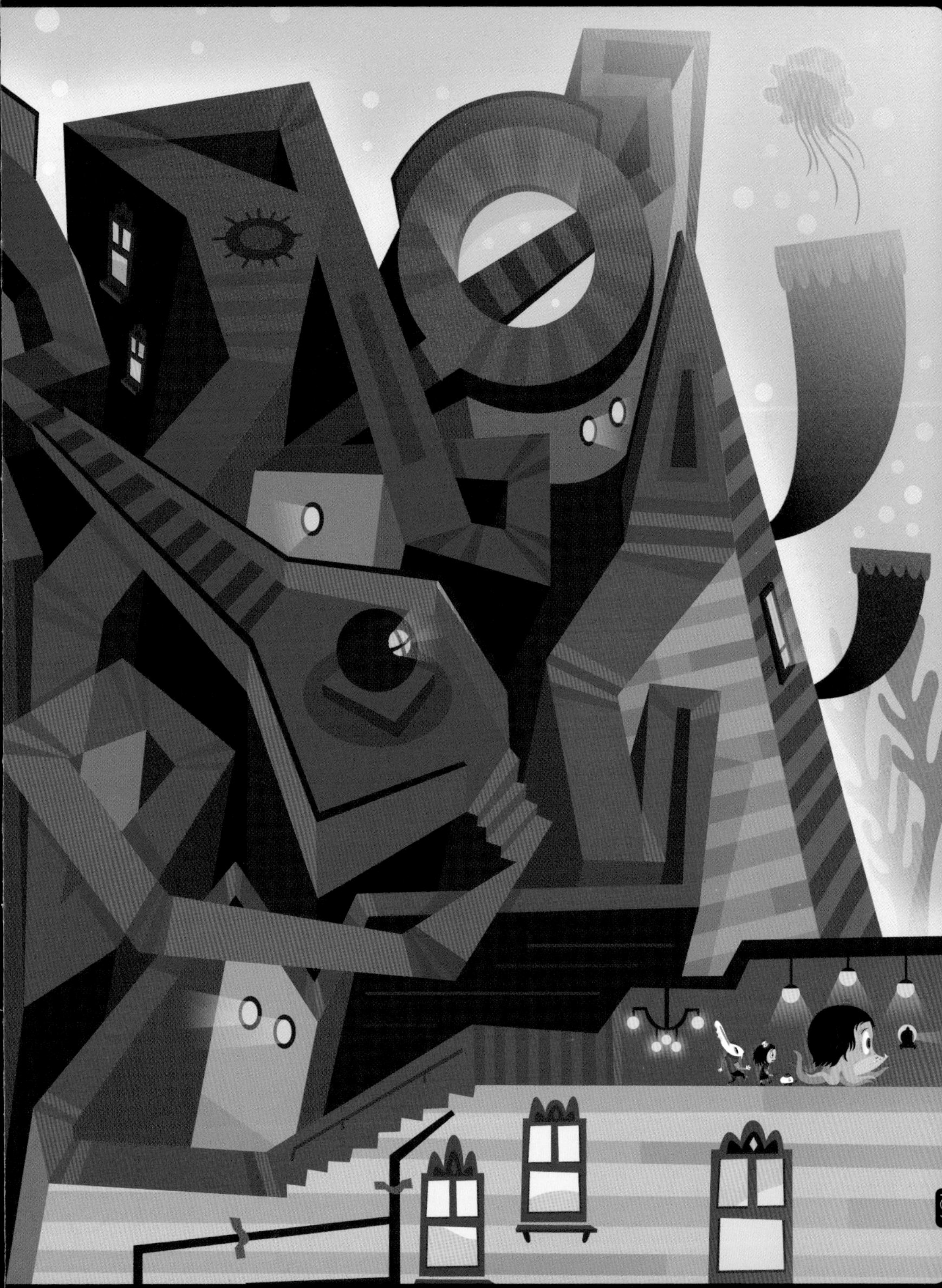

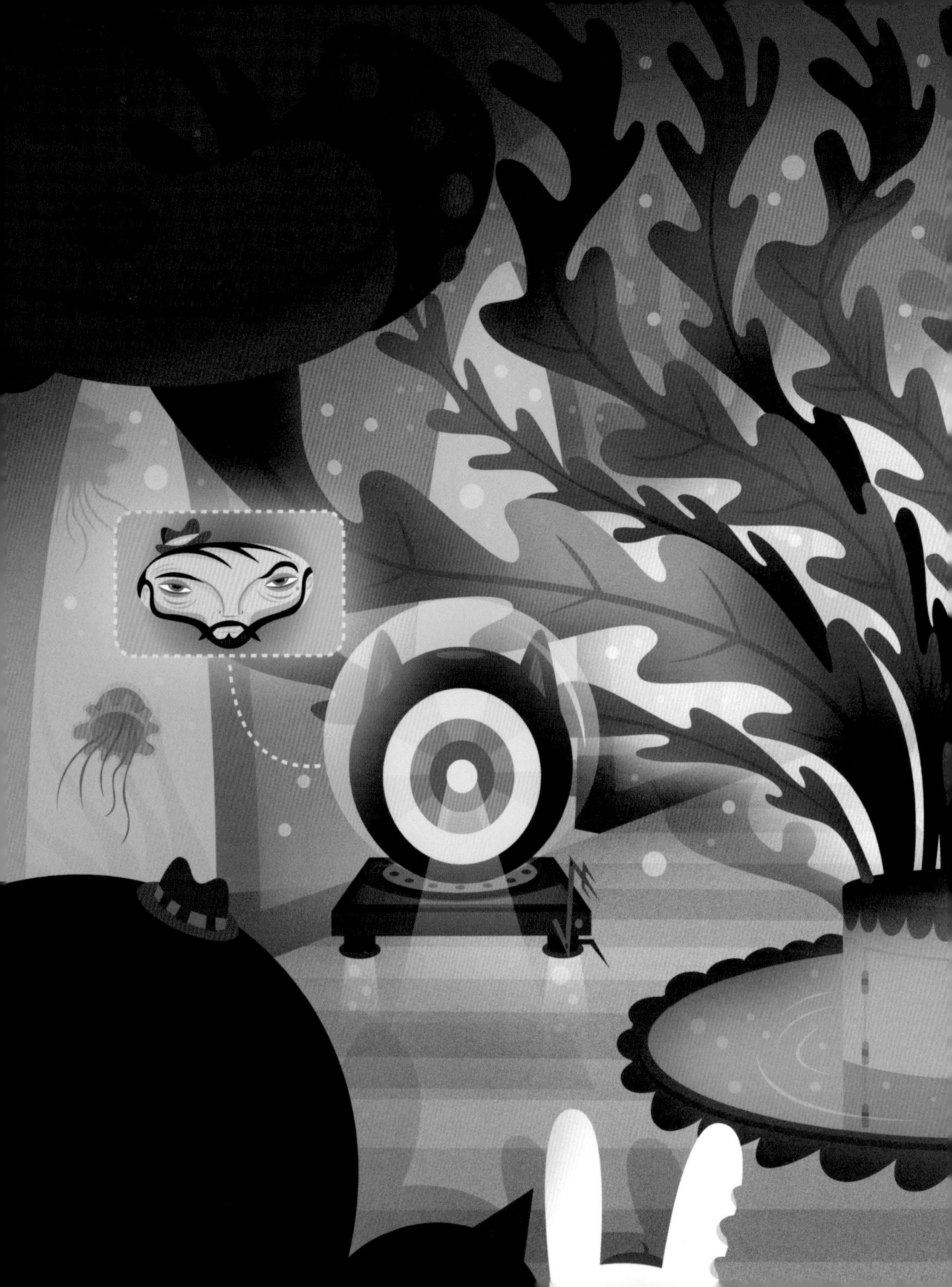

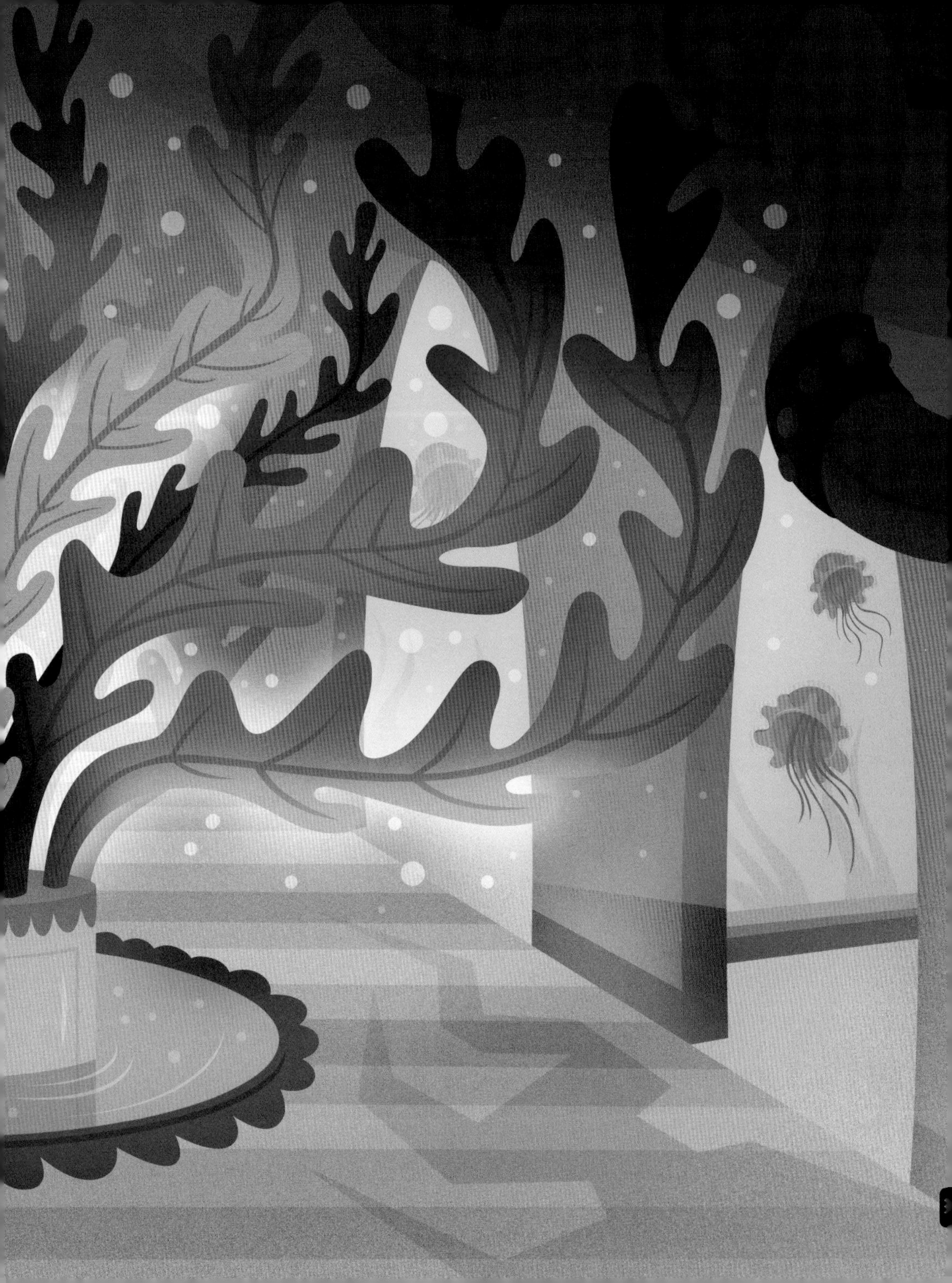

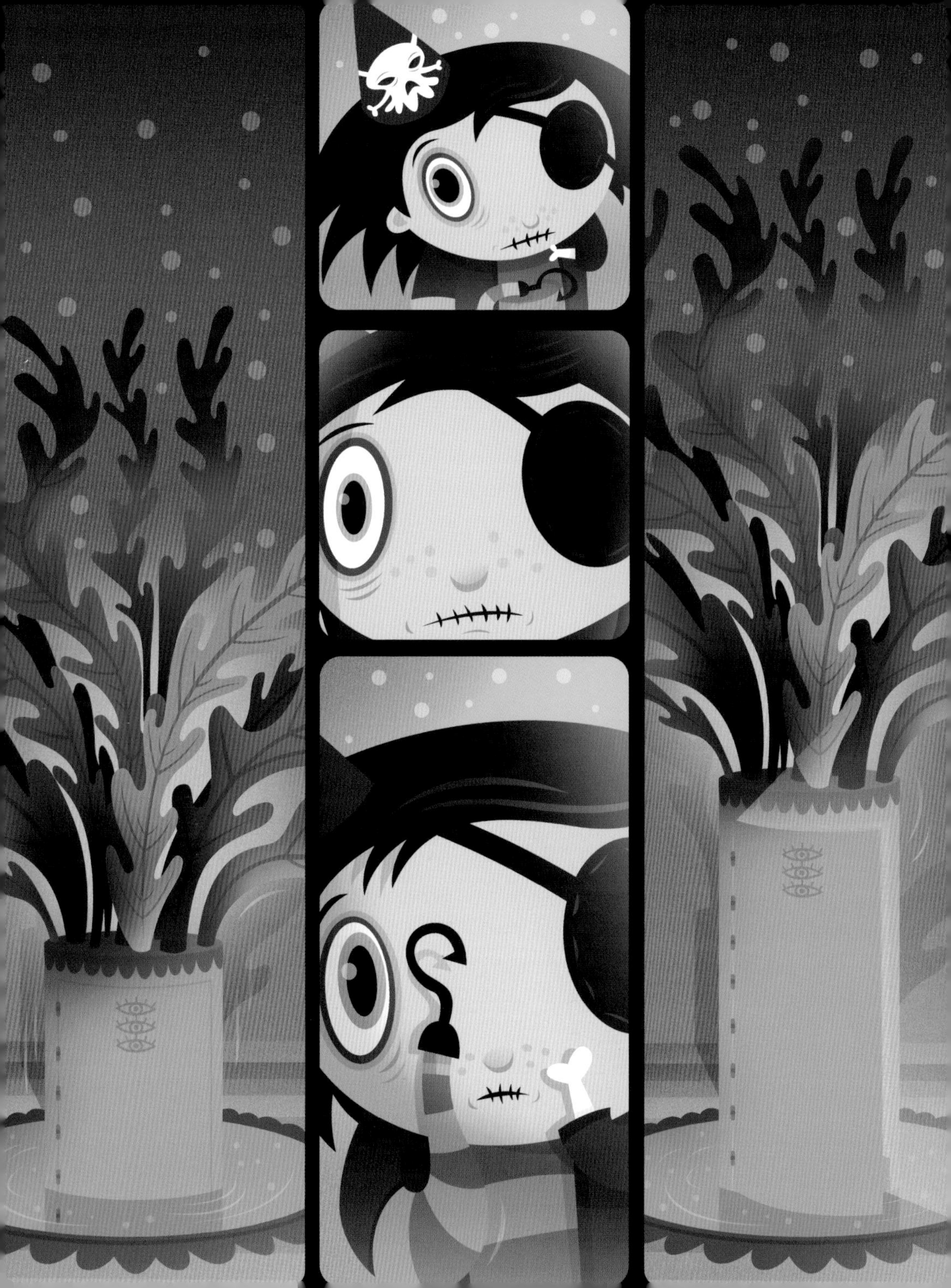

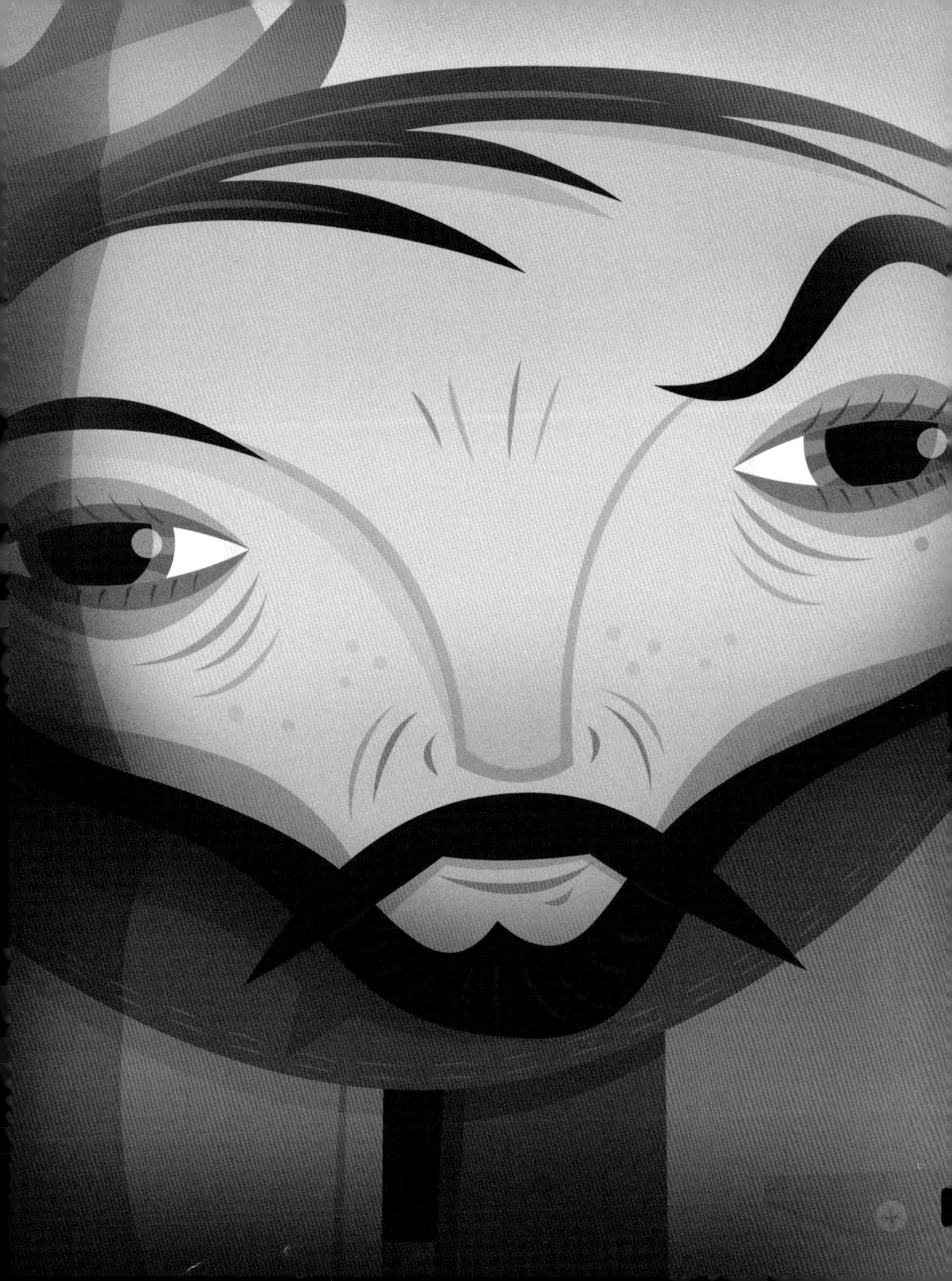

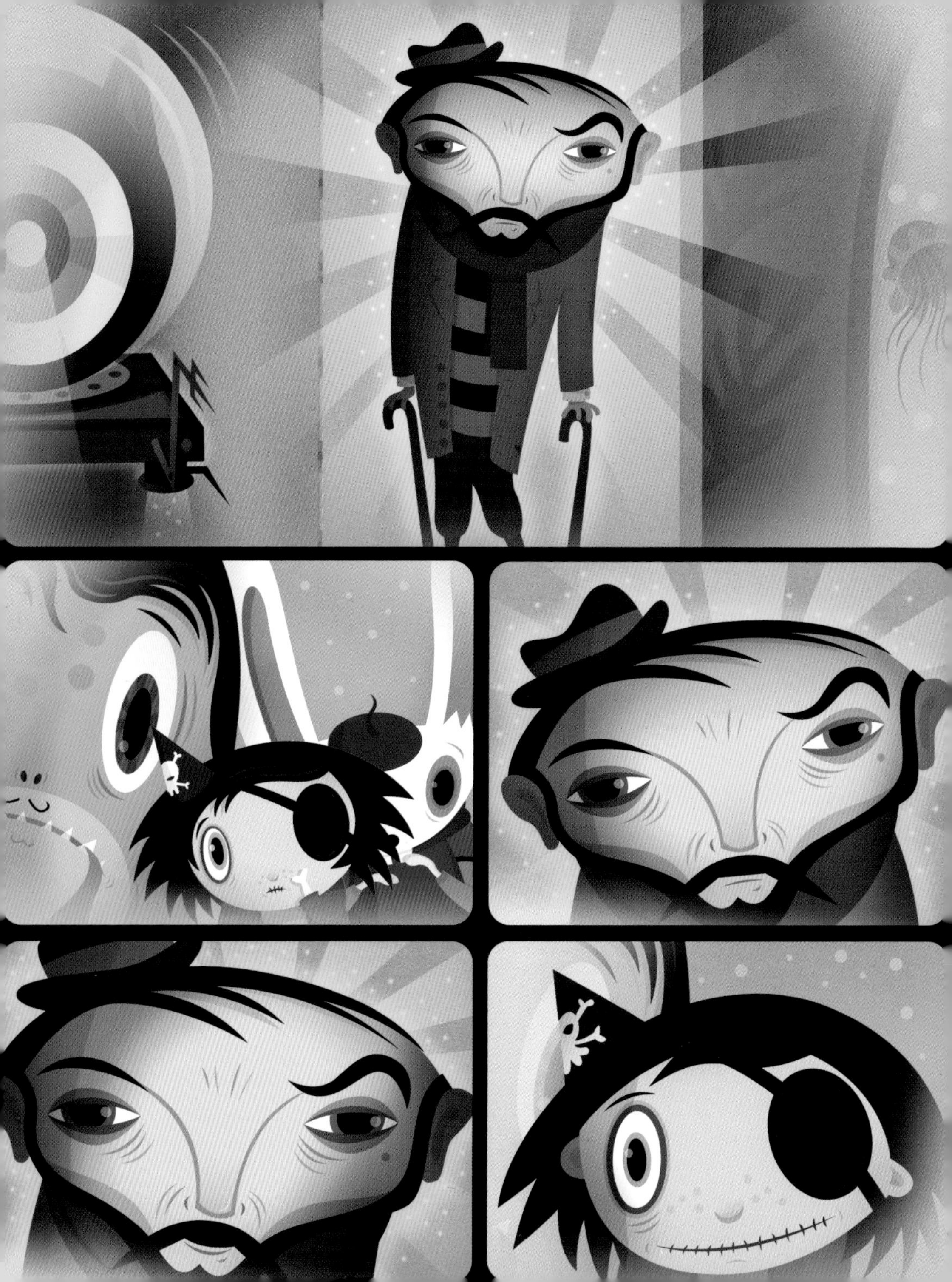

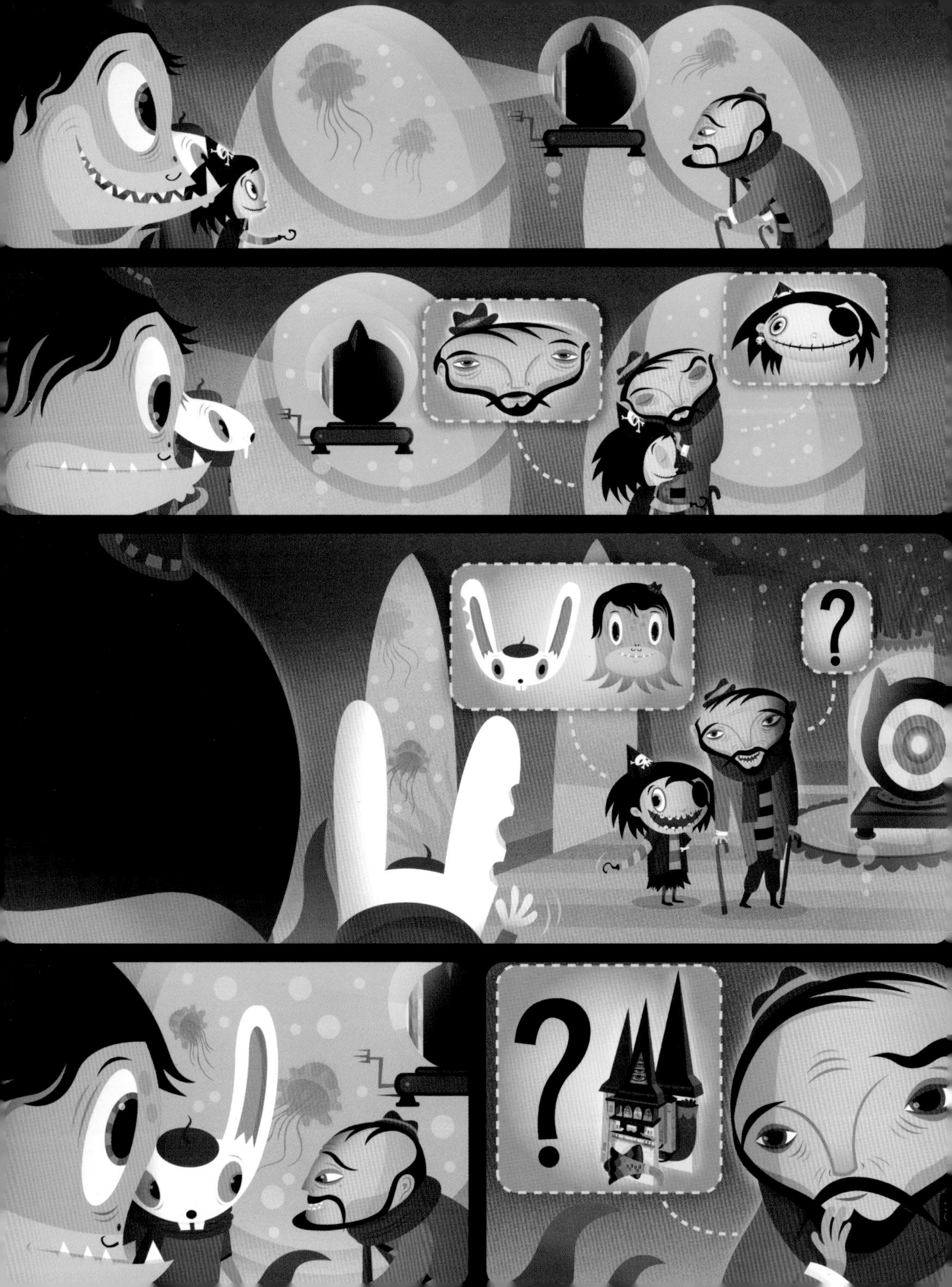
?
?

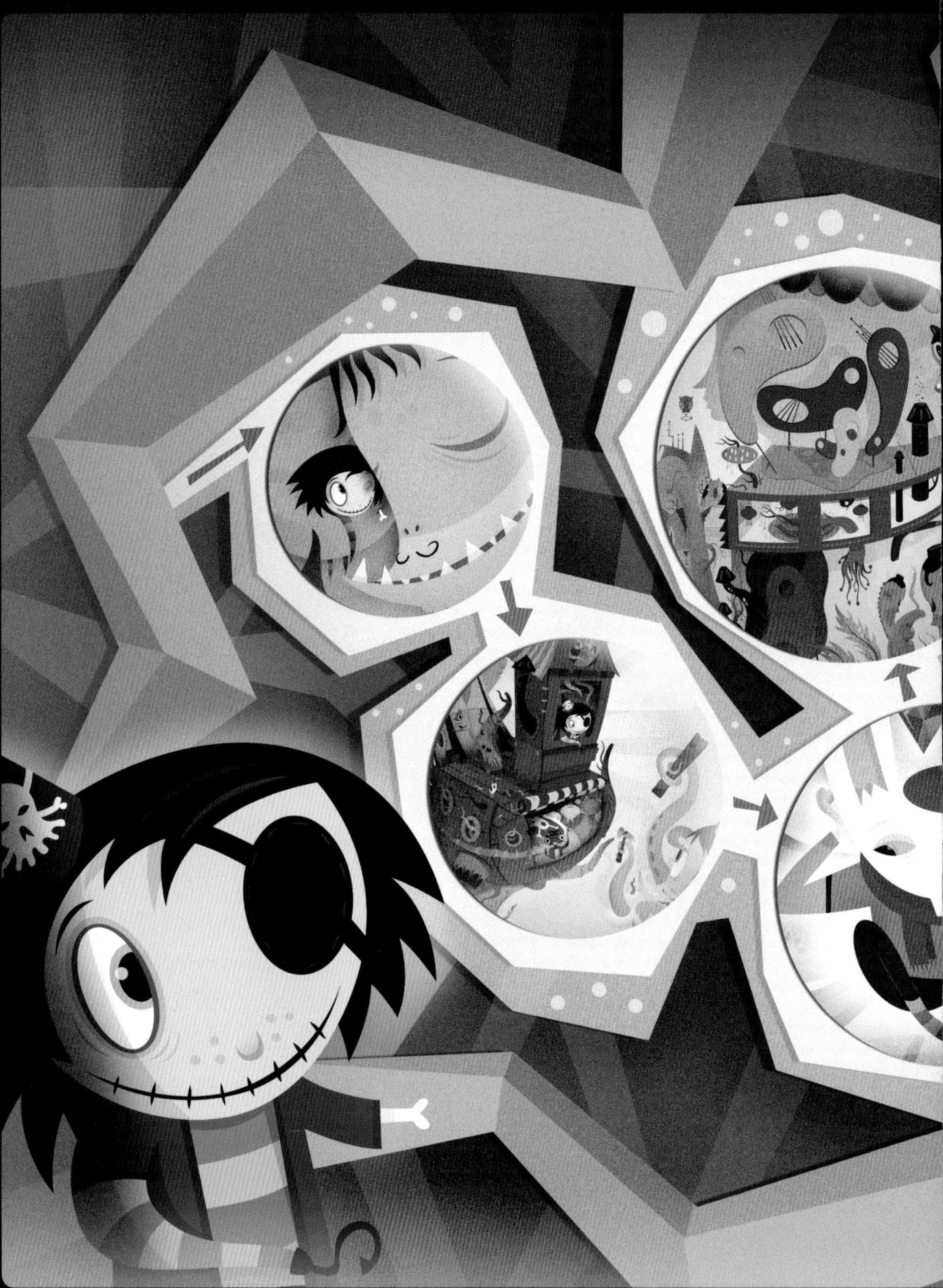

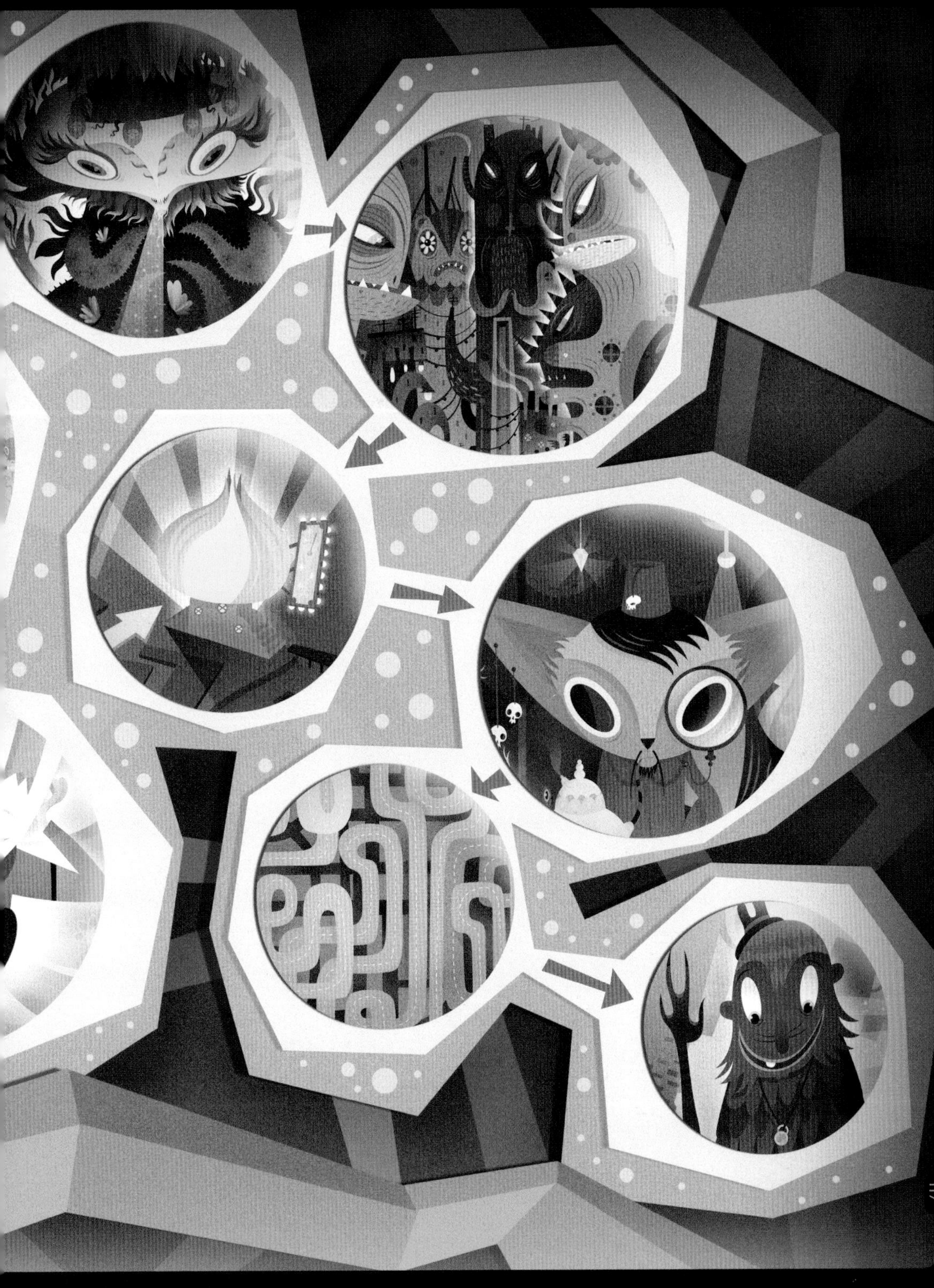

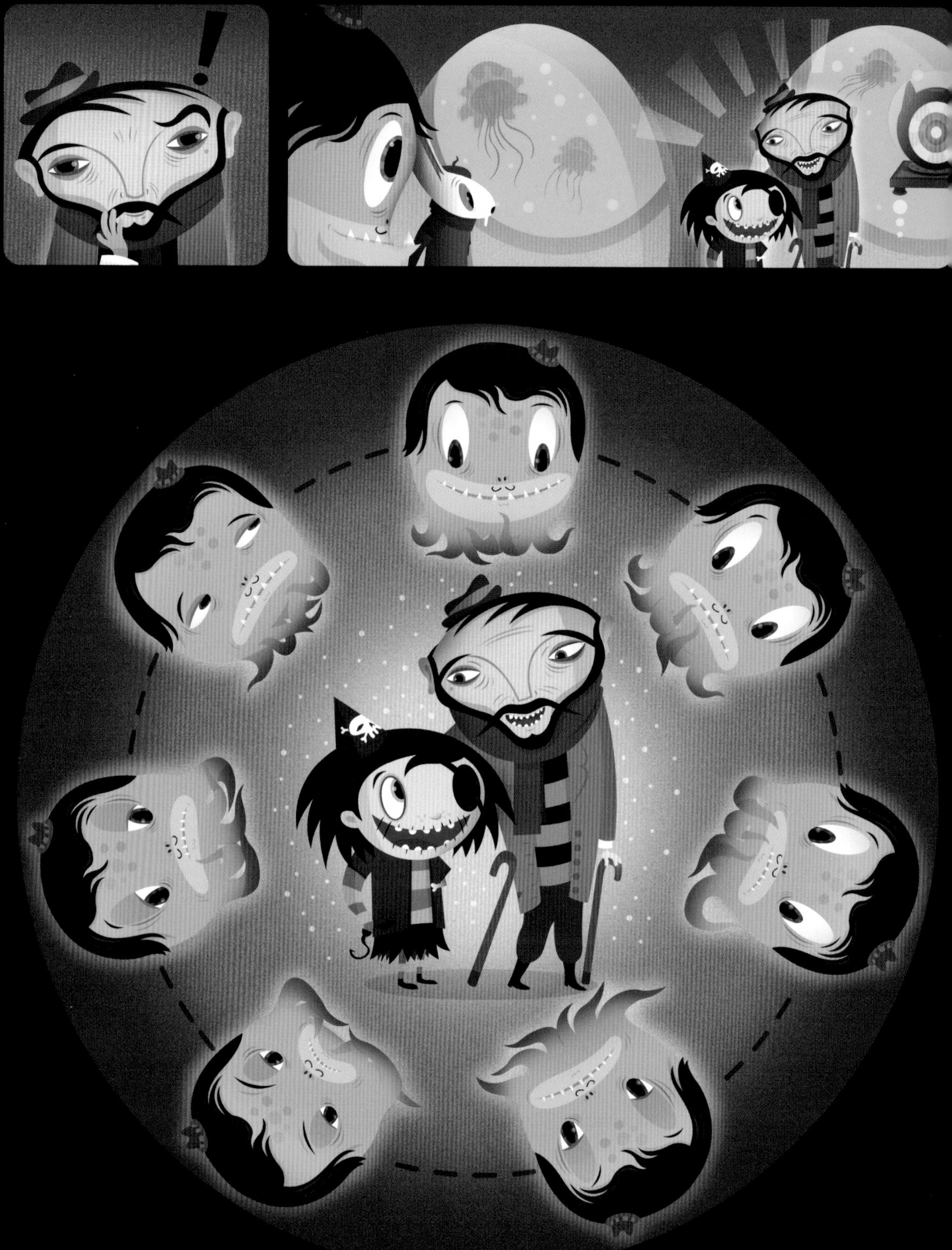

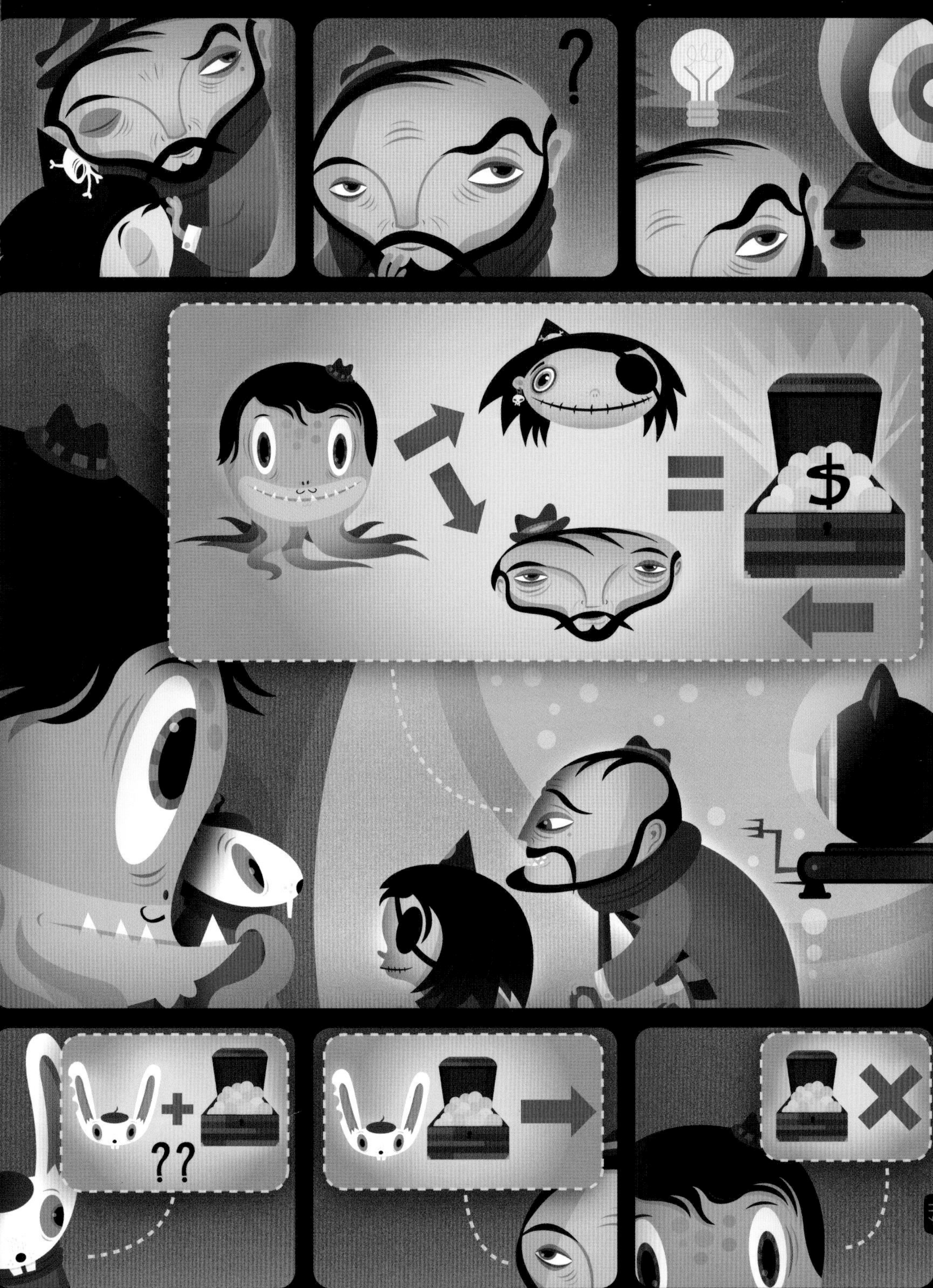
?
$
??

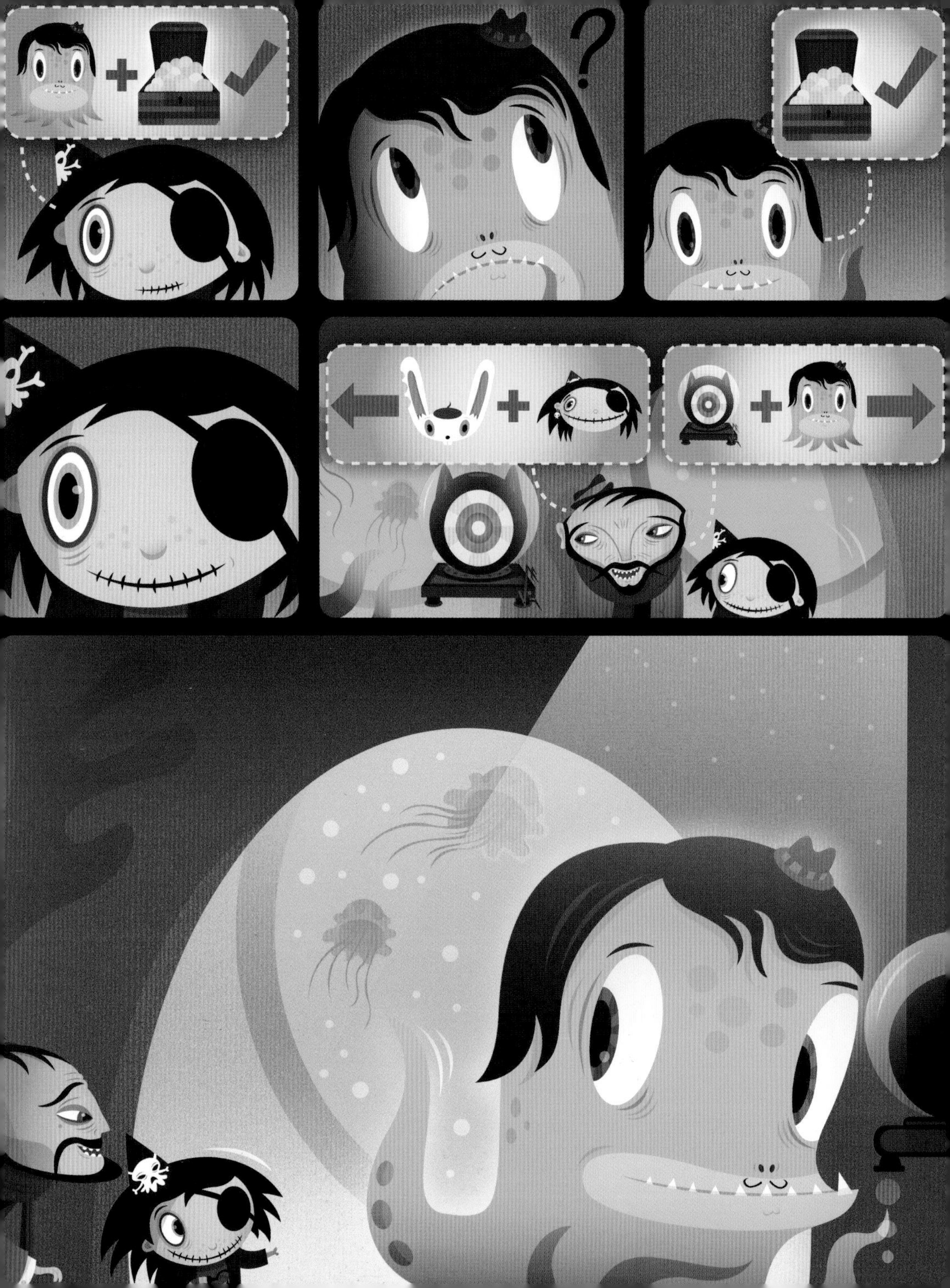
?

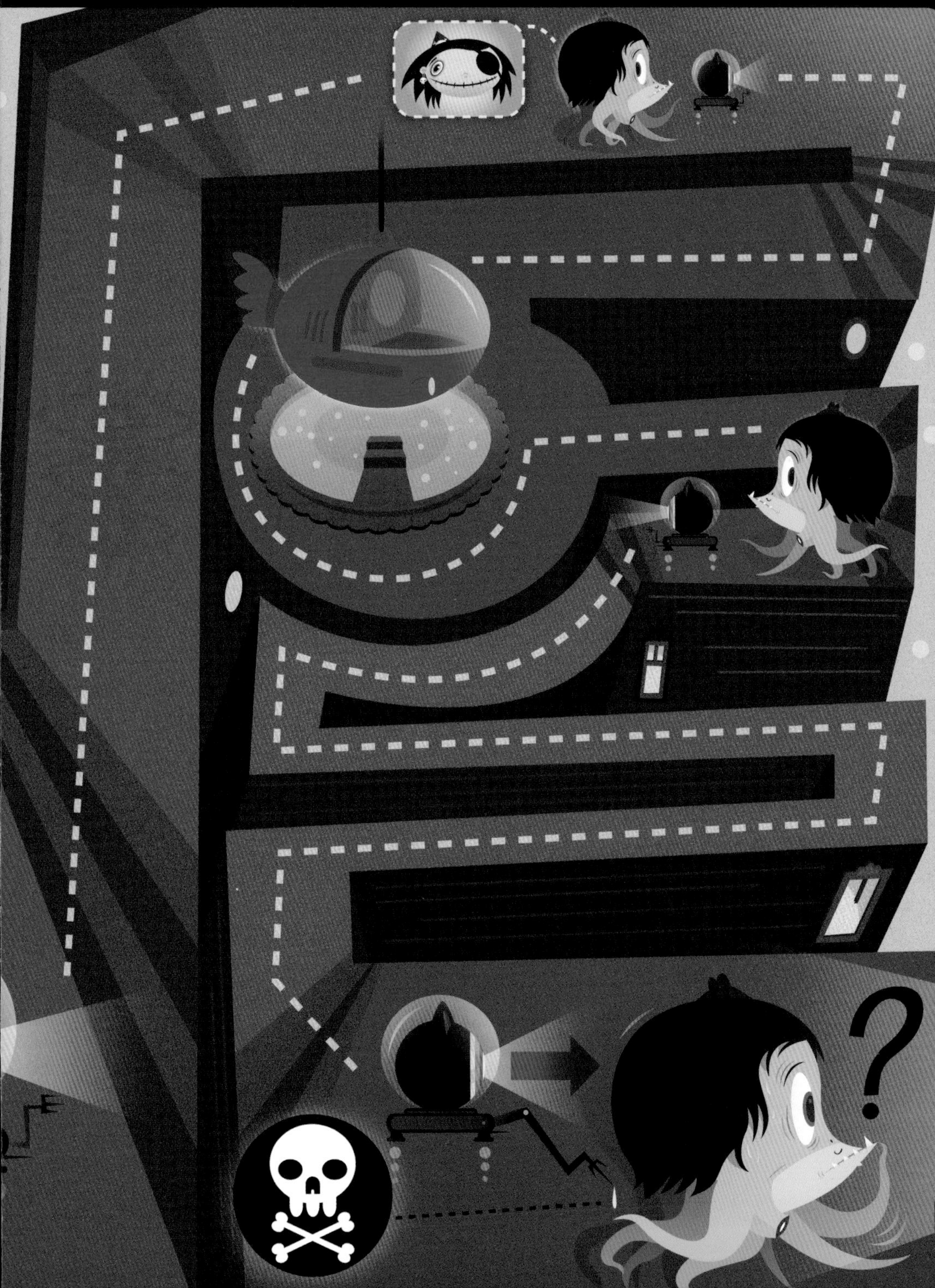

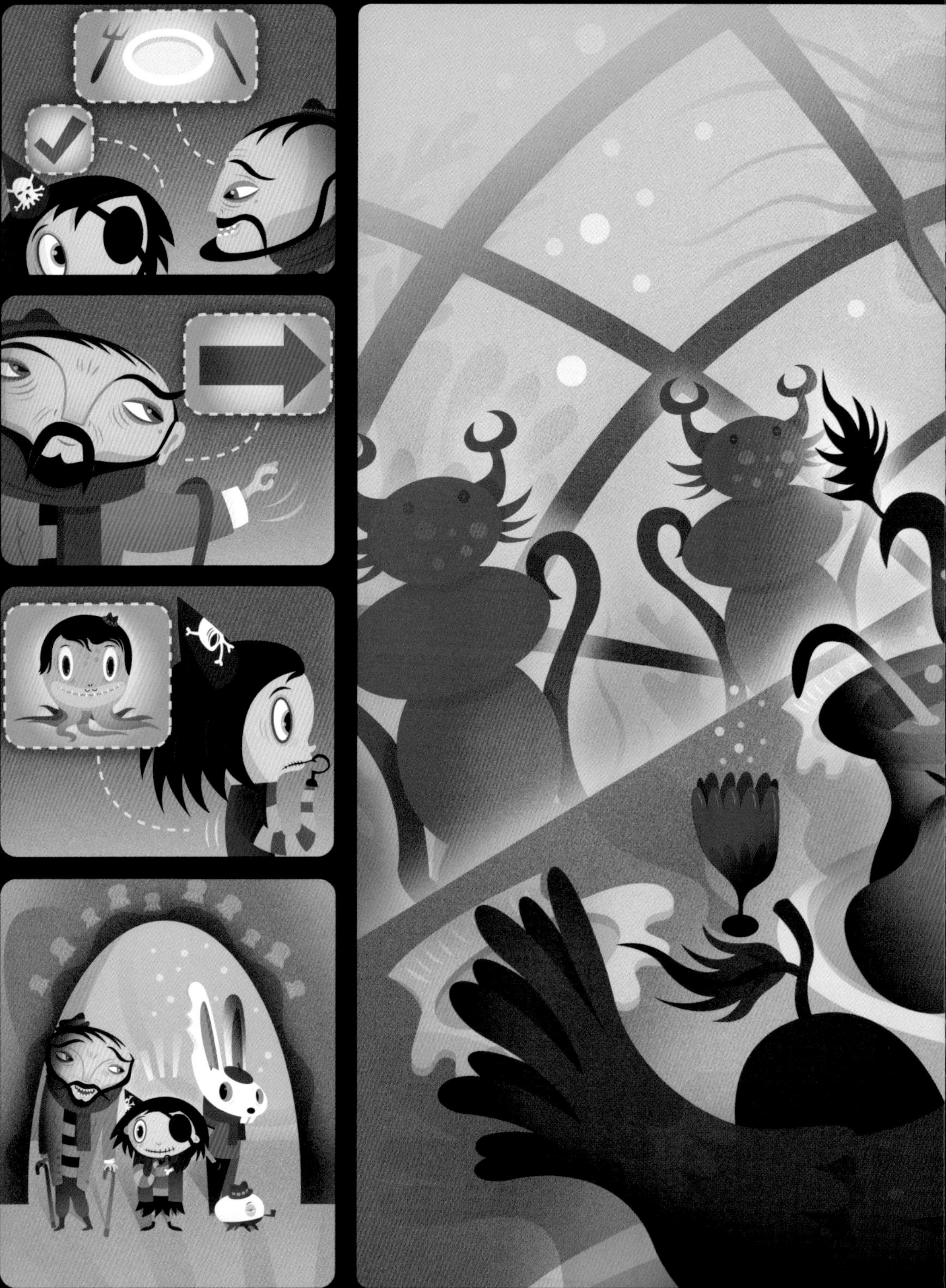

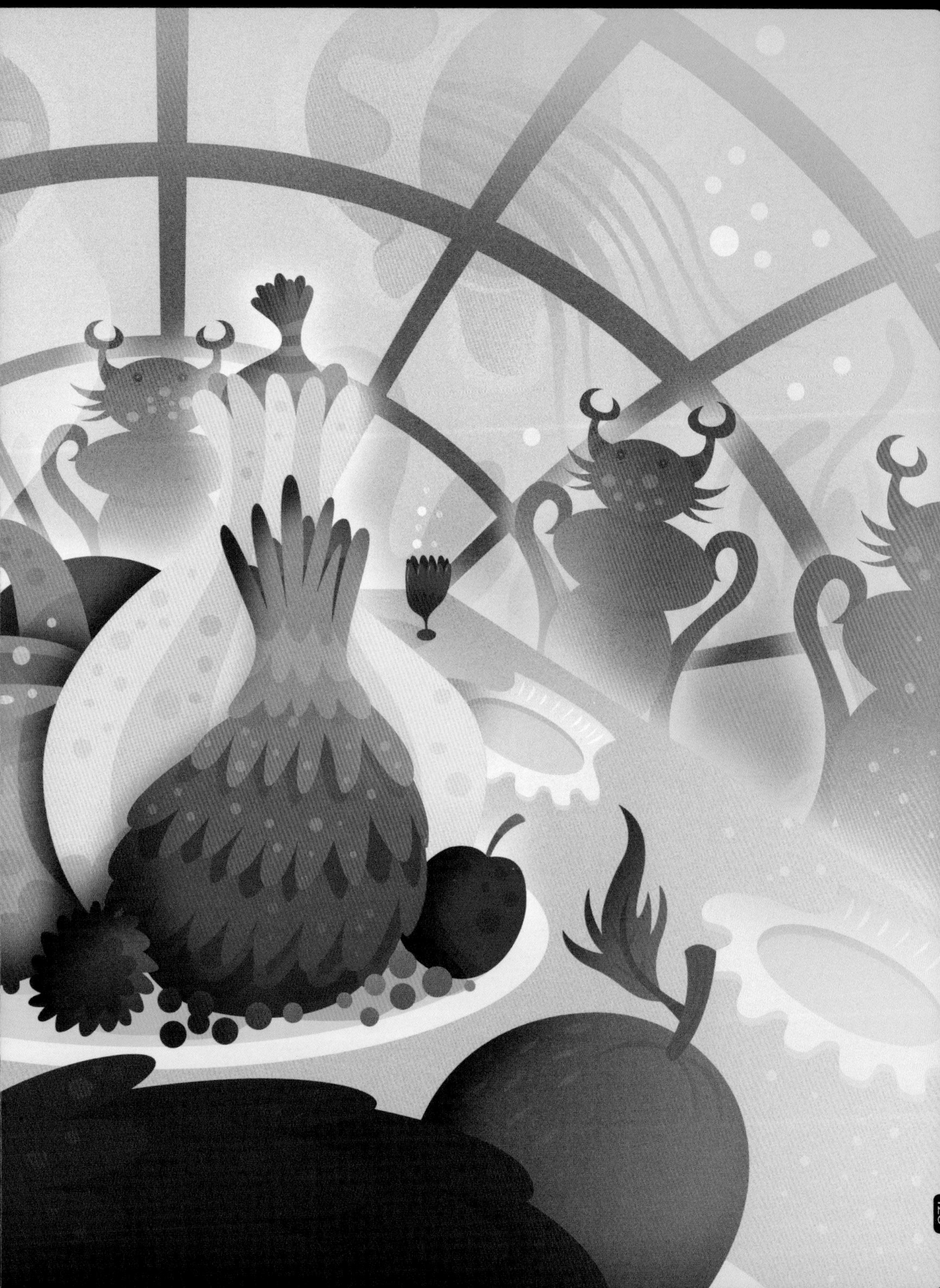

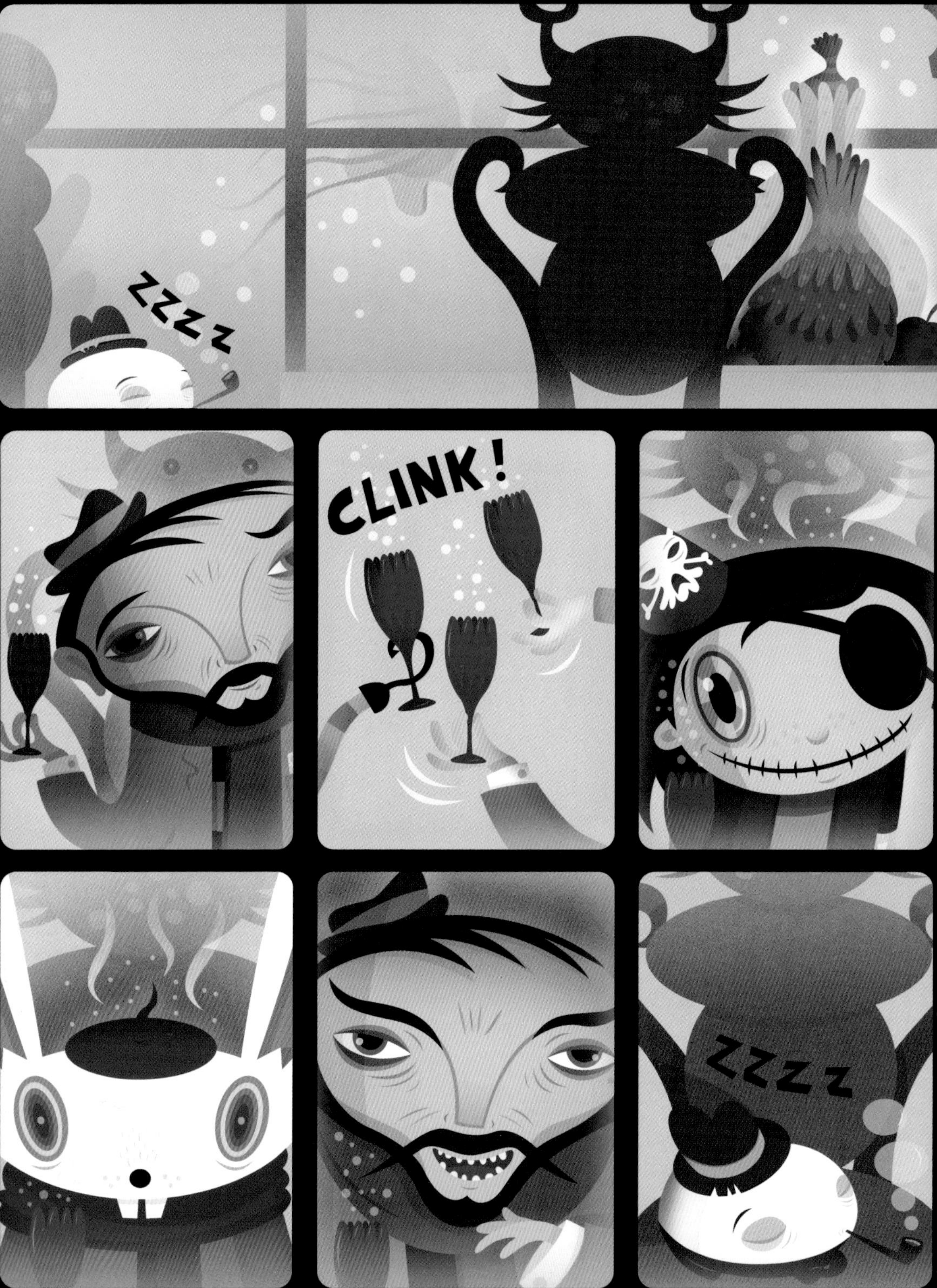
ZZZZ
CLINK!
ZZZZ

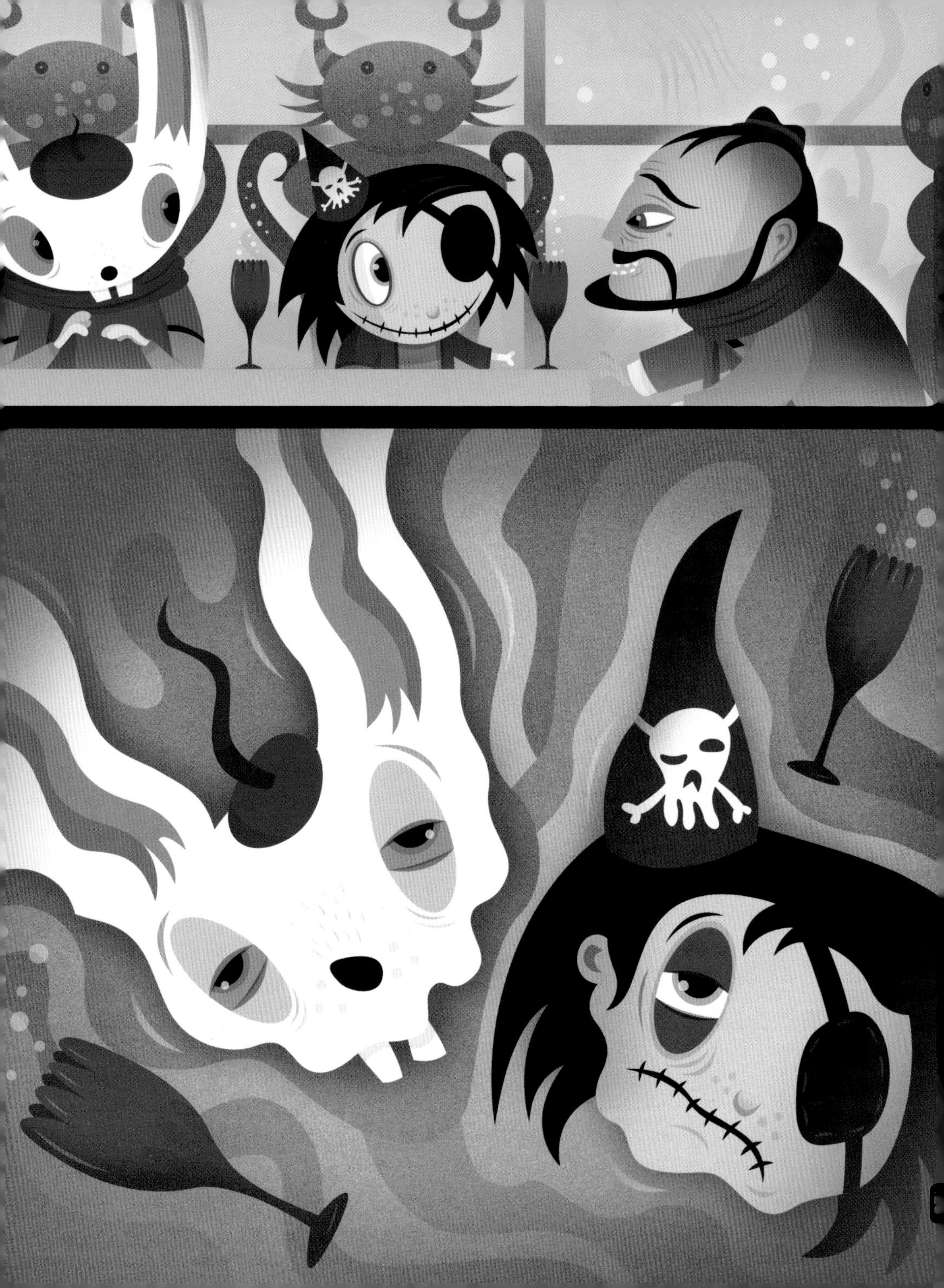

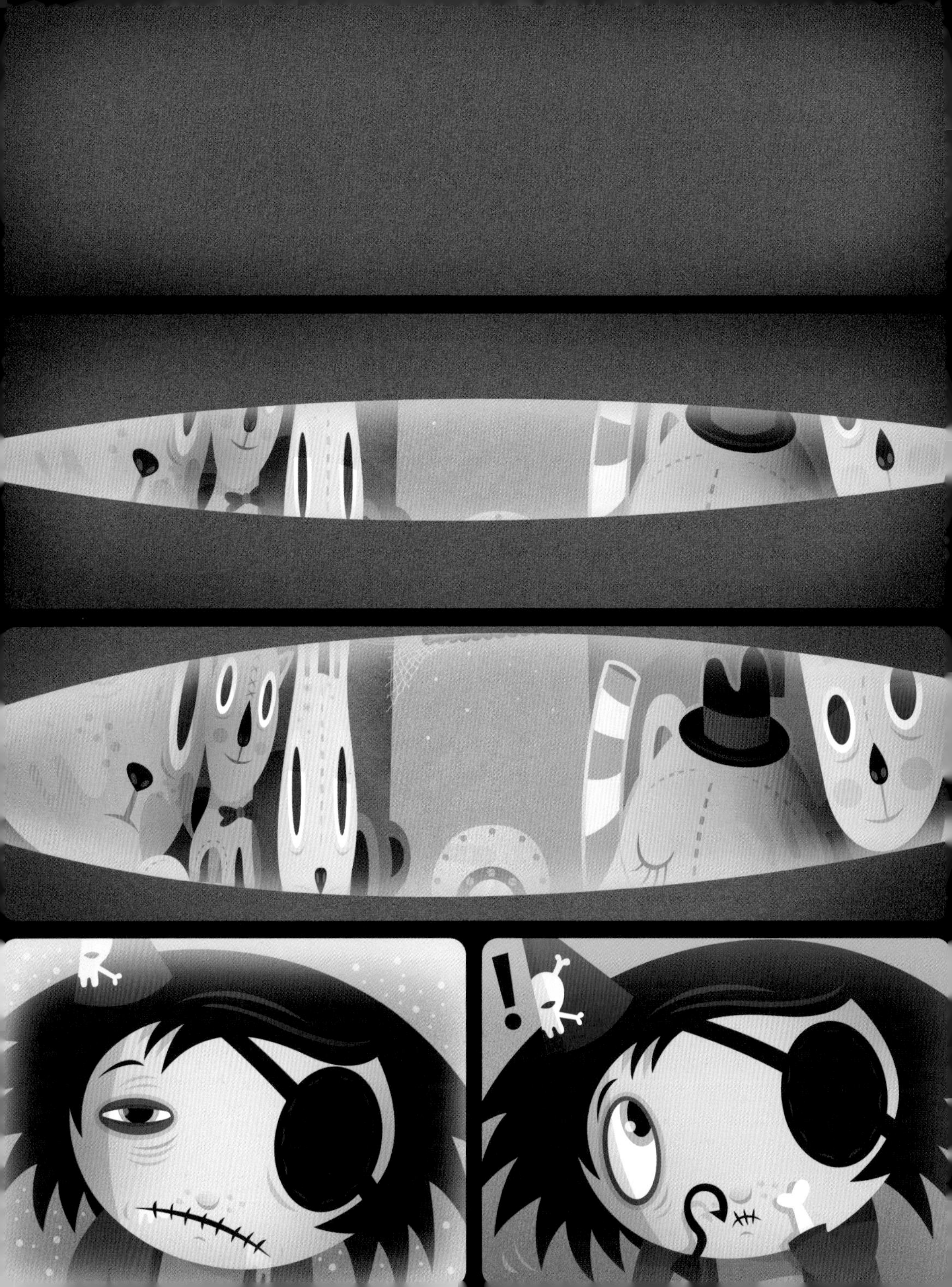
!

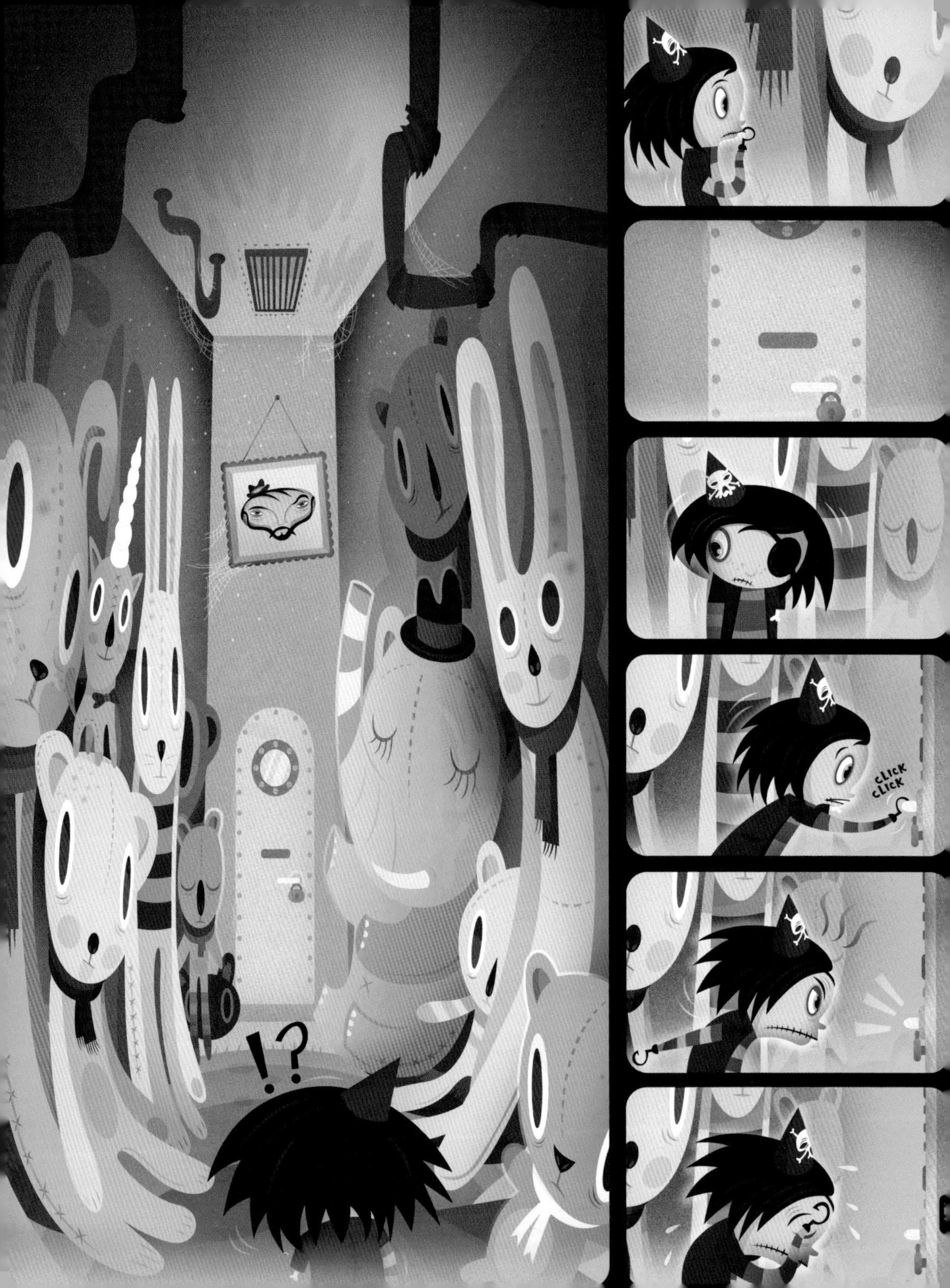
!?
CLICK
CLICK

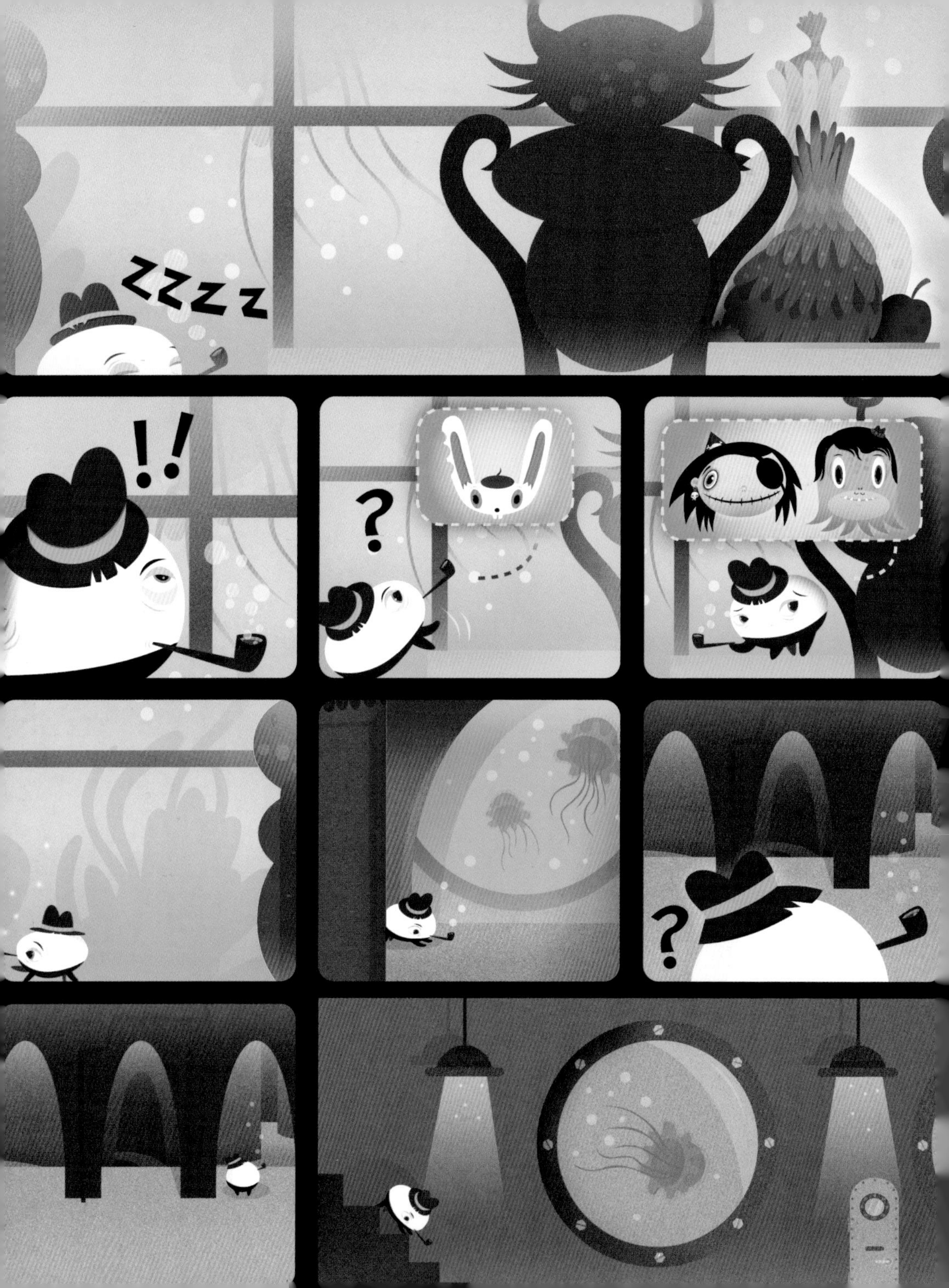
ZZZZZ
!!
?
?

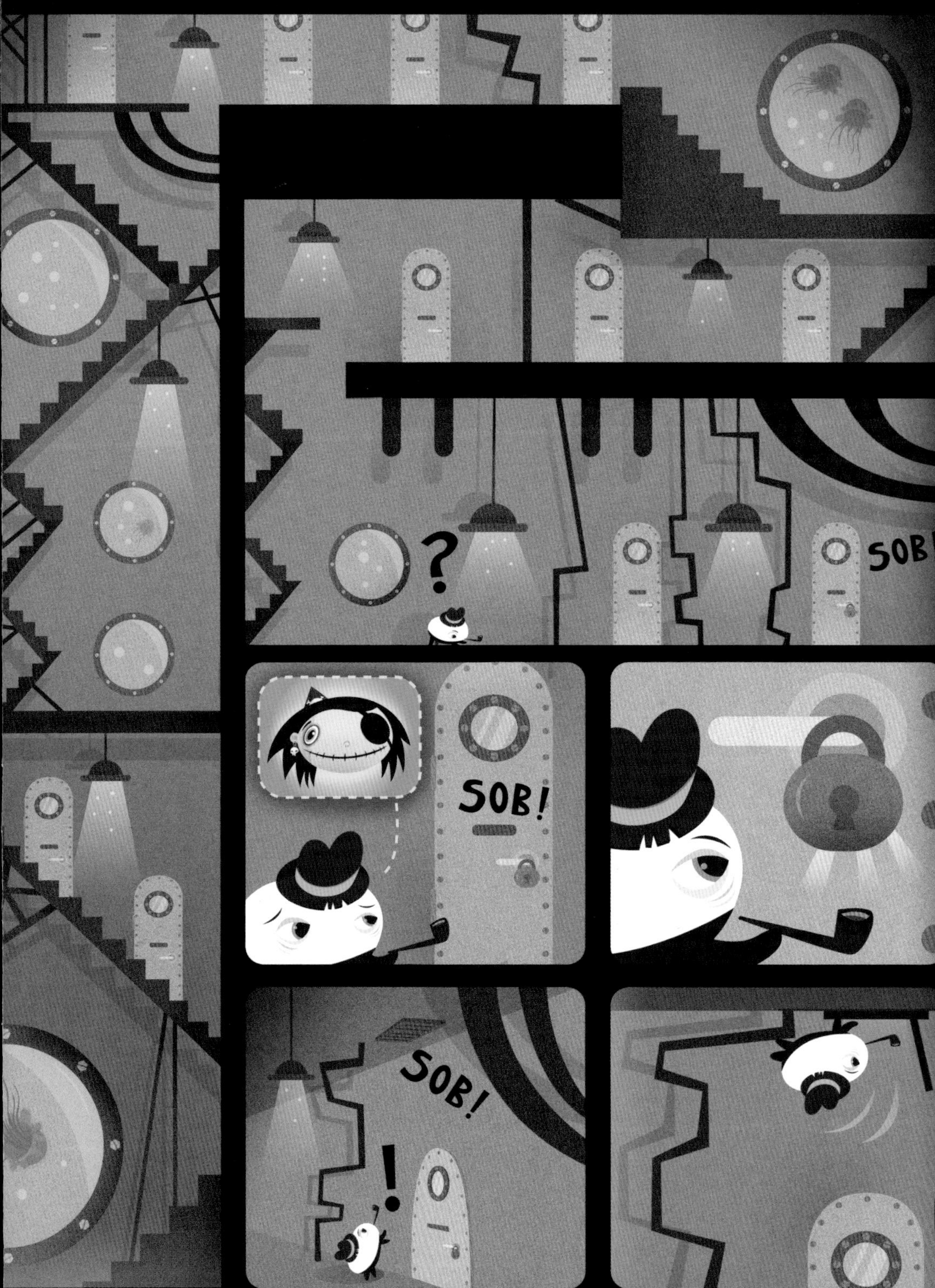
SOB!
SOB!
SOB!

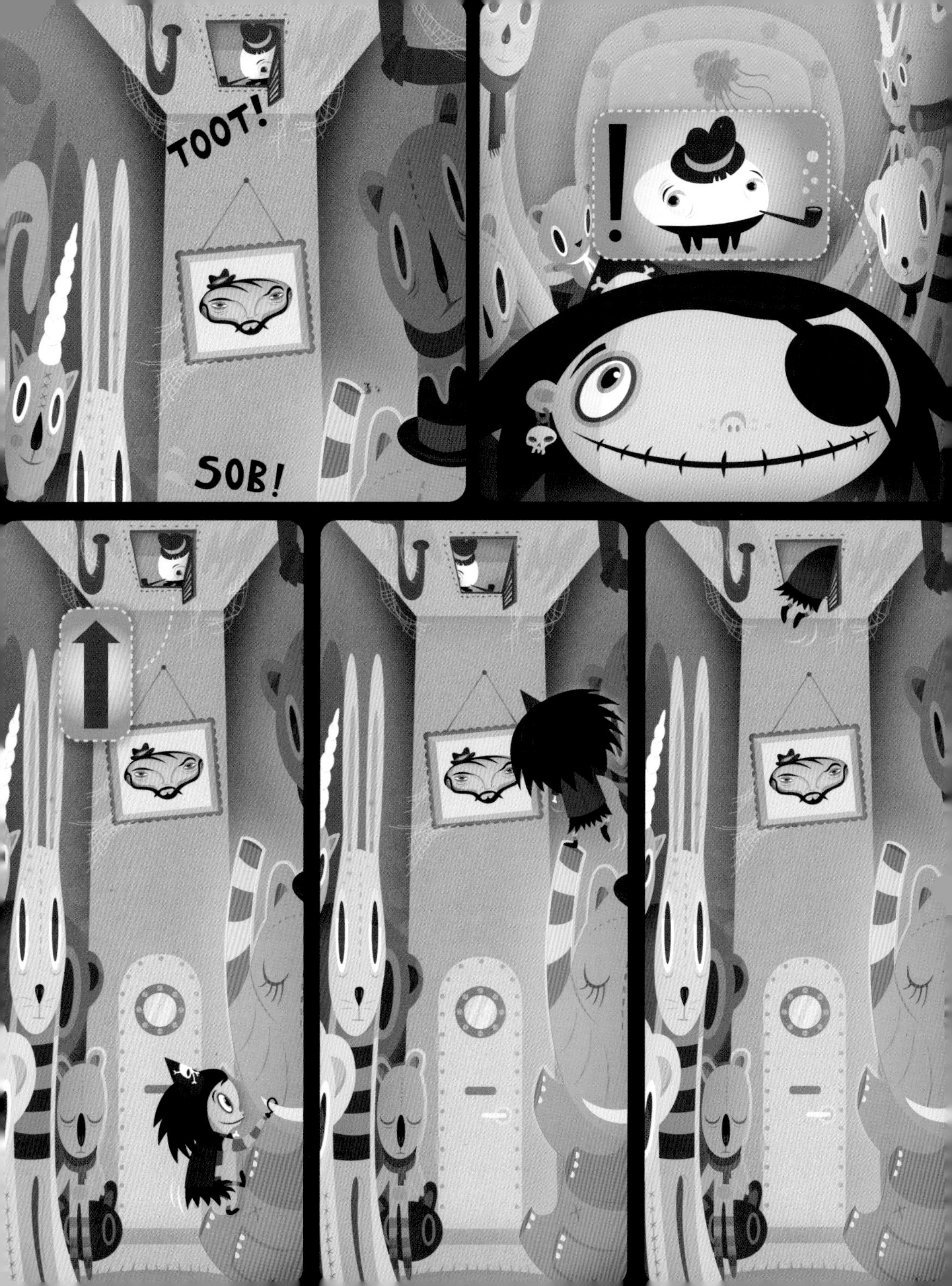
TOOT!
SOB!
!

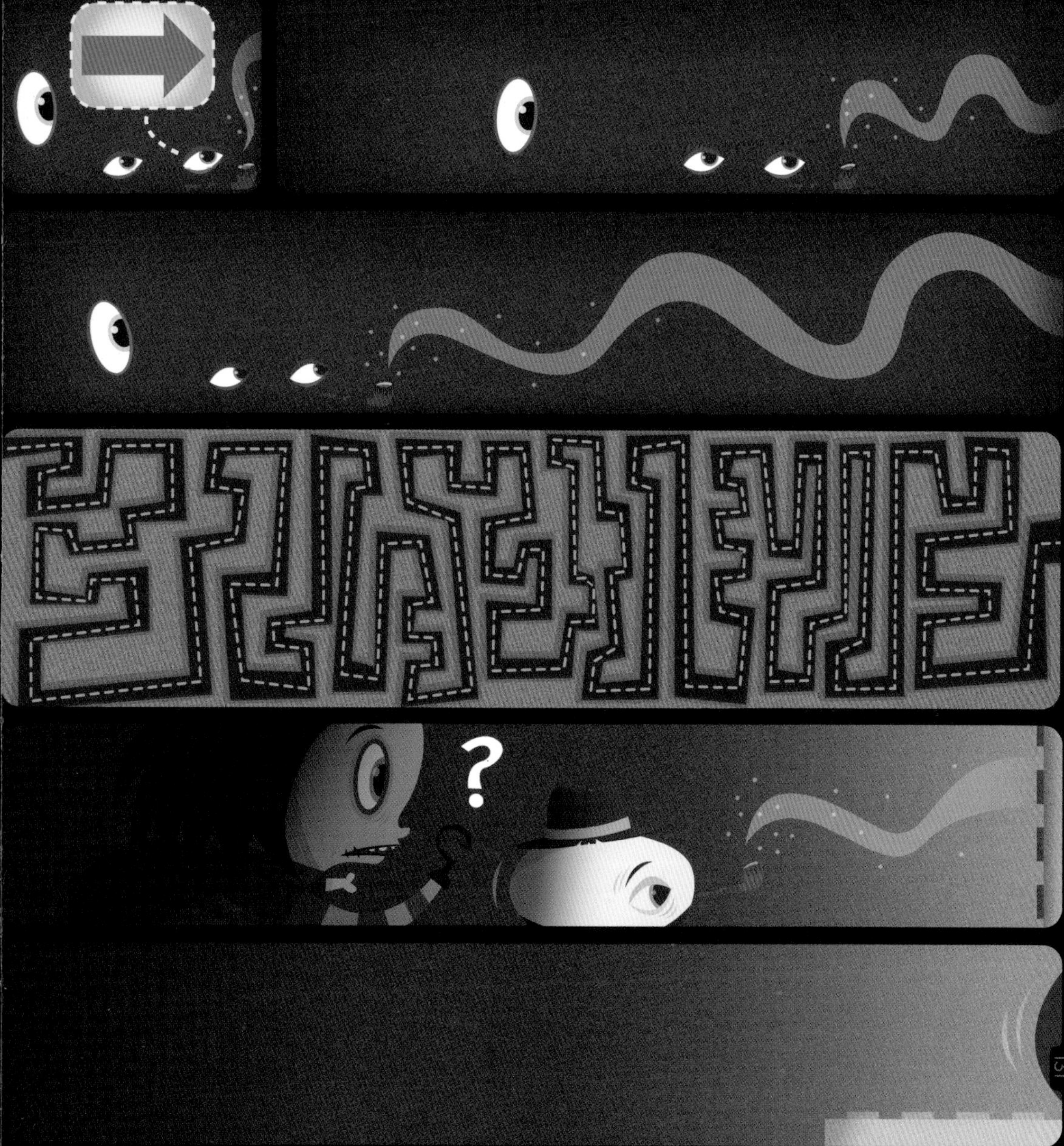
?

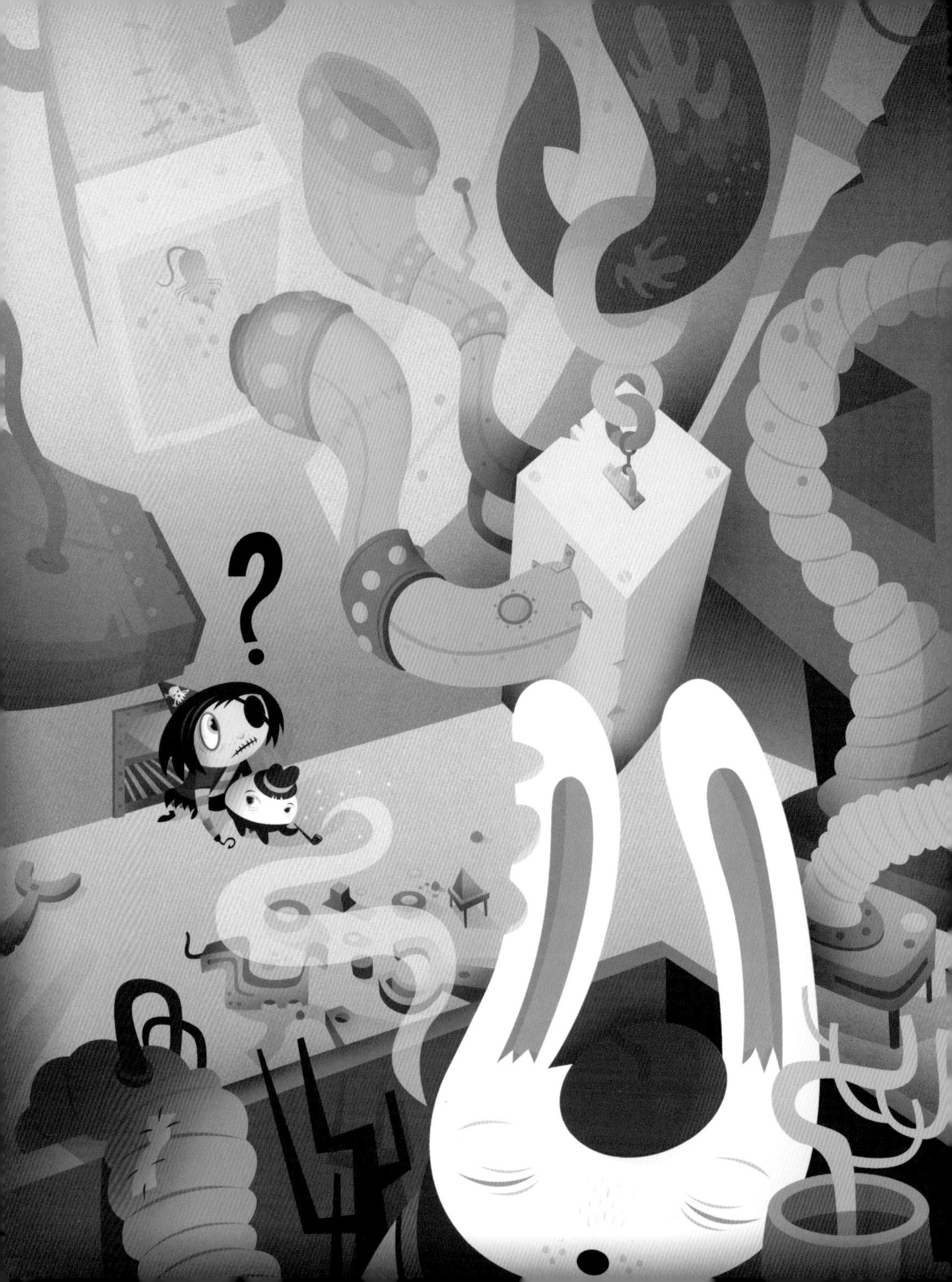

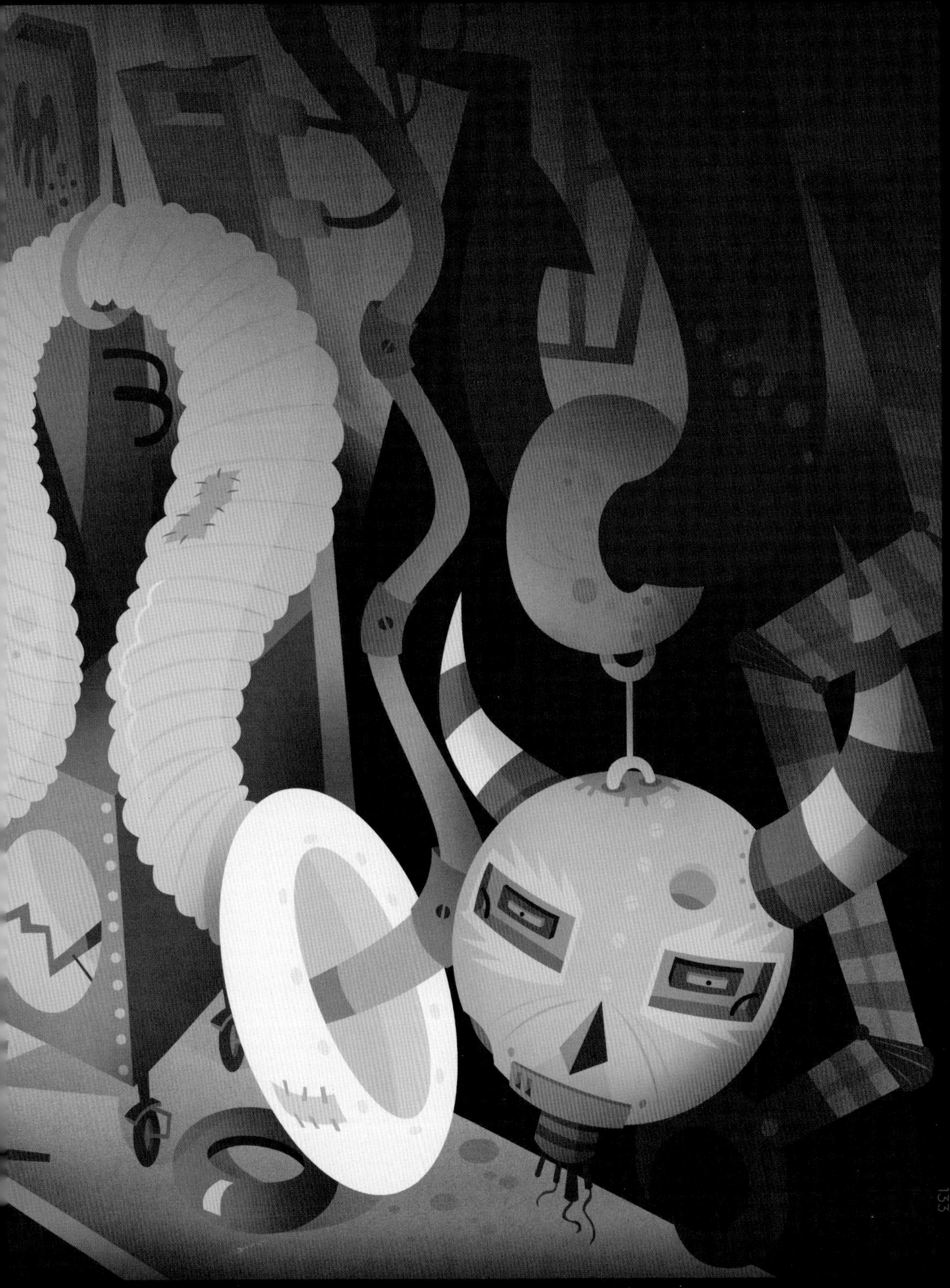

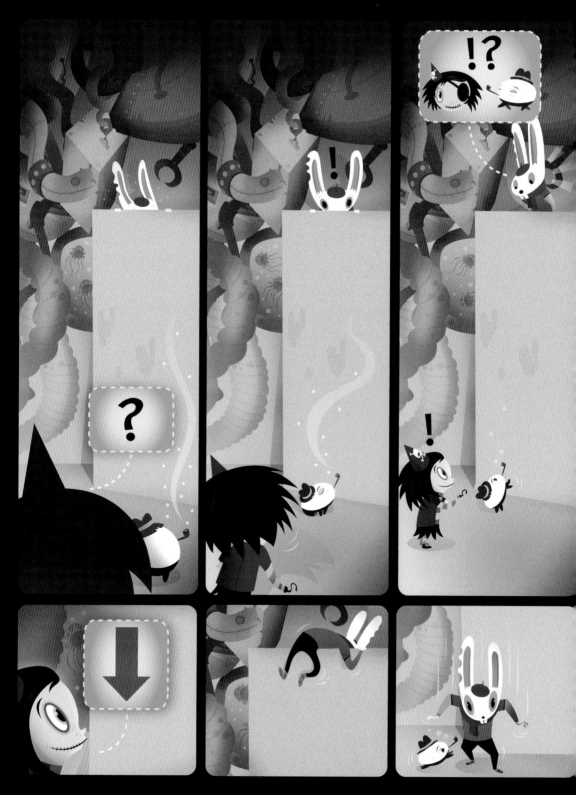

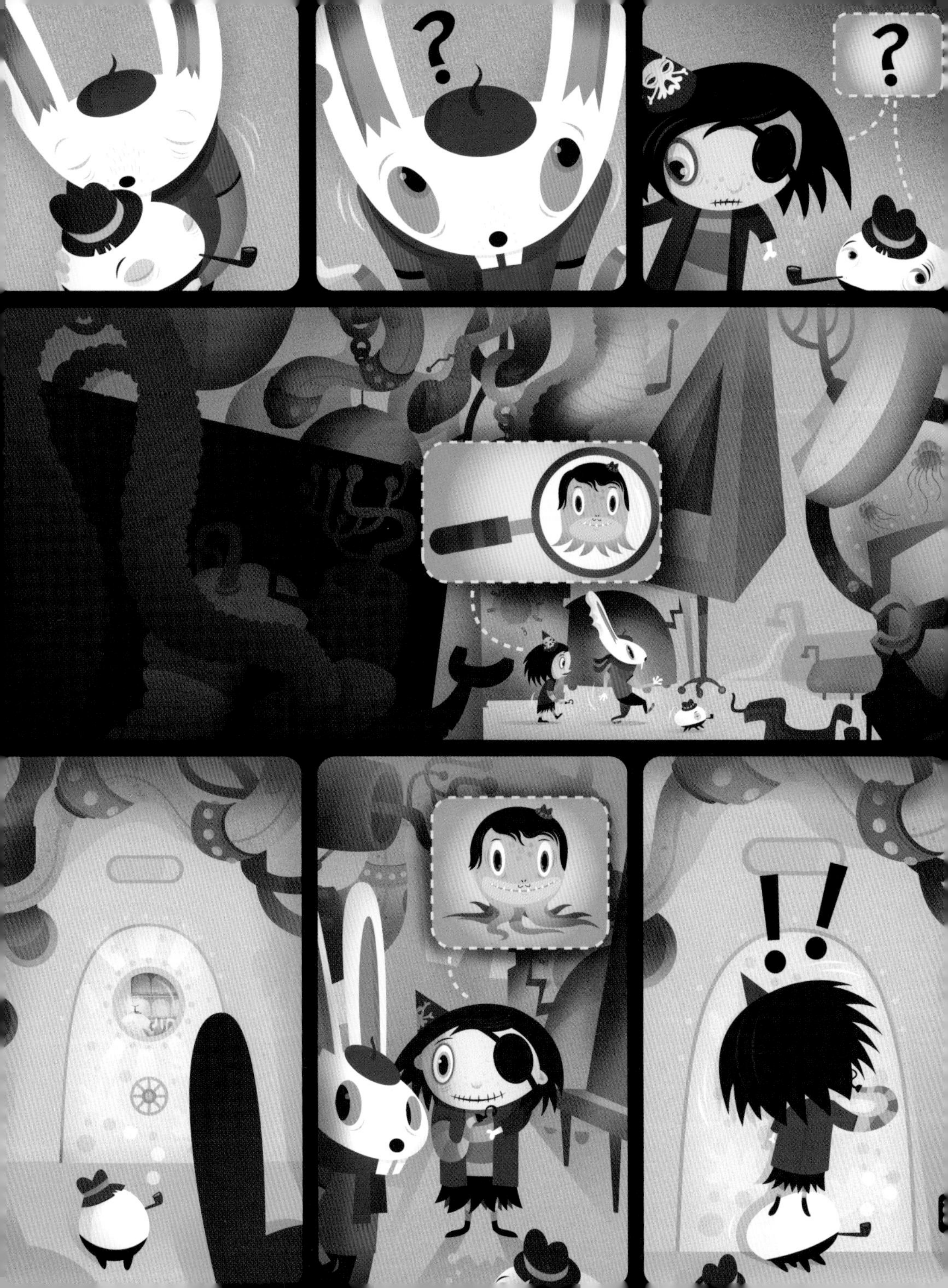

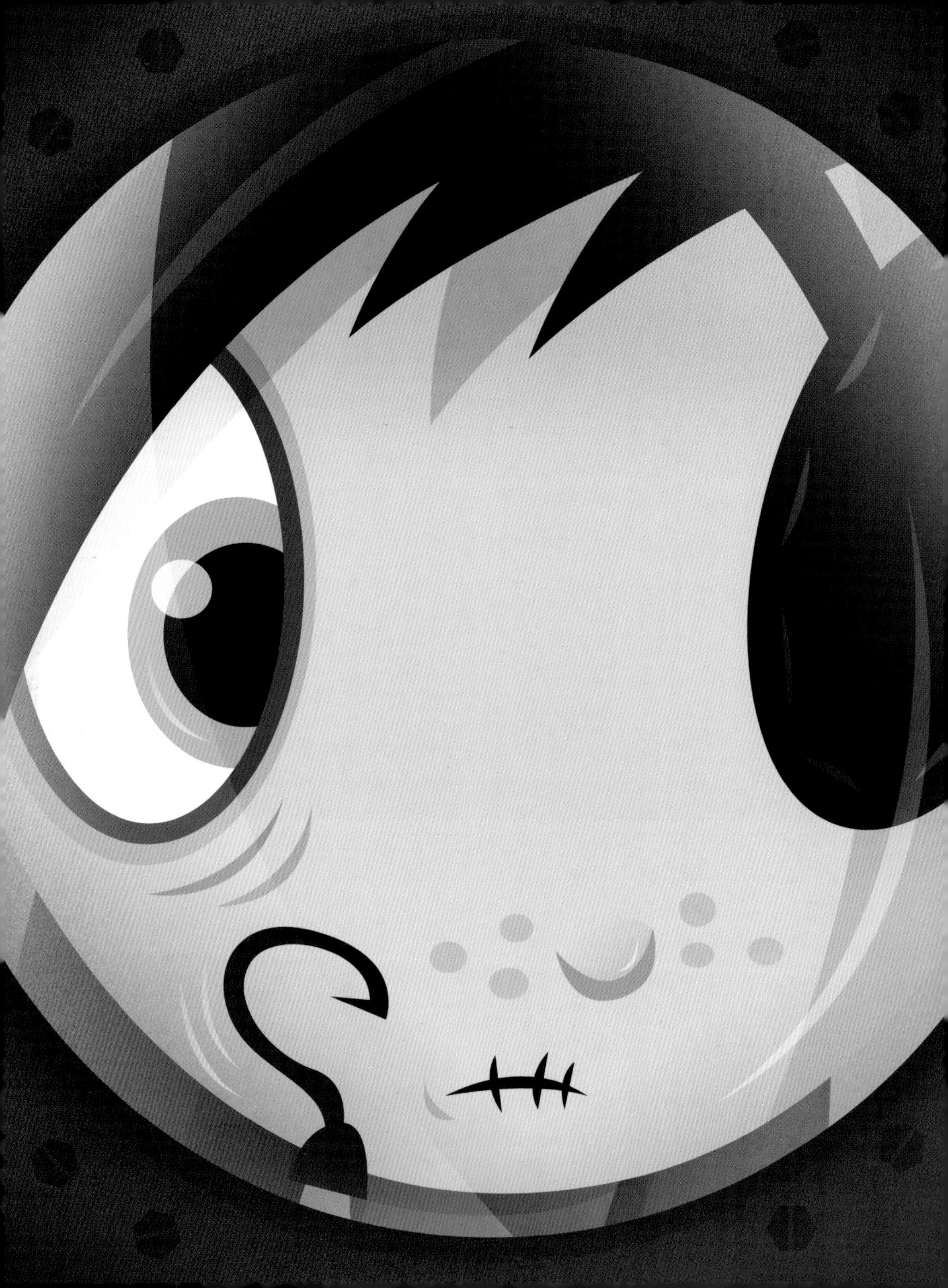

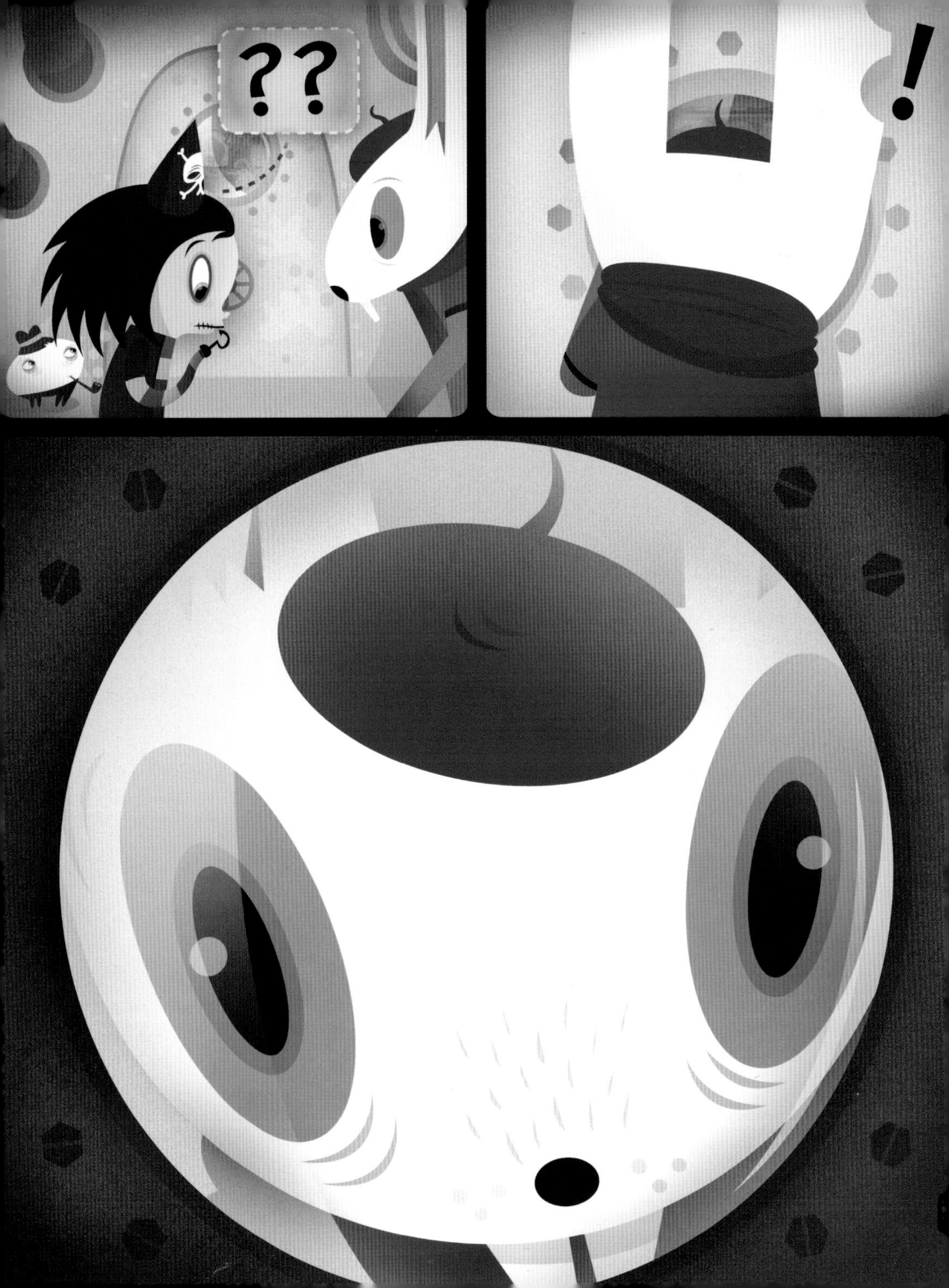
??
!

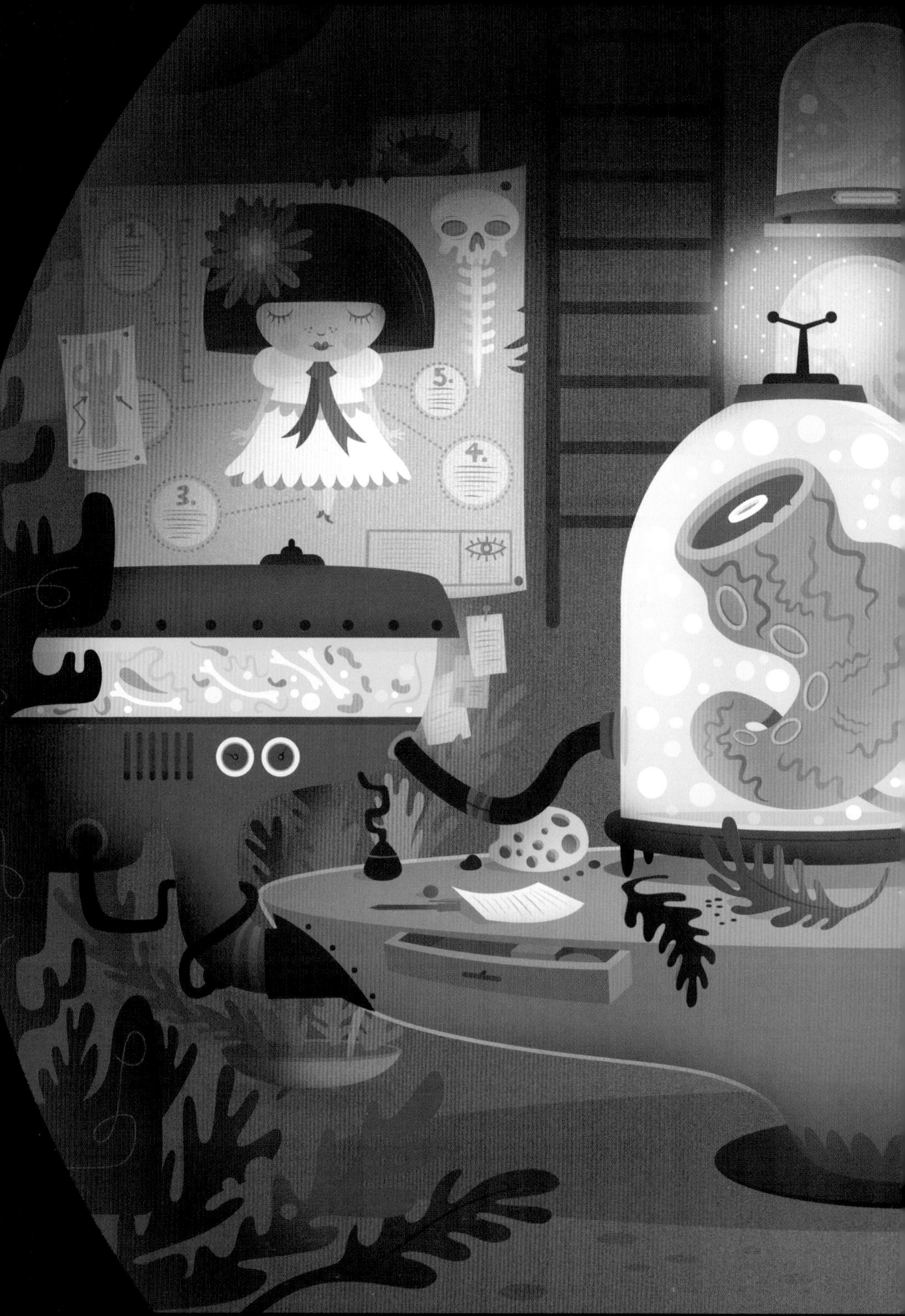
1.
5.
4.
3.

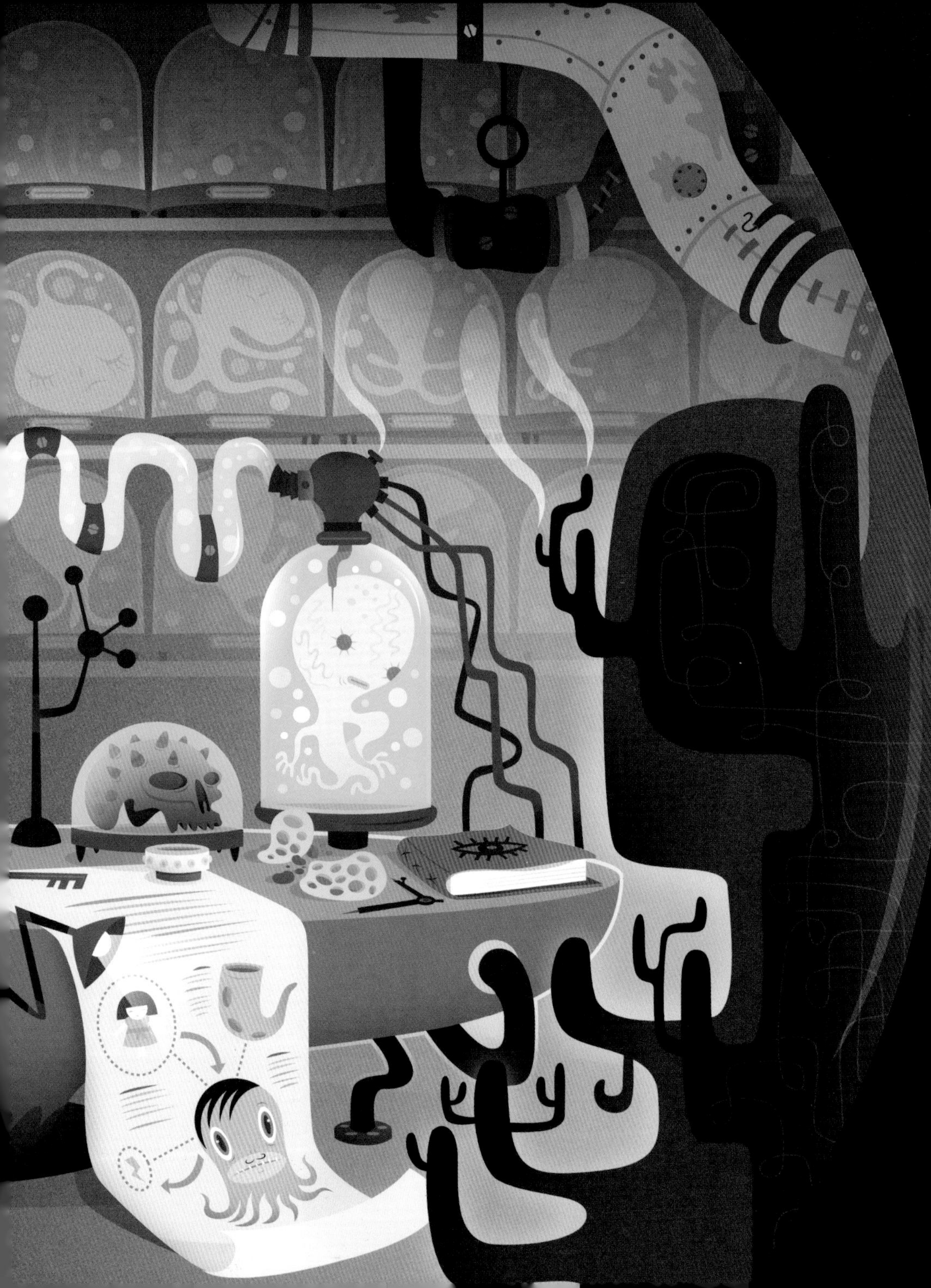

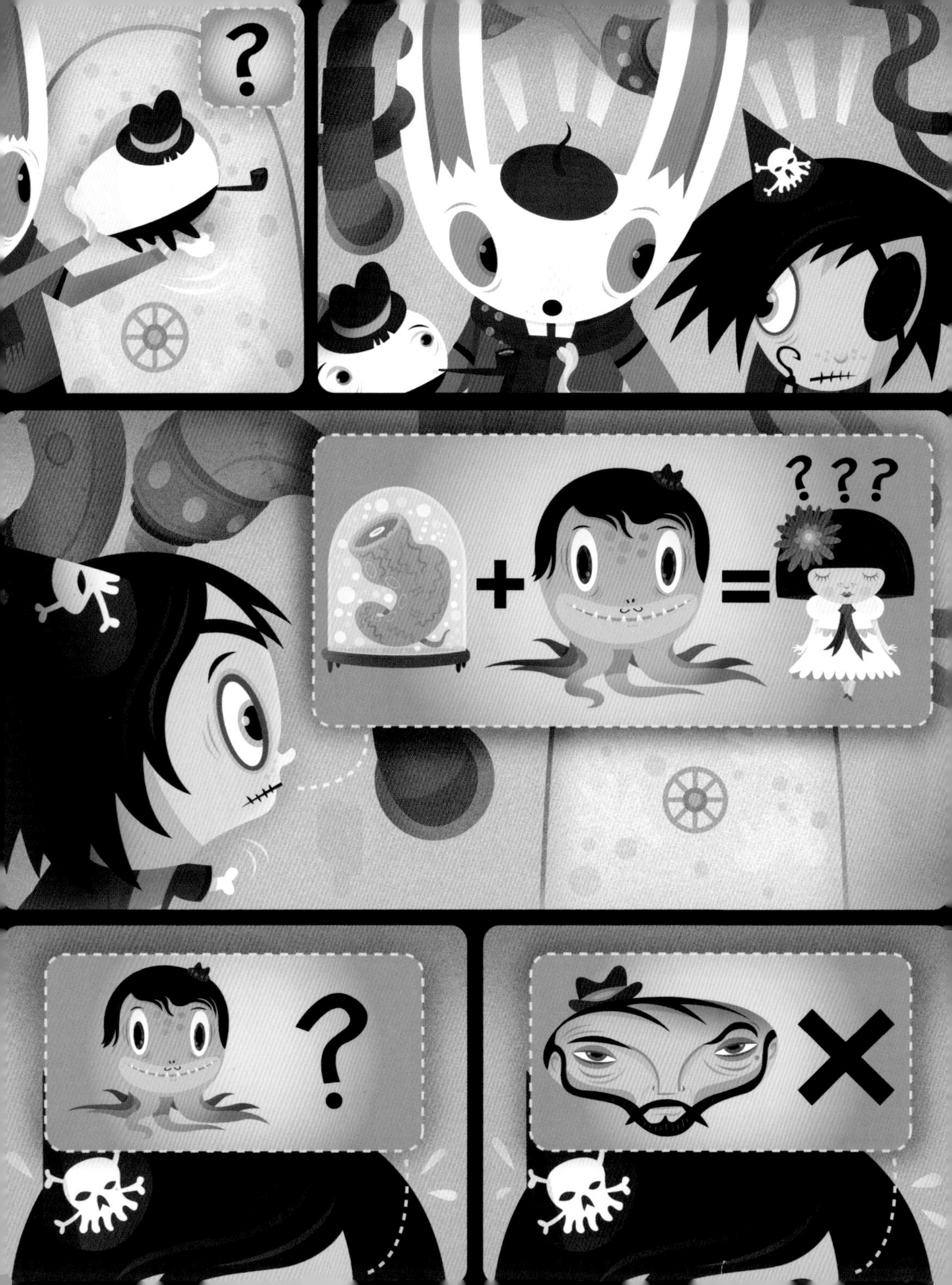

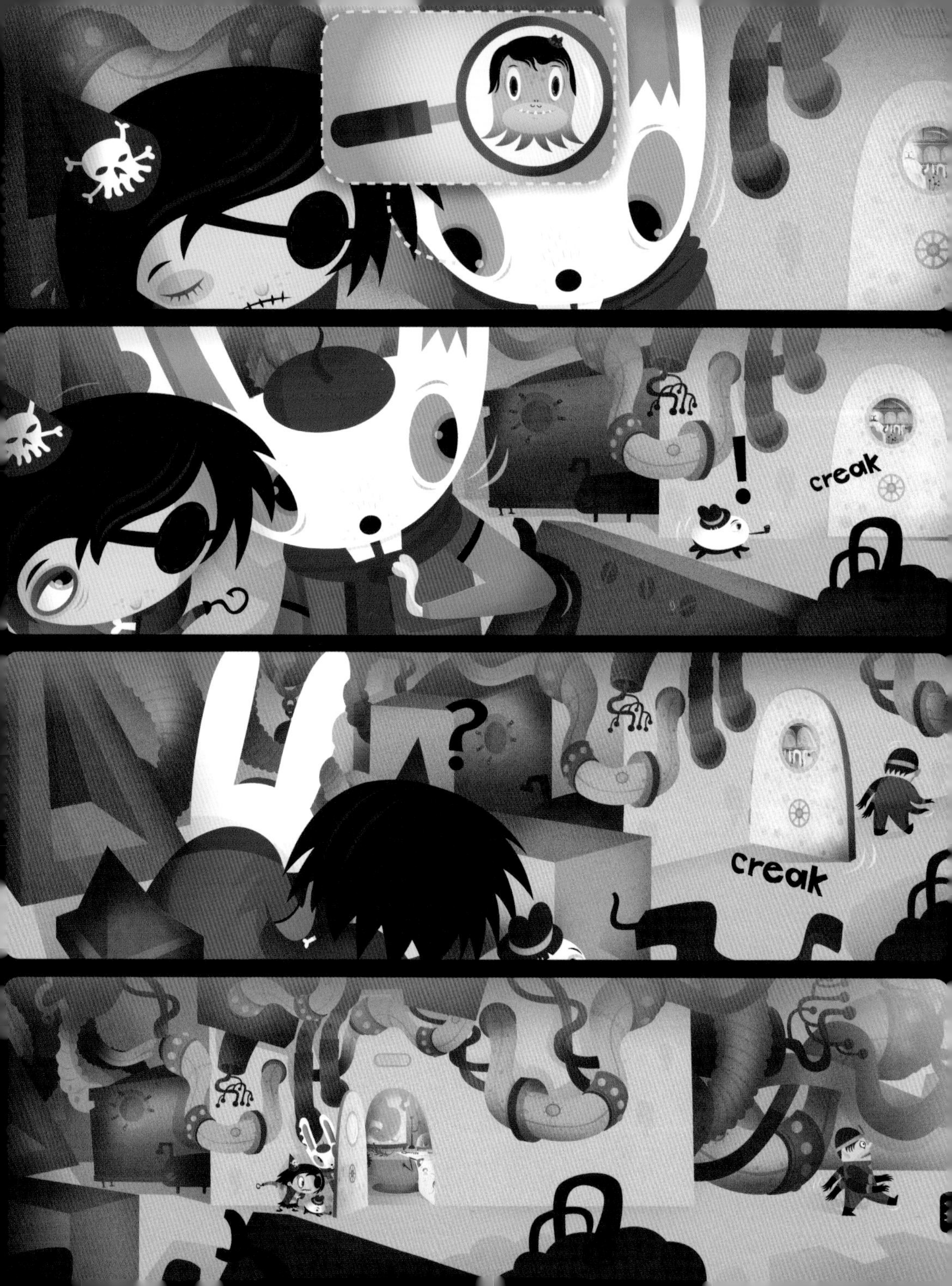
!
creak
?
creak

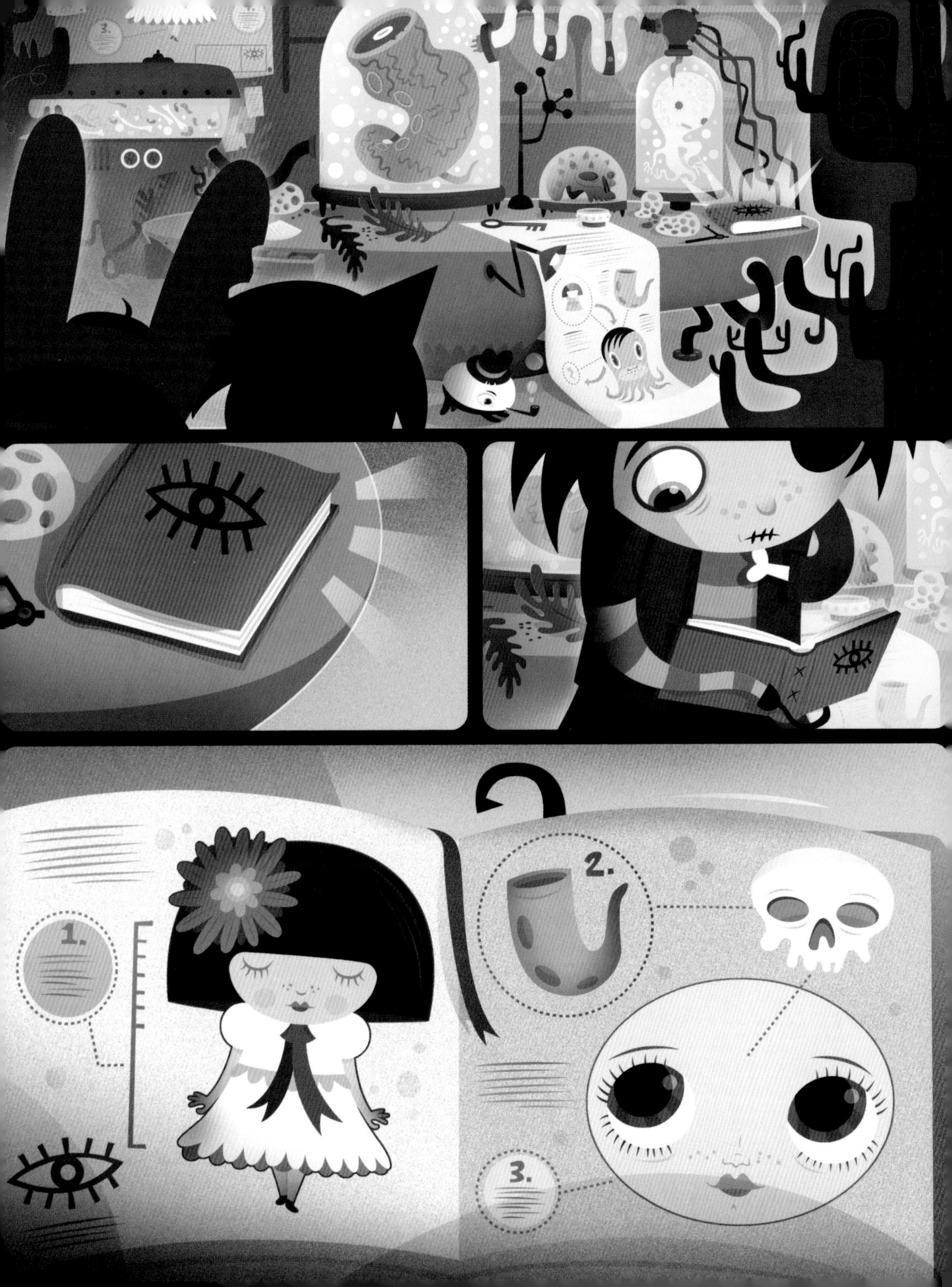

1.
2.
3.

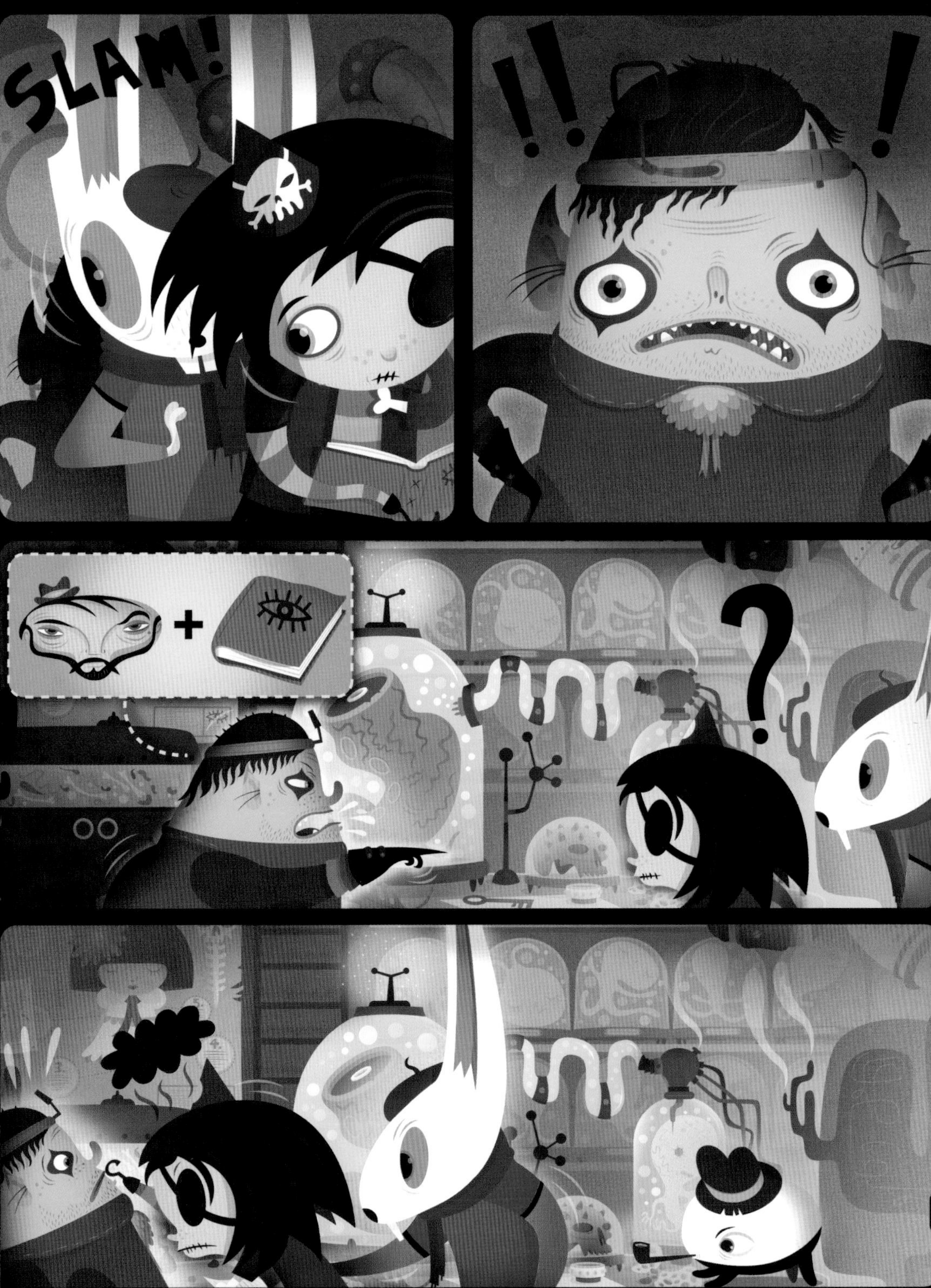
SLAM!
!!
!
?

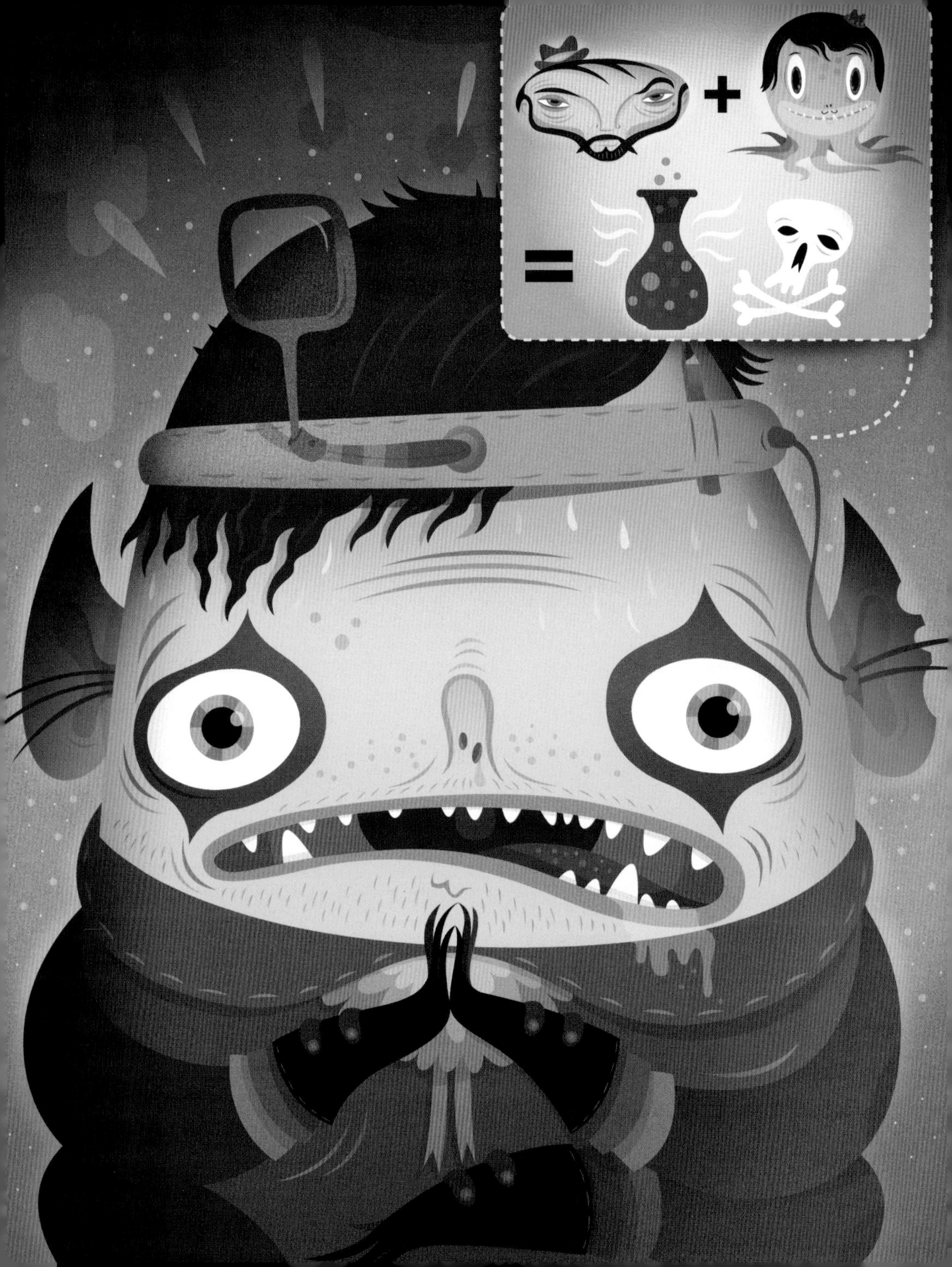

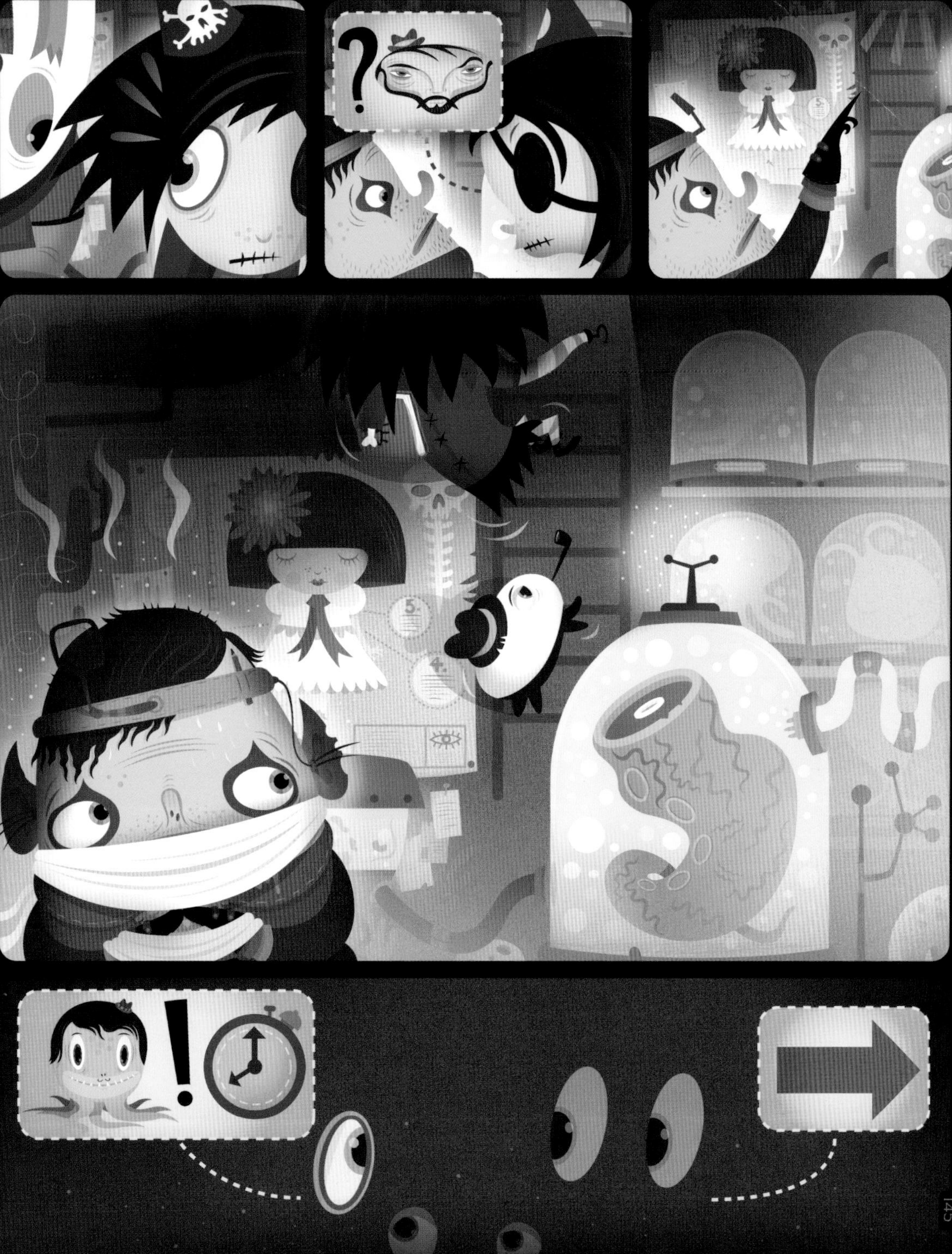
?
!

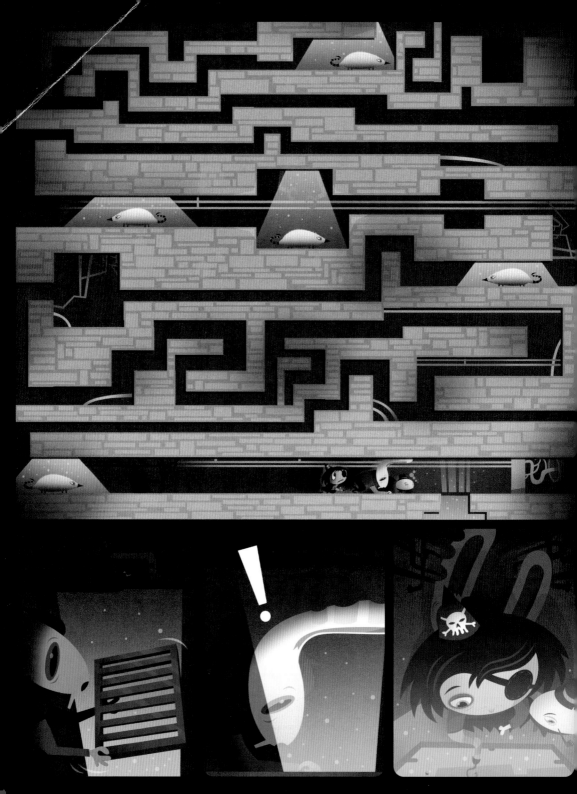

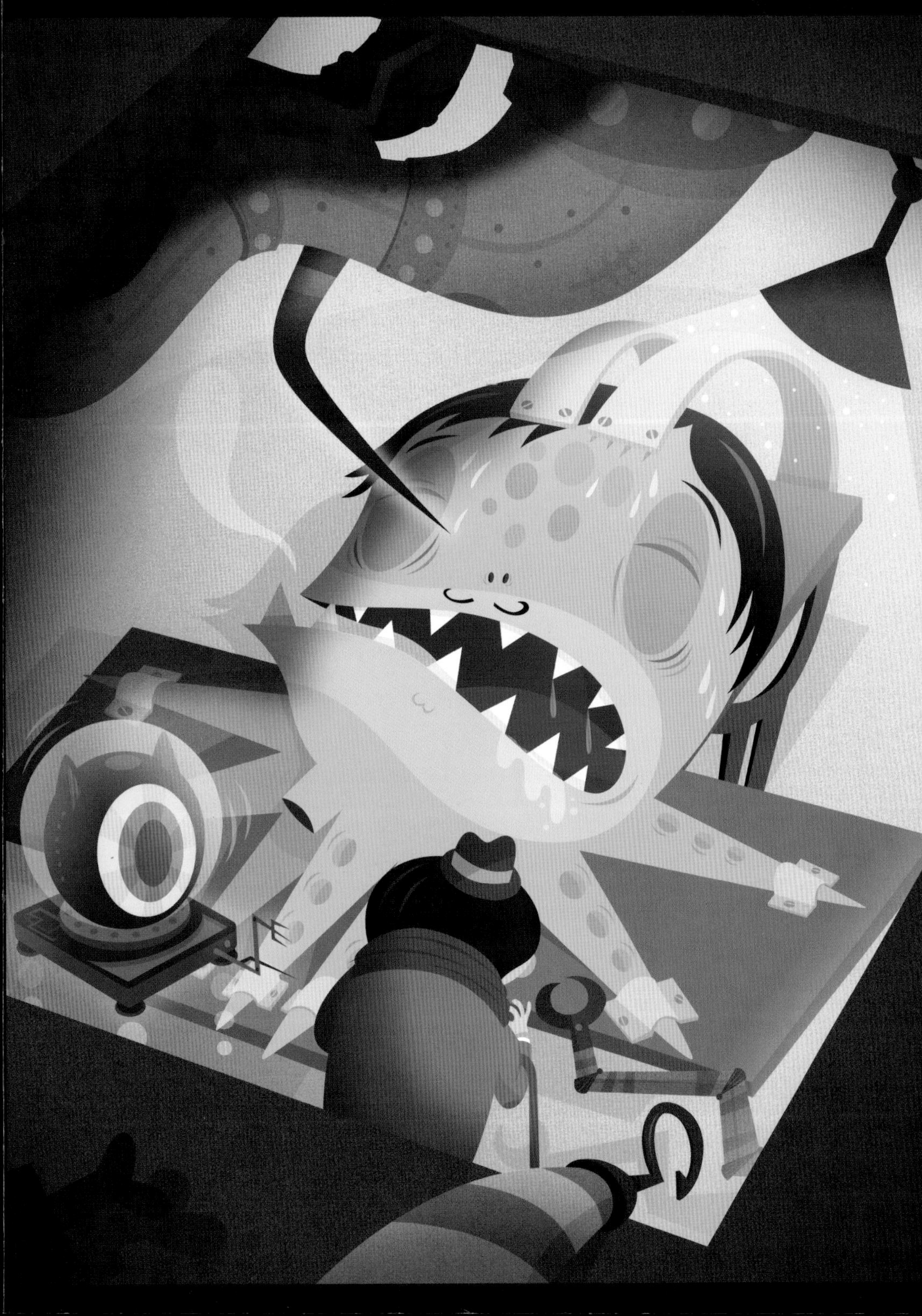

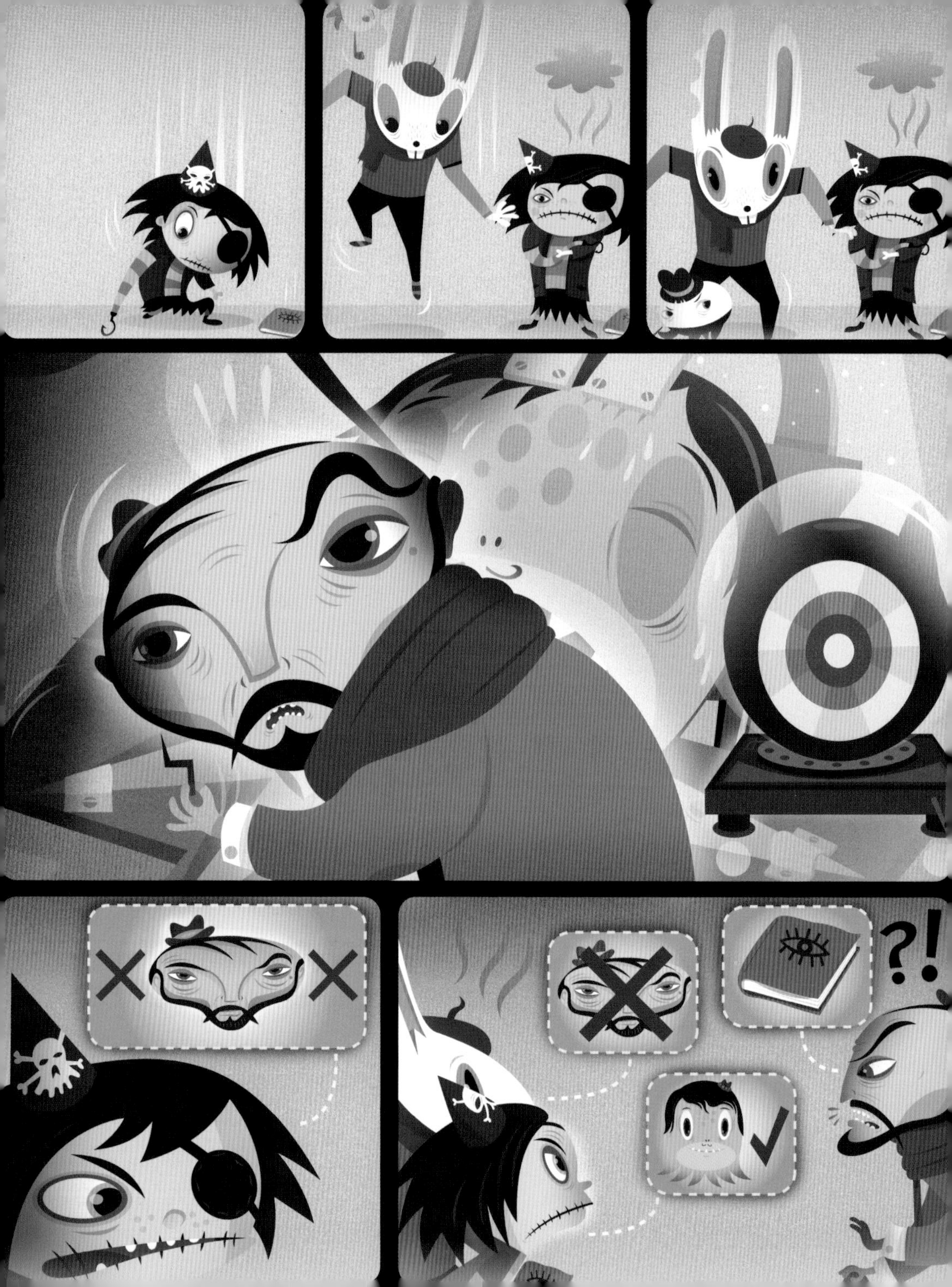
?!

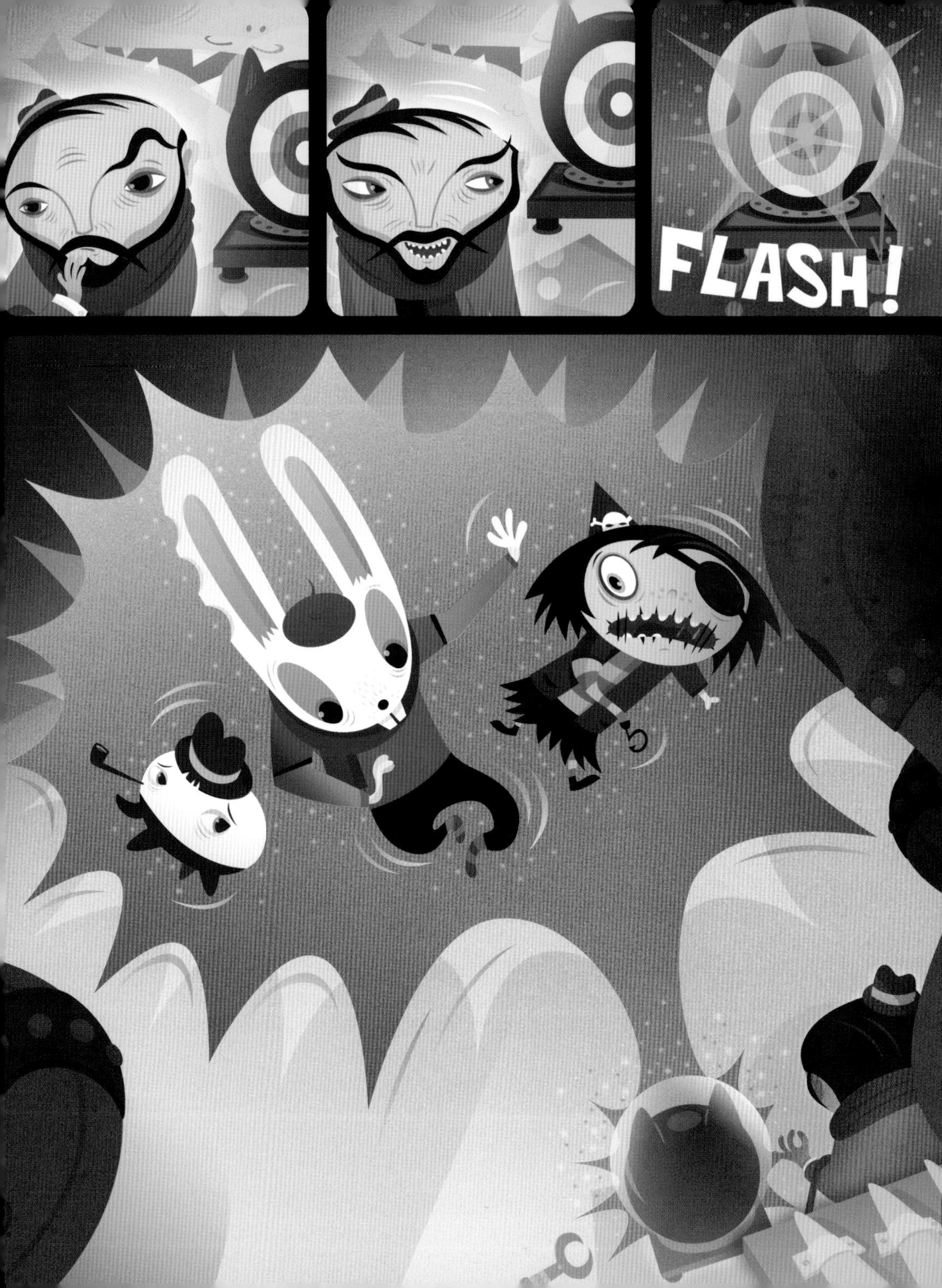
FLASH!

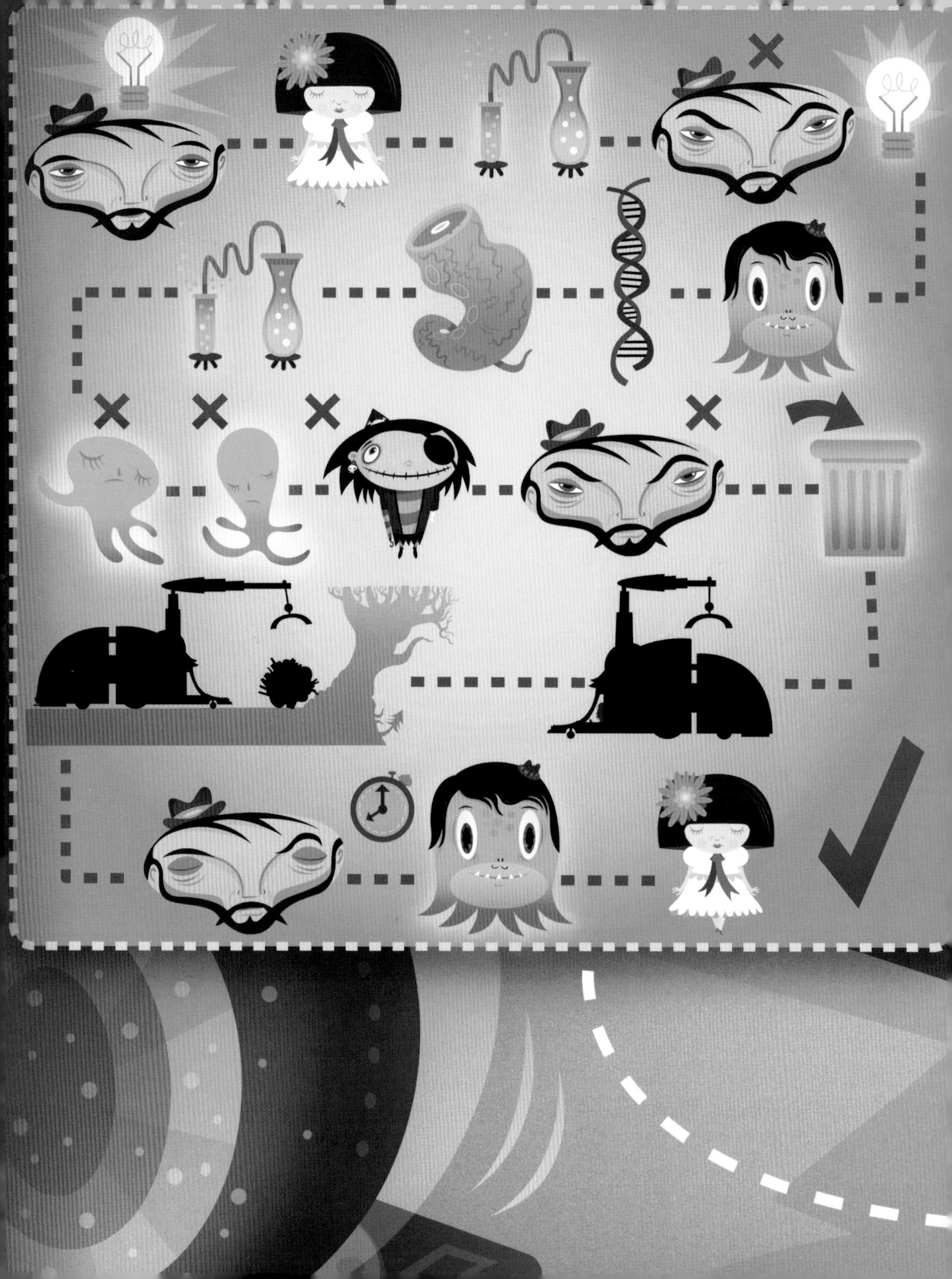

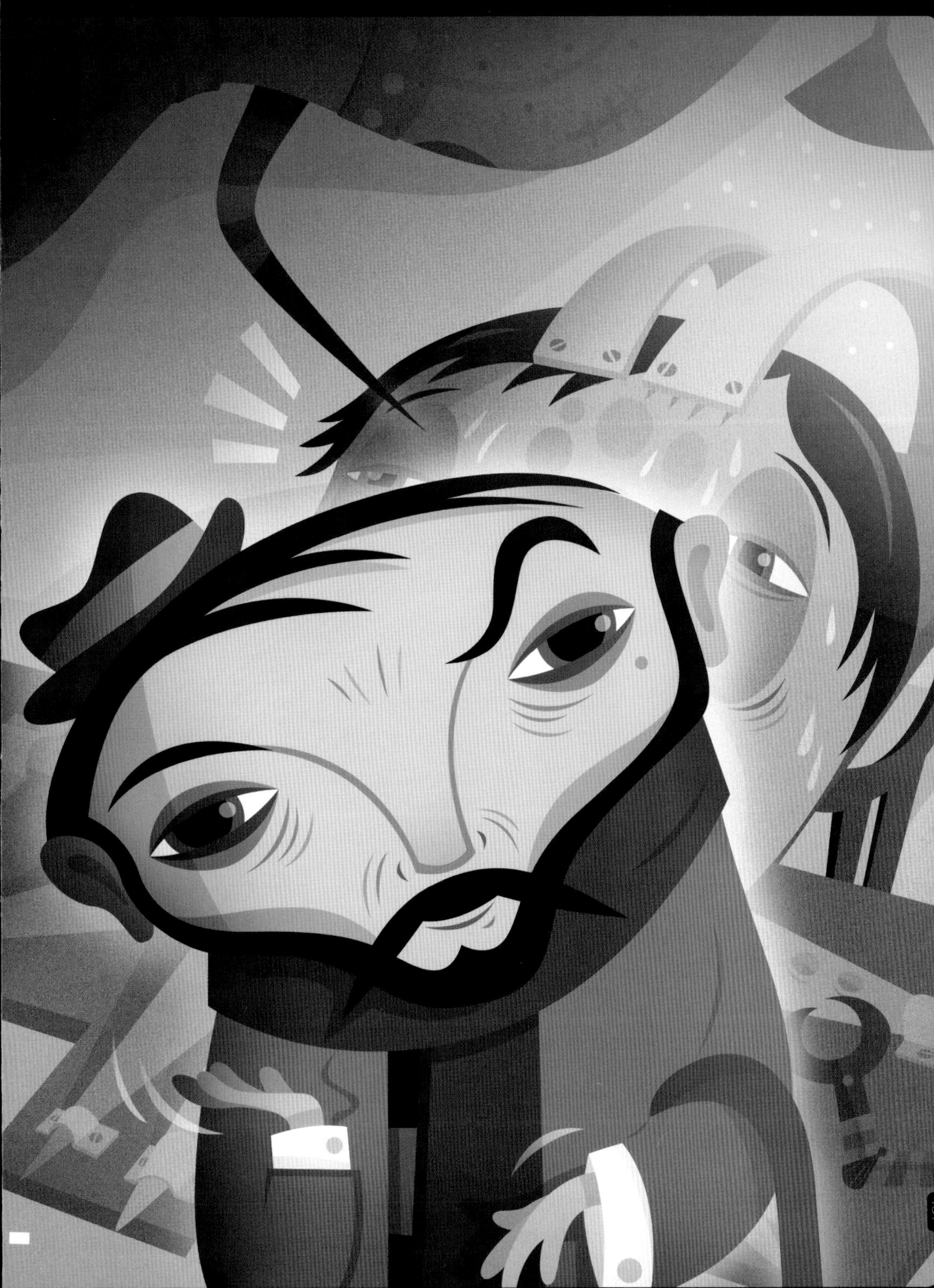

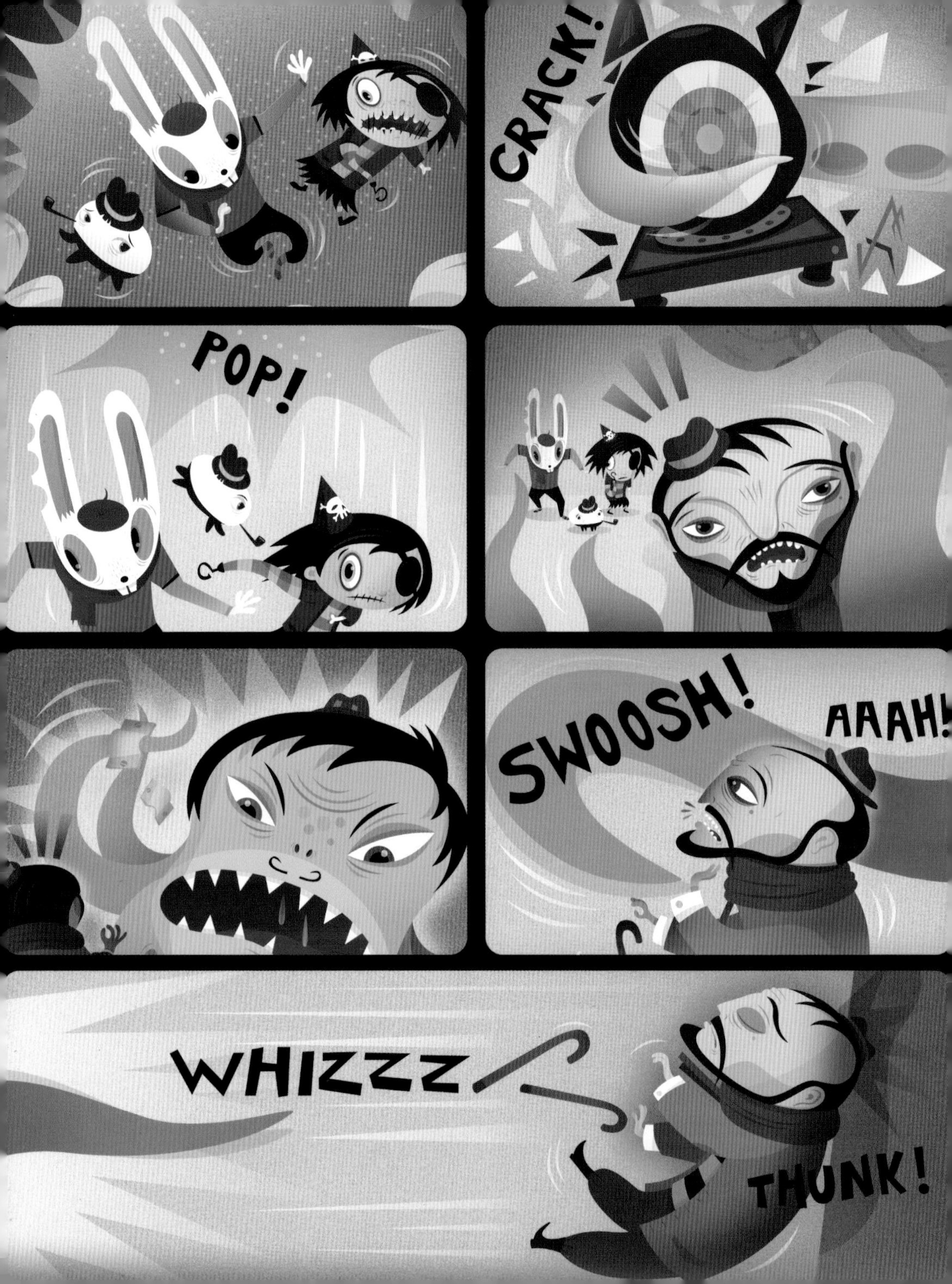
CRACK!
POP!
SWOOSH!
AAAH!
WHIZZZ
THUNK!

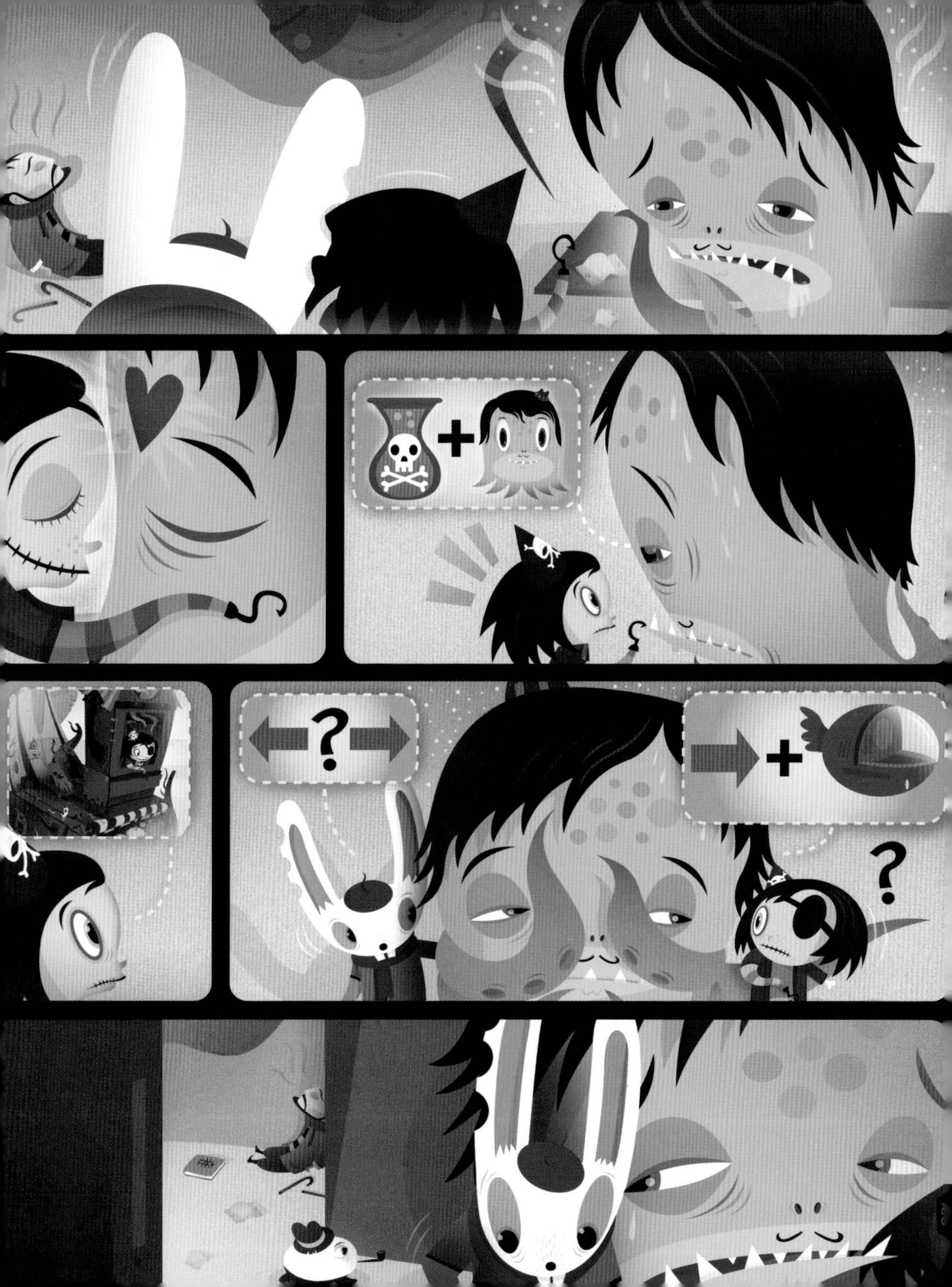

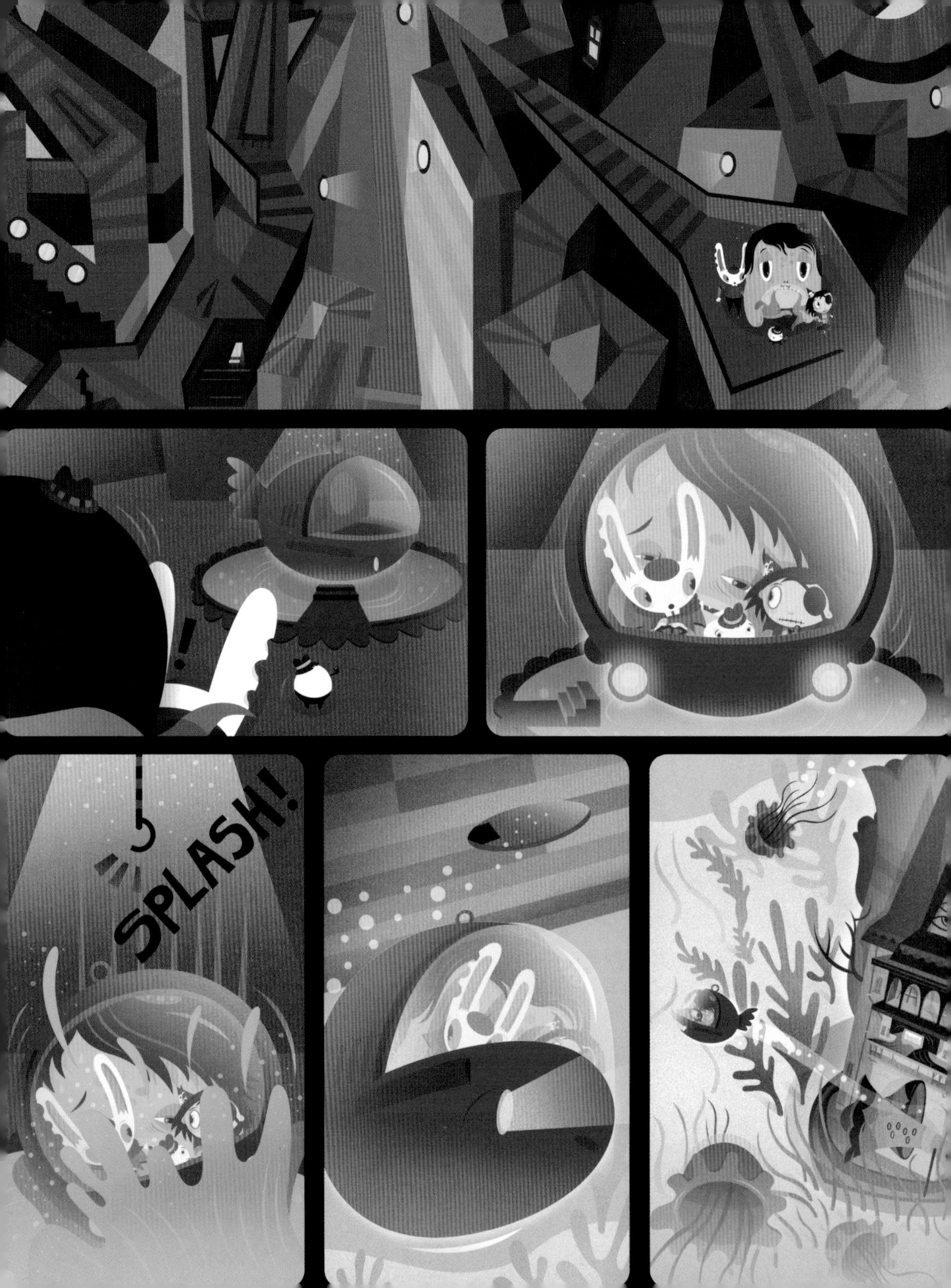
!
SPLASH!

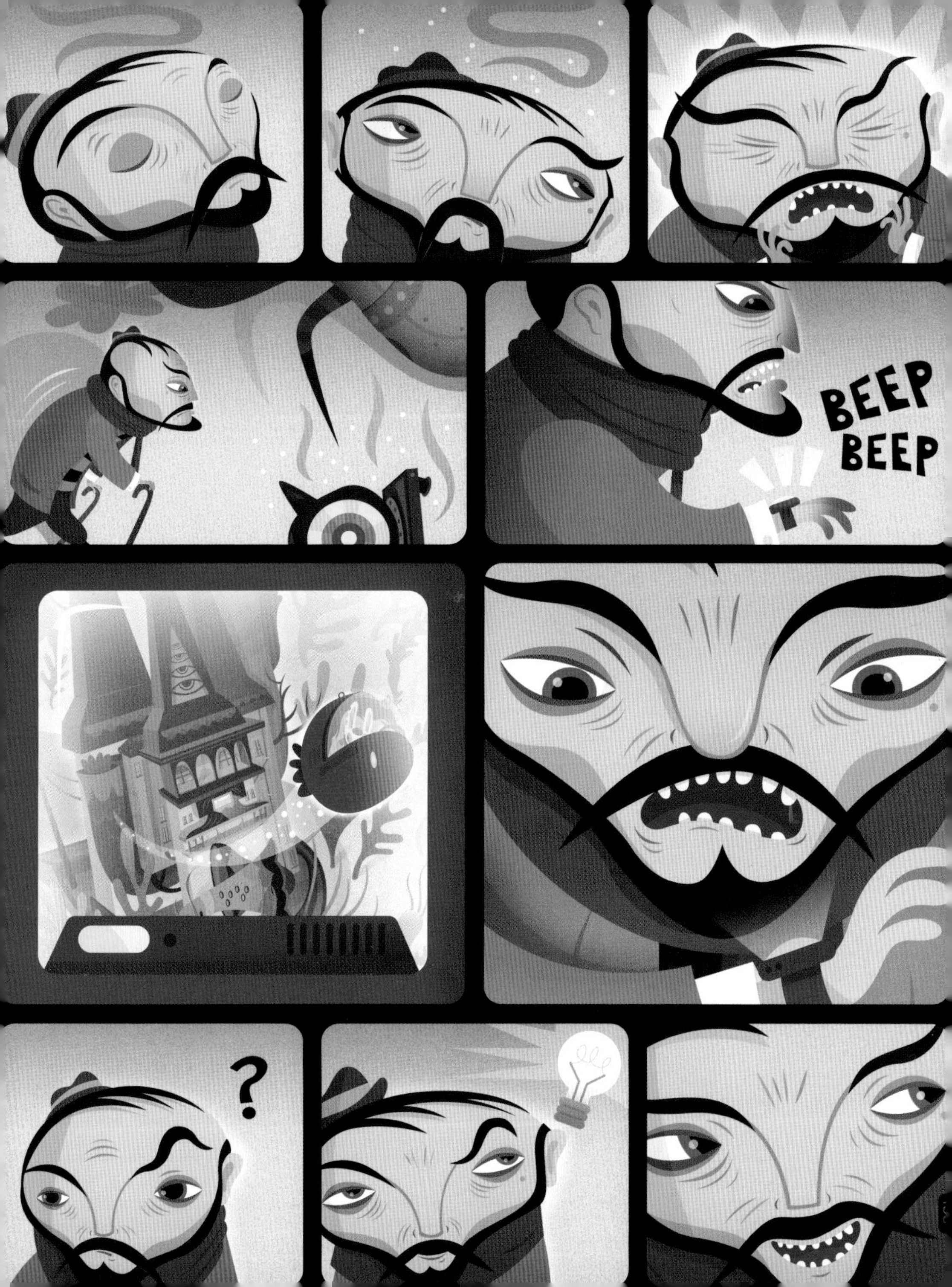
BEEP
BEEP
?

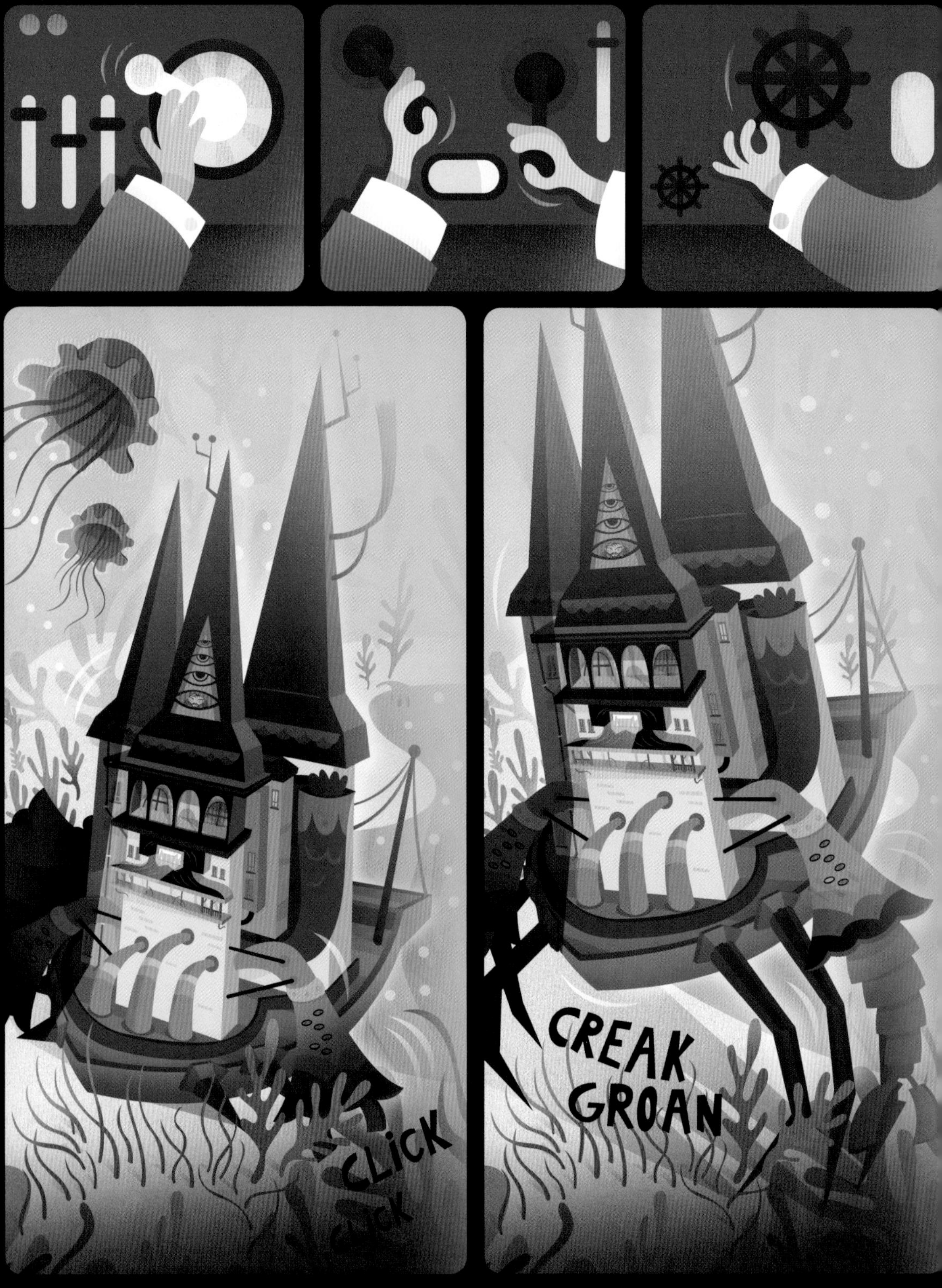
CLICK
CLICK
CREAK
GROAN

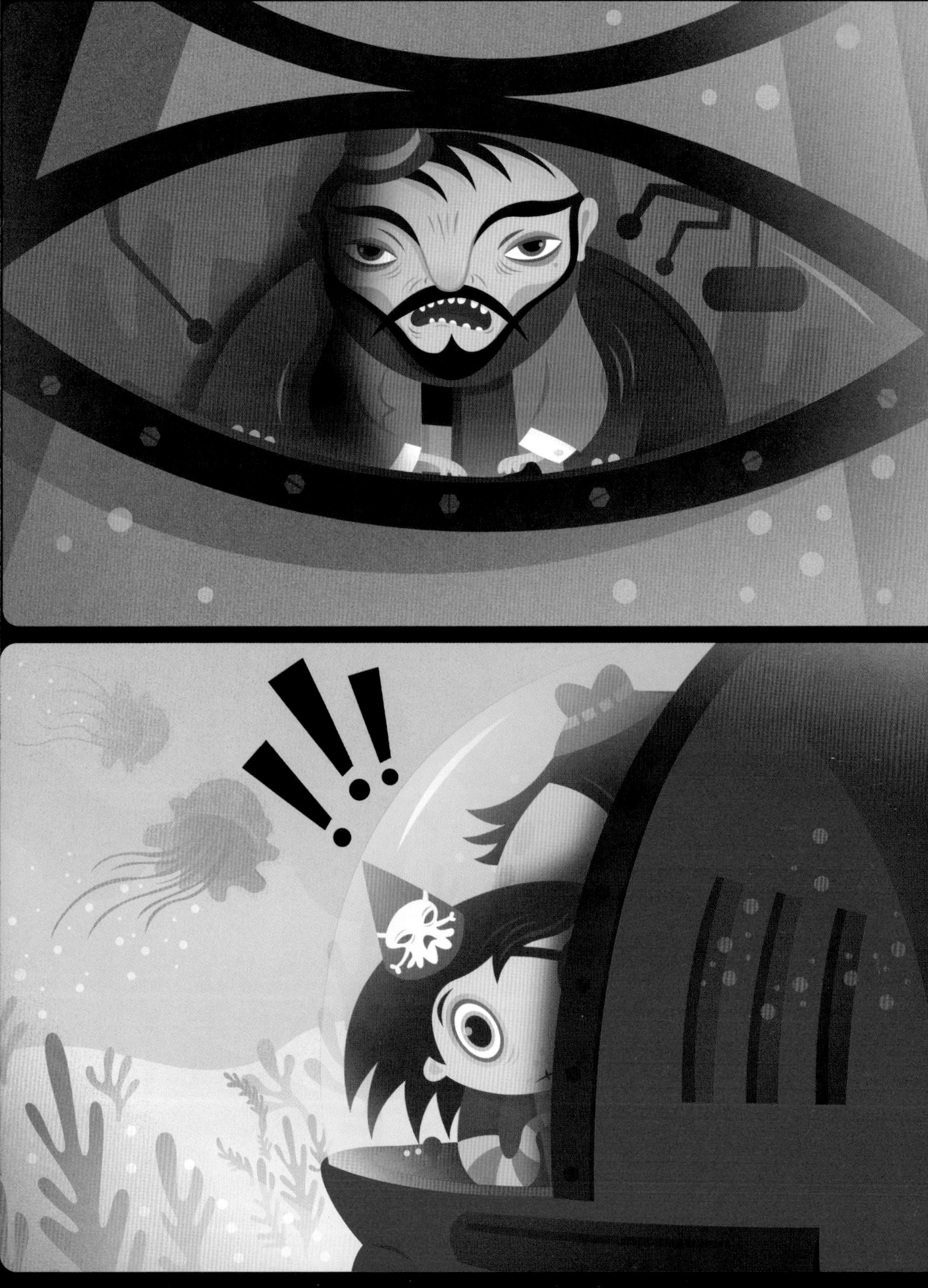
!!!

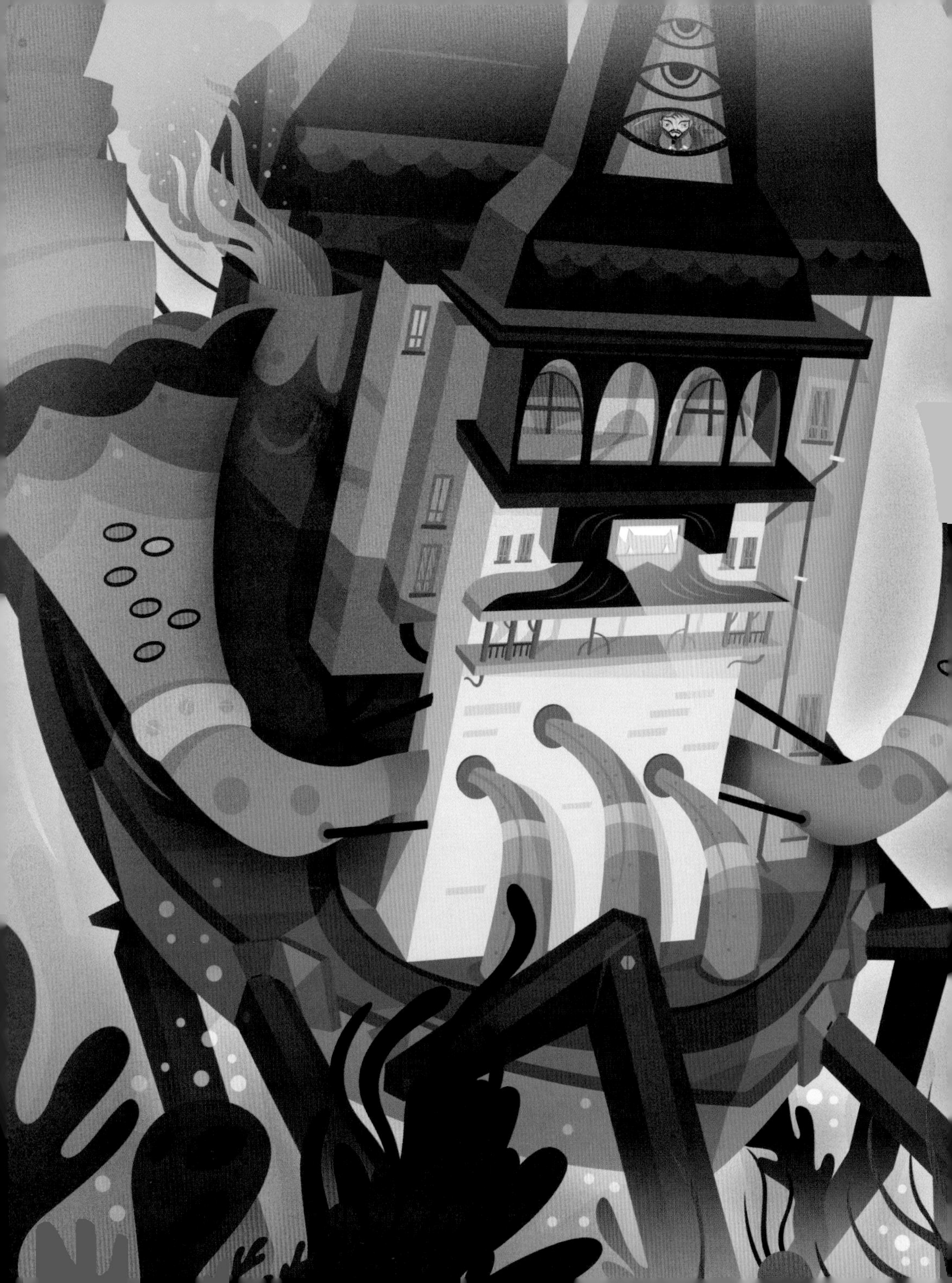

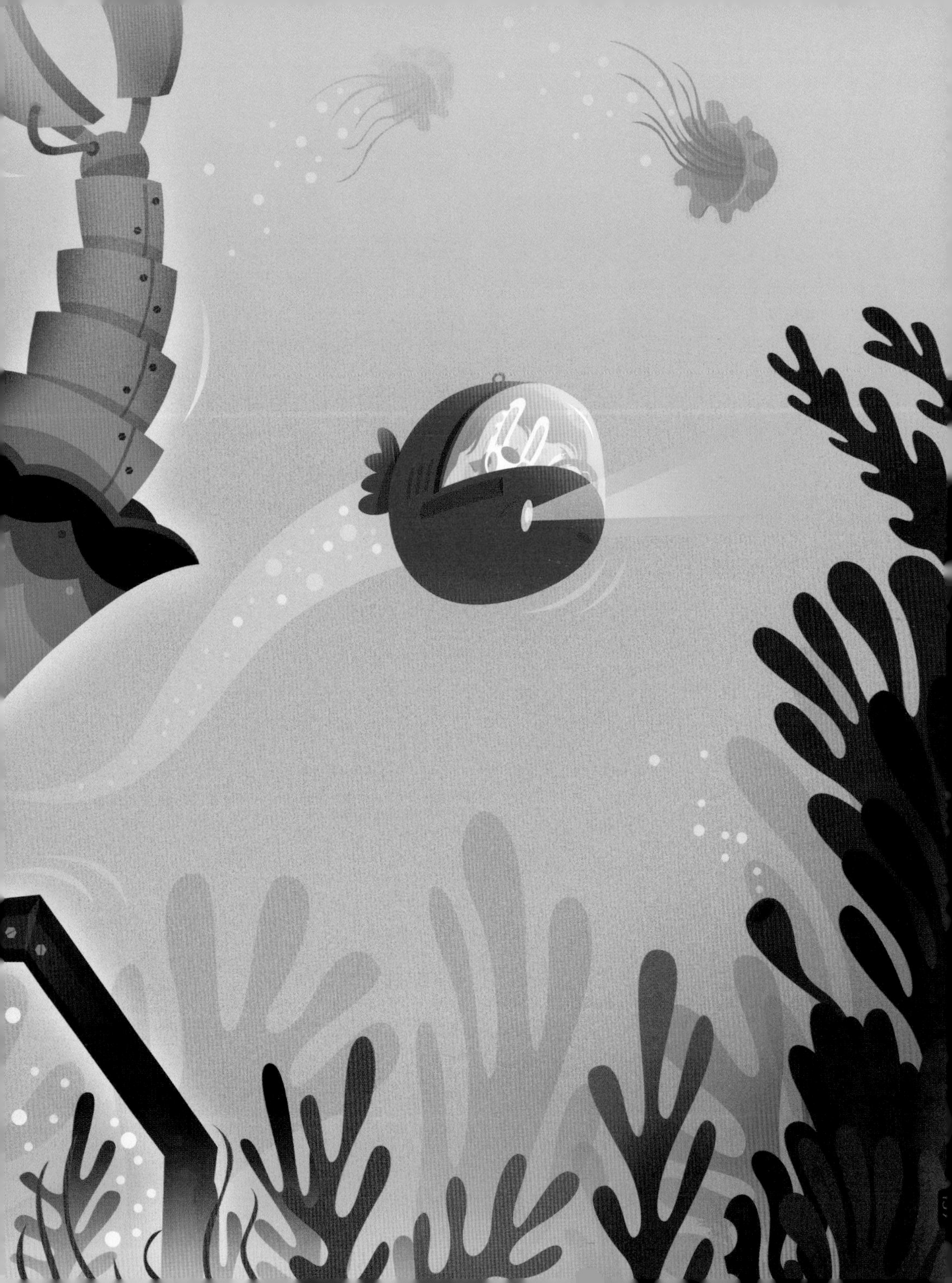

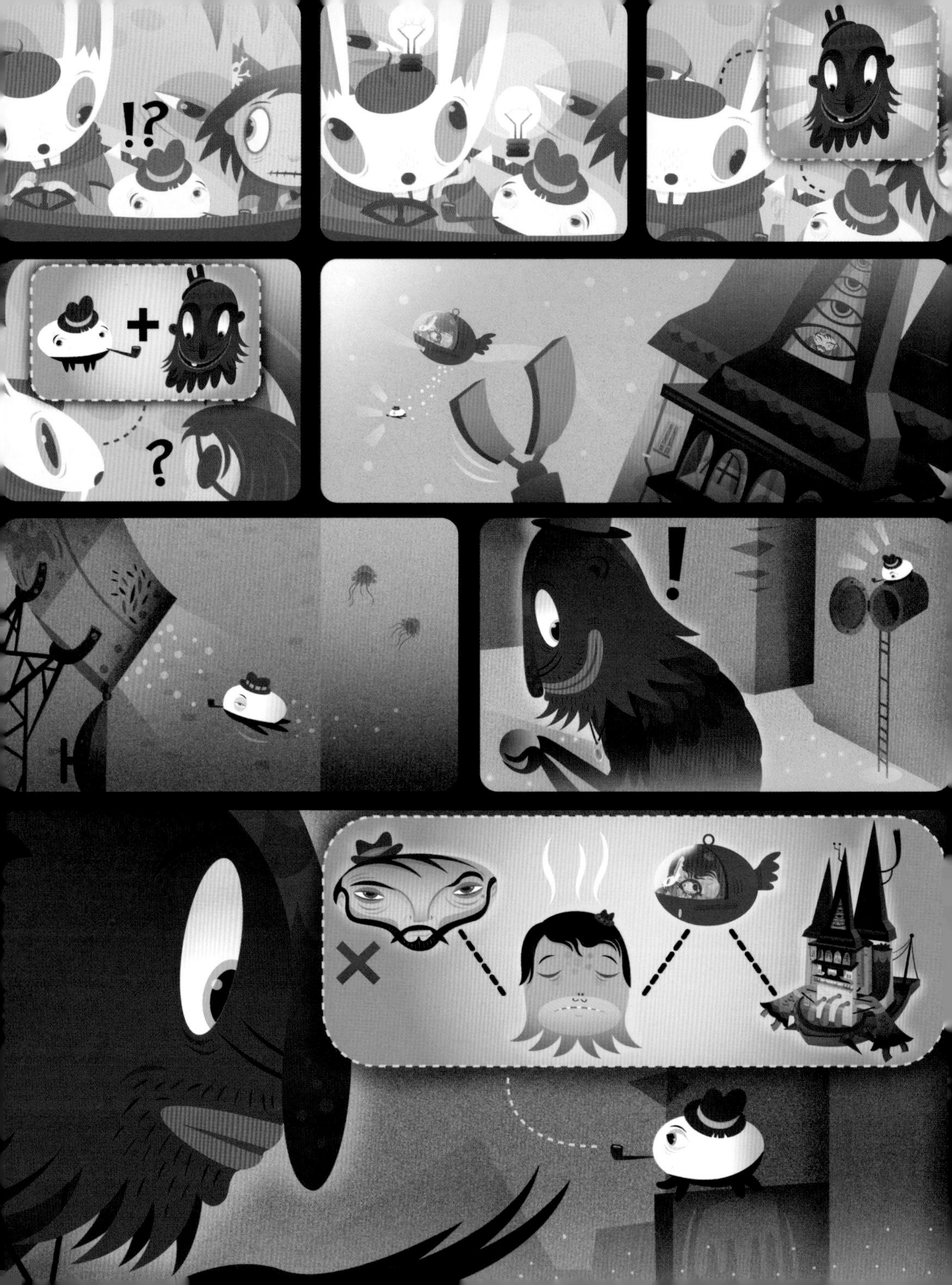
!?
?
!

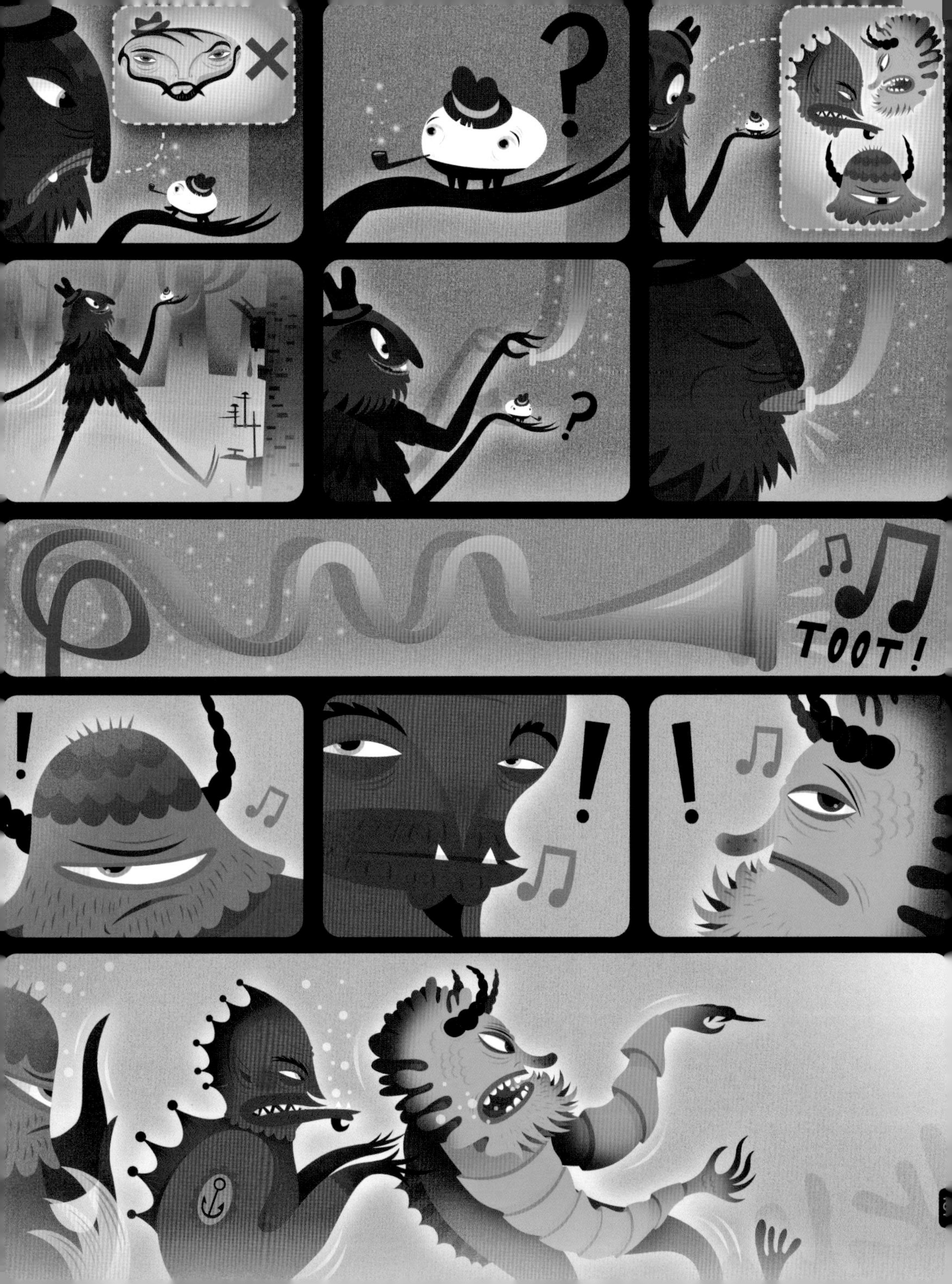

TOOT!

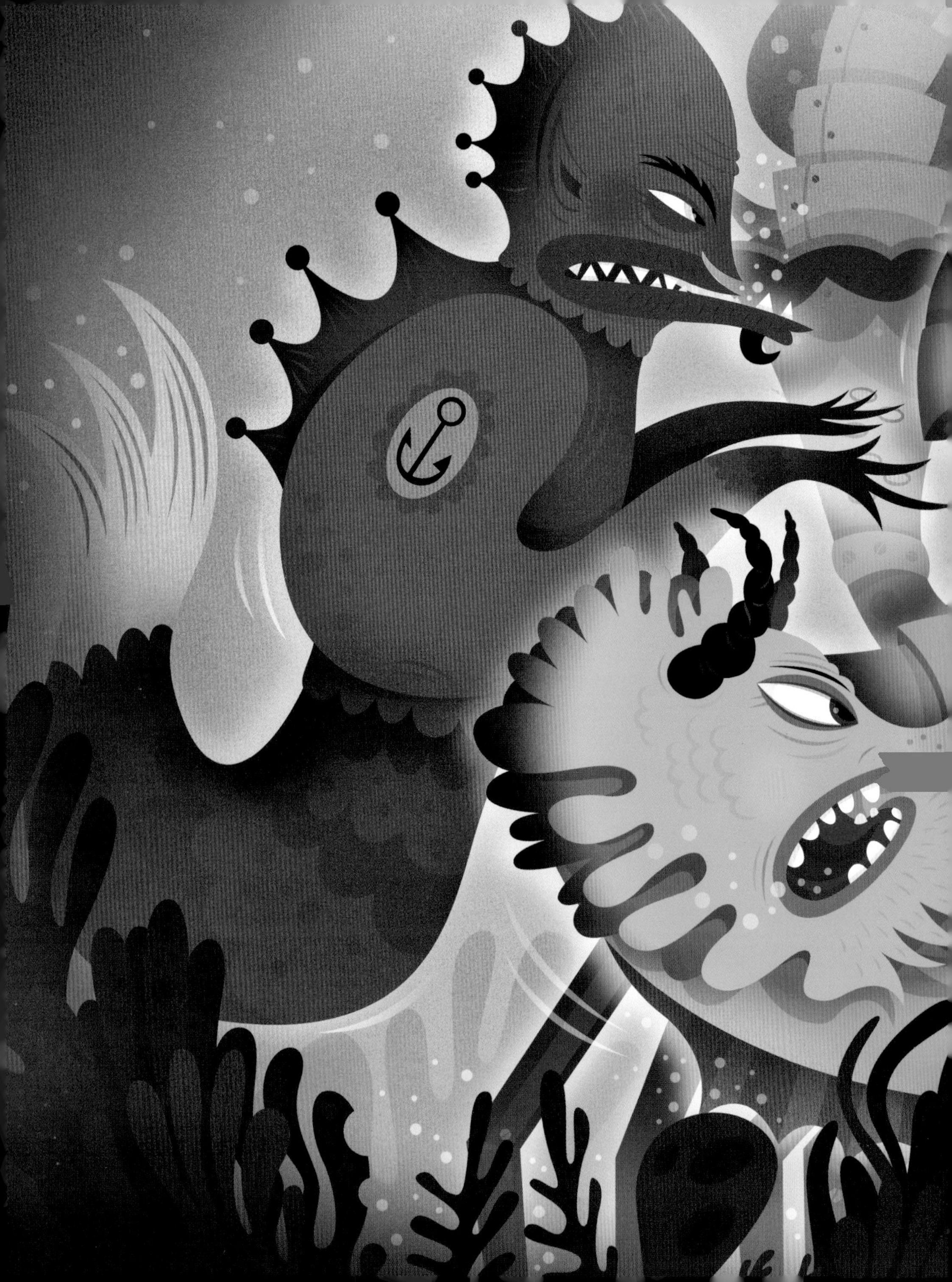

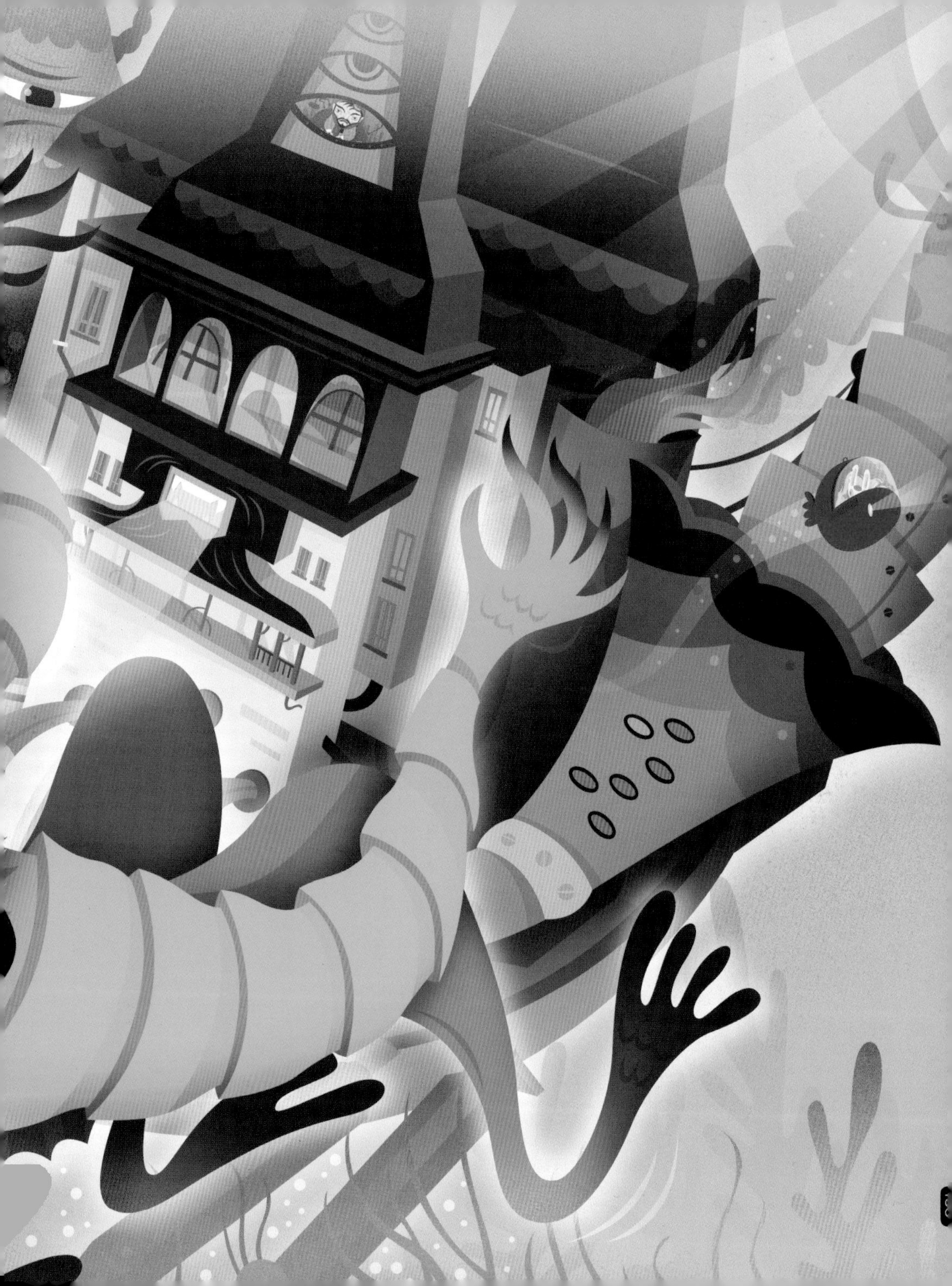

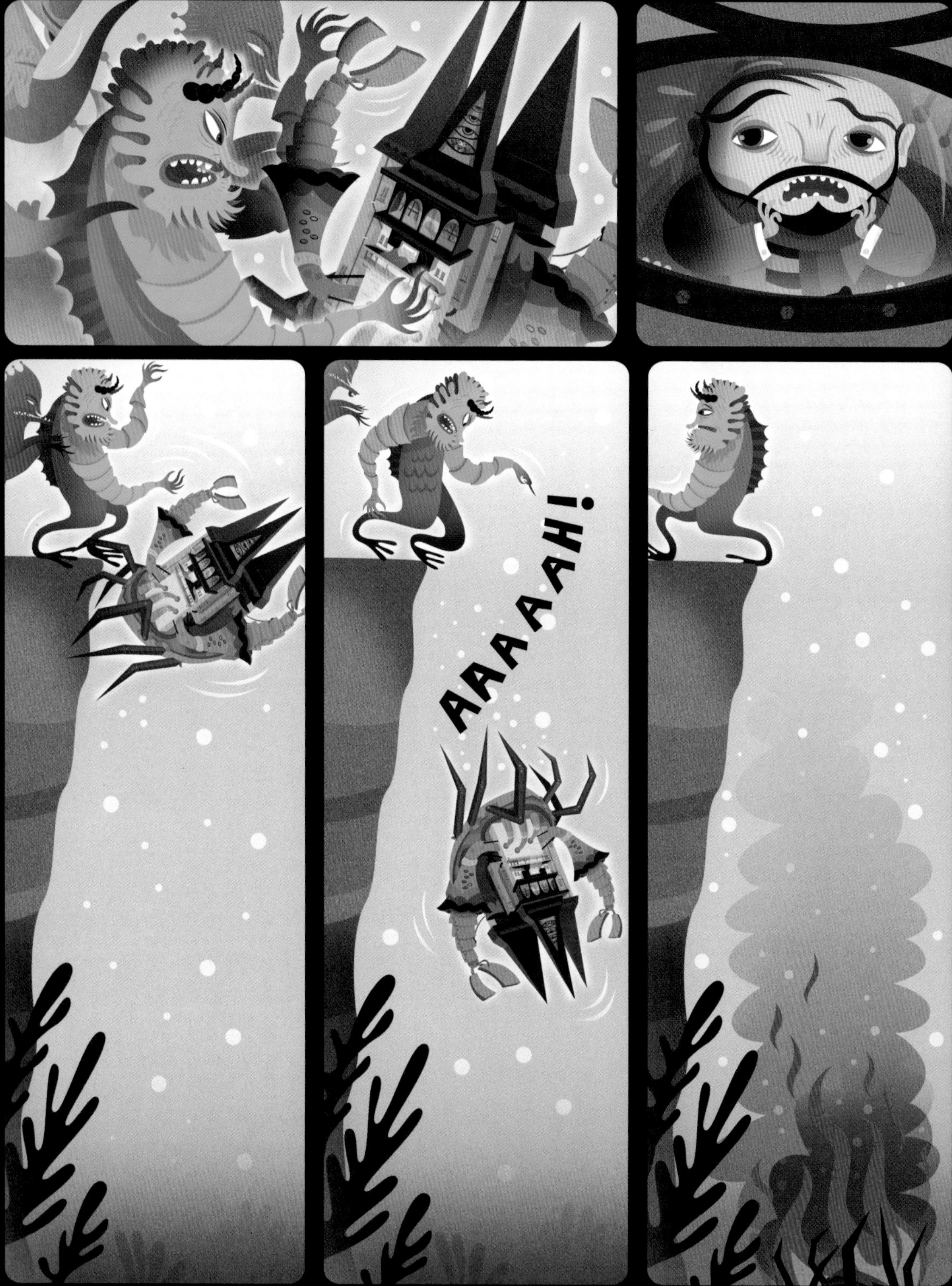
AAAAAAH!

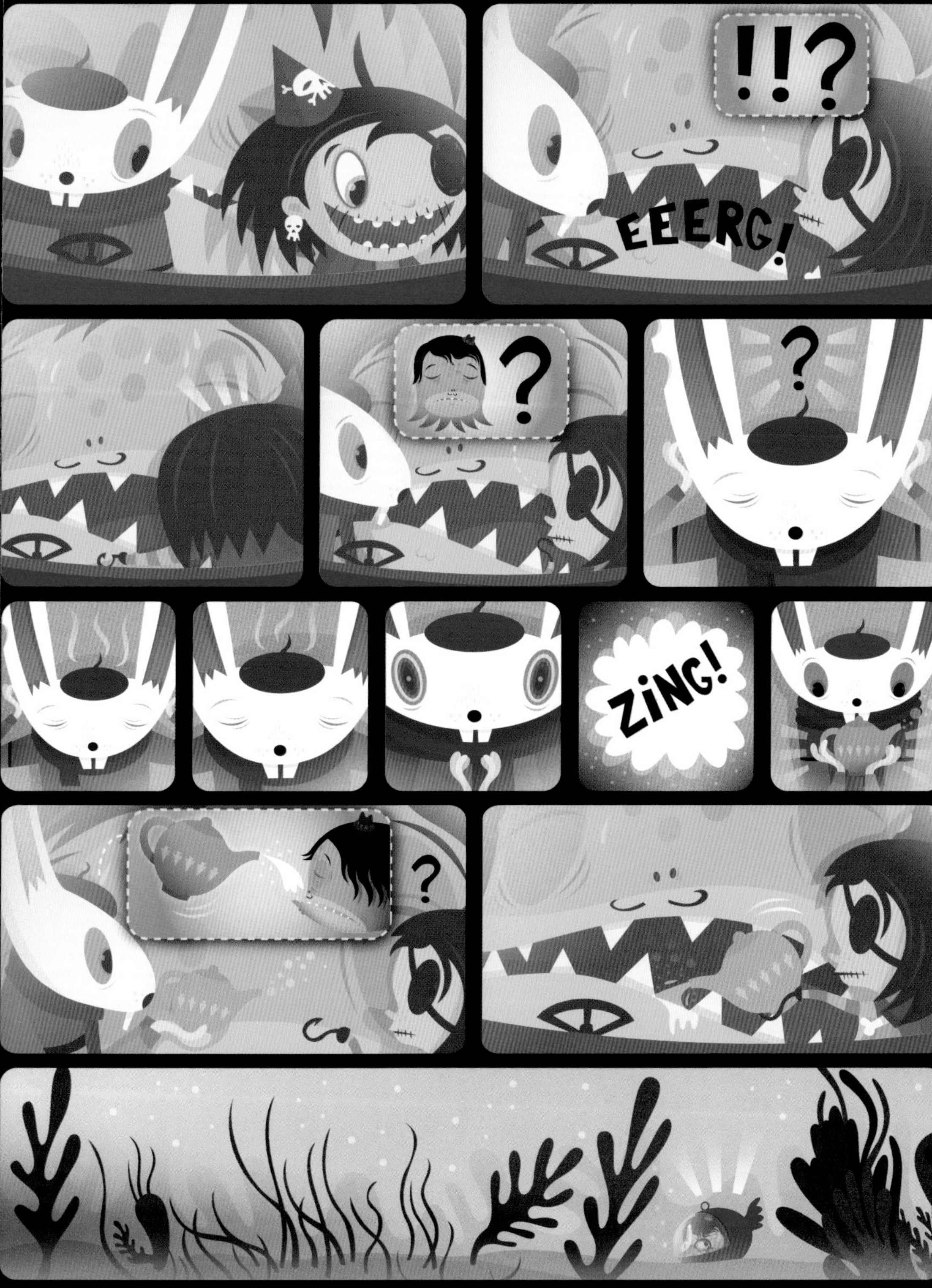
!!?
EEERG!
?
?
ZiNG!
?

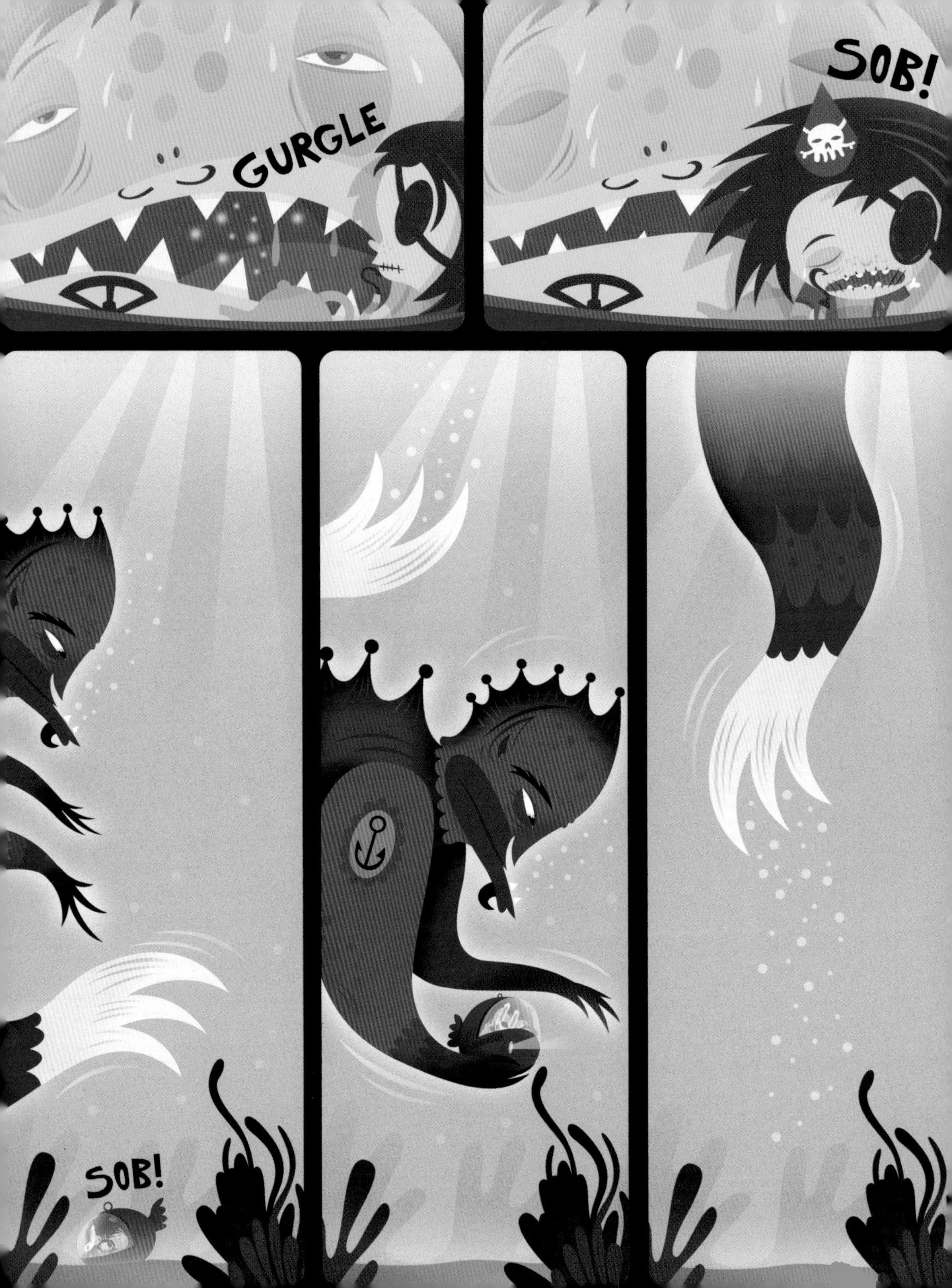
GURGLE
SOB!
SOB!

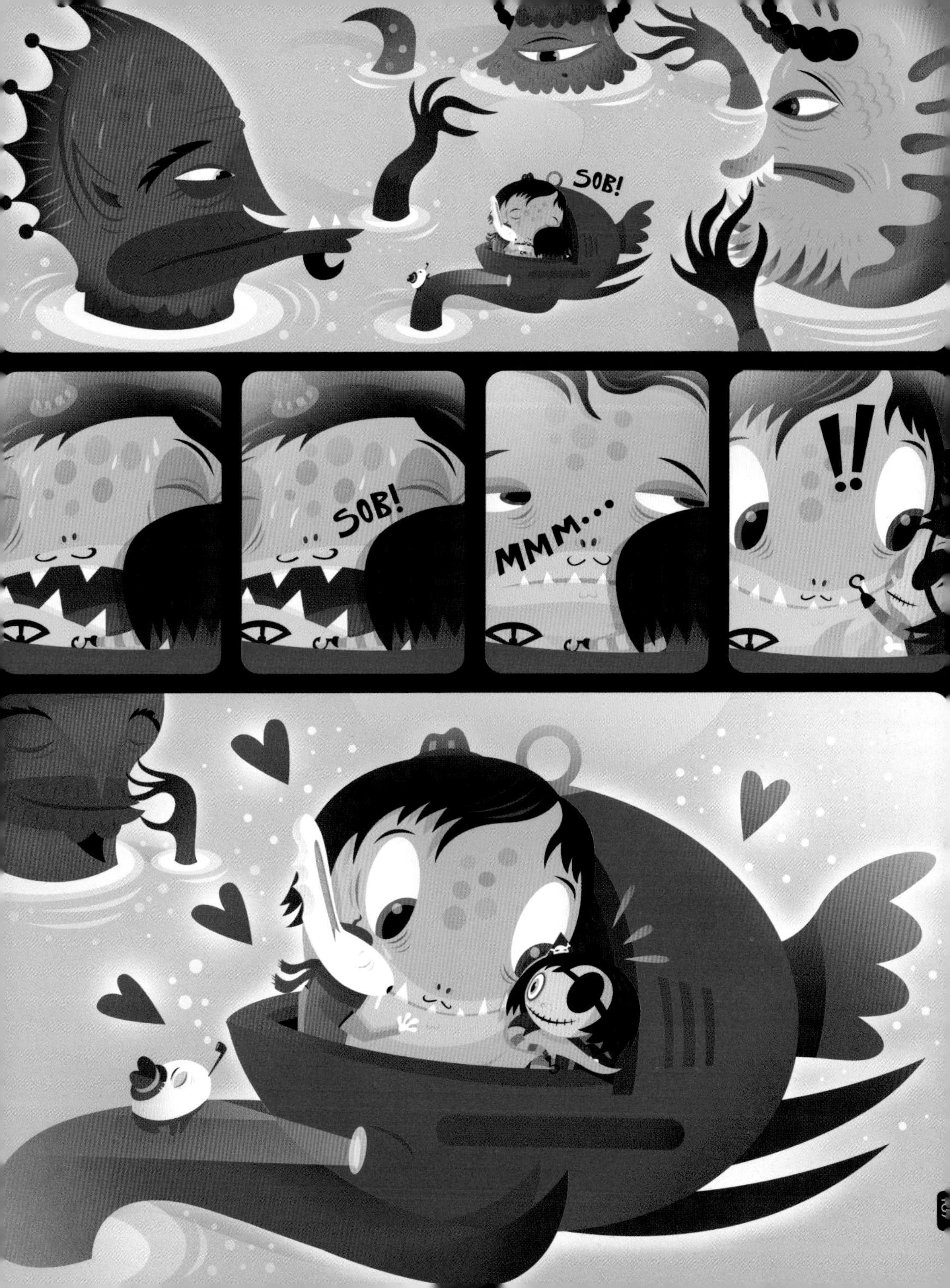
SOB!
SOB!
MMM...
!!

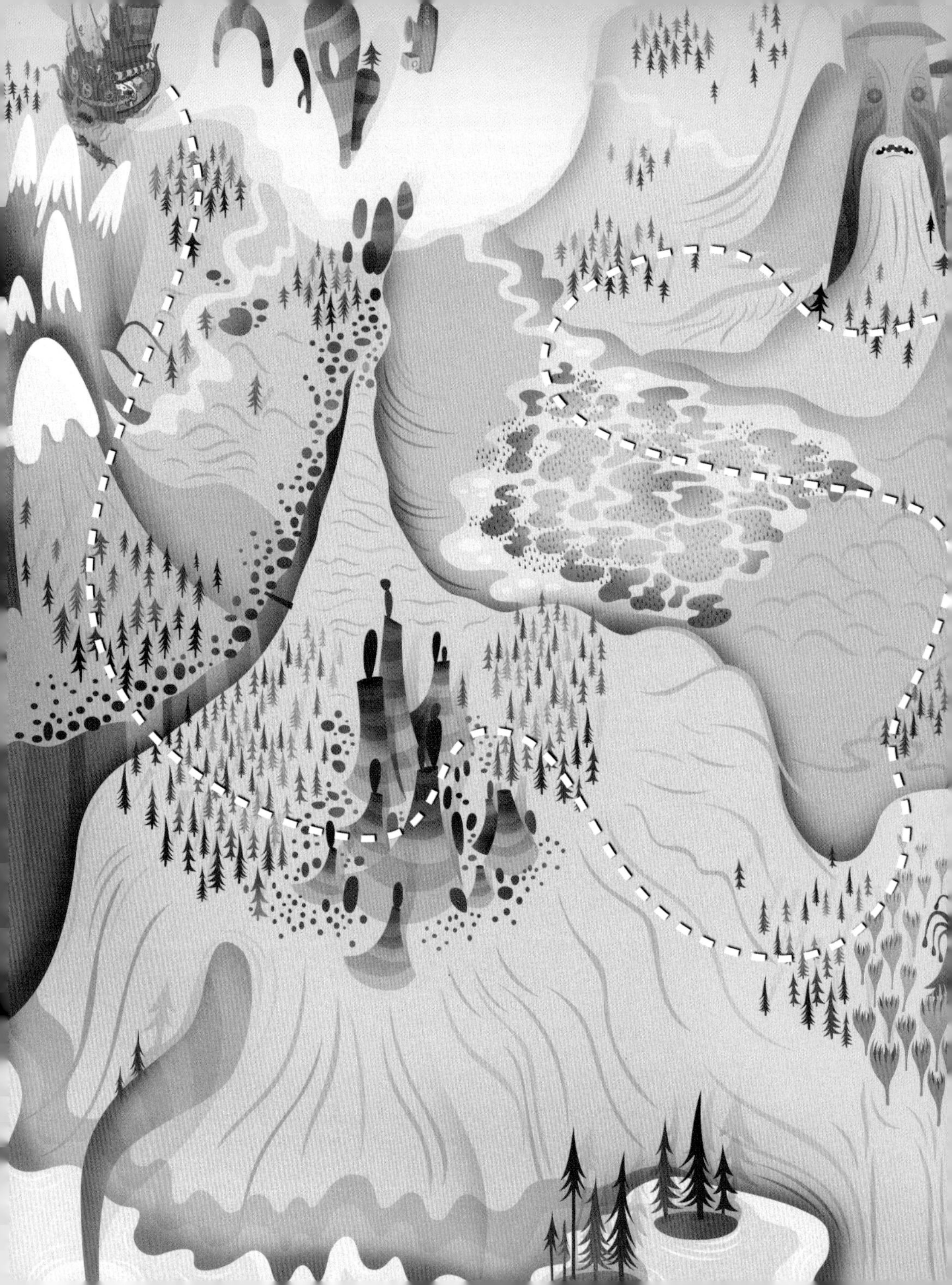

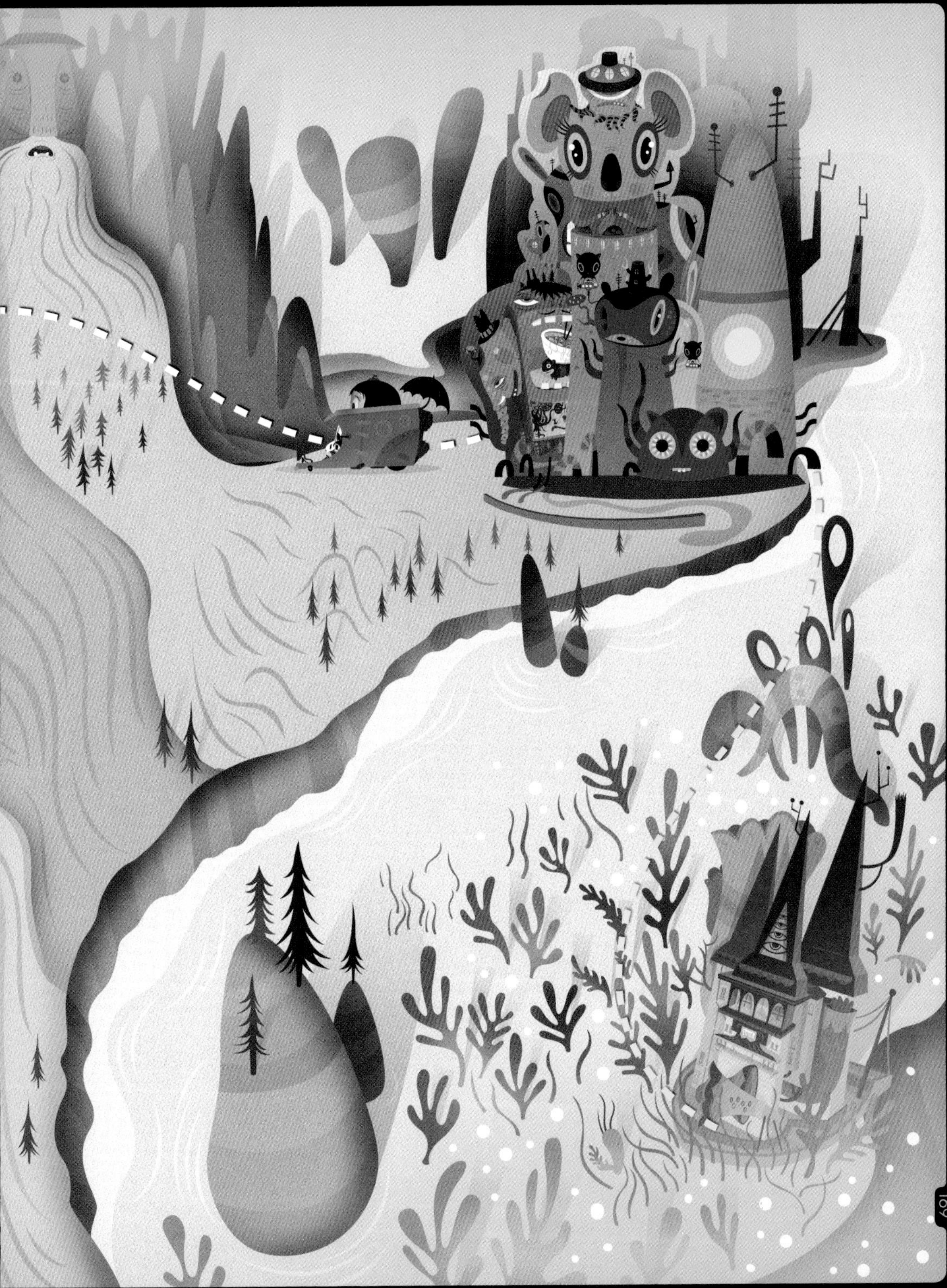

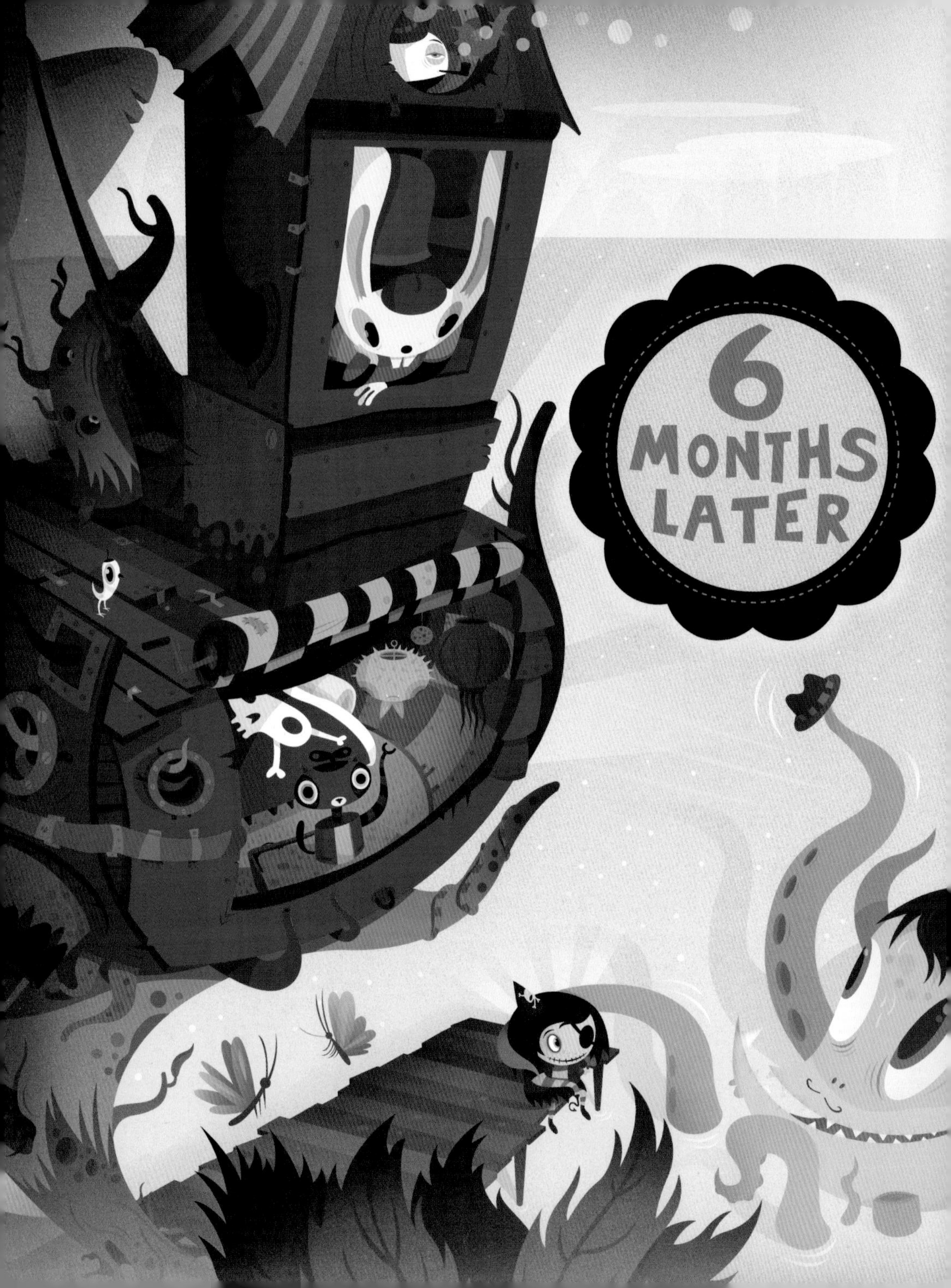
6
MONTHS
LATER

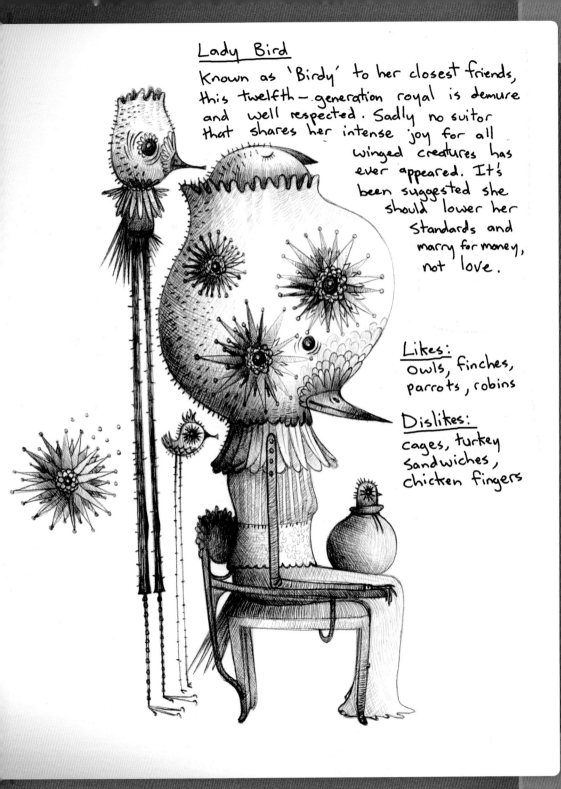

Lady Bird

Known as 'Birdy' to her closest friends, this twelfth—generation royal is demure and well respected. Sadly no suitor that shares her intense joy for all winged creatures has ever appeared. It's been suggested she should lower her standards and marry for money, not love.

Likes:
Owls, finches, parrots, robins

Dislikes:
cages, turkey sandwiches, chicken fingers

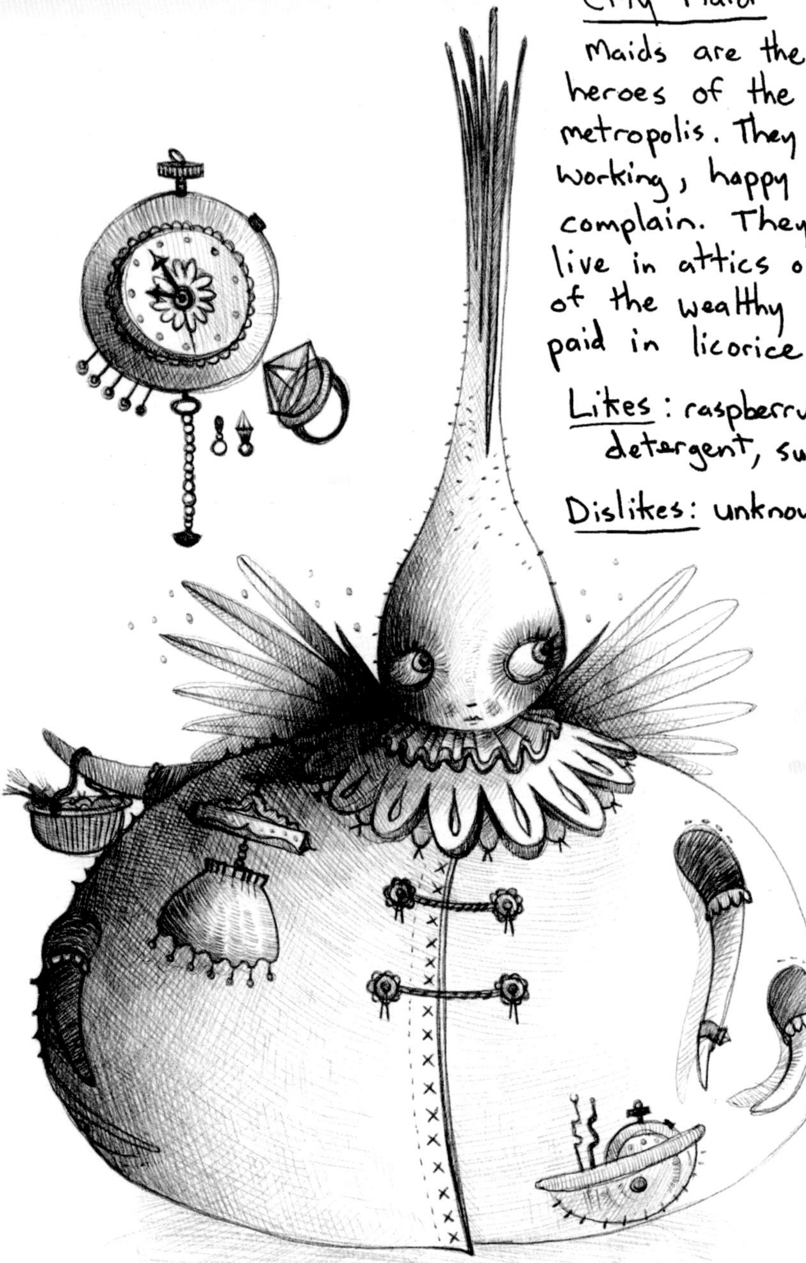

City Maid

Maids are the unsung heroes of the sprawling metropolis. They are hard-working, happy and never complain. They generally live in attics or basements of the wealthy and get paid in licorice.

Likes: raspberry sundaes, detergent, summer breezes

Dislikes: unknown

Forest Knitter

Quiet and studious, the ~~Knit~~ Knitter is a valuable asset to the environment. Every month at half-moon this tiny creature collects depressed forest-waste particles, forming them into ~~ectopla~~ ectoplasmic scarves and cute mittens.

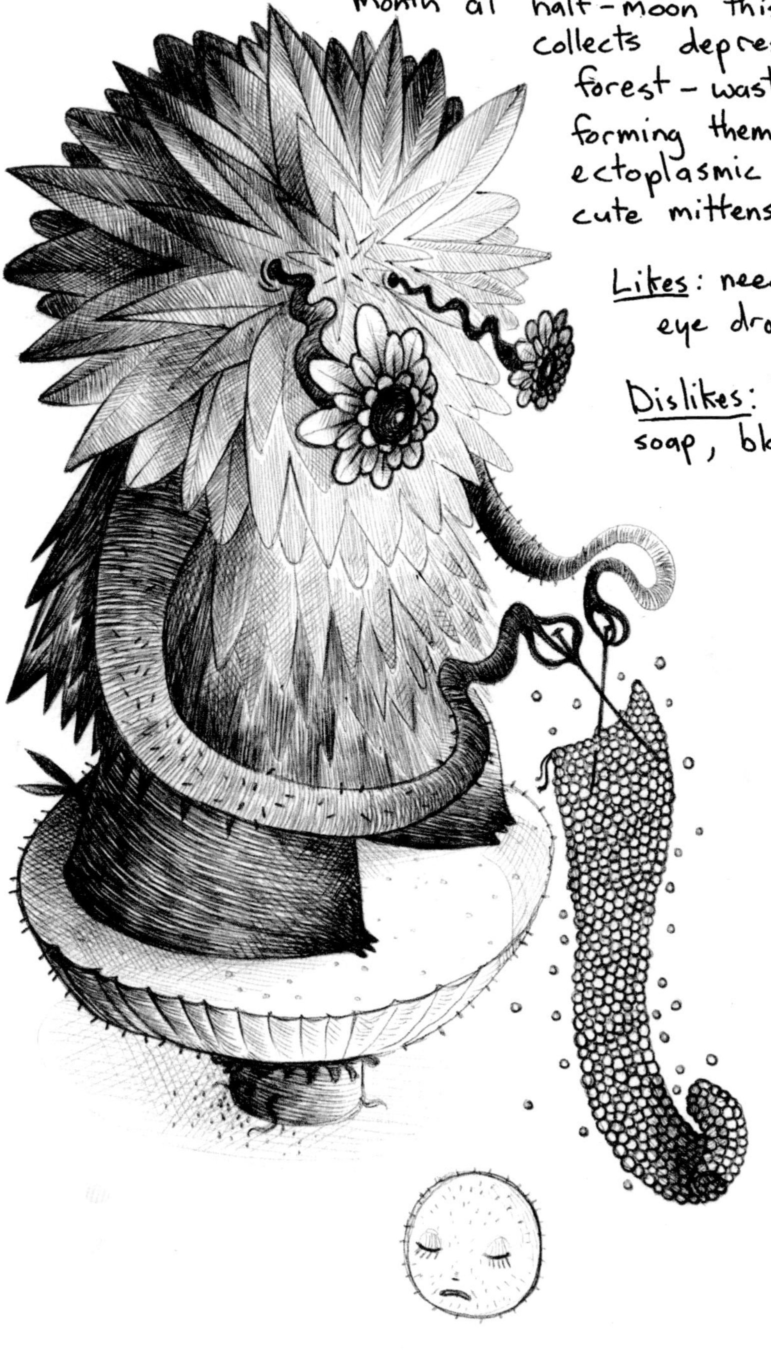

__Likes__: needles, happiness, eye drops

__Dislikes__: lemon-scented soap, blackboards

Fruit Head

Long ago, this once-handsome farmer selfishly hoarded his entire apple orchard during a famine. The local (and very angry) warlock placed a curse on him causing his cranium to swell to the size of a melon and fill with fruit sap and floral-scented mucus.

Likes: revenge

Dislikes: the world and all who inhabit it

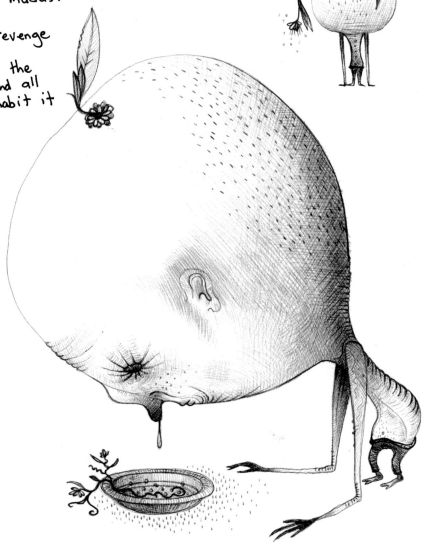

Ghostsquid

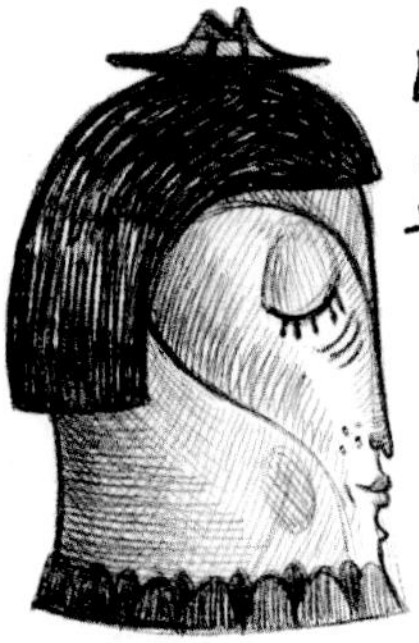

~~of~~ Often working side by side with the Lost Child, the Ghostsquid is a parasitic creature known for its deception and its taste for beating hearts and warm brains.

Likes: pleather handbags, lip gloss, fake eyelashes

Dislikes: daylight savings, chewing gum

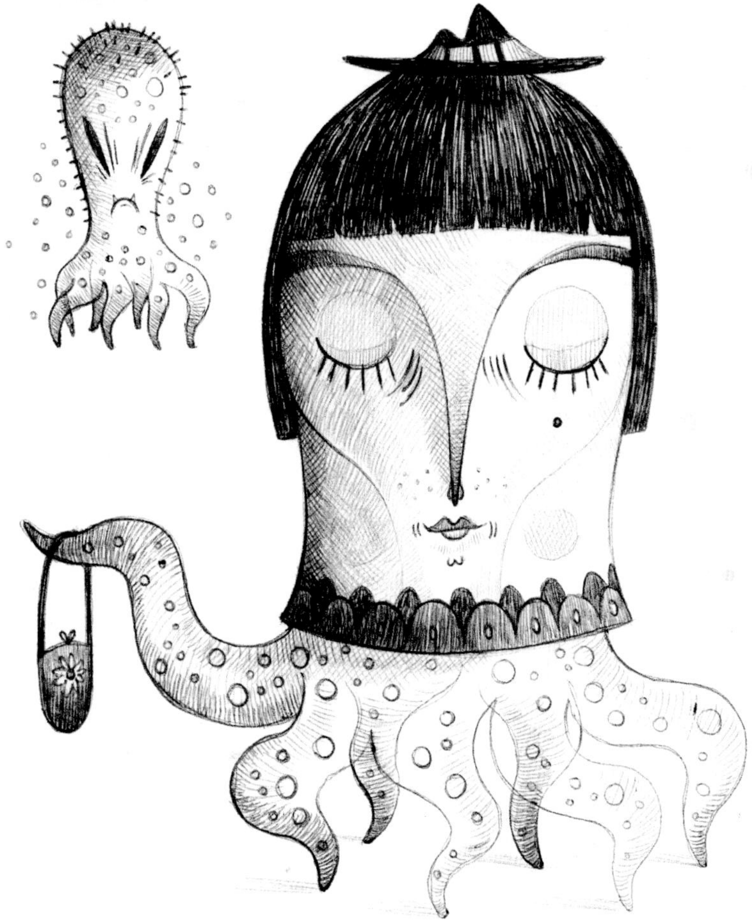

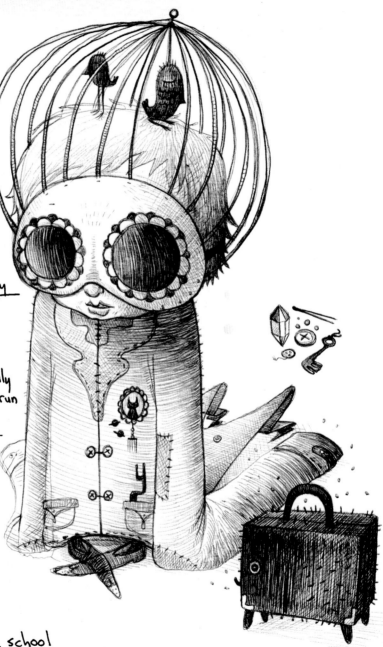

Homeless Wharf Boy

Bespectacled and sweet-faced, this seemingly innocent Wharf Boy is actually co-leader of a kid-run crime syndicate. While he begs for scraps of food, his highly trained stealth-briefcase steals the onlookers' valuables.

Likes: gelato, poker, cigars

Dislikes: gravy, imitation cheese, school

Homeless Wharf Girl

With vacant eyes and a downturned mouth, this seemingly innocent Wharf Girl is actually co-leader of a kid-run crime syndicate. While she begs for scraps of food, her highly trained, flea-bitten cat steals the onlookers' valuables.

Likes: strawberries, whipped cream, costume jewellery

Dislikes: teachers, muesli, combs

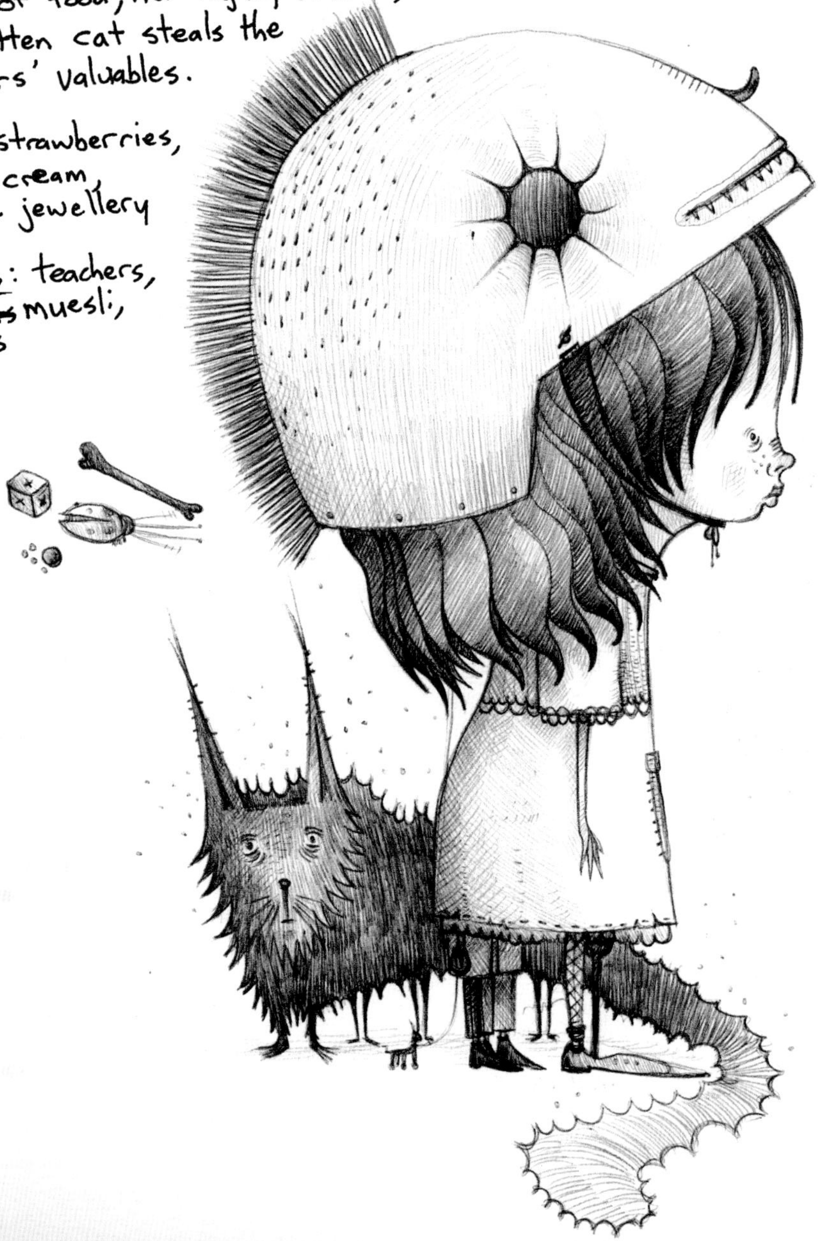

Onion Seller

This shrewd and hot-tempered businessman was once a courageous army general. On retirement he channelled his tactical battle skills into an obsession with growing onions and boiling ~~cabbage~~ cabbage stew. He is unmarried.

Likes: onions, cabbage, noughts and crosses

Dislikes: losing, mint toothpaste

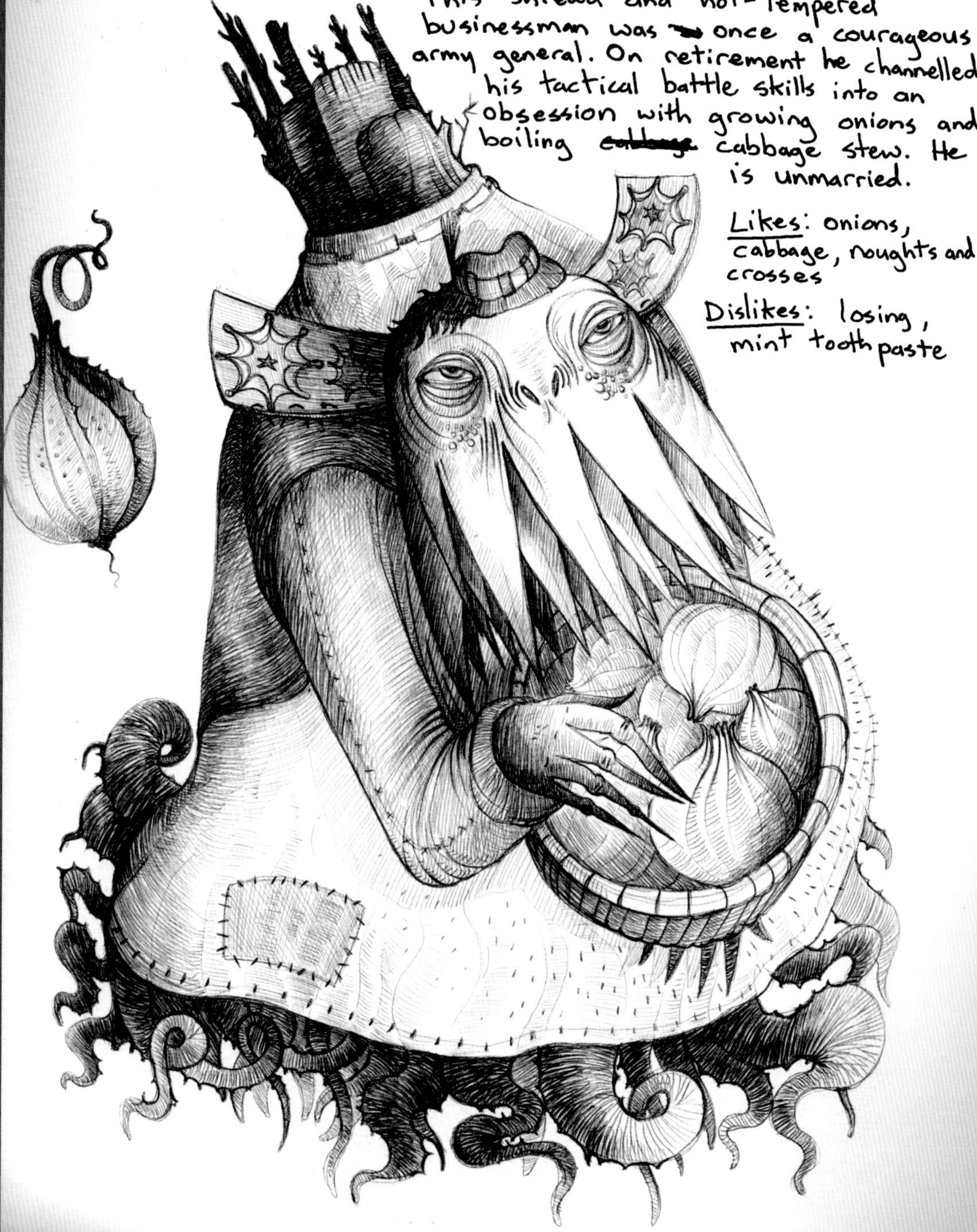

Lost Child

This evil being preys on innocent ~~travels~~ travellers, enticing them to help what appears to be a sweet, beckoning child. Once the hapless individual is within arm's reach, the Lost Child swivels at lightening speed and proceeds to eat the victim's face.

Likes: fava beans, chianti

Dislikes: chocolate sprinkles, cotton sheets, peanuts

School Girl

Intelligent and mischievous, private School Girls scoot around the city on their powered backpacks. Students are generally tutored in ancient law, modern art and household economics.

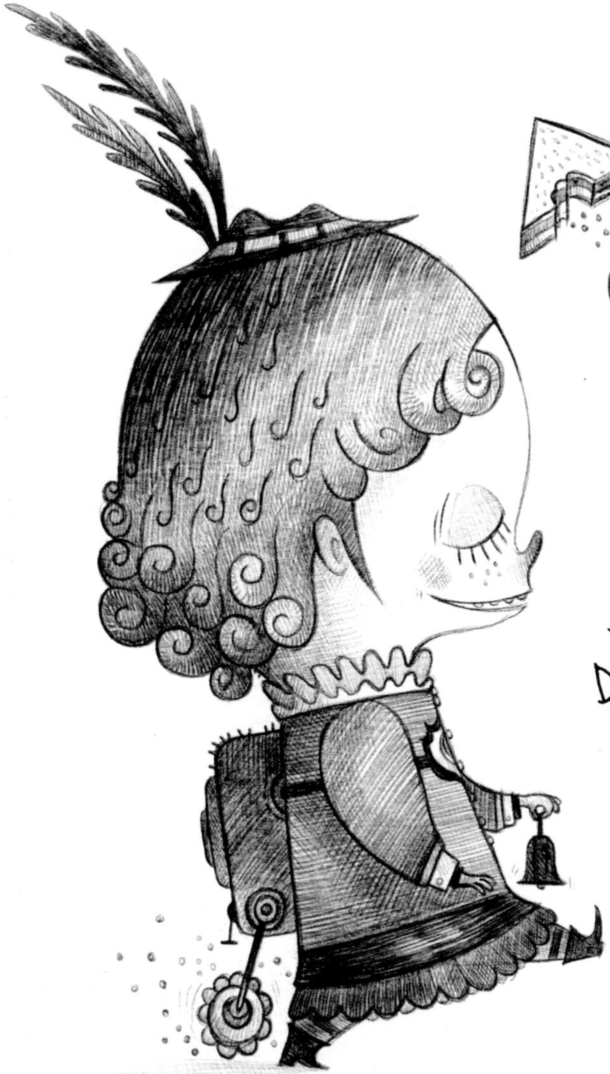

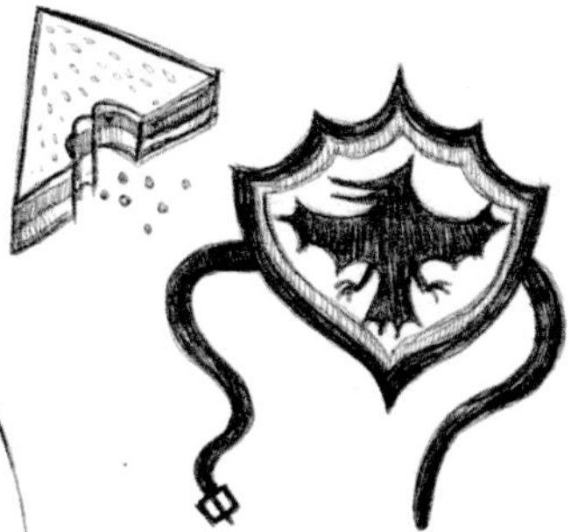

Likes: lemon drops, jump-rope, kittens

Dislikes: beans, cheese on toast, sunglasses

Swamp Peasant

Once part of an exclusive club of wealthy landowners, Swamp Peasants are now a lowly group of untouchables. These deformed beings roam the marshes looking for lost dreams and past lives.

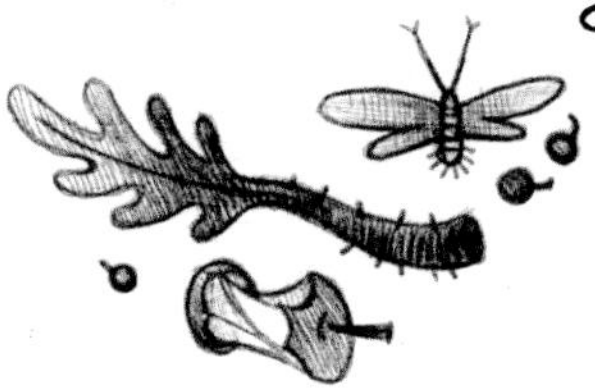

Likes: white wine, abstract art

Dislikes: lice, rough toilet paper

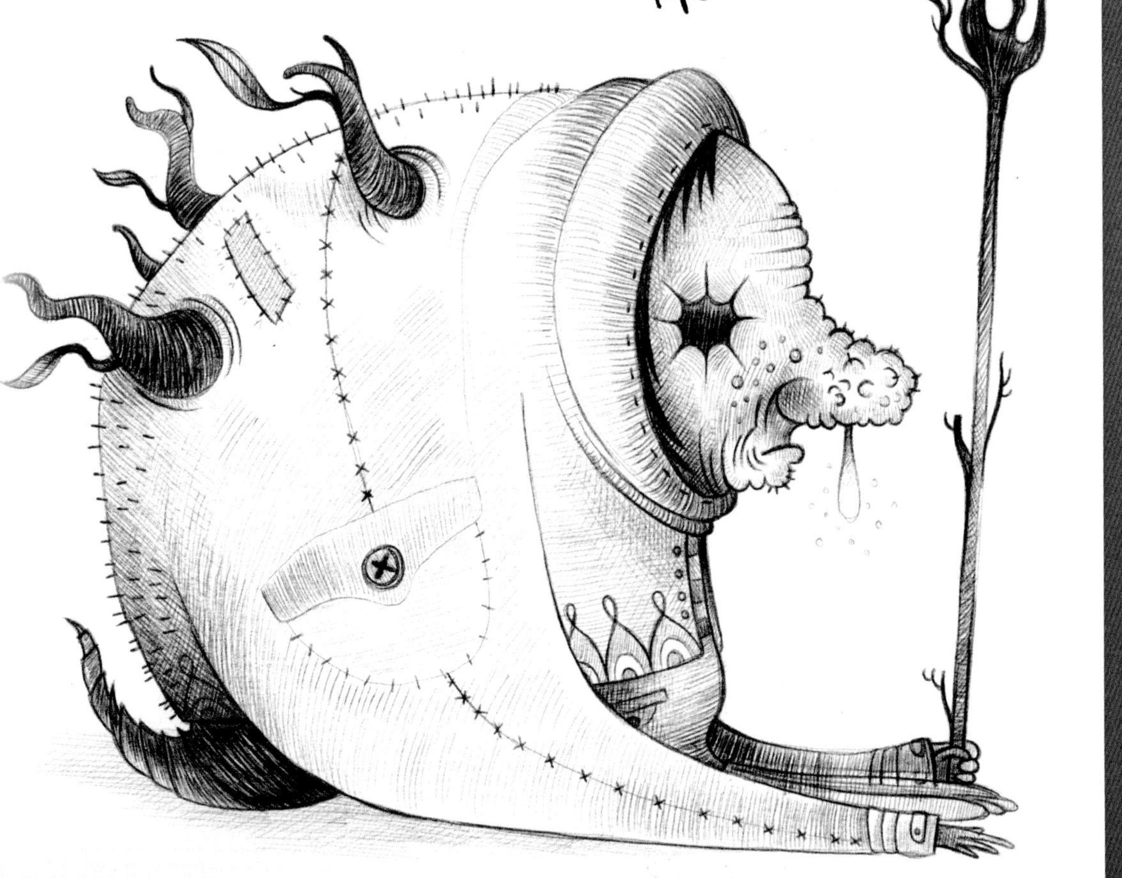

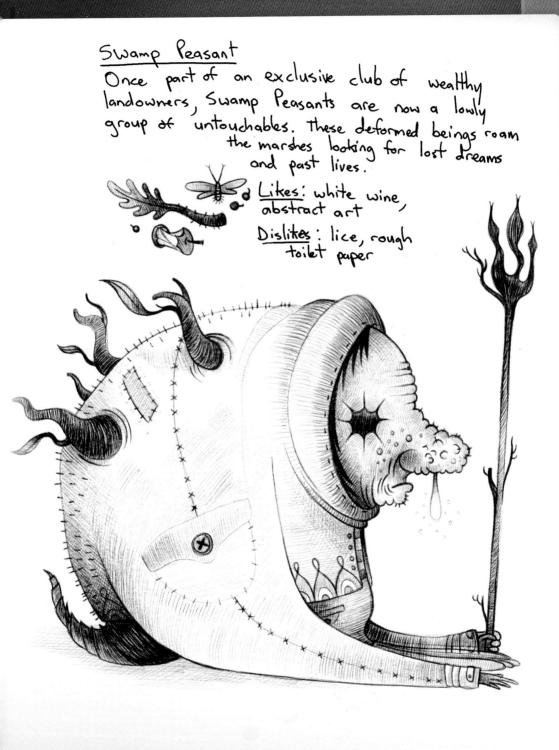

Swamp Elder

As old as the trees and almost as stationary, the Swamp Elder is a wise and fearful creature.
It was only recently discovered that the Elder was once a reanimated skeleton, who escaped his ~~enchants~~ enchanter and hid deep in the forgotten swamp lands.

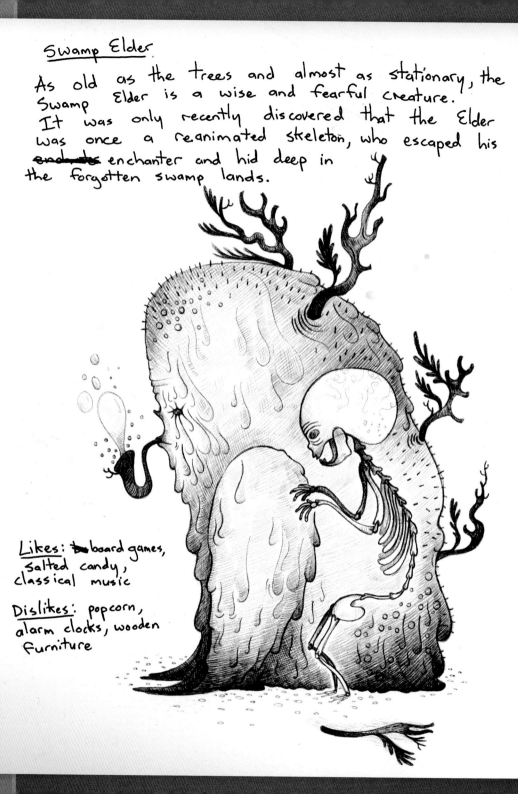

Likes: ~~b~~ board games, salted candy, classical music

Dislikes: popcorn, alarm clocks, wooden furniture

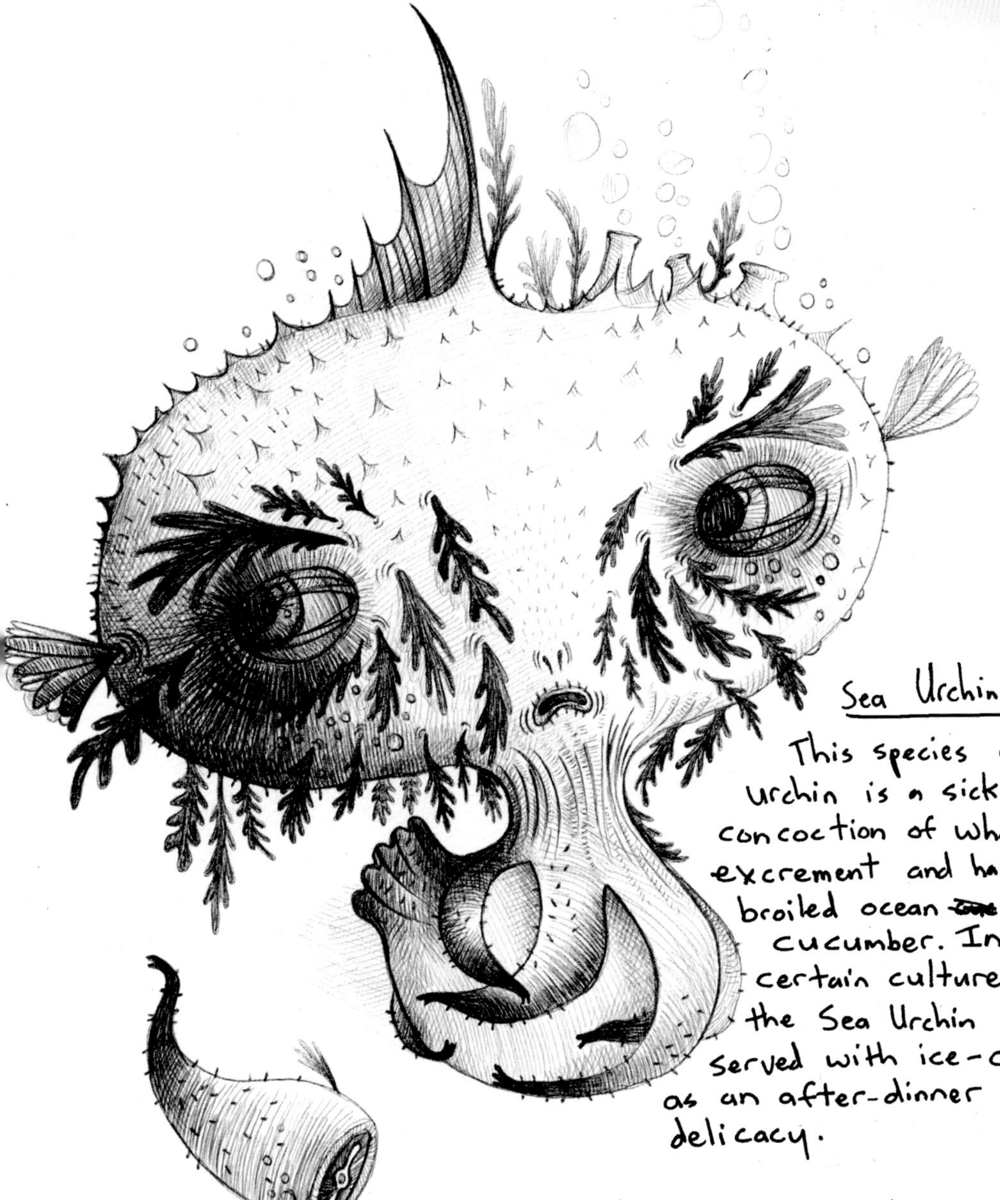

Sea Urchin

This species of urchin is a sickly concoction of whale excrement and hard-broiled ocean cucumber. In certain cultures, the Sea Urchin is served with ice-cream as an after-dinner delicacy.

Likes: sewage pipes, rubber tires

Dislikes: clam chowder, chefs, french fries

Snakeowl

Unexplained fusions of species are a regular occurence in the swamp lands. though mostly unsuccessful, on rare occasions an exceptional specimen is discovered — the Snakeowl being one such example.

Likes: leather-bound novels, mice

~~Dislikes~~ Dislikes: earthquakes, bright lights, cats

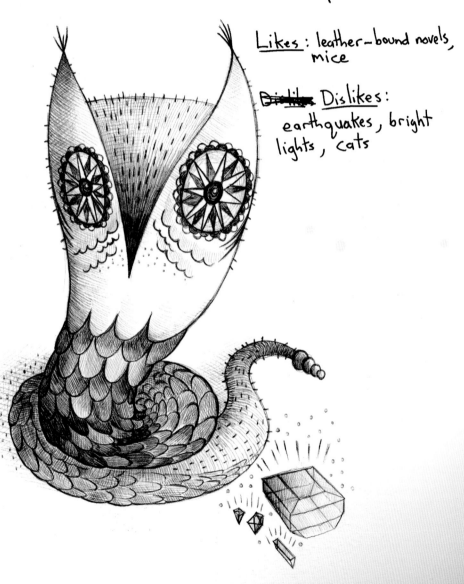

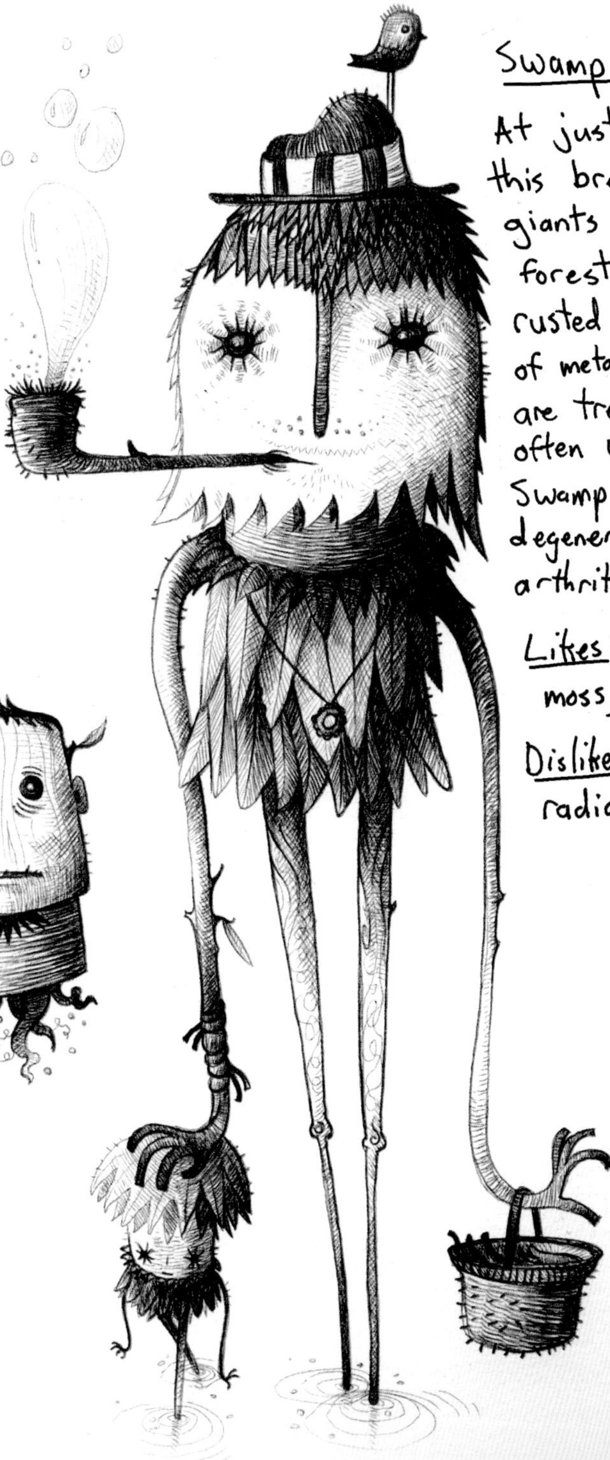

Swamp Giant

At just over 100 feet, this breed of mid-sized giants trawl the forest's bogs collecting rusted pipes and scraps of metal. These items are treasured and are often used to heal the Swamp Giants' rapidly degenerating bodies and arthritic limbs.

Likes: shiatsu massage, moss, bubble baths

Dislikes: rats, gas leaks, radiation

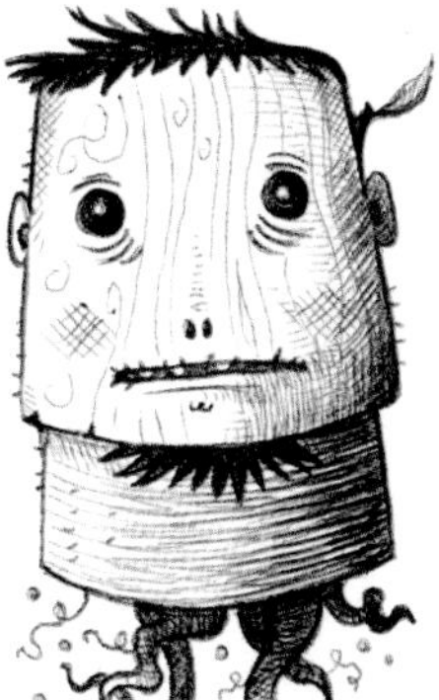

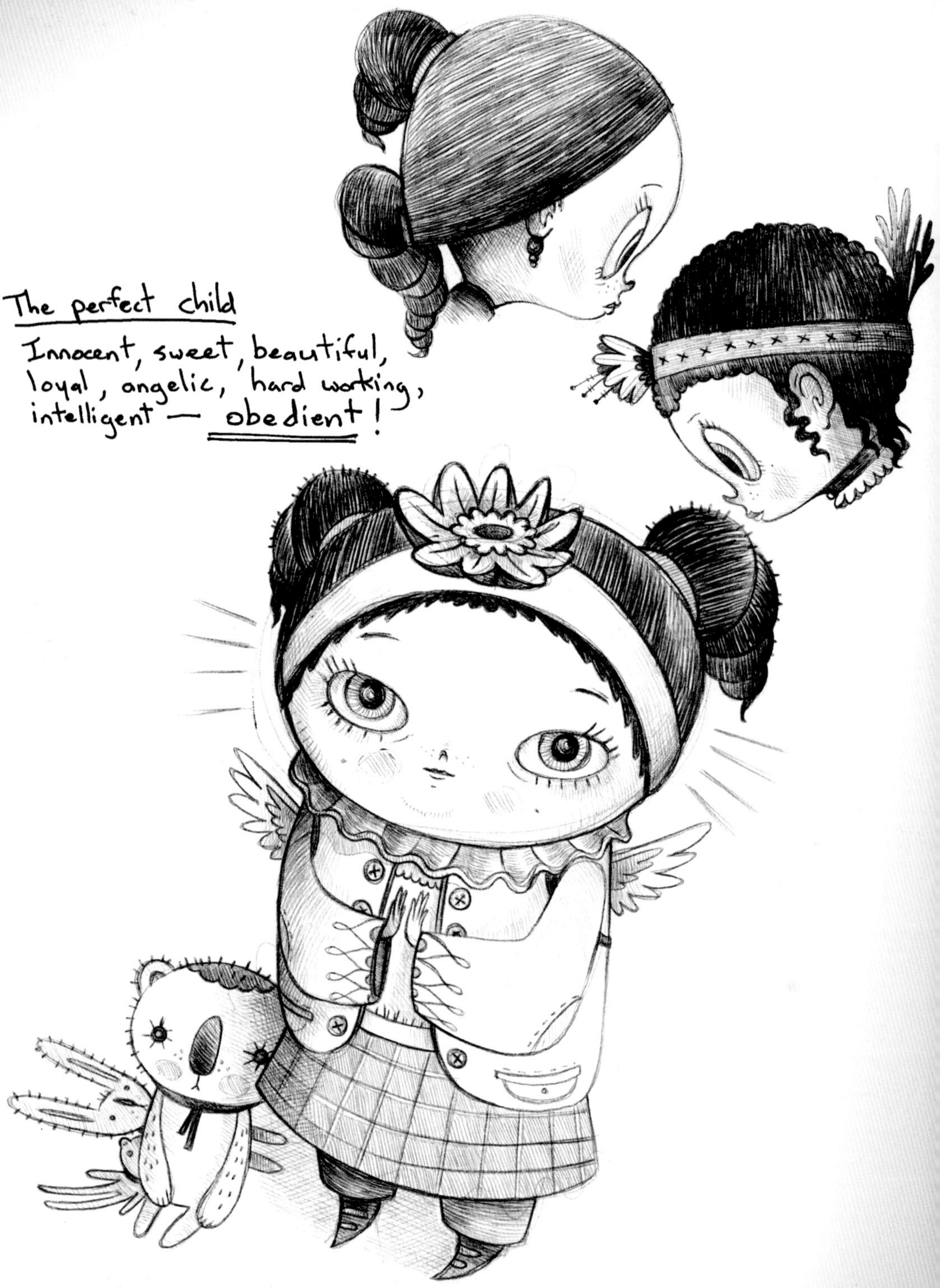
The perfect child
Innocent, sweet, beautiful,
loyal, angelic, hard working,
intelligent — obedient!

NATHAN JUREVICIUS is an Australian artist whose diverse range of work has appeared in numerous publications and galleries around the world. His most acclaimed project to date is the Scarygirl universe, a vision that is filled with psychedelic colours, dreamlike compositions and heartfelt stories that recall fables and folklore from our shared cultural memory. Since its creation in 2001, the brand has developed an underground following of fans across the globe through its limited edition toys, designer products, games and travelling art shows.

Nathan is currently in a partnership with Sophie Byrne, his good friend and producer of the Oscar-winning short film *The Lost Thing*. Together they are developing an animated feature film based on Scarygirl.

Nathan would like to thank:

Mum and Dad
Luke and Amber
Milo, Arkie and Sass
Andrea Kang
Sophie Byrne
Magic Pony
Outre Gallery
Erica Wagner
Bruno Herfst
Susannah Chambers
Remy